FIREFIGHT!

At the first sound from Randall, Huynh spun to face the opposite direction, flicked his safety off, and opened up. His aim wasn't as disciplined as Randall's was, but his bullets flew through the right area.

A few meters away, Vega and Tho were caught by surprise. They were almost as surprised as the NVA were. Tho was already facing in the right direction, so when he heard the first cry of alarm and scream of agony from the snipers, he fired at them. Vega had to scramble around before he could shoot. Instinctively, he did the same thing Randall did, kept 'em low and spread 'em around.

The four NVA hadn't gotten very far beyond the four-man ambush before they were fired on. . . .

Also by David Sherman
Published by Ivy Books:

The Night Fighter Series

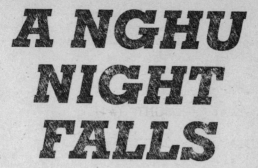

A NGHU NIGHT FALLS

The Night Fighters, Book 5

David Sherman

IVY BOOKS • NEW YORK

Ivy Books
Published by Ballantine Books
Copyright © 1988 by David Sherman

Library of Congress Catalog Card Number: 88-91149

ISBN 0-8041-0267-8

Printed in Canada

First Edition: September 1988
Second Printing: December 1988

For Corporal Dick Unger, USMC
Killed in action, May 1966, while leading a Combined Action night ambush patrol, Ky Hoa village, Quang Ngai Province, Republic of Vietnam

AUTHOR'S NOTE

The U.S. Marine Corps' Combined Action Program was real. It was probably the least known American project in the Vietnam War. Structurally, the Combined Action Platoons (Combined Action Companies in the early days of the program) were similar to the Army's Special Forces—a small number of Americans working with, training, and leading local troops in combat against the communist insurgents and North Vietnamese Army units. Their basic function was a little different, though. The CAPs had as their main objective keeping a village safe from the enemy, not going on operations against enemy soldiers outside the village. In combat abilities the CAPs were worthy successors to the Fourth Marine Brigade at Belleau Wood in World War I, where a few thousand Marines stopped a German advance that had the French army reeling; Echo Company, which took Mount Suribachi on Iwo Jima; and the First Marine Division in Korea, which fought its way through eight Red Chinese Army divisions during its withdrawal from the Chosen Reservoir. Actively participating in civic actions, the CAPs were everything the Peace Corps ever hoped to be. These young American Marines, mostly eighteen, nineteen, and twenty years old, were true American heroes. I am proud to have been one of them.

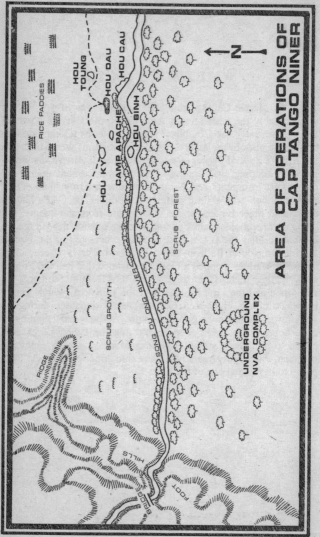

AREA OF OPERATIONS OF
CAP TANGO NINER

N

RICE PADDIES

HOU TOUNG

HOU DAU

HOU CAU

HOU BINH

CAMP APACHE

HOU KYO

SCRUB FOREST

SCRUB GROWTH

SONG DU ONG RIVER

UNDERGROUND
NVA COMPLEX

RIDGE

FOOT
HILLS

BRIDGE

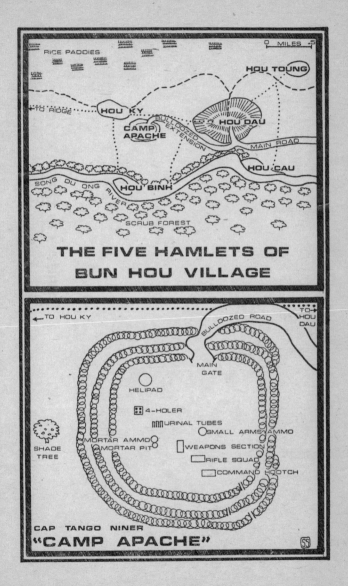

RICE PADDIES

0 MILES 5

HOU TOUNG

TO RIDGE ← HOU KY

CAMP APACHE

BULLDOZED EXTENSION

HOU DAU

MAIN ROAD

HOU CAU

SONG DU ONG RIVER

HOU BINH

SCRUB FOREST

THE FIVE HAMLETS OF BUN HOU VILLAGE

← TO HOU KY

BULLDOZED ROAD

TO HOU DAU →

MAIN GATE

HELIPAD

4-HOLER

URINAL TUBES

SMALL ARMS AMMO

MORTAR AMMO

MORTAR PIT

WEAPONS SECTION

RIFLE SQUAD

COMMAND HOOTCH

SHADE TREE

CAP TANGO NINER

"CAMP APACHE"

UNITED STATES ARMY

Military Assistance Command, Vietnam

Saigon
Office of Public Information

26 December 1966

For Immediate Release:

During the forty-eight-hour Christmas cease-
fire that ended at 0700 hours this date, allied
forces reported sixty-three violations of the
cease-fire by Vietcong insurgent and North
Vietnamese Army forces. The exact number of
Vietcong and NVA casualties is not available at
this time, but their casualties are believed to
have been heavy. American casualties were
light.

For immediate release to all accredited news
agencies.

CHAPTER ONE

Christmas Day, 1966

"You sure she's bringing some girlfriends, Tex?" Sergeant J. C. Bell asked.

"That's what she said yesterday," Corporal "Tex" Randall replied, and turned slightly pink under his sunbaked bronze tan, remembering the two days and one night he had just spent with Bobbie Harder on his way back from R&R.

"Think any of them know what end to stick it in?" asked Corporal "Wall" McEntire, eyes bugging wide and jaw slackening. "Been so long I forgot."

Corporal "Stilts" Zeitvogel looked down at his husky friend and tapped the back of his head with his open hand. "Smack you upside the head, boy," he said. "These ain't no boom-boom girls coming to spend Christmas with us. They're friends of Tex's split-tail." His black face was split by a grin, a smile that made his mouth look like it held too many teeth, and he leaned close to McEntire's ear to whisper, "But I wouldn't worry about it too much, Wall. If she'll let you, it'll fit in either end."

McEntire beamed.

Randall blushed deeply at the word Zeitvogel used to describe Bobbie Harder. "Don't call her a split-tail, Stilts. She's a nice girl," he said through gritted teeth. Zeitvogel grinned at him, and Randall blushed even deeper; the derogatory term for a female reminded him of the nights Bobbie Harder had opened her legs underneath him on the beach at Da Nang.

The four Marines were standing inside the wire on the eastern side of Camp Apache, watching the horizon for the expected helicopter. It was early morning, and they had to squint against the sun, which was still low to the horizon.

"You shitheads're wasting your fucking time. Ain't no goddamn bird hauling ass out here before Christmas chow, no fucking way," said a new voice.

"Go play with your radios, Swearin' Swarnes," Bell said to the speaker.

"See if you can call an artillery strike in on you'self, Swearin' Swarnes," Randall added, trying to cover his embarrassment about being the only man in the unit who had a girlfriend in-country.

"Fuck you and the horse you rode in on," Swarnes replied with a laugh. He left them and headed toward the command hootch and his radios. PFC "Swearin'" Swarnes was Combined Action Platoon Tango Niner's radioman. He wasn't called Swearin' Swarnes for the way the words sounded together; he earned his nickname the old-fashioned way: he was the most foulmouthed man in the unit. He hadn't been with the sergeant and corporals watching for the helicopter; he'd left his radio watch to use the piss tube and seen them. He had guessed what they were doing and had wandered over to confirm his suspicions. On his way back to the command tent, which was divided into three parts—radio room, commander's living quarters, and combination storage room–medical corpsmen's quarters—he passed by Second Lieutenant Burrison, Tango Niner's commanding officer, who was lounging on a beach chair outside the tent.

"They think they see anything yet?" Burrison asked.

"Nah, Scrappy, only the fucking sun-ball."

"Maybe they shouldn't be looking at the sun so long?" Burrison asked, but he wasn't serious about the question. He was more curious about what kind of profanity Swarnes would use in answering it.

"No fucking problem," Swarnes said. "Goddamn silly-ass NCOs can't see diddly shit nohow. Don't make a damn bit of difference if they burn out their eyeballs eye-fucking the sun."

Burrison chuckled and shook his head. He wondered if Swarnes would ever be able to rejoin the civilian community back in The World, or if his foul mouth would force him to make a career of the Marine Corps—maybe the only place in the world he could get away with talking the way he did. He kept searching for a good way to describe Swarnes to his friends back home but hadn't been able to come up with a way to tell civilians. Swarnes was the kind of man who would go with his mother for dinner at the minister's house, Burrison wanted to write to his friends, and while sitting at the table with his mother, the minister, and the minister's wife, would say, "Pass the fucking salt," and think the reason for the sudden silence was that he forgot to say please.

Swarnes stepped through the open end of the tent and resumed his seat in front of the long, narrow table that held the radios Tango Niner used to communicate with its patrols and with the outside world. He tipped his chair back and propped his feet on the table. His head was near the radio headset hanging from a nail in the tent upright, right where it belonged so he could hear traffic without having to wear the headset. He picked up the girlie magazine he'd been reading before answering the call of nature and started again where he had left off. He licked his lips as he read the pictures.

Outside, Burrison watched Corporal "Big Louie" Slover join the sergeant and the other three corporals on the east side of the hill. Big Louie was just that—big. He was built like a professional football lineman. Big Louie wasn't as tall as Stilts Zeitvogel's six foot five inches, nor as wide as Wall McEntire—whom they called Wall because "he's not tall enough to be a tree and not fat enough to be a bear"— nor were his muscles as big and well defined as Tex Randall's—Randall had been a high school football player and wrestler. But still, Slover's bulk seemed to dominate the small group of Marines. As usual when inside the Camp Apache compound, he wasn't wearing a shirt, and his black skin showed stark against the sky.

One NCO was missing from the group, Corporal Jesus Maria Ruizique. Burrison looked to the left, expecting to see him in the tent the rifle squad used for its quarters, sleeping after having been out on patrol all night. He saw Webster, Pennell, and Neissi, the men of Ruizique's fire team, sleeping on their cots at one end of the tent. Elsewhere in the tent he made out "Dumbshit" Dodd's lumpy form. Slover had nicknamed Dodd "Dumbshit" when he'd learned the PFC had been drafted into the Marine Corps. "Dumbest damn thing I ever heard of anybody doing," Slover had pronounced. "What the fuck kind of dumbshit gonna go and get his young ass drafted into the Mo-reen Corps? You a dumbshit, Dodd, you know that?" Everybody in the platoon agreed, and that's what they called him.

One of the other junior men of the rifle squad was sitting in isolated splendor on the wall-less four-holer the compound had as its outhouse, contemplating life, the universe, or maybe just a difficult bowel movement. The others were grouped around a table made from a sheet of galvanized iron laid over a bed of sandbags, leisurely eating a C-ration breakfast.

Ruizique wasn't on his cot. Burrison craned his neck to look to the western side of the compound. Ruizique was sitting on the lip of the defensive trench that surrounded the compound inside the concertina wire fence. His rifle was broken down on a towel laid out at his side; he was cleaning his weapon and staring at the hills to the west. Might have known, Burrison told himself. And I bet I know what he's thinking, too.

If he had gotten out of his chair and walked over to ask the corporal from the Dominican Republic, Burrison would have won that bet with himself. Ruizique wore a fresh utility uniform. The short-sleeved shirt was open, and its tails hung outside his trousers; the trousers were bloused just above his ankles. He wore tire-tread Ho Chi Minh sandals on his feet and a straw, camouflaged bush hat was pushed back on his head. Crossed bandoliers, rough side out and with a bullet in every loop, were draped across his chest. He saddle-soaped the bandoliers daily, twice a day when he could, to keep the leather soft and pliable so it wouldn't creak when he moved at night. He looked at the rifle parts he was cleaning only when he needed to; most of the time his eyes swept the cleared area west of the hill and the forest edge beyond. Frequently he looked beyond the forest to the hills farther out.

When his patrol had come in at dawn, he had taken his cleaning equipment to the perimeter and settled down to watch until he saw somebody else watching the perimeter. He knew that in this area, as in most of the country, the Vietcong conceded the day to the Americans. But here, in Bun Hou, the Marines claimed the night as well. There was no watch set on the perimeter during the day in Camp Apache; whoever felt like it watched during the day. So Ruizique did the watching until he saw someone else take over. Then and only then would he lie down and sleep himself. His expression was grim.

We hurt you, Mister Charlie, Ruizique thought. We hurt you bad. Tell me, gook, do you have the machismo to come back at us, seeking vengeance? Or are you like the kicked cur who slinks off to lick his wounds until he feels better, and in the future hopes to avoid the man who kicked him. If you come back, Mister Charlie Cong, I will cut off your *cajones*. He started to reassemble his rifle. It didn't matter to him that they were in the middle of a forty-eight-hour Christmas truce, or that the Americans couldn't fire at any enemy soldiers they saw unless they were fired at first. Ruizique was confident that if he saw any bad guys, he could get them to shoot first. Next he saddle-soaped his bandoliers.

"Morning, bac si Chief," Lance Corporal "Short Round" Hempen said. "Pull up a sandbag and make yourself a cup of C-ration coffee. My heat tab's still going." He gestured with his fork at a C-ration can with triangular holes cut near its bottom. A chemical pill burned hot in the can's bottom. "You can use it." One heat tab burned long enough to boil a half-canteen cup of water and heat a can of C-ration entree. Hempen's heat tab was still burning, because he decided to eat his scrambled eggs and ham cold. Lance Corporal "Billy Boy" Lewis was looking at him oddly, and PFC Wayne "Homeboy" Mazzucco tried to ignore Hempen's eating. Neither of them could understand how he could eat the gelled, canned eggs cold.

"Thanks, Short Round," Hospitalman Third Class Tracker said. He used his heel to reposition a wooden ammo crate before he sat down. The canteen cup he half filled from the lister bag went onto Hempen's field stove. He removed the powdered coffee, powdered creamer, and sugar packets from his C-ration condiment pack and stirred them into the water. While his field coffee "brewed" he opened his can of beefsteak and scraped the coagulated fat from its top. When his water was steaming and the lip of the canteen cup was almost hot enough to burn his lips, he removed it from the field stove and put the beefsteak on to warm up enough to be edible.

Lewis finally grimaced and looked away from Hempen when the short Marine made smacking noises with his lips while scraping the residue of the eggs from his can. He saw the small group of NCOs clustered at the east side of the compound. He clenched his fists in front of his face and twisted. When his hands came away, the right end of his mustache looped up and around in an almost complete circle; the left end mirrored it downward.

"Look at them dumbasses," Lewis said.

"You mean to tell me there's more than one of you sitting here?" Hempen said, looking up from his now-empty C-ration can and glancing around the makeshift table. "You're the only one I see."

Lewis glared at Hempen, trying to look ferocious; the backward, sideways S of his mustache ruined the effect. He opened his mouth to snap something threatening but was stopped by a hand clamping down on his shoulder.

"You giving my little buddy a hard time?" PFC John "Big Red" Robertson asked.

Lewis switched his view up to Robertson's face. The big Marine's hair was a brilliant red above his florid face —he grinned broadly, but his teeth gave the impression of being too sharp to be friendly. "Ain't giving no one no hard time," Lewis said.

"Didn't think so," Robertson said, and sat heavily on an unoccupied ammo crate. "Who you calling dumbasses?" He looked at the top of his C-ration box and scowled. "How come I got the ham and fucking limas? Scrappy's supposed to get them."

"Them." Lewis jerked a thumb toward the wire. "Dumbass NCOs."

Tracker judged his beefsteak to be warm enough and started forking it into his mouth. He cocked an eye at Lewis, then looked at the group of men he was talking about. "Careful, Billy Boy," he said. "I'm one of them."

Lewis looked at Tracker, confused. "No you ain't, Chief. You're a medicine man, not an NCO."

Tracker shrugged. "HM three, samee-same a corporal." Tracker was a full-blood Kiowa Indian. Like nearly every Indian in the Marine Corps, he was called "Chief."

"Boo-shee-ick, samee-same corporal. You're a doc. Docs aren't corporals." Lewis lifted his eyes in momentary thought and added, "Docs aren't sergeants, neither."

"Same pay grade."

"So what?" Lewis glanced quickly at the other Marines at the table, looking for help. He suspected he was in an argument he might lose if he stayed in it alone. "You're a swabbie. Swabbies don't have corporals or sergeants." He darted looks at the others again. "Ain't that right, Short Round, squids don't have corporals or sergeants?"

Hempen looked at him wide-eyed. "Chief ain't a swabbie. He's an honorary Marine."

"But—"

"Short Round's right," Robertson said. "Chief's a Marine, just like you and me. Only difference is he didn't go through boot camp, and he wears these funny-looking rank insignia." He glanced at the corpsman's bare collars and added, "When he's not in the field."

"That's it." Lewis excitedly leaned forward. "He didn't go through boot camp. Can't be a Marine unless he went through boot camp."

"Scrappy didn't go to boot camp," Mazzucco joined in.

Lewis reared back, offended. "Scrappy's an ossifer."

"But he's a Marine officer," Robertson countered.

"If Scrappy can be a Marine without going through boot camp, so can I," Tracker said. The beginnings of a smile curled the corners of his mouth.

Lewis looked pained. Why's everybody ganging up on me? his expression seemed to say. "Scrappy ain't no swabbie. He's a fighting Marine, even if he is an ossifer."

"Chief's a fighting Marine, too," Hempen said.

"Huh?"

"Sure, don't you remember how he was with Jay Cee and Tex over there when Charlie tried to overrun us?" Hempen asked, pointing at the west side of the perimeter. "Or how he was humping a rifle when those sappers tried to come through the wire there?" He pointed to wire on the north side of the hill.

"But—"

"Shee-it, Billy Boy, Chief's got two Purple Hearts," Robertson said, glowering at Lewis. "And he got both of them when he was fighting, not doctoring." He screwed up his face at the corpsman. "What you doing, Doc, trying to get three and go?" A third Purple Heart and Tracker could go home to The World without finishing his thirteen-month tour of duty.

Tracker flinched at the reminder. "No way, Jose. Two's the limit for this Indian." He remembered when he thought one was the limit, and before that, when he thought one was over the limit.

Mazzucco shook his head. "No way around it, Billy Boy. Chief's a Marine."

"Even if he is a squid," Hempen added, nodding.

"But, but . . ." Lewis sputtered. He was trying to say something about those dumbass NCOs at the wire and didn't want to include the corpsman in the "dumbass."

"Billy Boy," Tracker said in a mild voice—he was growing tired of the teasing, even if it was in his defense. "I'm a petty officer third class. That's an NCO. Now, if you're talking about the corporals and the sergeant, not about NCOs, why don't you say what's on your mind?"

Hempen leaned toward Tracker; he looked earnest and serious. "Doc, are you sure he's got a mind? We wouldn't want Billy Boy to strain anything, you know."

Tracker and Mazzucco laughed while Lewis sputtered. Robertson cracked a smile and tried to look superior to the whole proceeding.

"Yes, Short Round, he's got a mind," Tracker said when he was through laughing.

"He may have to look for it awhile before he finds it, but he's got one," Mazzucco added. He and Tracker started laughing again. This time Hempen and Robertson joined them.

"Fuck you and the horse you rode in on," Lewis shouted. He jumped to his feet, knocking his ammo case chair over, and stomped toward the west side of the compound, where Ruizique still sat watching alone. The others might think he was a jerk-off except when he was on night patrol, but Ruizique had respect for him. He would sit and talk for a while with someone who took him seriously and didn't make wisecracks about his mind.

The corporal from the Dominican Republic looked up

when Lewis neared him. "Glad to see you, *pano*," he said. He was through cleaning his rifle and saddle-soaping his bandoliers. Now that someone trustworthy was here to watch over the west side of the hill, he could get some sleep. "I haven't seen any bad guys this morning. If you see any coming, be sure to wake me up." He rose to his feet, gathered his gear, and headed toward the squad tent and his cot.

Lewis looked hound-dog after him. So much for friends, he thought. It's days like this that tell who they are. Now all he could do was sit alone, unless he wanted to go back to those jokers and let them jerk his strings some more. No, he decided, he wasn't going to go back to them. They'd have to come to him and apologize before he'd talk to them anymore. At least none of them were in the same fire team with him; he wouldn't have to go on patrol with them. Same for Ruizique.

CHAPTER TWO

Noon, Christmas Day, 1966

Swearin' Swarnes jerked taut at his radio bench and held the headset tight to his ear. "Roger that, Flyboy," he said professionally into the mouthpiece. "Our man in the black flak jacket will direct you in. Ah, Flyboy"—there was hope and uncertainty in his voice when he continued —"do you have the special passengers we was told was coming? Over." He listened to the response and his face stiffened for a moment, then a broad smile spread across his face. "Thank you, Flyboy. We're most definitely ready for 'em. Even put a curtain around the shithouse. See you soon, Flyboy. Earthbase Camp Apache, out." In his excitement, Swarnes almost knocked over his chair getting out of it, but by the time he was halfway to the tent's open entrance he had calmed down and was almost marching. Despite his open utility shirt with the sleeves cut short and the Ho Chi Minh sandals on his feet, he almost looked properly military when he stepped outside and stood almost at attention next to the beach chair Lieutenant Burrison was still lounging in.

"Sir," Swarnes said smartly to the dozing officer, "I

have a message that requires the Lieutenant's immediate attention."

Burrison flinched out of his light nap and, with a crooked finger, tipped the brim of his bush hat to look one-eyed up at his radioman. "Where's Doc Rankin?" he asked. "Get your ass in your rack. I'll have the corpsman check you out, Swearin' Swarnes, get a med-evac for you most ricky-tick." He shook his head. He'd never before heard Swarnes speak formally—or call him "sir." The man must be sick.

"Bullshit, med-evac," Swarnes snorted. "No fucking way I'm dee-deeing out of here now, Scrappy." He spoke in his more normal way, and his body switched from almost at attention to a slouch so fast he didn't seem to move in the process.

"That's better." Burrison let the brim of his bush hat drop back down over his eyes. "What's the message?"

"Buncha birds about zero five out be shitting on our pad most ricky-tick."

Burrison uncrossed his ankles and sat straight. He pushed his hat back until it was square on his head. "Any visitors?" he asked. Even though Tex Randall had said his girlfriend was coming out and bringing other women with her, he wasn't going to believe it until they showed up.

"Yep. Got a Big goddamn Six from Box fucking Top and a railroad tracker."

"Shit." Burrison grimaced. It was nice that the lieutenant colonel they called "Tornado" and Captain Hasford were coming to visit, but it just wasn't the same. He glanced down at himself and stood up. He thought he should change from the cut-off utility trousers and green T-shirt he was wearing into a more suitable uniform to receive the two officers. "Any cargo?" he asked, heading into the tent.

Swarnes followed him. "You got it. Four cases of World tiger piss and a turkey dinner with all the droppings. No bullshit." He followed the young lieutenant all the way into the squad tent's middle room, the one used as quarters by

Burrison and Bell, and stood looking expectant while the officer started to change.

Burrison noticed him standing there, watching. "Swarnes," he snapped, "will you get out of here and give me some privacy while I change?"

"Ain't gave you all the damn message."

"What is it?" he asked impatiently, and continued stripping his casual clothes.

"Three birds coming down." Swarnes paused for dramatic effect. "Got a shitload of fucking split-tails."

Burrison froze, one leg in his trousers, the other raised to insert into the other. "Say what?" He started hopping around to face Swarnes and jiggling his raised leg to get it into his trousers.

"Shitload of split-tails." Swarnes grinned so broadly his head seemed about to split across the middle.

Burrison started hopping and jiggling faster to finish pulling his trousers on. The back of his knee hit the side of his cot, and he lost his balance and tumbled back onto it. "What are you gawking at, Swarnes?" he said mock seriously. He lay on his back. He raised his legs to pull his trousers over his knees and arched his back to yank them above his hips. "Haul your young ass out there and tell Big Louie to get his paddles over to the landing pad most ricky-tick."

Swarnes spun and darted out so fast any words he might have used acknowledging the order were lost on the young lieutenant, who was now on his feet, buttoning his fly and cinching his belt.

Within two minutes all the Marines of CAP Tango Niner—except Swarnes, who was at his radios, and a few others, who were manning defensive positions around the perimeter—and half of the Popular Forces, PFs, were gathered in a semicircle around the white-painted circle of dirt in the compound's northeast corner, watching the circling birds. They were all standing far enough away from the pad that they'd be missed by most of the dirt and debris thrown out by the downwash from the rotors. Except for Big Louie Slover.

The PFs were dressed in motley, few of them in complete uniforms. Some of them wore the traditional black pajamas with only the camouflaged straw bush hats worn by the CAP to distinguish them from the other peasants; others wore utility shirts over the black silk trousers. None of them wore shoes or boots. The Americans wore their cleanest uniforms: trouser legs pegged, shirtsleeves cut short, shirttails outside, bush hats on their heads; few of them wore boots, mostly just Ho Chi Minh sandals or rubber shower thongs from The World. Except for Big Louie Slover. All of them, American and Vietnamese, had their weapons held ready. Except for Big Louie Slover.

Slover stood off from the others, closer to the landing pad, his back to the wind. His bush hat was crushed low on his head with the chin strap under his jaw instead of tucked inside the hat. His trousers were squared away over Ho Chi Minh sandals. He held an orange Ping-Pong paddle in each hand, and his rifle was slung over one shoulder. His coal-black torso shone magnificent in the brilliant sunlight. Big Louie Slover never wore a shirt inside the compound.

Four helicopters orbited the hill. The one that flew low and swung wide over the tree lines east and north of the hill and the thicker forest edges south and west was providing cover for the others; the other three birds circled higher and tighter. The low bird completed one circuit of the hill and swung out wider. One of the three higher choppers dropped and aimed itself at Slover. It came in fast and barely stopped when it touched down. Four men jumped off the bird; two of them, dressed in white cooks' uniforms, turned back to the helicopter's door, while the other two ran ducked-over from under the whirring blades. The bird was rising again while the men in white used their guiding hands to break the fall of four five-gallon insulated containers the crew chief shoved out at them. Then the white-uniformed men crouched low and covered their heads to protect themselves from the rotor's powerful downblast.

The first two men—one tall, angular, and nearing middle age, the other more average in height, strong, and younger than the first—stopped in front of Burrison, Bell, and Lieutenant Houng, the PF commander. Several of the Marines broke from the semicircle as soon as the helicopter was a few feet above the ground, speeding away. They ran onto the landing pad and helped the men in white haul the containers from the landing pad.

Big Louie Slover grimaced at the second high bird, which was now making its run at him. He held the orange paddles straight out at his sides to show the pilot he was level, then held them out front and drew them briskly back and forth toward his shoulders, signaling "come in." When the bird was close enough he patted the paddles down: "settle down." This helicopter didn't come in as fast as the first one and squatted low on its wheels when it touched down. It didn't lift off until all of its passengers were off. Tex Randall met them at the door and shooed them toward the waiting Marines and PFs outside the downwash. The three birds continued to circle the hill.

Big Louie Slover's torso no longer shone in the brilliant sun; it was now dull gray, covered with dust and flecks of white paint. But he didn't care; he was too busy grinning at the passengers who'd departed the second helicopter. He guided in the final bird. Stilts Zeitvogel and Wall McEntire met its passengers and guided them to safety.

While Burrison, Bell, and Houng greeted Lieutenant Colonel Tornado and Captain Hasford, Randall tried to restrain himself with Bobbie Harder—he felt he couldn't even kiss his girlfriend in front of the other Marines. Randall and Bobbie tried to introduce everybody all around, but there were too many and not everyone got named. But that was all right; nobody would have remembered all the names anyway. They had the rest of the day to get it straightened out.

"Welcome back, sir," Burrison said to the lieutenant

colonel, and shook the hand offered him. "It's good to see you again." He said it with a sincerity junior officers don't usually have when they talk to a higher-ranking officer.

"Good to be back in-country," the lieutenant colonel said. His eyes swept the compound in a practiced manner; there wasn't much that could avoid his gaze. "I hear you had some major excitement while I was gone."

"Excitement, sir?" Burrison swallowed a little. "Not really."

The lieutenant colonel cocked an eyebrow. "Someone got Captain Phang off your backs, and someone made a bonfire in a valley bowl on the other side of those hills"— he nodded toward the west—"and you say there wasn't any excitement?"

"We didn't have anything to do with that, sir," Burrison said, meaning the death of Captain Phang, the corrupt assistant district chief.

Bell kept his mouth shut, and Houng pretended the lieutenant colonel was talking too fast for him to understand.

The lieutenant colonel looked hard at Burrison's youthful face, then his own craggy visage almost cracked a smile. "I know you didn't have anything to do with Captain Phang's death," he said slowly enough that even Houng couldn't pretend not to understand. "There's still the business on the other side of the hills." He suddenly broke off and slowly turned in a circle. "Form on me," he said softly.

Burrison blinked at the abruptness of the unexpected order but recovered immediately. "Sergeant Bell, line them up," he said.

Bell had already started turning toward his men, who were milling around the dozen and a half women who'd come out to the boonies to share Christmas dinner with them. Everybody on the hill jerked and spun toward him in disbelief when he bellowed, "Platoon, fall in!" He stood at attention in front of the officers. Houng shrilled orders in rapid Vietnamese at his men, and Captain Hasford, who was fluent in Vietnamese, was unable to restrain a smile at what Houng said. The Marines had trained the PFs well as night fighters, but they hadn't bothered with garrison discipline: instead of shouting orders, Houng explained to them what they were supposed to do. The Marines of Tango Niner had stood in parade-ground formation only twice before in the unit's seven months of existence; the PFs had joined them only once.

It took Ruizique only an instant to be the first to realize the fall in order was serious and start shouting at his men to line up. The other corporals caught on instantly and called to their men. There was momentary confusion while the Marine corporals figured out how to line up their men, and Collard Green and Willy, the two PF squad leaders who were in the compound, ran among their men, getting them properly assembled in this unfamiliar formation.

Swarnes stuck his head out of the command hootch, slack-jawed and google-eyed, wondering if he should abandon his radios to join the formation. He managed to catch Burrison's eye, and the lieutenant patted the air: stay put. Swarnes closed his mouth, wondered what had gotten into somebody that this strange thing was happening, and darted back to the safety of his radios.

Bobbie Harder and the other women also wondered what was going on, but nobody thought it could be bad. One of them, an Air Force first lieutenant, shrugged, said something to the other uniformed women, and marched to join the other officers. The uniformed women, Navy and Air Force—the Marines didn't have any women in Vietnam—lined up behind the men and stood at attention. Bobbie and the other civilian women stood in a cluster off to one side.

Bell executed as sharp an about-face as he could in his Ho Chi Minh sandals and saluted Lieutenant Burrison. "Sir," he announced in a parade-ground voice, "Tango Niner all present and accounted for."

Burrison returned the salute and glanced uncertainly at the lieutenant colonel.

He need not have bothered; the lieutenant colonel was already stepping forward to address the men. Captain Hasford stepped alongside him. "Marines and Popular Forces of CAP Tango Niner," the lieutenant colonel said in a voice that carried far beyond the hilltop, "I just want to tell you this is one outstanding unit." Next to him, Hasford translated into Vietnamese for the PFs who didn't have enough English to understand. "You have met the enemy time and again," the lieutenant colonel continued, "and each time you have met him he has tucked his tail between his legs and run off in defeat, even when he has bloodied you. I am proud of you, the Marine Corps is proud of you, the Republic of Vietnam is proud of you, America is proud of you. And you had best believe they know about you at Three MAF headquarters in Da Nang." His face almost cracked again in a smile. "Every time the powers that be in Saigon object to Marines being assigned to CAP duty instead of all hands going on battalion operations, our Marine leadership tells those powers about the most recent things Tango Niner has done, and those powers back off, grumbling to themselves but knowing there's nothing they can do about it. Men of Tango Niner"—this time he did smile—"and honored guests, I wish you a very merry Christmas and offer a hearty 'well done.' I even brought two messmen out here so you don't have to serve your own holiday dinner." Then he did something that surprised them all; he brought his hand up in a salute. Hasford followed half a beat later.

Bell caught the movement out of the corner of his eye and barked, "Present arms!"

The Marines in the formation brought their rifles up vertically in front of their bodies, grasped the stocks with their left hands, and dropped their right hands to the rifles' grips. They didn't do it sharply; none of them had any recent practice with the manual of arms, and some of them had to think about what the command meant before they could do it. The PFs watched the Marines and copied them, though three or four had their hand positions reversed. The uniformed women in the back row saluted. Burrison, Bell, and the Air Force first lieutenant faced the lieutenant colonel and saluted.

The senior officer held his salute for a beat before cutting it. He turned to Burrison. "Have your radioman signal my bird to come get me."

Bell started toward the tent and saw Swarnes's head sticking out again. The radioman was staring in disbelief at the speech and the salute. He didn't quite know what to make of the sight of a lieutenant colonel saluting corporals, lance corporals, and PFCs. He wished he were in the formation so he could tell the grandchildren he imagined he'd one day have about how a senior officer once saluted him. Oh, well, he thought, it was so improbable his grandchildren would probably think he was just bullshitting them anyway. Swarnes saw Bell come toward him, stop, and make hand signals. He interpreted the hand signals, nodded, and returned to his radios.

Half a minute later the helicopter Lieutenant Colonel Tornado had come on was dropping down again, and Slover was in his accustomed place at the landing pad, facing away from the wind. The lieutenant colonel and Hasford shook hands with Burrison, Bell, and Houng, and the senior officer winked at the Air Force lieutenant—or at least she thought he did.

"One last thing," the lieutenant colonel said before the landing helicopter was too loud for Burrison and Bell to hear him. "Don't worry about Major Y; he's being dealt with at a different level." Mayor Y was the district chief. Tango Niner hadn't had any dealings with him until after Captain Phang's death. He turned out to be as corrupt as his assistant had been.

Then the bird was too close, and neither of the CAP leaders was able to ask him at what level Major Y was being dealt with and what was being done. The lieutenant colonel they called Tornado and Captain Hasford dashed onto the bird and it lifted away. The four helicopters headed east and were soon too far away to hear.

Before dismissing the men from the formation, Bell reminded them of the Christmas presents they had gotten for their visitors and told them to get them ready.

CHAPTER THREE

Let's Boogie!

Field grunts. Nearly anyone can tell you of all the low-lifes in existence, field grunts were the lowest of the low. Field grunts were dirty, their clothes were filthy and torn, they usually needed a shave, they were surly and ill-mannered, they were foulmouthed, they drank too much when they could get it, and they were always looking for an excuse to get into a fight and break up things and people. And they smelled bad.

Rude, lewd, and crude was how the field grunts put it.

Ask any field grunt who wasn't a Marine, and he'd tell you the Marines were far and away the worst of the lot. Mud Marines is what they called them.

Nobody liked field grunts or had any respect for them except other field grunts—and the women who loved them, and not even always then. It was especially the women who didn't like field grunts. Every woman knew the only interest field grunts had in her was what was between her legs, and almost any woman could tell you Marines were the worst of all. To hell with their virginity.

Getting raped was one thing; they didn't want to get killed in the process.

At least this was the impression field grunts and Mud Marines had of how the world perceived them.

'Tain't so, though, not really. Field grunts were simply decent young men who happened to have a very dirty, very difficult, very dangerous job to do. It was a job that nobody in his right mind wanted to do. When field grunts came in out of the field they needed to blow off some steam, and all they asked was some appreciation and respect. But they got in trouble for blowing off steam, and too few people wanted to give them any appreciation or respect. Mud Marines had the dirtiest, most difficult, most dangerous job, so they had more steam to blow off. But the reception they got when they came in out of the field was enough to make them think nobody loved them except their own mothers. And maybe not even them.

It pissed field grunts off, the way they got treated when they came in out of the field, so they naturally tended to associate with those few people who did appreciate them and respect them and let them blow off steam—one another. Made other people think they were clannish and only strengthened the opinion that they were worthless troublemakers. It was a damn shame this should happen to such decent young men, but it did.

So how did it happen that Bobbie Harder, a very decent young woman if ever there was one—not to mention beautiful enough that she probably could have snatched up any man she wanted—met Tex Randall, Mud Marine, and became his girlfriend? Well, some would say there's no accounting for taste. That's not why, though. There's a better reason. The more important question is how on earth did Bobbie Harder, decent young woman, ever manage to talk a dozen and a half other decent young women into forgoing the best Christmas dinner the Da Nang mess halls had to offer and the parties at the officers' clubs to spend Christmas Day out in the boondocks with a bunch of Mud Marines? Mud Marines most of whom hadn't seen a round-eyed woman in seven months or more? Even the helicopter pilots and crews who flew them out to Camp Apache—and knew the Marines of Tango Niner well enough to know that under their murderous exteriors lurked decent young men—couldn't figure that one out.

Bobbie Harder was a civilian employee of the Department of Defense, working in a records office in Da Nang. Two months before, Corporal Tex Randall had accompanied Lieutenant Burrison on a trip to Da Nang to check out a report that an elder in a neighboring village had been killed by Marine H and I—harassment and interdiction artillery—fire. Bobbie Harder worked in the office they went to. At first glance—she saw him staring at her— Bobbie Harder thought Tex Randall was just another jerk field grunt. And that's the way she treated him, with disrespect and absolutely no appreciation. She shared the common view of field grunts and was, frankly, rude to him.

In a combat situation Tex Randall was a vicious man, a ruthless and cold-blooded killer. Of course he was; that's survival. His life and the lives of his men depended on his being a master killer. If you asked him how many men he'd killed, he'd shrug and mumble an I-don't-know. He didn't know, and he never wanted to think about it. Combat and killing weren't things he enjoyed; he was a Marine and a good, patriotic young man with a job to do—a job to survive. Take away his utilities and combat boots, soak him in a tub of fresh flowing water with lots of soap long enough to leach the ground-in dirt out of his pores, and dress him in a tuxedo and he would have been that slightly bashful older guy who took your sister to the senior prom. Not a lot older; he was twenty.

Bobbie Harder had expected Tex Randall to be rude, lewd, and crude. She beat him to the punch. He knew his staring was out of line; it was just that he'd been in the field for five months and hadn't seen such a beautiful woman in a long time. He was embarrassed. He blushed when she was rude to him.

Tex Randall had a deep, sunbaked, bronze tan. The red

showed through it. The fact that he could blush all the way through his tan told Bobbie Harder she might have been wrong about him. She gave him a chance to prove it and found the decent young man behind the killer; she came to understand that he was a killer only when performing his very dirty, very difficult, very dangerous job.

Captain Phang, the late but not lamented assistant district chief, had been a very corrupt official. Tango Niner had interfered with his extracurricular money-making activities too often, so he'd decided to get rid of them. The way he did it was plant two kilos of pure heroin in Camp Apache and arrange to have it discovered by Marine authorities. Lieutenant Burrison, Sergeant Bell, and all five of the CAP's corporals were arrested and charged with drug smuggling. Lieutenant Houng and his PFs decided to find proof that Phang planted the heroin. They did, and the CAP Marines were freed. They held a party at Da Nang— the supplies were provided by Lieutenant Colonel Tornado —to celebrate, and Bobbie Harder managed to talk a few of her friends into attending the party. Not only did nobody get hurt or raped at the party; everybody had fun. And the women learned that Mud Marines weren't necessarily the beasts they'd thought—they really could be some very decent young men. The women who'd been at the party on the beach at Da Nang thought going out to Camp Apache for Christmas dinner would be an exciting adventure. They helped Bobbie Harder talk more women into joining them.

So there they were, a bunch of basically decent young men who were starved for feminine companionship, a group of American women out in the boondocks where there was an actual fighting war going on, and a platoon of Vietnamese farmers who were part-time soldiers most of whom had never before seen an American woman. All gathered together for Christmas dinner. Everybody involved suffered a bit of culture shock.

CHAPTER FOUR

Mad Dogs, Englishmen, and Marines in the Field on Christmas Day

It was a hot day. Not as hot as it had been in July and August, when the Marines of Tango Niner didn't want to know how high the temperature really was. But it was a good fifty or sixty degrees hotter than it was in Minneapolis on that day, say, in the low to mid-eighties, with the high tropical sun beating down and no natural shade on the hilltop. That sun was why most of the Marines wore their bush hats; the only shade available was inside the three squad tents and the four-holer. The squad tents had their sides rolled up for ventilation; the four-holer had sheets raised as privacy side curtains because the women were there. The few small trees on the hilltop didn't really cast any shade.

Once the women who'd come with Bobbie Harder got over the excitement of the helicopter ride and the landing on the almost barren hilltop and the brief ceremony conducted by the lieutenant colonel, they finally noticed the heat. Most of them started wondering why they had agreed to come out here. But they weren't allowed to wonder for long. The Marines did their best to make the women feel welcome. They started by giving each of them a bush hat just like the ones they wore. For most of the Marines it had been too long since they'd been this close to a round-eyed woman—they didn't want to disappoint their visitors.

Nancy Carter was an almost beautiful woman. She wasn't quite tall enough to be called tall and was a little too ungainly to be called statuesque. Her hair was light, but not quite blond, and her eyes were an intense blue, but not enough to be called sky or piercing. She was a tad too angular to be called "built." Her self-esteem was high, but a little too weak for her to be noticeably self-possessed. She wore snug-fitting red pedal pushers and a white blouse that looked as if it would turn transparent if she sweated through it. In short, she was almost—but not quite—the stuff wet dreams are made of. Not that it made any difference to Wall McEntire.

Nancy Carter wasn't one of the women who had partied at the beach; she hadn't met any of the Marines of Tango Niner before, so she was uncertain when an odd specter confronted her. A tall, grinning man stood five feet in front of her. He looked to be a little over six feet tall and gave the impression he was as wide as he was high. She gingerly took the straw camouflage bush hat he offered her and equally gingerly placed it on her head and tipped it back far enough that she wished she had some bobby pins to hold it on with. She looked at her benefactor. His hands hung limp at his sides, then planted themselves firmly against his thighs, then clasped in front of his lower abdomen, then tucked into his pockets, then went akimbo on his hips, then gripped each other behind his back, then wove into a cross over his chest. Nancy leaned forward slightly at the hips and tilted her face up at him.

"Hi, I'm Nancy Carter. What's your name?" She realized she had no choice but to tough it out.

The tall, broad man grinned wider and his lips quivered, but he didn't say anything.

Did I make a mistake coming here? she wondered. Is

this giant going to do something to me? She was about to take a tentative step backward when a second man appeared beside the first one. A shock of bright red hair stuck out from under the second man's bush hat. While he was neither as tall nor as wide as the first man, he somehow gave the impression of being bigger. He tipped his hat, a bush hat like the one just given to her, and spoke to her.

"Nancy Carter, I'm pleased to make your acquaintance," the redhead said. "I'm PFC John Robertson. They call me Big Red." He doffed his hat and raised his eyes to point out his hair. "Silent Sam here is Corporal Dennis McEntire. We call him Wall, because he's not tall enough to be a tree and not fat enough to be a bear." Robertson looked at McEntire, who was still grinning at Nancy and now had his hands behind his back. "He's shy," Robertson said to her, then to McEntire, "Mind your manners, Wall. Say hello to Nancy Carter."

McEntire's mouth writhed, and he finally managed to say in a voice that seemed impossibly small to come out of such a huge man, "Hello to Nancy Carter."

Robertson nodded, satisfied. "He's shy," he said again. "Would you like to take a tour of Camp Apache, Nancy?"

She wasn't sure she wanted to take a tour—getting away from here seemed to be a much better idea—but she was stuck until the helicopters came back for them. And anything had to be better than standing there being stared at by this silent, grinning man. "Sure. Why not?"

Robertson swept one hand out, pointing the way for her to go, and curved his other arm in invitation. If she wanted to walk linking arms or with their arms around each other, that was wonderful with him.

Nancy went in the direction he pointed and avoided his curved arm. McEntire, still grinning, hulked along in their wake. The trio walked past another Marine, involved in conversation with one of the Waves who'd come with her, and McEntire mumbled something to him that Nancy thought she misunderstood. But she didn't misunderstand;

he actually did mumble, "It's been so long I really did forget what end to stick it in."

"These are our hootches," Robertson said. "Well," he continued awkwardly, "actually they're tents, but we call them hootches. This one"—they were south of the center of the compound—"is the one we live in. . . . Ah, I mean the rifle squad lives in it. Wall doesn't; he's the machine gun team leader. He lives over there." He pointed at another tent to the right. Both tents had their sides rolled up and the cots and makeshift tables were piled high with miscellaneous gear. In the field these Marines weren't much on having their gear properly stowed away. "That's my rack there." He pointed out one of the cots. "I sleep in it every morning."

Nancy looked at him quizzically, and he shrugged. "I'm out on patrol every night; most of us are on patrol or perimeter duty every night. We get most of our sleep during the day. This here"—they were going up the last, slight slope toward the south side of the hill—"is the command hootch. Swearin' Swarnes—he's our radioman—is in this end of it with his radios." He held the open flap of the tent open more so Nancy could look in. She saw a scrawny-looking Marine hovering over two of the other women; they were also wearing bush hats. One of them was seated in a folding chair in front of a narrow bench, and Swarnes was explaining to them how his fucking radios worked and how his was the most goddamn important job in the unit. The more the scrawny Marine talked, the stiffer and more uncomfortable-looking he became and the more the two women he was talking to shook with repressed laughter.

"Does he always talk like that?" Nancy asked Robertson, who was looking pained.

He shook his head slowly, then said, "No. Usually he swears more. Let's keep going." He stepped out of her way and started to go around the tent.

Nancy turned and stopped abruptly. McEntire was standing flat-footed. His mouth still bore its wide grin, but his forehead was wrinkled. She felt sudden compassion for this huge man, who so obviously wanted to talk to a good-looking woman and just as obviously was afraid to. "It's okay, big boy," she said, patting his arm. "You'll get over it." Everything on McEntire's face seemed to sag, but he kept grinning.

"Scrappy and Jay Cee sleep in the middle room of that hootch." Robertson was still talking, not having noticed the brief byplay between the other two. "And the two corpsmen have the other end, which is also a supply room. Over here is our trench. It goes all the way around the perimeter inside the wire. A month, two months ago some sappers got through the wire there." He pointed. "Wasted one man, wounded two others." He looked at her grimly. She looked back, startled, suddenly aware of the life-or-death situation these men faced daily. "We wasted both of them." His expression immediately softened, and he continued. "Out there—" He pointed his arm in a sweep to the south. "—is the Song Du Ong River. Lots of fishermen fish on it at night. You can see the lights on their boats from here." He looked at her again. "Anytime we see a boat on the river at night without a light, we know it's Charlie, and we blow its ass away."

She was startled again. She looked toward the river winding its way east to the South China Sea. A narrow band of large trees bordered it, and between the hill and the river the band of trees was wider. There was beaten-down scrub growth between the hill and the trees. "Does that happen very often?" She licked her lips, which were suddenly dry. "That you see boats without lights, I mean."

Robertson shrugged. "Once in a while. We probably sunk forty or fifty boats since I've been here." He paused a second, momentarily lost in thought. "I've been here since September." He turned right and spoke again in a more normal voice. "Over there's the piss tubes, and the thing that looks like an Arab sheik's desert tent is the shithouse." He stopped talking and looked away from her, astonished. "Goddamn my fucking mouth, I didn't mean to—ah, shit, I—" He stopped talking and looked embarrassed.

McEntire finally said something in a voice that sounded to Nancy as if it belonged in a body that big. "That's right, dipshit. Watch your fucking language, before you say something you don't mean to. . . .Ah, shit, I did it, too." He turned his back to Nancy and hung his head.

Nancy suddenly saw **the two** young Marines as **more** human than she had before, and she laughed. "Come on, you guys. It's okay. You should hear the way us girls talk when there aren't any men around."

"You sure about that?" Robertson asked, half looking at her over his shoulder.

"I'm sure." She laughed again, a friendly laugh. "It's all right." Impulsively, she reached out and grabbed them each by the arm. "Come on. Show me the rest of Camp Apache." The two Marines started strutting, with her arms linked through theirs. Robertson became expansive, and McEntire lost his shyness and found his voice. He was even able to forget for a few minutes that it had been so long he forgot which end to stick it in.

Halfway around the compound, Tex Randall was giving Bobbie Harder the same tour. She wore her bush hat backward, right side of the brim up, and cocked at a rakish angle over her right eye. It wasn't much of a tour; Camp Apache was a half mile in circumference and had only a few things in it other than the defensive positions around the perimeter. Once the trench that circled the hill inside the three banks of concertina wire—two banks along the steeper, eastern face of the hill—had been seen, there really wasn't that much more other than the squad tents the men lived in, unused living bunkers, mortar pit, and two ammo bunkers.

"This is the main gate," Randall explained when he stopped at an opening in the wire where a bulldozed road wide enough to drive a truck through entered the compound. "We close it at night with those plugs—" He pointed to an assembly of wire sitting next to the opening. "—and the machine gun covers it."

Bobbie nodded politely and walked through the opening to look at the other side of a plywood panel standing on two iron posts next to it. She read the hand-painted sign and burst out laughing. It said:

CAMP APACHE
USMC
Home of Combined Action Platoon T-9
It Takes Two to Tango
Charlie Gonna Die Here
Barry Sadler, Eat Your Heart Out

"Who's Barry Sadler?" she asked when her laughter stilled.

Randall shrugged. "He was some doggie in the Green Beanies. He wrote the song 'The Ballad of the Green Berets.'"

She cocked her head and thought for a moment. "You mean the one that starts 'Fighting soldiers from the sky'?"

"That's the one."

"Tex, are you trying to tell me you're tougher than the Green Berets?"

"You know it." He grinned, then added proudly, "Maybe Force Recon is tougher than we are. If they are, they're the only ones."

Bobbie smiled at him, then marched almost close enough for her breasts to press against his chest and stretched up to kiss him lightly on the lips. She took his hand and said, "I'm hungry. Let's go see what's for chow."

He blinked. "I didn't know you called it chow."

She laughed. "Normally I don't, but now I'm in the field with Marines. Marines in the field call it chow, don't you?"

"We sure do." His grin turned into a tender smile; his chest swelled with pride as he returned with the most beautiful woman in the world to the rest of the platoon, where Burrison, Bell, and the Air Force lieutenant were beginning to line everybody up to be served the Christmas dinner. Bobbie Harder wasn't really the most beautiful woman in the world, even though she was beautiful. But when a man's in love—or on his way to being in love—the woman he's in love with is the most beautiful to him.

Later, over roast turkey, roast ham, candied yams, mashed potatoes with gravy, cranberry sauce, French-cut green beans, apple pie, and the rest of it, Houng and Collard Green sat talking with J. C. Bell. There were twenty-three Marines, two Navy corpsmen, and nineteen women. That's why Bell hadn't managed to pair off. Not everyone was as fastidious as he was; the other extra American men were willing to double up. The three men talked in broken English and badly inflected Vietnamese, as well as the patois that incorporated English, Vietnamese, and French. They understood one another well enough.

"So these are your American women," Houng said, looking around at the fair-complexioned blondes and brunettes and redheads. He had thought that maybe the Marines did something to their hair, because they had so many different colors. Since the women also had many different colors of hair, maybe that's the way Americans were, instead of sensibly all having the same color, like Vietnamese did with their black hair. He openly looked at the chests and hips and thighs of the women and remarked, "They go out and swell large in many places where our women go out or swell only a little. It seems strange that women, who are smaller than men, should be so big as they are." He looked at Bell and grinned crookedly. "But then, American men are giants, so I guess American women should also be bigger than normal men." The average Vietnamese man stood only an inch or two over five feet tall—only three or four of the visiting American women were that short.

Bell looked longingly at Tango Niner's visitors and mentally kicked himself. As a sergeant and the unit's number two, he should have had his pick of them, but he had made the mistake of taking too long in making sure there was adequate security set to protect the visitors before circulating among them himself. By then it had been too late. He sighed. "Yeah, these are normal American girls. When I go home, I'm going to get me five or six of them and do some heavy-duty partying."

Houng chuckled. "I understand you, my friend. When I came home to Hou Ky from the Arvin, had I not been married I, too, would have gotten several women to help me celebrate." But only two or three, he added mentally. He looked appraisingly at Bell and wondered if the American really could handle five or six women at one time. He was big and young and strong enough, but the American women were also big and young and strong.

"What do you think of American girls, Collard Green?" Bell asked.

The PF squad leader scowled at him. "The American women are very. . ." He used many words to describe the physical attributes of the women, but the one that he would have used if he'd known it was "pneumatic." "I want very much to talk to them, but—" He swept his gaze around the compound, pausing briefly to glower at each of the women. "—when they see me coming they all turn and walk away. They make it obvious they do not wish to talk to me." He shook his head vehemently. "I would like to take one of them home with me and lay her on my bed and rest on her. They are so—" He moved his hands through the air to describe what they were "so." "—and I would like to rest my tired head on one of their chests when I come in from patrol." He looked longingly at them, but his expression was not one that someone who didn't know him would call longing. "They are big enough I could lay on one and use her as a sleeping mat without causing her hurt. Any one of them would be the most comfortable sleeping mat I could imagine."

Bell laughed. "Bet I can tell you why they walk away when they see you coming," he said. Houng joined in his laughter.

Collard Green glared at them as fiercely as he could.

Most men would instantly have jumped away from him, but the two knew there was no need to move. "Is it my fault my skin has an odd color?" he snapped. "I am not to blame because the bones of my face are shaped the way they are, that the muscles and skin flow over them the way they do. It is only you strangers who see me the way you do," he finished haughtily. Collard Green's complexion had a greenish cast to it, and his expression, whether he was scowling, glaring, looking fierce, grimacing, smiling, or looking any other way, was that of a man suffering from severe stomach distress—Collard Green always looked as if he was no more than a second or two away from throwing up.

"No, it's not your fault," Bell said, and tried hard to control his laughter. "Tell you what. When we finish eating I'll introduce you to one of them, explain to her it's okay to talk to you."

Houng's eyes sparkled mischievously. "Oh? Which one of them do you know? Why are you not sitting with her now?"

Bell glowered at him. He changed the subject. "You know, I never noticed before how good these bush hats look." The others looked at the women, all wearing the camouflage bush hats, none worn straight on their heads but at different angles. The hats looked marvelous.

"Boy that was good, Tex," Bobbie Harder said when they were through eating. "I need to walk it off." She looked beyond the hill. "Is it safe to take a walk down by the river?"

"You bet it is," Randall said. He'd been wondering ever since she called the evening before how he was going to be able to get her alone for a while. "Give me a minute to tell someone where we're going." He was back in about two minutes. A cartridge belt with canteen, first aid kit, bayonet, and four magazines was around his waist. His rifle, with a magazine in it and a round in the chamber, was slung on his shoulder. A light pack hung on his back.

She looked at him, a little worried. "If it's safe, do you really need all that?"

Randall shrugged. "It's safe, all right, but better to be extra safe than sorry."

CHAPTER FIVE

All Things Must...

"We never go outside the wire unarmed, Bobbie," Randall said. "Besides"—he glanced at her—"I'm so used to carrying a rifle I feel kind of naked without one. Really, it's Christmas. There's a truce on." They were walking through the low scrub that was still trying to recover from the time more than a month earlier when an entire grunt company bivouacked on it following a concerted attempt by the Vietcong to wipe out the Marine outpost. She had expressed concern that he felt the need to carry a weapon on their walk to the river. "And remember, they don't have anybody out looking for trouble, and neither do we. Hell, if there's any Charlies in the area, they're taking the day off, samee-same us. You're going to like this," he said. The final fifty meters between them and the large trees was rapidly shrinking. "It's cooler in the shade."

It *was* cooler under the trees, by ten or fifteen degrees. Unfortunately, the trees didn't only block out the sun and some of its heat; they also cut down on air movement. The sweat that coated Bobbie Harder's body from the mild exertion of the walk from the hill to the trees just sat there.

She fanned herself with her hat and wiggled and tugged at her blouse to keep it from sticking to her. Randall watched out of the corner of his eye; he enjoyed watching her move.

"The breeze picks up again by the river," he said.

Ruizique watched the two disappear into the trees and called for Webster to join him.

"What's up, honcho?" Webster asked, joining him at the wire.

"Get Fast Talking Man and the newby and your weapons. We're going for a walk." He had already gotten his own rifle and cartridge belt from the squad tent.

Webster stared at him. "You dinky dau or something? Shit, we don't want to go for any damn walk. We're trying to make time with the girls."

"You don't need to make time with them now, Malahini. You're going on R and R tomorrow. Fast's already been there. He can hold out for a little longer. Get them." The "newby" didn't count.

Webster didn't move.

Ruizique turned to him. "That's an order."

"That's a bullshit order. We don't run patrols during the day. When we take walks, it's because we want to. Anyway, there's a truce on."

"Tex is out there with his girlfriend. We should have some security for them. Move it."

"You want to watch while they do it or something? They don't need security because of the truce."

Ruizique glared at him. His machismo was insulted at the implication he was a Peeping Tom. "Now."

Webster stirred uncertainly and looked back to where the other Marines were talking and laughing with the girls —and at the one he'd been talking to. He saw Bell eyeing her, the only woman on the hill who was alone at the moment. "Can we take the girls with us?"

Ruizique looked disgusted. A security patrol was no

place for women. But there was the truce. "Bring them. Let's go," he snapped.

"Right away, honcho." Webster spun and trotted back to the woman he had left. He didn't look directly at Bell but could see disappointment on the sergeant's face when he reached her before Bell did. He didn't notice Houng and Collard Green lean close to each other and shake with laughter.

"How'd you like to go for a walk down by the river?" Webster asked.

"Is it okay?" she asked; she was thinking, Will I be safe from you?

"No problem," he said. "Let me get a few other people." "Fast Talking Man" Pennell and the newby, Neissi, were both nearby with the two women they'd eaten with. Shortly, the four Marines and three women were all filing out the back gate, a series of narrow, offset openings through the barbed wire on the south side of the hill.

"Oh, boy, you all look tough and ready for action," one of the women said. "Shouldn't you be wearing helmets?"

Ruizique shook his head. "We are night fighters," he said. "We don't wear helmets, because they cut down on your hearing." He looked her in the eye. "At night, hearing is more important than vision." Eyes alert, he looked toward the trees they would soon enter for any clue someone might be in them. "I don't even know where my helmet is. I haven't worn it in three months. These hats"—he glanced at her and nodded at the bush hat perched on her head—"are ideal for night movement."

"Besides," Webster joined in, "daytime's the safe time around here. Even if there wasn't a truce on, Charlie don't come around during the day. We kick ass on him so hard at night he just knows we'll put him even deeper in the hurt-locker if he comes around during the day." He grinned and looked at the trees, thinking of their shade and privacy. Going on one of the informal daytime patrols Tango Niner called "taking a walk" was beginning to seem like a good idea.

Under the trees, Pennell took the point. Talking softly and slowly, the quiet black man from South Dakota explained to the light brown woman walking by his side how a point man operated. Pennell was called "Fast Talking Man" in ironic counter to the quiet manner in which he spoke. He told her what signs he watched and listened for and pointed out things he saw or heard and how he would react to them on a night patrol. But he didn't tell her the signs he was alert for now. He had been a mortar man when he joined Tango Niner but had been transferred to the rifle squad when casualties stripped the platoon and replacements took too long to arrive. He liked going on the night patrols and had proved adept at point man.

The Song Du Ong was a broad river, several hundred meters wide at the point where Randall and his girlfriend reached it. Its bank here was low, only a foot or so above the sluggish water. Bobbie Harder looked at it and chewed on her lip.

"Is it clean?" she asked.

He nodded. "It comes down out of the mountains. There aren't any villages upstream."

"Is that important, no villages upstream?"

"Yes. The river's the only running water the peasants have." He grinned at her. "They use it the same way we use running water, to bathe in and as their toilet. Riverside villages use the rivers to take craps in." He looked at the water. "This river's probably clean enough to drink here."

She looked at it doubtfully. "Even moving this slowly?"

He nodded again. "It's only moving slow close to the bank. A few feet out, it goes faster. Nasty little bugs don't have much chance to breed in it."

She looked thoughtfully at the water, then out across and up and down the river. She pulled on her sweat-soaked blouse and made up her mind. "Tex, turn your back." She smiled impishly at him. "I want to wash some of this sweat off me. No peeking."

"Ah, come on. . . ."

"I said no peeking, Tex. Now, turn around."

Grumbling, he turned his back and shucked his pack. He went off a few yards and emptied it. It held a poncho, a blanket, and a few cans of Coke that had been cold when he packed them but were now almost hot. He spread the poncho, laid the blanket over it, and sat cross-legged in its center with his rifle over his legs. He faced into the trees and watched and listened for intruders.

Bobbie watched him and smiled softly. When he settled, she stripped off her hat, blouse, and slacks but left her bra and panties on. Kneeling on the bank, she dipped her blouse into the water and wrung it out. She used the wet garment to wipe herself off, rinsed it out again, and wiped her chest, belly, back, and legs again. A third time the blouse went into the water. She wrung it as dry as she could, fluffed it out, and hung it on a low-hanging tree branch. Her slacks went next to it. Then she put the hat back on, crouched low, and tiptoed to the blanket. She opened her arms wide and lunged to grab her man from behind.

And found herself wrapped in his arms.

He gently brushed her thick auburn hair from her face, knocking the hat off, and said huskily, "I'm a night fighter, Bobbie. You can't sneak up on a night fighter."

Then their mouths crushed together.

Pennell easily followed the path Randall had taken. It was obvious the Texan didn't expect any trouble; he wasn't making any attempt to conceal his passage. The occasional boot print, crushed leaf, or broken twig was a clear indicator of where he was going with Bobbie: straight to the river. Less than fifty meters from the water, Pennell turned right to follow a well-used path. If Randall was directly to the front, which seemed likely, Pennell didn't want to walk in on him and his girlfriend suddenly when they were in a clinch. He went a hundred and fifty meters west before he stopped and waited for Ruizique.

The corporal from the Dominican Republic looked at

him, and Pennell shook his head; Randall hadn't come this way. "Circle back and go the other way, Fast," Ruizique said.

Pennell nodded and turned away from the river before heading east, curving his route to hit the trail east of where he'd first stepped onto it.

"What's this about?" asked the light brown girl beside him. She fanned herself with her hat as they walked.

Pennell thought about her question slowly, the same way he talked, and decided to tell her the truth. "Tex is out here with his girlfriend. We're providing security for them, just in case. I think I know where they are. We're avoiding them." A soft smile reformed his face. "A good grunt never goes back the same way he went out. That's why we didn't just turn around on the path after checking things this far."

She thought about that for a moment, then looked at him admiringly. "Somebody following you might set an ambush along your path and wait for you to come back, right?"

His smile became less soft, and he nodded.

"You're smart," she said, and gave him her warmest smile.

His smile turned into a proud grin. "I'm a night fighter," he said, "and I'm good at it."

Randall and Bobbie were oblivious to the seven people circling outside their view or hearing. They were in love and loving each other. Each marveled at the near perfection of the other's body and at how lucky they were to have found each other. When their passion was sated, they dressed and lay side by side on the blanket, their shoulders and thighs touching and their hands clasped. They didn't want to get dressed so soon, but there was the possibility of someone coming by. Bobbie's blouse was still damp, but she knew it would dry soon from the heat. They talked of small matters for a while until they got to the important matters: how much longer he had to go on his tour in Viet-

nam, how much time she had left on her contract with
DOD. How he was going to take thirty days leave on his
next duty station when she got back to New York City and
they'd spend the month together. They skirted the question
of whether she would move to Texas when he got out of the
Marines or he would move to New York. They didn't mention marriage at all, though they both thought about it.

The four Marines and three women found a place where
they could sit in a tight circle and talk—Ruizique made
them talk quietly. The Marines knew they were not more
than seventy-five meters from where Randall sought privacy with his girlfriend. They didn't know what the two
were doing with their privacy, but they knew what they'd
be doing under those circumstances and didn't want to disturb them. The three women talked and joked and giggled
—softly, of course—and wondered why one or another of
the men they were with always seemed to be watching and
listening outside their circle.

Webster was listening and watching outside the circle
when he said, "They're going."

The women looked at each other, confused. Who was
going? What did that have to do with the question? One of
them had just asked Webster where he was going on the
R&R he was leaving for tomorrow.

The Marines knew what he meant and stood up. The
three women scrambled to their feet and donned their bush
hats.

"Bangkok," Webster said, and grinned.

Neissi punched his shoulder. "Go get 'em, tiger," he
said. Bangkok had a reputation among the Marines in
Vietnam as the biggest whorehouse in the world. A man
could go there, get drunk out of his mind, and fuck his
brains out for five solid days and four solid nights before
being poured onto a plane for the flight back to VC Land.

"You better believe it," Webster said, grinning.

When they reached the edge of the trees, the three

women were surprised to see Randall and Bobbie ahead of them, halfway to the hill. The four Marines weren't surprised. Then they heard a distant *carrumph*. The women didn't know what it meant and ignored it. The Marines did know what it meant and said, "Ah, shit." A puff of smoke blossomed on top of the hill. A second later they heard the dull explosion of the mortar round and the nearer, sharper crack of a bullet. The four Marines dropped at the sound of the crack and knocked the women down with them.

"Where is he?" Ruizique demanded.

"Came from that way," Pennell said, pointing.

"Everybody, back into the trees," Ruizique ordered. "Stay low, and go fast."

"Fast, newby, come with me," Ruizique said when they were back in the cover of the trees. "Malahini, stay with the girls." There hadn't been any more shots or mortar rounds.

Ruizique didn't look to see if his orders were being followed. These men were Marines; he expected them to obey. He didn't look back when one of the women screamed. He knew a security patrol was no place for women, and the scream proved it. The three Marines went hunting for whoever had shot at them.

"Over here, I got something," Neissi shouted a few minutes later. He angled to the side and knelt on one knee. He picked something up and displayed it to the others: a spent cartridge. Bent grass showed where the sniper had lain, waiting for them. One man, one shot.

The corporal wanted to go after him, but he knew the sniper had to be running faster than he would dare pursue with only three men. He also knew chasing the sniper might lead them into a trap. And there were the women he'd left behind with Webster. "You've got a souvenir," he told Neissi. "Let's go back."

Webster and the three women weren't where they'd been left; they were in the open, where they'd been when the shot had rung out. Webster was lying on the ground.

Two of the women were kneeling over him, their shoulders heaving. The third woman was a few feet away, bent over, throwing up. The three Marines ran to them.

Webster's surprised eyes stared, sightless, at the sky. Blood flowed from his side. One man, one shot, one kill.

CHAPTER SIX

**The Wee Hours of the Morning,
December 26, 1966**

Corporal Tex Randall peered through the brush lining the Song Du Ong. A hundred meters away, across the rapid-running water, was the spit island where the abandoned hamlet called Hou Binh rotted away. Next to him, napping quietly, lay Vinh, one of the PF squad leaders. On Vinh's other side, Billy Boy Lewis watched the island. A dozing PF was beyond Lewis, and two more were to Randall's right, one watching the approach to the ford from this bank to the island, the other getting what sleep he could. Behind him, PFC Lawrence Dodd slept and two PFs kept watch on the ambush's rear. They had been sitting in this ambush for over an hour. It had been nearly a month since one of Tango Niner's three night patrols had watched Hou Binh. At one time the Vietcong had frequently used the small hamlet as a rest spot; they'd liked it because they were able to observe all approaches and escape if they saw anyone coming. But the Marines had learned how to deny safe use of the island to the VC, and they'd stopped going there.

At one time the Vietcong had gone through Bun Hou village any time of day or night they wanted; they moved with impunity. Even after the Marines arrived they continued to do so. Until the Marines killed too many of them—the Marines and their Popular Forces partners. Eventually Tango Niner settled into a routine of putting out three patrols per night, and those three patrols proved strong enough and flexible enough to deal with any new tactic Charlie came up with to safely move his men and supplies along the Song Du Ong flood plain from the mountains, in the west, to the coastal areas, where so much of the fighting was taking place. Bun Hou had become peaceful in the process.

But the sniper round that killed Webster and the single mortar round that hit inside Camp Apache changed Tango Niner's nighttime routine. The platoon was suddenly operating as it had in the past when it could expect to run into the enemy several nights a week. In a way they all knew it was too good to be true; there hadn't been any action in nearly three weeks.

Randall glanced at the luminous hands of his watch, held his PRC-6 walkie-talkie-type radio to his head, and listened. He heard a brief exchange and then pressed the speak button on the raido's side. "Donald Duck, this is Dewey. Situation as before. Nothing's happening. Over."

Sergeant Bell's voice came back almost immediately. "Roger, Dewey. Duck out."

A moment later Randall heard Ruizique identify himself as Lewie and say his situation was the same also. Bell "Donald Ducked" out. Randall's patrol had been out two hours; two more and they'd go back in. They were to patrol the area south of Camp Apache, as far east as the market hamlet of Hou Cau and west to beyond Hou Binh. The only stipulation was to set an ambush for an hour or so overlooking the island hamlet.

Randall put the radio down and went back to watching the island. He thought about the scene on top of the hill

when he and Bobbie Harder had reached it immediately
after the mortar round exploded.

Loud voices were bellowing orders for the women to get in
the sleeping bunkers and for the defensive positions to be
manned. Shriller voices shouted in Vietnamese. Women
were screaming and crying. Randall paused long enough at
the entrance to the bunker next to the command tent to
shove Bobbie into it.

"Stay there until I tell you to come out," he shouted at
her, but she didn't hear all of his words, because he was
running away.

All across the hilltop, PFs were racing for the trench
around the perimeter to prepare themselves for the assault
that might come next—once the expected mortar barrage
lifted. Lieutenant Burrison ran about, organizing half the
Marines in the compound to defend the south and west
sides of the hill. Bell was supervising the rest of the Marines hustling the women into the three bunkers. Randall
glanced around and saw both corpsmen kneeling, treating
two people on the ground.

He spotted an obviously panicked woman streaking toward the main gate and took off after her. Her foot came
down on one of the many irregularities on the ground, and
she collapsed forward. When Randall reached her she was
rubbing her ankle and trying to stand at the same time,
heading toward what she hoped was safety, beyond the hill.
He grabbed her shoulders to pull her to her feet, and she
gasped at the pain in her ankle. She tried to wrench herself
out of his grasp to continue her flight, but he was too
strong and twisted her around.

"This way," he shouted, and gripped one arm to pull her
along.

"No," she wailed, "I've got to get out of here." She put
her weight on the twisted ankle and, screaming from the
pain and panic, fell heavily to her knees.

Randall didn't waste any more time; he bent over,
wrapped an arm around her waist, and ran, carrying her to

the nearest bunker, the one near the weapons section squad tent. She flailed her arms and legs, trying to break free, but couldn't. He hustled her into the bunker and, in one quick motion, lowered her to the floor and pinned her there with one hand held firmly below her breasts. He looked at the women huddled in the bunker and snapped, "She panicked. Hold her down until she's under control, or she'll try to run out. Keep her here."

One of the women, seeming calm and controlled, cradled the screaming woman's head on her lap and ordered the others to surround her. Then she started stroking her hair and crooning at her.

Randall didn't stick around to find out what happened next. Outside, he saw Bell waving at him and ran in the direction indicated. Lewis and Dodd were just finishing putting the concertina wire plug in the main gate. He joined them, assigned fields of fire, and hunkered down to wait for the barrage and the assault.

"What the fuck's going on?" he asked his men. "Charlie's never tangoed with us during the day before."

That wasn't exactly true. Tango Niner had been hit once before during the day. In September, North Vietnamese sappers under the command of Major Nghu, sent to wipe out the Marines of Tango Niner, had hit them during the day. One mortar round wounded three of the Marines and two PFs. One of the Marines was Lieutenant Masterman, the platoon commander. Masterman was wounded so badly he never returned.

Randall watched the island and knew in his heart no one was on it, no one other than him and his men would visit it tonight; no enemy slinked through his patrol area. If Charlie wanted to tango, where was he? It frustrated him.

A kilometer and a half west of Hou Binh, Ruizique and his two remaining Marines, along with Willy and five of his PFs, lay in ambush. The band of trees bordering the river here was little more than fifty meters wide, and Ruizique split his small unit into two segments, one watching the river, the other observing the scrub north of the trees. The patrol leader was splitting his time between the two groups and resolved to stay awake for the six-hour duration of his patrol. It was a roving patrol that had gone out an hour before midnight and would come back in before dawn. The patrol had a rough route to follow, but he was free to alter his route anywhere he wanted within the boundaries of his patrol area: six square kilometers that ranged from a few hundred meters south of the main east-west trail between Bun Hou and the western hills, south to the river, from a klick west of Camp Apache to a klick east of the hills.

Ruizique planned to make a slow, clockwise circuit of the area and sit in ambush three times during the night. He put his radio down after checking in and glanced at his watch one more time. He decided to give Charlie another ten or fifteen minutes to come to him here, then he'd go looking for him somewhere else. His right hand kneaded the scar on his left arm where a VC machine-gun bullet had ripped through it, making this war very personal and giving him a blood lust for the men on the other side. The corporal from the Dominican Republic had not enjoyed the three weeks of peace Tango Niner had just experienced as the rest of the Marines and PFs had; he wanted to kill Charlie. Now his face looked grim, but he was happy on the inside—Charlie was back, and he could kill him again for the wound he had suffered. He fingered the soft leather bandoliers that crossed his chest and remembered what he found on the hill when his men carried Webster's body onto it that afternoon.

Few people were visible on the hilltop; the women were all hiding in the bunkers, and most of the Marines and PFs were in the perimeter trench. Through the open side of the command hootch Ruizique saw Swarnes at his radios, calling for a med-evac.

"Jesus H. fucking Christ," the radioman said when he saw them. "How bad is he?"

"Wasted" was Ruizique's terse reply. Webster was dead; the corporal was already putting him out of his mind. The living were more important; the living were the only ones who could keep one another alive. "How are you?"

"Been better—that's for goddamn sure," Swarnes said. He had one arm in a sling, and a bloody bandage was wrapped around his head. "Shit, I'm a fucking radioman. Ain't no dinks supposed to go zinging my young ass." He talked into his radio, amending the casualty report he'd just made, adding one KIA.

"Jay Cee, secure this place with the people you have," Burrison shouted. "Stilts, Tex, get your teams over here. Doc Rankin, I want you."

Houng was also shouting orders, to his PFs. In less than a minute Burrison and Houng had seven Marines, twenty PFs, and one corpsman filing rapidly out the back gate, a recon in force to find the mortar that had fired one round at the hill and stopped.

Ruizique watched them enter the trees west of the hill from his position on that side, where Bell had assigned him and his team. He was not sorry not to be with them; he was certain they wouldn't find the enemy mortar team or anyone else. Fifteen minutes later he heard the *whumpa-whumpa* of approaching helicopters and turned to watch. The first one to land was a med-evac bird. It took a wounded PF, the woman who sprained her ankle in her panicked flight, and another woman, who had been hit in her thigh by a piece of shrapnel. It took off immediately and flew east without waiting for the others. Two more helicopters landed for the rest of the women, got back into formation with the gunship that had orbited the hill while they loaded, and then headed east, away from the truce violation. Swarnes refused to be med-evaced; he said his arm didn't hurt, and besides, some asshole was sure as hell going to fuck up his radios while he was away.

Three hours later the thirty sweaty, dirty men who had gone looking for the enemy came back. Their mood was sour. They hadn't found anyone; they couldn't even find where the mortar had been.

West of where Ruizique and his men lay in ambush, Corporal Zeitvogel listened to the patrols report their situations while his eyes continued to search the finger ridge leading down from the hills. It was too quiet tonight, he thought. It was too unlike Charlie to zing in a round during the day. He expected the enemy to try something tonight. Where were the little fuckers? he wanted to know. His night fighter's ears listened for any sound, or lack of sound, that indicated anything out of the ordinary. All he heard were the buzzing of insects, the *fuk-yoo* calls of lizards, the homing shrieks of night-feeding birds. He couldn't even hear the soft breathing of the PF who lay alert within his long arm's reach to the right, or the sleeping breath of Short Round Hempen, on his left. It was too quiet.

In a little while he'd pull his ambush and move to the cleft in the hills where the Song Du Ong came out of them onto its flood plain. He patiently waited, watching, listening. But he wasn't able to drive the spooky memory of the afternoon's fruitless search from his mind.

The thirty men ran to the trees; dust rose from the beaten-down scrub into the air in their wake. Burrison hustled the Marines and half of the PFs into a skirmish line across the band of trees and pushed them fast. Houng, Doc Rankin, and the rest of the PFs held back fifty meters as a reaction force if part of the line met the enemy.

Zeitvogel was in command of the left side of the line and kept looking from side to side as well as to his front, keeping his men up in a staggered line. The woods felt empty to him, emptier than they'd ever felt before. The Marines and PFs crashed through the thin brush, their footfalls echoed off tree trunks. They yelled at one another, "Keep it up," "Do you see anything?" "Keep it staggered, people." The noise of their passage was too loud for the tall black corporal to hear any birds crying, insects buzzing, or lizards *fuk-yoo*-ing, but Zeitvogel was positive that even if they had crept through in night silence, he wouldn't have heard the birds, the insects, or the lizards. They trampled through an empty world, one void of quarry foe. Still he rush-walked; still he cried out to the men at his sides, keep it up, watch your front and sides, keep it staggered. They hustled on.

Then they reached the cleft where the Song Du Ong River flowed onto its plain.

"Stilts, bring your people and a couple fay epps. We're going to check the bridge," Burrison ordered. "Tex, you're in command here. Let's do it."

"In column, people," Zeitvogel shouted. He looked to see who the nearest PFs were. "Pee Wee, Hank, you come me. Big Red, lead it out."

The five Americans and two Vietnamese trotted the ground-eating, energy-preserving trot called the "paratrooper shuffle" up the path alongside the rushing river. The hillside above them climbed faster than the path they followed. The river didn't climb as fast, and it wasn't long until they were high above the white-rushing water and in permanent shadow deep below the crest.

"Watch for footprints, Big Red," Burrison shouted. He didn't need to; Robertson was watching the ground in front of him for passage of men without being told to. The pebble-strewn ground was covered with a light coating of dust that puffed up at each step——the path looked like no one had passed this way in the three weeks since Tango Niner had gone to tango with Charlie in his hidden communications center three ridges to the west.

Then the rope-and-plank bridge across the river appeared ahead of them. The seven men gathered around the end of the bridge. Burrison and Mazzucco looked at the frayed ropes and rotted planks and knew no one had crossed it in a long time. Zeitvogel and the others remembered crossing it in September and knew there was no way they'd attempt it now. Three months earlier the ropes had been fraying, some of the boards had been broken, a few of the vertical ropes had been dangling, and the main support spans had been weakening. Now one hand rope was down and one of the two bottom ropes looked as if any weight put on it would bring down the whole structure. Only a few of the planks looked strong enough to support the weight of a light man—if he stepped easy.

Burrison looked farther up the trail, but he knew there was no point searching further. The sniper and mortar team hadn't come this way. He turned around. "Let's go back," he said.

The thirty men got on line and trudged through the meadows and scrub between the river and the paddy land north of it. They walked at a normal pace, neither patrol slow nor at a quick march. They watched for any sign someone had been there and paid particular attention when they reached the area where the CAP leaders agreed the mortar had to have fired from. Nothing.

Ruizique, at peace and happy within himself, watched the river, on which he knew no boats plied tonight but honest fishermen, watched the scrub forest, where he knew no enemy prowled. He was happy because he knew tomorrow night Charlie Cong would come to tango. I will kill you then, he thought.

Zeitvogel unfocused his eyes the way men who know how to see at night do and looked at the skyline. His eyes moved in an almost jerky manner, frequently stopping, never staying long on one spot. The skyline was stark and motionless against the starry black sky. He wondered where Charlie was. The sniper and mortar round weren't isolated; he knew that. The two shots were a warning of more to come. The first shots in what he believed was a campaign to demoralize the Marines and PFs of Tango Niner. Charlie was here to tango. But where was he? It was maddening.

* * *

The sinewy hawk-nosed man on the hillside let the sun rise above the horizon before putting his eyes to the 10×50-power tripod-mounted binoculars. Lean fingers made fine adjustments to the focus. The bunched muscles of his jaw regrouped themselves into different bunches, drawing his face into a leering smile as he watched the small amount of early-morning movement on Camp Apache's hill. He recognized a few of the men: the black-haired Trung si Bell, blond and muscular Ha si nhat Randall, impossibly tall Ha si nhat Zeitvogel, who was leading his all-night patrol back into the perimeter, the monster black man Ha si nhat Slover. Some of the others, he also recognized. And there were some he had never seen before: the eager-looking young man with a child's face that must be their new lieutenant, the scrawny one that must be the replacement for their radioman, and another one who looked lost and alone. Most of the Marines were lying on cots in the dimly seen interiors of tents or lying in randomly placed hammocks. It was quiet in Camp Apache. Only a few of them were up; fewer were on the perimeter watching outside.

When the hawk-nosed man withdrew his face from the binoculars, the heavy eyebrows that crawled across his head in a barely-broken line between his eyes looked almost like a prankster's mark. He chortled low in his throat —it was a soft sound but one that could chill a brave man's blood. "You are predictable, Tango Niner," he said to himself. "I knew you were predictable when I was here before, but then I did not understand how good you were at night fighting. This time I know, and I concede the night to you —you will not find me at night." He bared his teeth in his death's-head smile. "This time I will find you during the day, Tango Niner, and I will kill you when you can watch your blood soaking into the earth." He looked away from Camp Apache's hill and focused his eyes on an almost invisible hamlet far to its east and a little north, almost obstructed from his view by the hill on which sat Hou Dau hamlet. "But first I will destroy your spirit. Before you die, you will be alone and empty. You will desire the physical death I will finally grace you with."

A sweep of the area showed a helicopter low against the horizon. He watched it for a moment until he knew it was headed toward Camp Apache. He would like to stay and watch longer, especially to see when the Marines received word of what was now happening in Hou Toung, but a helicopter in the area made sitting on the hillside too dangerous; it was time to move back to his hidden place. He stood and made a curt gesture at a nearby private. The private hurried to remove the binoculars from their tripod and collapse the tripod for carrying.

"You caused me to lose face once before, Tango Niner," the hawk-nosed man said. "But Major Nghu never remains with lost face; he always wins back his honor."

CHAPTER SEVEN

Early Morning, December 26, 1966

"You're in luck," Captain Hasford said. "Storey and Hunter were already assigned to replace Wells and Reid." He had come in on a chopper in the morning with three new men, replacements. "Vega just happened to be available. He was on his way back to his unit from the hospital —down with malaria—but his old battalion isn't in country; it's back on Okinawa." He smiled and shook his head at the good luck of having so easily found an available man with no nearby unit to claim him as its own. "So I touted you up to him and he volunteered for CAP duty." Hasford smiled wider, looking very smug. "Something even better, all three are PFCs. That means you get to promote one of your own for a change." Then he remembered the reason Tango Niner had an opening for a lance corporal, and his smile disappeared.

Burrison and Bell looked at him solemnly; they knew too well why the opening existed. The corporals just looked. The two officers and six NCOs were crammed into the tent section Burrison and Bell used as their quarters. Burrison and Bell had removed their extra uniforms from

56

the rafters where they'd hung and folded them neatly under their cots for the occasion. Hasford sat on Burrison's folding chair in front of the small field desk, the lieutenant and sergeant sat on Burrison's cot, and the five corporals sat on Bell's cot and the footlocker.

"Who should get the BB guns?" Hasford asked, trying to erase the memory of his out-of-place smile. The rank insignia for lance corporal was a chevron over crossed rifles. The crossed rifles were commonly referred to as "BB guns"; the insignia was also called "one-and-a-half stripes." "The lieutenant colonel said if you don't pick somebody today, he'll give the promotion to someone else."

Nobody spoke for an uncomfortable moment. They were all glad one of their own was going to get promoted. Tango Niner had been at Camp Apache for nearly seven months, and in all that time no one had been promoted; replacements had always been assigned who already had the rank.

Finally Bell said, "Robertson, Pennell, and Knowles all rate it."

"Only one," Hasford said.

Burrison and Bell looked at each other, then at the corporals. The corporals looked away.

There was a jingle in the room's doorway, and Bell barked an unamused laugh. The others looked. Swarnes stood in the entrance, one-handed flipping two quarters, his other arm still in its sling. "Two mouths, two holes, or one of each," Swarnes said, his eyes gleaming. "Whatever way you fuck them, that's who gets the BB guns. Call it in the air." He tossed the two coins again and let them fall to the straw-mat floor. "No fair peeking."

"Swearin' Swarnes, you're a dumbfuck," Zeitvogel said. He leaned toward the radioman, resting one long arm on a broad knee, and smiled with what looked like too many teeth. It was a smile calculated to frighten. "We didn't say who was heads, who was tails, and who was both. Your coin toss don't count." He shook his head and repeated, "Dumbfuck."

Swarnes knew the tall corporal too well to let the smile scare him. "Ain't my goddamn fault you're too fucking slow, Stilts. You people wearing too damn many stripes on your shoulders, dragging down that headshit you call brains." He carefully avoided including the officers in what he said—or even looking at them. There was no way to predict when an officer would get upset about something somebody said.

"No coin toss, Swarnes," Bell said gruffly. "We're going to do this the military way. Get back to your radios."

Swarnes raised his eyebrows and elaborately shrugged one shoulder before pocketing his quarters and slouching out the entryway and back to his radio bench.

Burrison cleared his throat and looked at Bell. The decision should be made by the two of them. "Knowles is in the gun team; we don't need another lance corporal there," he said. "Do you agree?"

Bell nodded. "It's between Big Red and Fast."

"They've both been in Tango Niner the same length of time."

"If Big Red gets it, we have to reorganize the squad, give him to Zeke." The sergeant looked at Ruizique, who shrugged. The Dominican didn't care. He knew all the men in Tango Niner were good Marines; any of them would do a good job helping him to kill Cong.

"I'd like to think about it," Burrison said to Hasford.

"You don't have time. I leave in—" Hasford glanced at his watch. "—fifteen minutes and have to have the name when I go, or someone else gets the promotion."

Burrison and Bell looked at each other for a moment.

"Big Red," the lieutenant said as the sergeant lipped the words simultaneously.

Ruizique nodded his acceptance. The other corporals breathed light sighs of relief; they all thought while each of the three men deserved the promotion, Robertson deserved it most. Zeitvogel's mouth twisted in a wry grin; he didn't want to lose Robertson, but the man deserved the promotion.

"You got it," Hasford said briskly. "I'll bring the paperwork the next time I come out." He paused and grinned crookedly at the NCOs. "The promotion warrant will be back-dated, so you can pin on his stripes today if you want; you don't have to wait until we can make a formal ceremony out of it. Now," he continued, businesslike once again, "who's next for R and R? I have to take two bodies back to Da Nang with me."

"Doc Rankin and Webster were supposed to go," Burrison said. His voice became husky when he said the name of the dead man.

"All right," Hasford said quickly, not letting any pause develop for the men to have a chance to dwell on the untimely death, "Doc Rankin and someone else. Who's next on the list?"

Zeitvogel and McEntire looked at each other and nodded. "Athen," they said. After the mortar gunner, they were the only two left who'd been in Tango Niner more than three months on top of their previous four months' required service in-country before being assigned to the Combined Action Program.

"No way," Bell quickly said. "Athen goes now, that means both of you get the next R and R. I don't want both of you gone at the same time."

"What we have here, gennelmens—and I mean you commissioned ossifers as well as the noncommissioned ones I'm flipping this here coin for," Swearin' Swarnes said in his best sports announcer voice, "is a gen-you-wine U.S. of A. quarter dollar."

Captain Hasford, Lieutenant Burrison, and Sergeant Bell were standing together, watching from near the command hootch. Zeitvogel and McEntire stood to Swarnes's front and sides. Despite the fact they were facing each other, they seemed to loom threateningly over the smaller Marine. They were standing in the area between the tents that housed the rifle squad and the weapons section, with the Marines of Tango Niner standing around them. A few of the PFs were also in the compound, watching with amused interest.

"This side here, with the visage of George Washington's profile on it, is called heads. The other side here"—he turned the coin over—"with the American Eagle spread-legged on it, is called tails. The way we do it is I toss the coin up into the air, and while it is up there one of you calls out 'heads' or calls out 'tails.' Whichever way it lands, if the person who called guessed right on the way it lands up, that person wins. If it lands with the other side facing up, the person who called it loses. Do you both understand that?" He looked at each of them. Fortunately, they both already knew how a coin toss worked—if they didn't, Swarnes's directions might have confused them. "Here goes." He flipped the quarter high into the air, and grimaced from the pain in his wounded arm.

"Heads," Zeitvogel snarled at the same time McEntire grunted, "Heads."

"Misdeal," Swarnes said, and snatched the quarter off the ground before anybody could see how it landed. He looked up at the very tall corporal and the huge one. "What say only one of you wet dreams calls it? Decide who's gonna call it." Sweat was beading on his forehead.

Zeitvogel bunched his fist in front of his chest and made a slight pounding motion. McEntire nodded and balled his fist as well. "One, two, three," Zeitvogel counted. At each count the two men pounded the air. On the third count Zeitvogel's fist remained bunched; McEntire extended his index and middle fingers. "Rock breaks scissors," the tall man breathed. "I call it."

McEntire nodded intently. He stared at Swarnes's hand holding the quarter.

"You two final-fucking-ly ready?"

"Flip the coin, Swarnes," Zeitvogel grunted. He looked as intent as McEntire did.

"Toss it," McEntire snarled.

The coin flew into the air, tumbling around, sparkling in the sunlight. "Tails," Zeitvogel said.

The quarter reached its apex and plummeted downward to bounce once on the ground. Swarnes dropped to a crouch, and his hand beat the hands of the two corporals, who were also stooping to the coin, cupping it where it lay. He shook his head reproachfully. "I run a clean-ass coin toss," he told them, loud enough for everybody to hear the catch in his voice. "Don't no-fucking-body fuck with my coin before I eye-fuck it to see what fucking side is up."

The two corporals drew themselves back indignantly, but not so far back they couldn't easily see the coin when Swarnes uncovered it.

Swarnes jerked his hand back and stared at the quarter for a long moment before announcing to everybody how it landed. Both Zeitvogel and McEntire looked unhappy. "Tails." Swarnes craned his head back and looked all the way up from his crouch to Zeitvogel's six-and-a-half feet of height. "Saddle up, Stilts. You won the toss— you gonna boom-boom boo-coo boom-boom girls in Bang-fucking-kok."

"No, I'm not saddling up," Zeitvogel murmured.

"Say what?"

"I won the coin toss, right?" Zeitvogel continued in a stronger voice.

"Yah, it means you got R&R."

The tall man shook his head. "No it doesn't. It means I get to make the choice."

Swarnes screwed his face into a question. He scooped up his quarter and stood. "Say what?" He wondered what was wrong with this dumb-ass corporal, standing there so goddamn tall and lean he looked like the fuckstick the jolly green giant's wife used to diddle her brains out with when ol' Jolly was away from home. Man even sounded like he didn't want to go get a chance to fuck his brains out and get drunk out of whatever the hell it was he used for a mind.

"I won. I get to pick who goes. Wall, you dumbfuck,

saddle up. You embarrassed me, not being able to talk to a pretty girl. Man, we got to get you laid." A grin slowly split his face. "You get five days and four nights to get all the boom-boom girls you need to remember what end to stick it in. Once you remember that, you'll be able to talk to the next pretty girl you see."

McEntire looked dumbfounded at the taller man for a moment; he wanted to respond to the embarrassment he was feeling now about being publicly reminded of how he'd fumbled with Nancy Carter. Instead, he exploded into action. Everybody had known the big man was strong and had untold reserves of endurance, but nobody had suspected him of being a whirling dervish. In what seemed like no time at all, he dashed into his tent and reappeared, dressed in his best utility uniform, complete with metal chevrons on his collars and a regulation soft cover on his head, instead of the nonregulation camouflage bush hat normally worn by the Marines and PFs of Tango Niner. A battered suitcase containing a khaki uniform and his civilian clothes hung from his left hand. He joined Doc Rankin and a sheepish-looking Swarnes at the helipad, where they waited for Captain Hasford to signal them onto the waiting helicopter.

"I had Chief take a look at his arm while I was packing," Doc Rankin said, jerking his thumb at Swarnes. "Some infection is setting in. I told him I'd have you practice on him before we left for R&R if he didn't get his young ass to a hospital most ricky-tick."

Swarnes grinned weakly. "I'm saving myself for marriage."

Captain Hasford beckoned from the door of the chopper.

"Don't worry, Wall," Robertson shouted as the three men ran for the helicopter. "I'll tell that split-tail you got your tongue back." Maybe, he thought. If I ever see her again. Think I'd rather keep that one for myself, though.

* * *

"Come on, Jay Cee. It's only half a stripe, not a whole one," Robertson said, a touch of anxiety in his voice. "You should only give me a half a hit, not take my fucking arm off."

Bell wrinkled his forehead and cocked an eye at the burly redhead. His left hand was tucked between Robertson's upper arm and the man's side. "Only half a hit, huh," he said. "Tell you what. Instead of pinning it through your arm, I'll only pin it *to* your arm. How's that sound?" He looked in the other's eyes, distracting his attention to what his own right hand was doing—it balled into a fist and suddenly slammed into Robertson's deltoid. Bell let go and stepped back.

Robertson twisted in pain—less pain than he showed—and clutched his injured shoulder. "Shit, Jay Cee, I told you not a whole punch."

"Hold it right there, Big Red," Zeitvogel said. "I've been waiting for this chance for a long time." He didn't let any suspense build; he hit Robertson on the arm below his protective hand.

"Goddamn, Stilts, any more of that shit, my arm's going to be too sore for me to go on patrol tonight."

"Not my problem anymore, Red," Zeitvogel said, and shrugged.

"My turn," Randall said from Robertson's other side, and hit him on the right shoulder.

"Ow!" Robertson screamed in mock agony. "Tex, I thought you was a wrestler in high school, not a boxer."

Randall gestured with open hands. "Wrestling, boxing, samee-same. Both need strong arms." He grinned. "And I played varsity football, too." His heart wasn't in it, though. He was thinking about the previous day's attack and wondering what Bobbie Harder was thinking, did she still like him after he exposed her to that danger.

"Stand still, Big Red," Ruizique said. "I don't want to miss your arm and break your jaw by accident."

"You hit me like Tex just did, I won't be able to go out tonight," Robertson threatened.

"The hell you won't. You have both arms in slings, you're going out tonight." Ruizique swung but pulled back before hitting. Robertson flinched. "Only way you don't go on patrol tonight is somebody breaks your arm and you have to be med-evaced." He looked hard at the new lance corporal. "You get med-evaced, you'll have company, because I'll break the head of whoever breaks your arm." His fist moved with lightning speed and stopped just as it touched Robertson's arm, barely tapping it. "You're my AR man tonight, Red."

Slover was up next, then Hempen, Lewis, Athen, Flood, Kobos, and Willard. They let Doc Tracker take a turn. It was the time-honored custom of "pinning on the stripes." When an enlisted Marine is promoted, every other enlisted Marine of equal or greater rank has the privilege of hitting him on the shoulder one time for each stripe of his new rank. It's a bond of blood, sort of. Despite the big redhead's cries of pain and the seeming ferocity of the blows to his arms, nobody hit him hard—nobody wanted to risk hurting him badly enough to affect him on patrol that night.

After Robertson's stripes were properly pinned on, the Marines celebrated with toasts of warm soda and a few lukewarm beers. The celebration was short-lived, though; they had an unexpected visitor.

"Hey, Pee Wee, little bro," Zeitvogel shouted when he saw the PF platoon's smallest member half run, half stumble through the main gate. "You come to me, have a drink for Big Red. Sucker just got promoted."

Pee Wee scrambled, gasping, to the side of the giant Marine. Zeitvogel draped an arm over the small man's shoulders. Pee Wee looked like he could easily have hidden behind that arm; the top of his head barely reached the Marine's chest. "Stilt, you come me," he stammered anxiously. "We go Hou Toung toot-sweet." He grasped Zeitvogel's arm with both hands and yanked. He hardly budged it.

"Okay, little pano, we'll go to Hou Toung. First have a brew, celebrate Big Red's promotion." He tried to force a half-drunk can of Falstaff into the PF's hand.

"Maybe he prefers Schlitz," Kobos said when Pee Wee refused the beer.

"No beer, no beer," Pee Wee gasped. He heaved deeply, getting his breath back. "We go Hou Toung toot-sweet, most ricky-tick." He tugged on Zeitvogel's arm again.

"Whoa there, little fellow. What's your hurry?"

"You come Hou Toung now. Vee Cee come Hou Toung today, kill chief."

CHAPTER EIGHT

That Same Day

Bell floored the navy-blue Jeep's accelerator, speeding the vehicle along the bulldozed road toward the hill Hou Dau hamlet sat on. They almost took the turn to the south of the hill on two wheels. Five minutes after roaring out of Camp Apache's main gate, he braked hard to avoid over-running the wide trail leading north to Hou Toung. Hou Toung was the easternmost hamlet in Bun Hou village, and slightly north of the others. The village's rice paddies were north of the Song Du Ong River, separated from it by scrub forest west of Hou Dau hill and Hou Cau hamlet and sugar cane fields east of there. Hou Toung was almost in the paddies, forming a small island connected to the cane fields by a short causeway. This hamlet was the farthest from Camp Apache and the least visited by the Marines during their unofficial daytime patrols; because most of the danger in the village came from the west, it was also the hamlet least often covered by a night patrol. The people who lived in Hou Toung didn't know or trust the Marines of Tango Niner as well as the residents of the other hamlets did.

Bell grumbled deep in his throat and white-knuckled the Jeep's steering wheel. He was in a hurry to reach Hou Toung and resented having to drive as slowly as the wide footpath forced him to: the only vehicles that ever visited Hou Toung were bicycles and buffalo-drawn two-wheeled carts that didn't need speed. Burrison sat in the passenger seat; Doc Tracker, Zeitvogel, Hempen, and Pee Wee crowded into its back.

Once, a white-clad man had to step into the field the trail cut through to let the Jeep by; another time, two old women, also dressed in white, made him come to a full stop before they stepped aside. All three peasants stared at the Marines blank-faced. They hate us, Bell thought, and shivered. It was the first time in months he hadn't felt welcome by a villager. He pounded his frustration on the steering wheel—it wasn't right for them to hate the Marines. The other Marines were silent: Burrison looked straight ahead, Zeitvogel and Hempen watched the sides, Rankin watched the rear. Pee Wee tried to be invisible. They all knew white was the Vietnamese mourning color; they all knew the people were blaming the Marines for the murder of the hamlet headman. No one was visible working in the fields.

Bell had to park the Jeep outside the gate through the palm tree and hedge fence around the hamlet. He pulled over as far to the side as he could without crushing any cane to leave a passage for people walking in or out. The six men walked somberly in a column to the hamlet square; Burrison was in the lead.

It wasn't much of a square, just a space with paths between hootches leading into it. As closely as the homes were packed in the hamlet, two of the smaller ones could have been packed into the square. All of Hou Toung's adults could cram into it, if they were friendly enough. A ring of young women, middle-aged women, old people, and children stood around the square now. In its center stood a narrow wooden bed. A wizened man lay on it, his tuft of white chin whiskers drooped down on his throat, incompletely hiding the gash that had killed him.

A *bonze*, a Buddhist monk, dressed in a saffron robe, sat cross-legged on the hard-packed earth next to the bed. Burning incense swirled around the bonze as he chanted and clanged cymbals and waved the incense smoke over the corpse. An old woman squatted at the head of the bed. Her hands cradled the dead man's cheeks, and she keened wordlessly; she was obviously his widow. A few other people, other family members, moved about the bed, garlanding it with flowers and palm fronds and hanging prayer wheels. The bustling relatives all wore white tunics and pants.

Everybody stopped what they were doing when the foreigners entered the square, except the widow and the bonze, who ignored them. A white-bearded man separated himself from the circle and approached the Marines. Burrison and Bell folded their hands and bowed low to him. The old man bowed back perfunctorily.

"Why have you come here?" the old man asked, speaking slowly so the foreigner in front of him could understand.

"We have come to pay respect to your chief," Bell replied in faltering Vietnamese. He translated for the other Marines; they stood uncertainly, aware that they weren't wanted here. Pee Wee stood a step or two aside from the Americans, hopelessly wishing the villagers would think he wasn't with them.

The old man looked impassively at him for a long time before pointing to the bier and saying, "He is there. Be quick about it, then leave us to our grief."

Bell tried not to grimace; he wasn't totally successful. "We also want to find who did this," he said. "It must not happen again."

The old man tipped his head without taking his eyes from the big American sergeant and shot a long spew of spittle to the side. "It is too late. It has happened. How it will not happen again is for you to go away." He turned half away, dismissing them from his sight. "Pay your respects, then dee-dee mau."

Bell bowed deeply to the old man, and the others did likewise. He led them to the bier, and they stood in a semicircle around it, avoiding the bonze and the widow, who were both still ignoring them.

Doc Rankin looked at the corpse's slit throat and murmured, "At least it was fast. The old geezer didn't have to suffer long."

"We don't know that, Doc," Zeitvogel said. "They might have tortured him first and the marks are covered by his clothes." The other Marines nodded agreement.

The corpsman nodded. After a moment he said, "I'm here and got my medkit." He turned to Pee Wee, who was still trying to look like he was in Hou Toung on his own. "Ask if anybody needs a bac si," he said in a soft voice.

Pee Wee swallowed nervously and looked like he wished he hadn't been spoken to. Finally he nodded and cried out in a thin voice. No one spoke back to him; only a few cast blank glances in his direction. It was obvious they all thought he was included in the new headman's injunction to dee-dee mau.

Burrison looked around at the silent villagers ringing the square—more had crowded in since they'd arrived. Everyone was staring at them expressionlessly, but he still thought he saw glimmers of anger in several eyes.

Burrison turned to Bell. "Ask the new chief when and where it happened."

Bell did. The headman said a few words in answer. The most clear were "Dee-dee mau"—get out of here.

"He said at first light this morning," Bell told the lieutenant, speaking softly. "Vee Cee were waiting for the people to wake up. When the villagers came out of their hootches, the Vee Cee grabbed the headman and one of them made a speech about how he was cooperating with foreign devils against the people and must pay for his crimes. Then they slit his throat and walked out, headed south." Bell's eyes displayed nervousness as he looked at the surrounding people. "That's all. He's not going to talk to us. None of them are. Let's go. Maybe Thien can talk to him later, find out something that'll be useful to us."

Burrison grunted.

"Let's go, people," Bell said to the others. The six filed slowly out of the hamlet square back to the Jeep. "Ah, shit," the sergeant said when they got back to it, "why would somebody want to go and do that."

"Sure as shit looks like it," Hempen said, looking at the brown pile on the driver's seat. Burrison, Zeitvogel, and Rankin looked and grimaced. One of them groaned. Pee Wee tried to look as if he were somewhere else.

"Good thing we got to Hou Toung so late in the day," Zeitvogel finally said, and looked out over the cane fields. He tore a handful of leaves off a bush and handed them to Bell.

Bell snatched the leaves and angrily said, "What's so fucking good about it?"

"If it was early, the honey buckets would have been full, and there'd be more than just a few baby turds sitting there."

Bell's expression was a mixture of anger, humiliation, and distaste as he used the leaves to pick up the human feces from the driver's seat and cast it aside. He grabbed another offered handful from Zeitvogel and wiped at what was still there. His nose wrinkled and his lips puckered as he stared at the small wet spot left on the seat; he didn't want to sit on it.

"Put these on it, honcho," Hempen said, and handed Bell a few leafy branches. "Might keep you dry until we get home."

Bell slapped the branches down on the seat. He grimaced. Time to let someone else drive, he thought, and looked at Burrison. "Scrappy, you keep saying you want to drive the Jeep," he said in as innocent a voice as he could muster. "Your turn." He waved at the steering wheel.

Burrison didn't manage to look innocent when he said, "Thanks, Jay Cee, but you requisitioned it. In our respective positions here, I think it's proper for you to be my driver."

Bell's jaws clenched. "Thank you and the horse you rode in on, too," he said. If that wasn't going to work, he could always pull rank. "Junior man drives. Short Round, take the wheel."

"No can do, Jay Cee," Hempen said immediately. "I don't have a driver's license." He made his eyes large and round, tried to look like a five-foot-four teenager, too young to drive, rather than the short, twenty-year-old man he was.

"Jay Cee," Doc Tracker said, clapping a hand on the sergeant's shoulder, "is that what the Crotch is teaching its NCOs these days; hand out the shit details you aren't willing to do yourself?"

"R-H-I-P, squid," Bell snarled. "Rank Has Its Privileges. And I already did my share of shit details. That's why I'm a sergeant."

Rankin laughed. "Come on, Jay Cee. I can give you a full battery of shots when we get back to Camp Apache, should knock out most things you can pick up from that— if anything gets through your seat cushion." He stripped a few more clumps of leaves off a bush and added them to the pile of branches on the seat. "And I got some pills can knock out most parasitic worms found in this part of the world, too," he added with a smile.

Bell pursed his lips tight and bulged one cheek out with his tongue. "All right, people," he said, "I'm driving. Your turns will come." He swung into the Jeep and settled gingerly on the pad of leaves and branches. He made a series of tight back-and-forth turns to point the Jeep back the other way, then barked, "Mount up."

The others climbed into the Jeep. Their departure was watched by a half-dozen seemingly impassive villagers. All the way back to Camp Apache, Bell squirmed. He kept imagining he felt the seat of his trousers turning wet, but it was only his imagination.

"Billy Boy, get Houng and Thien, toot-sweet," Burrison

ordered as soon as they arrived back at the Marine compound.

"Can I take the Jeep?" Lewis asked, but the lieutenant was striding rapidly toward the command hootch and didn't answer. Lewis looked at Bell for permission, but the sergeant was following close in Burrison's wake, pulling at the seat of his trousers and flexing his hips away from the material and didn't see him. Lewis shrugged and got in. He stepped back out and started to knock the crushed leaves away from the seat.

"I wouldn't do that if I was you," Hempen said to him.

"Why the fuck not?"

"Just take my word for it—you'll be a lot happier."

Lewis looked quizzically at him and at the leaves. He shrugged and got in on them. Fifteen minutes later he was back with the Popular Forces lieutenant and the Hou Ky hamlet chief. He wondered why Bell was taking a shower right now and how come he was scrubbing so hard at his ass. He swore long, loud, and hard at Hempen when he found out later and then took a shower himself. He scrubbed his backside very thoroughly. A little soap and water was all it took to wash the wet spot off the leather of the driver's seat.

CHAPTER NINE

That Night

The PFs who were patrolling with the Marines that night came to Camp Apache in time to share the Marines' flown-in, hot evening meal and stayed until time to leave on the patrols. The sun was almost down to the ridge line to the west when the Marines started drifting into their squad tent to prepare for the night.

"No shit tonight, people," Ruizique said to his men. "Mister Charlie is back out there, and I want to find him." He paused and looked each of his men in the eye: the newly promoted Robertson, looking half smug and pleased, half scared because of his new responsibilities; Pennell, straight-faced, only the barest tension showing; Neissi, openly nervous, not having been with Tango Niner long enough to know in his guts they owned the night in Bun Hou. "I do not want Charlie finding us," the Dominican corporal continued.

He opened his ammo crate table and pulled out three green camouflage paint sticks, one light, one dark, one medium. He used them to draw irregular lines and splotches on his arms and hands, paying particular attention to his elbows, biceps, and knuckles. As he finished with each of the sticks, he handed it to Robertson. Robertson handed them back when his own arms and hands were lined and spotted in a way that didn't hide the color of his skin but rather broke up the outline and covered the high spots. Ruizique drew war paint—like stripes and forms on his own face, then did the same to Robertson. Satisfied with Robertson's appearance and his own mirror reflection, he handed the sticks to Pennell and Neissi. "Do your arms and hands," he said, and watched closely as the two men painted themselves. When they were through, he did their faces.

Tango Niner hadn't used camouflage paint since Neissi had joined it, and Ruizique supposed Neissi was wondering about the broken pattern of paint, instead of the full-face mask he probably used in a regular line company, so Ruizique explained as he painted their faces. "There are three things that make you visible at night. One is movement, one is outline, the other is reflection. The color of your skin cannot be seen; everything is gray under the moon and the stars. The high places—forehead, cheek arches, bridge of the nose, nostrils, and point of the chin —are the main places that reflect and show outline. Camouflage paint dulls them, cuts down the reflections, and breaks the outline. The other thing that makes reflections is sweat. If you paint your whole face, sweat breaks through it and shines on the high places. If you leave most of the skin bare, it allows the sweat to come through in places other than the high places, and you don't reflect as much. So we don't paint full masks onto our faces for night patrols, only the high spots and random lines." He stared at Neissi for a beat or two before adding, "And keep your mouth closed so your white teeth don't show and give us away."

Neissi's mouth twisted into a half smile—but he kept his lips together and didn't show his teeth.

Ruizique stood in the narrow space between his cot and Robertson's. He moved slowly and with exaggerated movements to demonstrate what he wanted his men to do. One dogtag was wrapped in black fabric tape and tucked on its chain inside his shirt; the other, also tape-covered, went into his boot lacings. He used the same tape to secure the front sling keeper on his rifle stock. "No slings," he reminded them. One canteen was on his cartridge belt. He shook it to make sure it was full and wouldn't slosh, then tucked it into a cut-off sock and put it in its pouch. He strapped the cartridge belt on and tied the bayonet scabbard to his thigh. Two star clusters, hand-held flares, went into the pockets of his shirt. A hand grenade went into the inside pocket of his shirt, and two more, their pull pins held down with tape, were attached to the left side of his belt. Then he picked up his M-14, held it out to the side, and hopped in place. The only noise he made was the soft thudding of his boots on the duckboard floor of the tent. The whole time, he carefully watched his men prepare themselves the same way.

Ruizique grinned, then slung the crossed leather bandoliers, a gift from his uncle, over his shoulders and clapped his bush hat on his head. He hopped again, noiselessly. "Let me hear you, Big Red." Robertson hopped just as quietly as his leader—he'd been going on night patrols in Bun Hou for a couple weeks longer than Ruizique. The big redhead looked wistfully at the bipods he was leaving behind. They'd make the automatic rifle he was carrying for the first time more stable if someone walked into their ambush, but he knew there was no way to keep them from making noise while they patrolled. They had to stay behind.

"Fast" Pennell hopped. He was as silent as Ruizique knew he'd be.

"Neissi," Ruizique called. The camouflage paint might have been new to Neissi, but noise discipline wasn't. He, too, was quiet.

"Now for our little people," Ruizique said, a slightly manic gleam in his eye. The others grinned back at him less maniacally. It was unusual for the PFs to be checked for noise by the Marine patrol leader. The Marines normally met them after leaving Camp Apache; they relied on the PF squad leaders to check their own men—men who traveled more lightly than the Marines did.

Randall and Zeitvogel watched from about forty meters away while Ruizique inspected the five PFs going out with him that night.

"Think the man's overdoing it, Stilts?" Randall asked.

Zeitvogel shook his head. "Man wasn't much to write home about when he joined us," he said, "but he's got his shit together now." He looked down at his stocky companion. "I think what happened yesterday, and killing Hou Toung's headman last night, means Charlie's back and got some new tricks up his sleeve. I'm going to inspect my fay epps before we go out tonight, too." He looked thoughtfully at the ridge the sun was half below and said slowly, "I think I'm going to talk to Jay Cee and Scrappy, tell them it's a good idea have our fay epps join us in here every night for a while."

Randall didn't say anything at first; he just kept watching Ruizique inspect his people and rolled and bunched his football player's shoulders to ease his mounting tension. Then he said, "Stilts, you're smarter than any tall man has a right to be."

"What do you mean? I'm not supposed to be smart?"

Randall looked up at the six-and-a-half-foot-tall corporal. "Shit, Stilts, man as tall as you, he's always hitting his head on things. Trees, skyscrapers, low-flying aircraft. You know—knocks dumb into you."

"Little bro," the tall man said in a pained voice, "if you weren't so much smaller 'n me, I'd take you out behind the barracks, kick your ass, you saying things like that." He shook his head. "But I can't. People would say I'm a bully, I kicked your ass."

"Shit, Stilts, when you was playing roundball I was on my way to the Texas state wrestling championships. No way you can kick my ass."

"Uh-huh, Tex, Greco-Roman wrestling. All you know

how to do is try to knock down a man already on his hands and knees."

Randall swiveled into a karate stance. "Think so, Stilts? I'll take your ass right now."

Zeitvogel positioned himself so the shorter-than-average Randall had to crane his head back to look up at the taller man's face. "Bullshit, Tex, you need at least a 106 recoilless rifle to take me, and you ain't armed."

Suddenly, Randall did something with his arms and his feet that was too fast for the eye to follow, and Zeitvogel was flat on his back with the smaller man lying across his chest, pinning his shoulders to the ground. Zeitvogel arched his back and pushed hard with his legs to bow himself high. Randall gave two jerky pushes down, flattening him again.

"Fight!" someone shouted in the background. Running feet thudded toward them.

"You weren't already on your hands and knees, Stilts," he said through clenched teeth; he was putting a lot of effort into keeping the bigger man down.

Zeitvogel went limp. "You're right, Tex. You got me down. Let me up."

"That string bean fucking with you, honcho?" Lewis asked, running up with several other Marines.

"You picking on my honcho again, Tex?" Hempen demanded.

"What the fuck you two doing?" Slover boomed.

Randall stood and extended his hand to help Zeitvogel up.

"Man's been getting laid too much," Zeitvogel answered Slover. "He's trying to find another hole now his girlfriend isn't here." He took Randall's hand and pulled himself up. Then he did something too fast to see with his arms and the leverage of his height, and Randall was turned around, kneeling, head pressed to the dirt, right arm twisted behind him. Zeitvogel straddled his back and kept pressure on the arm he held captive.

"Now what you gonna do, Tex?"

Randall took a deep breath, then snaked his free arm around Zeitvogel's left ankle and threw his weight in that direction, bowling the taller man over. He rolled with him and across him; Zeitvogel loosened his grip enough that Randall was able to slip out of it and keep rolling to his feet. He danced backward a few steps and stood in a ready stance. "Two for me, Stilts. Want to go for three out of five?"

"What the hell's going on here?" Bell shouted, striding between them. He stared hard at them each in turn—Randall smiling and bobbing slightly in a fighting stance, Zeitvogel propped up on his elbows, laughing.

"Nothing, honcho," Zeitvogel said, and laughed louder. "Just a little grab-assing."

"Well, shitcan it," Bell ordered. He looked at both of them and snarled, "Couple of little fucking kids. I don't know how you got into my Marine Corps in the first place."

Zeitvogel and Randall exchanged looks. Since when did Bell talk like a lifer? they both wondered.

Zeitvogel held his hand out to Randall.

"Bullshit," Randall said. "You think I'm going to fall for that again?"

Slover reached down and yanked the tall man to his feet.

"I wasn't going to do it again," Zeitvogel said, "not with the honcho standing there." He smiled in a way that said, When he's not around, though.

Randall nodded at him, and they both laughed and clasped hands, thumbs linked around other. "Anytime, Stilts, anytime. Still think all I know how to do is try to knock a man down when he's already on his hands and knees?"

"Shit, I'll knock you both upside the gourd," Slover snorted.

"You and who else?" they both asked.

"You two just be cool, understand?" Bell said.

"Sure thing, honcho. No problem here."

"Just a little grab-assing, Jay Cee. We're cool."

Bell snorted and turned back to the command hootch. He had too much on his mind after the events of the past twenty-four hours to waste time on a couple stupid corporals grab-assing.

Ruizique joined them while they watched the sergeant walk away. "Jay Cee, he talks like he's a lifer," he said when Bell was far enough away.

Slover nodded once, slowly. "Sure do."

Bell reached the command hootch and looked back at them. "Zeke, you've got a patrol to run," he called. "Do it."

"Aye-aye, Jay Cee," Ruizique called back. He popped his right hand sharply to the brim of his bush hat and shot it up and outward and let it trail off into a wave, a sarcastic "high-ball" salute. "On our way, honcho." Leaving the other corporals, he muttered loudly enough for them to hear, "What the fuck's his problem? We're the best damn Marines in the whole Crotch, and he's acting like he's got a hair up his ass about something." He reached his men and pointed them out the main gate. Pennell was on the point. They would patrol north of Hou Dau hamlet and the area between it and Hou Toung for three hours before setting an ambush for half the night and then patrolling again. The patrol would come back in after sunup.

The other corporals watched him leave, then looked at one another. Ruizique was right; something was bothering Bell. What was it?

"I'll talk to the man tonight," Slover said. The other two nodded. If anybody could find out what was on Bell's mind, it was Big Louie Slover. Then they could take care of the problem—whatever it was.

An hour and a half after sundown, Randall tapped Billy Boy Lewis on the shoulder. Unseen in the darkness, Lewis scowled. He stepped out, leading the patrol through the back gate. He scowled because Randall had inspected him with everybody else, even made him hop in place. This was the only time since the first month Tango Niner had been in Bun Hou that he had been inspected before going out on patrol—his feelings were bruised. This patrol would roam west of Hou Ky, from the paddies on the north to the river on the south, and return to Camp Apache during the wee hours of the morning.

An hour later Zeitvogel whispered, "Go get 'em, Pee Wee," and the diminutive PF led the short patrol out the back gate. It was going to be a short night for these men; they'd be back from patrol and sleeping by the time Randall and his patrol came back in.

There were twenty-seven Americans in Tango Niner— twenty-five Marines and two Navy corpsmen. Twelve were out on patrol, two were on R&R, and Swearin' Swarnes was in the hospital. That left twelve to hold Camp Apache overnight. Under normal circumstances there'd be fifteen men in the compound at night. Burrison, Bell, and Swarnes would cover radio watch, Slover and Athen would spend the night in the mortar pit, and McEntire and Kobos would man the machine gun at the main gate. The other eight men would be in four two-man holes around the perimeter. To have only twelve men on watch wasn't normal, but to call the times when they had fifteen men in the compound normal nights wasn't exactly right. Between R&R and casualties there normally weren't fifteen men at home.

Tonight Bell and Burrison shared radio watch and didn't get much sleep, because every two hours one of them went out to check the lines while the other listened to the radio. McEntire was on R&R, so Kobos and Knowles manned the machine gun. Slover and Athen held the back gate. If they had to use the mortar, Slover and Athen could dash to the mortar pit and be relieved at the back gate by Burrison and Bell, who would take the radios with them. Not the best possible arrangement, but it was workable—more or less. Vandersteit, from the gun team, was with Flood near the helipad. Graham and the new man, Hunter, were at the southwest corner of the compound. Doc Tracker and Willard, the M-79 grenadier, spent the night watching over the east side of the hill. One man was awake at all times in each position; the other got to sleep. They had two-hour watch rotations.

An hour or so after the night's last patrol went out, Bell made the rounds.

Hunter was awake while Graham slept. The new man was edgy. He was too vividly aware of the two hundred meters in each direction to the next defensive position, two hundred meters where Charlie could try to come through the wire.

"No sweat, Hunter," Bell tried to reassure him. "We've got so much shit in that wire—trip flares, Claymores, noisemakers—Charlie's never going to get through without setting something off. He's tried to boo-coo times. Gave himself away every time." Bell didn't mention the time a sapper squad had managed to get inside without setting anything off. That time Doc Tracker and Kennith Kelley, who was then the platoon's radioman, were the only ones in the compound. They were alone because the rest of the platoon was south of the river, wasting the rest of the sapper platoon that had been sent in to destroy Tango Niner. Kelley hadn't had a chance. If Tracker hadn't gone out to meet Slover and his mortar team on their way back, he would have been killed also. Slover led his men in through the wire and killed the NVA supersoldiers.

"You sure about that, Sergeant?"

"Yeah, I'm sure. And call me Jay Cee."

They sat in silence for a few more minutes until it was time for Bell to move on. Hunter was glad of the steadying company of the seasoned sergeant who'd lived through nearly seven months with Tango Niner. When Bell left, Hunter was less nervous than he had been before—but not much less.

Flood was looking for Bell when he arrived; the sergeant had used the ground-wire phone that linked all the defensive positions and the command hootch to let him know he was on his way.

"Quiet night, honcho," Flood murmured in that voice night fighters develop; it wasn't a whisper but was easier to understand and didn't carry as far.

Bell listened to the muted night sounds for a brief moment. "Just quiet or too quiet?" he asked in the same voice.

A slight rustling told Bell the other man shrugged. "Just quiet," Flood said. Successful night fighters quickly learned the normal sounds of night and what it meant when those sounds weren't there. A really good night fighter could follow the passage of an enemy and tell how many were in his group just by listening to the silent spot moving through the night noises.

"Tell the main gate I'm on my way," Bell said after a few minutes of sitting silently. He didn't spend much time talking with the men on the perimeter, mostly sat with them, listening to the night, hearing what they heard, feeling for himself whatever they said the night was like. He heard the handle on the ground-wire phone crank as he headed off along the trench toward his next stop.

Kobos, the machine gunner who'd joined Tango Niner a month earlier, leaned his folded forearms on the tripod-mounted M-60.

"You know, Jay Cee, I'm bored," he said. "Sitting on this fucking perimeter every fucking night is fucking with my brainbox. I'm about ready to request a transfer to the rifle squad. Humping the boonies every night can't be as bad as this." He shook his head. "I'm going bugfuck here."

The Vietcong hadn't tried to overrun the compound since he had joined.

Bell grunted softly; it passed for a humorless laugh. "Next time Charlie hits us, you'll probably be glad you're in a hole behind wire, instead of out there." He stayed at the main gate a few minutes longer before moving on to the position on the east side of the hill.

Doc Tracker was on watch.

"What's happening out there, Chief?" Bell called softly.

Tracker looked at Bell's silhouette. "What's the matter, paleface?" he asked. "You've been out here as long as I have. Can't you tell for yourself yet?"

Bell laughed softly; it wasn't a grunt like he'd given Kobos. "Sure I can," he said. "Just making sure you can."

They sat quietly for a short while, then Tracker said, "The winds tell me Charlie isn't going to bother us here for a while. Not at night, anyway. But he is out there, many of him."

Bell didn't say anything. What Tracker said was too close to what he felt. Then he moved on to his last stop.

"How's it hanging, Jay Cee?" Slover asked.

"Straight and hard."

"You need something to stick it in, Jay Cee? Say you want some lessons on how it's done? Come talk to me after dawn." Two-and-a-half weeks earlier, Slover had been shacked up with a Chinese woman when he went on R&R in Taiwan. He wanted to talk about how good it had been.

Bell lightly punched the big man's shoulder. "Don't need any lessons on how to stick it in, Big Louie."

They were silent for a moment before Slover made a light rumbling that might have been clearing his throat and asked, "Then what's bothering you?"

"Nothing's bothering me," Bell said too fast, his voice was strained.

"Talk to me, Jay Cee," Slover said after another silent moment. "How come you're acting like a lifer?"

"I'm not acting like any goddamn lifer, Corporal," Bell snapped, louder than anything else he'd said on his rounds. He jerked to his feet and headed back to the bunker the radios were kept in at night.

CHAPTER TEN

Sunup, December 27, 1966

The buzzing and chirping of night insects started changing to the simple buzz-buzz of day insects about the time the eastern sky turned a lighter shade of black and the stars started blinking out. Bird cries began to sound with the wakening of the avian world. Nature's noise increased so much in the course of the half hour before dawn that this would be the ideal time to launch an assault against a lightly defended position such as Camp Apache. At least Knowles thought so. That's why he woke Kobos to help him watch and listen during that last half hour. And why when he had the last sleep he always insisted whoever he was on with wake him for that last half hour. Somewhere he had heard the Australian army had a routine they called "stand to"; during the first and last half hours of darkness, everybody was awake and on the perimeter. He'd also heard the U.S. army didn't. Didn't make any difference to him; he was a Marine. So far as he knew, all Marines in the bush were awake and alert during the first and last half hour of darkness.

The sun rose and flooded the land with its brilliance.

Knowles swept his gaze over the countryside to the north. All was quiet and as it should be. Then he squinted to the east and made out Ruizique's patrol emerging from the long shadows cast by the woods south of Hou Dau Hill.

Kobos also looked at the returning all-night ambush patrol. He stood and stretched. "Man, I'm going bugfuck sitting here all the time. I wish I was out there with them. At least they're moving around, doing something."

A single shot shattered the morning calm before Knowles could reply.

The Marines and PFs walking alongside the bulldozed road between Hou Dau and Camp Apache dove to the ground and started firing into the trees to their left rear.

"Oh, shit!" Kobos shouted. He grabbed the machine gun and moved it to the side of the hole they were in. "Spot for me." He started firing twenty-round bursts into the trees while Knowles linked more belts of ammo together and kept them feeding smoothly into the gun's breech.

Knowles, the gun team's assistant gunner, looked away from the trees and the ammo belts long enough to see that one of the men in the patrol lay crookedly and wasn't firing back. He swore under his breath.

Everyone awake in the compound and not watching in one of the two holes on the west side dashed to the east side and dove into fighting holes and the trench to add the booming of their M-14s to the fire being poured into the trees. The men of the two patrols that had returned before dawn and who were sleeping bolted awake and joined in. Confused shouting added to the din of the firing as men called out to one another, asking where the enemy was, where were they supposed to shoot. Only Willard didn't fire; the trees were too far away for his shotgunlike 40mm M-79 grenade launcher to reach.

The fire went on for about two minutes before Bell's voice cracked over the hilltop. "Cease fire, cease fire," he shouted. The shooting petered out and the defenders heard the silence—the patrol had already stopped shooting.

When they looked toward him, the Marines on the hill saw Bell and Doc Tracker jumping into the Jeep.

"Get that gate open," the sergeant shouted. He flipped the ignition switch and started toward the main gate. Kobos and Knowles scrambled to pull the plug of barbed wire that filled the opening. By the time he reached it, Zeitvogel, Randall, Lewis, and Hempen had piled into the back of the Jeep.

"You don't think you're going anywhere without us, do you?" It seemed to Bell all four asked the question at the same time.

Tracker held his medkit on his lap. Bell dropped a PRC-6 walkie-talkie radio on the floorboard between the front seats. "Hang on," he said. There was an edge of desperation in his voice. He floored the accelerator as soon as the gate was open, and the Jeep shot down the hill and took the turn at the bottom on two wheels—they almost lost Zeitvogel then, but Randall grabbed the front of his shirt and held him in.

From the hill, the Jeep seemed to disappear in a cloud of dust when Bell slammed on the breaks at the ambush. All but two of the men in the patrol were already running in a skirmish line toward the trees. The two left behind were the one Knowles had seen lying crooked and a PF kneeling over him.

"Who is it?" Bell asked as he scrambled out of the Jeep. The other four Marines who came with him formed a defensive square around the casualty, facing out, rifles ready to fire.

Pham, an assistant PF squad leader, raised his tear-streaked face. "Mike," he said, thick-voiced, "him dead."

Tracker moved fast; he was already on his knees next to the downed PF, holding a pressure bandage against the gaping wound on his side—a wound that had already almost stopped flowing blood into the huge puddle on the dirt near the small man's body. Tracker peeled Mike's eyelids back and checked for a pulse in his throat. He put his ear next to Mike's mouth to feel for breath. Nothing. He let go of the pressure bandage and rocked back on his heels. "Shit" was the only thing he said. After a moment he stood and slowly walked back to the Jeep and sat half in it, on the passenger seat.

The rest of the patrol trudged back from the trees.

"We found where the motherfucking sniper waited for us," Ruizique said. "Looked like he scrambled out of there so fast the fuckface was halfway back to Hanoi by the time we turned around and blasted at him. We followed his trail for about half a klick before we lost it completely. How's Mike?"

Bell looked down at the small body, which seemed shrunken in death. "Wasted." He reached into the Jeep for his PRC-6 to radio in a report.

Ruizique glanced briefly at the trees where the sniper had fired from while the remaining PFs clustered around the corpse of their dead friend. Then he looked far to the south and a little west and stared for a long moment. Randall came and stood at his side, looking in the same direction. The stocky corporal clapped a hand on his friend's shoulder. "No sweat, Zeke," he said, "we'll get the fucker."

"Mister Charlie," the proud Dominican corporal said softly and slowly. He seemed to ignore Randall standing at his side, hand on his shoulder. "When you came with special soldiers to kill us, we looked for the hidden tunnels and found them and we killed you." Zeitvogel joined him on his other side. Ruizique continued without acknowledging him. "You came after us in large force, and we killed enough of you, the survivors had to break and run. You kept coming at us and trying to sneak men and supplies through our village. We killed you then, and we kept killing you." He turned his face to the west. "When we got tired of you coming to us, we found your base and we killed you in your own home. Yet you still come after us. Your tactics are new now, Mister Charlie. But I, Jesus Maria Ruizique, Corporal, United States Marine Corps, I tell you, you will not win. We will kill you as we have killed you in the past. And we will keep killing you until you no longer come to us. Then and only then, Mister Charlie, will you be safe from us."

Zeitvogel looked down at Ruizique, stern-faced. Then he locked eyes with Randall. "I think what the man's trying to say is payback's a motherfucker," he said.

"And we're the meanest motherfuckers in the valley," Randall said softly.

"Zeke, get your people back to the hill," Bell broke in. He was revving the Jeep's motor after radioing in his report.

"Right," Ruizique said.

Bell spun the wheels of the Jeep, starting away.

"Hey, wait for us," Lewis shouted after the Jeep, but it was too late. Doc Tracker was Bell's only passenger; the others had to walk back with Ruizique and his patrol.

"We take Mike," Pham said. Ruizique handed him his poncho to carry the body in. The Marines and PFs separated into two groups and walked side by side next to the roadway. They maintained an alertness, but not too sharply. Nobody expected any more trouble this morning; Charlie knew he had done his damage. Most of the Marines turned off when the procession reached Camp Apache's hill.

"I'm going to walk into Hou Ky with them," Zeitvogel said. Hou Ky was a quarter mile west of the hill; it was where the men Ruizique had patrolled with lived.

"You and me both, honcho," Hempen said.

Without discussing it, the two Marines took opposite sides of the small group of PFs, providing security for those carrying the dead man.

An old, French-built masonry house shaped like an L was in the center of Hou Ky hamlet. A low wall extending from the ends of the L closed in a plaza that was the hamlet square. Thien, the hamlet chief, lived with his family in the shorter, fatter arm of the L. The longer arm contained stalls in which lived old people without families to take care of them—most of those old people had lost their families to the war.

A child, about seven or eight years old, was riding a water buffalo out the gate to Hou Ky and saw the PFs carrying Mike's body. The boy was taking the thousand-pound beast to graze in the brush south of the hamlet. He guessed immediately the meaning of what he saw and hit the buffalo on its forehead with a switch to make it stop. He bounded off and ran back to Thien's house to tell him —he couldn't turn the buffalo around and make it run through the hamlet; the huge animal would probably knock over a house or two and trample somebody just because it was so big and graceless. The buffalo stood there dumbly for a moment before it realized its rider was gone. Then it made the buffalo equivalent of a mental shrug and shambled a few feet to somebody's kitchen garden and started munching.

Thien and Houng were in the square when Pham arrived with Mike's body. The other PFs who lived in Hou Ky were also gathering in the square, and other people were beginning to crowd around its perimeter wall. Pham and his men laid Mike's body on the ground in front of the flagpole. There was a scream from the crowd and some excited jabbering. Zeitvogel looked and saw a woman almost fall, jumping over the low wall. Her scream trailed off into keening as she ran to the small body on the ground and collapsed over it; she was Mike's widow.

In moments the rest of the PFs were all in the square, and Houng told Collard Green to get them in formation. Houng squatted and tried to comfort the widow.

Stringy little fucker finally has a reason to look like he's going to lose his lunch, Zeitvogel thought, watching Collard Green line up the PFs and get the squad leaders' reports.

Collard Green reported Pheet missing. The Marines called the missing man "Pheet" because his feet were out-size for his body; they looked as if they belonged to a man six feet tall, and Pheet was hardly more than five feet.

Houng stood and looked around. He called out in Vietnamese for Pheet to report; he asked if the people around knew where he was. None did. Even the PF's wife and child weren't there. The PF lieutenant looked exasperated. Pheet was in Willy's squad. He told Willy to find him. The PF squad leader scampered away, calling Pheet's names, both nickname and Vietnamese name. He was back in a few minutes without having found the missing man. More of Mike's relatives were in the square now, squatting around the body, keening and mentally preparing themselves for the funeral.

The hawk-nosed man squatted behind his tripod-mounted binoculars on the distant hillside. His heavy brows made a sharp V over the bridge of his nose as he watched the gathering in Hou Ky's square. His thin lips twisted in a cruel mockery of a smile when he saw the men in the half uniforms of the Popular Forces shouting and running about, obviously looking for their missing man. He imagined their shock when they found the man with the huge feet, and an evil laugh cackled out of him. "You are mine now, Tango Niner," he whispered hoarsely. "I have now killed four of you and injured at least one of your women. One hamlet of Bun Hou is turned against you, and others will follow. Soon, Tango Niner, the running-dog imperialist Marines will be the only ones of you left. And then I will kill them most ignominiously." No aircraft were in sight, so he remained squatting behind his binoculars. All he had to do was shift their aim slightly to see where the body of the PF waited for discovery. He would gleefully watch that discovery.

He was wrong about the casualties, though. Swarnes wasn't dead and would return.

"Let's go, Short Round," Zeitvogel said after Houng had spoken his words over Mike's body and released it to his family.

"I'm with you, honcho," Hempen said solemnly.

They told Houng they were returning to Camp Apache and would give a full report to Bell and Burrison. The PF leader nodded wordlessly. Having a man die the way Mike had, without a chance to fight back, numbed him. Later he would feel the anger and fury. Later would come the vengeful bloodlust. But now he was numb and closed in on himself.

The two Marines left. On the way to the hamlet gate, they passed the forgotten water buffalo, contentedly munching on the remains of the kitchen garden, not yet aware it would soon be looking for another kitchen garden to browse.

They passed through the gate, and Hempen looked up at his fire team leader's drawn face. "Don't worry, honcho," he said. "We'll have you back in your hootch most ricky-tick. It's too early in the morning for night fighters to be up and out. You can get your beauty sleep." He shook his head. "I'm not sure it'll do much good, though. You're so damn ugly." He ducked from the sweeping punch the tall man slowly threw at his head.

They turned a final bend in the trail and stopped. They couldn't see Camp Apache's hill from here, but they could see the open ground north of it. Their rifles were suddenly ready in their hands, and their eyes searched the scrub trees around them.

"Shit," Zeitvogel swore. "Motherfucking cocksuckers."

"Gonna waste them little fucking bastards," Hempen said, "kill them till they're all fucking dead."

CHAPTER ELEVEN

December 27, 1966

"Let's take the poor fuckers down," Zeitvogel said. His voice broke on the words.

Hempen rasped something in agreement. They moved slowly; their hearts were heavy, and their limbs felt sheathed in lead. Three bodies hung from the branches of a tree alongside the path: Pheet, his wife, and his three-year-old son. The PF was naked from his waist down; dark red blood had flowed down and clotted on his legs from the gaping wound in his groin where he had been emasculated. His genitals protruded from his mouth, and his empty eye sockets stared out. His throat gaped in a broad slit. Somehow his feet didn't look so big in death. The body of the young child was not mutilated except for where his head had been split open by the machete blow that had killed him. Pheet's wife was also eyeless. Her body was shirtless, and her hacked-off breasts lay on the ground beneath her feet. She, too, had had her throat slit.

As tenderly as they could, the two Marines lifted the bodies off the branches they were impaled on.

Zeitvogel looked at the ground on both sides of the trail.

"Help me look, Short Round," he muttered. "They weren't killed here. Let's see if we can find a trail."

Hempen looked at the ground below where the bodies had hung. He saw very little blood. It was obvious the bodies had been drained someplace else and carried here. "Right," he said, and started looking.

"Maybe Billy Boy or Chief can find something," Zeitvogel said after a few minutes. "I sure as shit don't see any kind of trail here."

"Me, either," Hempen said.

They returned to the bodies. "Stay here," Zeitvogel said, and walked to where the trail emerged from the trees. He looked toward Camp Apache and waited until somebody looked in his direction. He waved to catch the man's attention. When he had it, he held his rifle in both hands above his head and pumped it up and down several times —the textbook signal for "enemy in sight." Then he doubled one fist and pumped it up and down, the signal for "hurry up." The distant figure spun around and ran. Zeitvogel could hear him shouting, though he couldn't make out the words. A moment later he saw the Jeep careening out of the main gate. Several men ran out behind the Jeep. He waited patiently.

The Jeep squealed to a stop, dust from the dirt trail billowing around it. Bell, Burrison, Mazzucco, and Storey piled out of it, rifles held ready.

"This way," Zeitvogel said. His voice was even, though dull. He led them into the trees where they had found the bodies. They all swore, except Storey. He'd only been with Tango Niner for one day and didn't know the dead man or his family. He was so new, his bush hat was still colored in the several bright greens of its camouflage pattern and didn't have any sweat stains on it yet; it was one of the leftover hats the Marines had bought for Bobbie Harder's friends when they had visited on Christmas.

"Goddamn fuckers," Bell said, pounding one fist into the other hand. "I thought we taught them not to fuck with the people."

"Pheet was a fay epp, Jay Cee," Burrison reminded him.

"Maybe so," the sergeant said, looking at the lieutenant red-eyed. "But his wife and kid weren't."

Burrison didn't respond to him. "Stilts," he said instead to Zeitvogel, "take your people and scout around, see if you can find anything."

The tall corporal nodded. He and Hempen had already looked, but maybe with four men they could find something the two alone had missed. "Homeboy, Newby, let's check it out." He didn't have to give Hempen any orders; the short rifleman was already headed into the trees.

Burrison turned to the other members of the rifle squad who were just arriving, panting, almost out of breath. "Billy Boy," he said hoarsely, "go into Hou Ky. Get Houng on the double. Don't let anybody but him know why."

"What if there are other people there when I see him?"

"Then don't tell him what I want him for until you get him away from them," Burrison snapped. "Do it."

"Aye-aye," Lewis said, and headed down the trail at a trot.

"Dumbshit, go with him," Randall ordered. Charlie never operated in Bun Hou during the day anymore, but he didn't want to take any chances with one of his men getting caught alone. And the way Charlie had been acting the last couple of days, anything seemed possible.

Dumbshit Dodd shrugged and, without seeming to go fast, caught up with Lewis before the wiry man was out of sight. Dodd understood probably better than anybody else in Tango Niner how dangerous days had suddenly become in Bun Hou, how any of their lives could end abruptly while the sun shone. But he shrugged off the knowledge; it was meaningless to him. Ever since he had failed in his attempts to talk his draft board out of drafting him into the Marine Corps he'd known the die was cast and his days numbered. Dodd counted himself among the walking dead. He was just a pudgy kid from the suburbs; he was sup-posed to grow up to be an accountant or a used-car salesman or an insurance salesman. He wasn't any John Wayne; he wasn't cut out to be a Marine. He didn't have the makings to be one of those bad-ass heroes. But here he was, so he'd do his job. What he didn't realize was his fatalistic attitude gave him a fearlessness that turned him into a much better Marine than he imagined. So he followed Lewis and watched for VC. His job was to kill the enemy before the enemy killed him. And that's what he intended to do to the best of his ability until the day when he got killed himself.

Ruizique stood isolated in the middle of the path, isolated even though another Marine stood not more than five feet from him and several more were within ten meters. He looked through the break in the trees above the path; his gaze rested on the hillside far to the west. He fingered the bullets in the loops of his crossed bandoliers. You are here somewhere, Mister Charlie, he thought. Have we underestimated you? Are you still ready to tango, even though we have shown we can find you and kill you where you live? Do not fool yourself, Mister Charlie. Whatever you do, you belong to us. His long fingers caressed his drooping Pancho Villa mustache, and he stared hard at the distant hillside, wondering if the Vietcong were out there, preparing new tactics for another attempt to wipe out Tango Niner.

On the distant hillside, Major Nghu watched Ruizique looking his way and shuddered. He fought with himself to avoid trying to shrink behind his powerful binoculars; he knew there was no way the distant Marine could see him with the naked eye. But the intensity of the imperialist's look was evident even without Nghu being able to see his eyes. This man is dangerous, Nghu thought. This man must die soon. He decided to instruct his men to kill the American with the mustache and crossed bandoliers at the first opportunity. He would have his men kill that one no matter how many of them had to be sacrificed in doing it.

* * *

Pheet still hadn't appeared in the Hou Ky square, and nobody had seen his wife or child. Willy, Pheet's squad leader, had checked out the missing man's hootch. No one was home, and nothing was disturbed or missing. That was the strange thing; even his wife's conical straw hat was hanging from the rafter where it would be if she were home. A worried Houng was organizing the twenty men he had present into search parties to find the missing man and his family when Lewis and Dodd burst into the square.

"Hey, Houng," Lewis almost shouted, "my honcho wants to see you most ricky-tick."

The PF lieutenant looked into the Marine's eyes and knew. He snapped orders in crisp Vietnamese, and several of the PFs gathered around him, ready to go with their leader.

"Only you, Houng," Lewis said.

"Why?"

Lewis shrugged, trying to look innocent and ignorant. "I don't know. He said he only wants you."

Houng shook his head vigorously. "This is my man," he said in broken English, "the friend of my men. They come with me."

Dodd thought fast and came up with a compromise. "You and Willy," he said. "Scrappy doesn't want panic."

Houng looked hard at the draftee and knew why it was so important not to bring his men. He didn't like it. Then he nodded. "Only Willy." He said something in Vietnamese, and Collard Green answered. The sickly-looking squad leader had the rest of the platoon back in formation by the time Houng and Willy followed Lewis and Dodd out of the square.

It wasn't far from Hou Ky to where the path came out of the trees; they got there in three or four minutes. Ruizique and his men were covering the bodies with pieces of tarp Bell had sent the Jeep back to Camp Apache for. Houng pulled up and looked at the sheets of heavy cloth, three of them covering lumps, one very small.

"His family?" Houng asked.

Burrison nodded. "Pheet, his wife and kid."

The PF lieutenant stood like he'd turned to stone. Only his body was still; his mind churned: We have not done this, he thought. We have killed Vietcong but never taken reprisals against their families. In the seven months Houng had commanded the Popular Forces platoon in Bun Hou, they and the Marines had killed too many of his countrymen for him to ever wish to count. In the beginning, the VC they'd killed had been neighbors, local VC recruited in Bun Hou so the Provisional Revolutionary Government— the political side of the revolutionary movement, of which the Vietcong was the army—could claim the village as being part of their territory. During June and into July they had killed these misguided villagers. Since then they'd killed South Vietnamese who had come in from someplace else. But they had never punished the families of the men who had turned to the VC.

Houng understood how those men had come to join the VC. They were poor men, farmers and fishermen, and few of them had more than a very few years of education—not all of them could even read. They knew little more than that which was their own lives. One thing they knew was that Saigon had set a limit on how much a landlord could charge in rent on farmland; the limit was one quarter of the principal crop. And the government officials charged with enforcing that law often looked the other way when the landlords charged as much as half of all crops, three times as much as they were legally allowed to. The farmers and fishermen knew there was a process for them to achieve redress for grievances, but they also knew they had to pay money to gain that redress. Money they often didn't have.

So when other men came into the village, men who dressed and looked and talked like them, men who seemed to also be poor farmers and fishermen, and told them that things would be better after the revolution, after the Communists took over the government, they believed. Of course, the strangers never said "Communists"; they always talked about the PRG or the National Liberation

Front, which was going to rid the country of foreign domination and reunite Vietnam. It was easy to believe someone who came and explained things. Easy because the Saigon government never came and explained things; it only demanded from the people and looked the other way when someone stole from them. Most of the people looked the other way and muttered to themselves how one government was as bad as another and didn't join the Vietcong or the PRG or the NLF.

Houng knew better. He had been conscripted into the army. While in the army he had the chance to study; he studied Vietnamese history and learned the truth of reunification and freedom. He learned it was true that Nam Viet, as the country had then been known, had been rebelling on and off for nearly two thousand years to throw off its Chinese overlords and gain its freedom. Then there had been on-and-off fighting against the French until they had finally been thrown out. Houng also learned about reunification. He learned that for the past thousand years there had been war between the Southerners and the Northerners of Vietnam, with the freer, happier Southerners wanting to rule themselves and the harsher Northerners wanting to control them and rule them as rural chattel. Reunification was a myth; it went counter to the freedom for which the South had fought for a millennium.

In the army he had also met many people who had fled from the North and he heard their stories. He knew it was true that there were no landlords in the North, robbing the people. This was because in the North, the state owned all the land and the farmers and fishermen paid to the state all of what they grew or caught and the state gave back as much—or as little—as it wanted to. In the North the people were at least as poor as they were in the South. He was not blind; he knew that in the South a man could be imprisoned or killed because he had something a government official wanted. He also knew that in the North a man could be imprisoned because a government official didn't think he—or a relative—should have what he did. South Vietnam was under martial law, and a man could go to jail or be executed because he stood against the government. It was worse in the North where a man could go to jail or be executed because of what he thought or what a relative or friend thought or what the government thought he might think in the future.

In the South the government often did not tell the people the truth. Houng knew this. In the South the government often stood aside and let others rob the people. But no matter how difficult it was, there was a means of complaining and making right what wrong had been done. In the North the government lied. It took everything from the people and gave back only what it wanted to, and it told the people they had to like it. Those were major differences that made the South a better place. There was another difference, one that made the fight and risk of life worth it all: in the South it was possible to change the government through free elections; not easy, but possible. In the North it was not possible for the people to change the government, no matter what lies the government officials told the people about a "People's" republic.

All the people wanted was to be left alone and allowed to make whatever decent living they could. But both sides came in and tried to persuade them to do things their way, to take sides. Sometimes they came in and told the people what to do. Sometimes they said things the people were able to believe; other times they didn't. The main way to distinguish between them was one side sometimes paid for what it took instead of always stealing it, and that same side more often than the other side killed when it didn't get enough cooperation.

Houng looked at the tarp-covered bodies of Pheet and his family and felt despair. He had come home and, with the help of the men he had recruited into the PF platoon and the Marines who had come to help, had killed the local Vietcong. Then he and his men and the Marines had killed so many more Vietcong who had come into Bun Hou since then. They had even killed the special soldiers, the sappers, who had been sent from the North to wipe them out. And the enemy kept coming. Was there no end to them? Were the lies of the Northerners and their dupes in the South so persuasive that those who knew the truth and wished nothing more than freedom for themselves and their families and their friends were doomed? Now the Vietcong were murdering the wives and children of the men who wanted freedom badly enough to risk their very lives for it.

"Yesterday the Hou Toung headman; today this," Houng said out loud, and stood erect. "They will pay." He had fought too long and too hard; he would not give up, no matter what.

"Payback is a motherfucker," one of the Marines said.

CHAPTER TWELVE

That Afternoon

"Yes, I really do think we should run our scheduled med-cap into Hou Cau," Bell said. There was determination and stubbornness in his voice.

"No getting out of it?" Burrison asked, another variation on the question he'd been asking his sergeant for the past couple of minutes.

Bell nodded vigorously. "Charlie's fucking with the people. Two days ago he wasted Malahini and wounded Swarnes. That's all he's done to us. Since then he's zapped two of our fay epps, killed one of their families, and murdered the Hou Toung headman." He looked seriously at the lieutenant. "If we back down from anything, the people will think we're going to let Charlie do anything he wants to them." He shook his head. "Worse, the fay epps will think we aren't interested in getting vengeance for Pheet's family, that we don't care what happens to their families. That happens, we're out here alone with no friends."

It was Burrison's turn to nod. "That's everything I thought of," he said, and then grinned. "But damn it, Jay Cee, you didn't say word one about us being Marines, and

Marines are supposed to aggressively pursue the enemy."

Bell cocked an eye at him. "That needed to be said? Scrappy, does the sun rise over the South China Sea? No shit, aggressive. Gung ho and all that."

Burrison laughed. "Who's going, and are they humping or taking the Jeep?"

Ten minutes later Ruizique and his men were gathered near the back gate with Doc Tracker. Knowles was with them for added security, as was the newby, Hunter. Hunter was with them even though he wasn't a known quantity, because Bell believed in getting his new men out among the people as soon as possible, getting them acquainted with one another. Nobody complained about having to walk.

Bell gave them a quick visual inspection. Each man had his rifle loaded and was carrying five additional magazines on his belt, except for Robertson, who had seven—and a bulge under his shirt looked like he had a couple more tucked inside it. They all carried bayonets or K-bars on their belts along with a few hand grenades. A PRC-6 radio hung by its strap from Ruizique's shoulder. Bell was satisfied. All that remained was what he hoped was an unnecessary admonition, "Look alive, people. Charlie's out there somewhere, and he want to tango."

"Don't worry, honcho," Ruizique said. "If Mister Charlie is between here and Hou Cau, we will find him."

"Just make sure you find him, and not the other way around."

Robertson was holding his automatic rifle loosely in his right hand. He brought it up sharply and slapped his left hand onto its forestock. "No sweat, honcho, this is our ville. Charlie can't find us unless we want him to."

Bell looked at the new lance corporal sadly. "Tell that to Malahini," he said after a moment. The seven men were somber when they left the compound.

Zeitvogel poked his head into the command hootch's middle room an hour later and said, "I'm taking my people for a walk, Jay Cee." Bell was lying back on his cot, reading a paperback book with a cover so worn the tall corporal couldn't make out its title.

"Where you going, Stilts?" Burrison asked. The young lieutenant was sitting at his field desk, trying to compose a report that would explain to Captain Hasford what had happened over the past twenty-four hours, and Zeitvogel hadn't immediately noticed him.

"Out that way." Zeitvogel looked at his commander and gestured roughly westward.

Burrison looked at him pensively for a moment, then said, "Take a prick six. Your call sign is Red Rover One. We're Dog House. Check in every once in a while." He paused again before asking, "Anybody going with you?" He meant from the PF platoon.

Zeitvogel nodded. "Willy's here with Long and Butter Bar and Huu."

Burrison and Bell exchanged quick glances. Do Chot Huu, the former VC who had surrendered to them a month earlier, had managed to be very silent about what had been going on these past two days. Huu's first job as an unofficial "Kit Carson" scout with Tango Niner had been to lead a reconnaissance patrol over the western hills to a Vietcong communications center. Huu had been wounded earlier, and when Doc Rankin treated him while on a med-cap patrol, he had become convinced of the basic humanity of the Americans. He knew that Rankin knew he was a VC, but the corpsman had treated his wound instead of killing him or taking him prisoner. When the VC had later attacked Hou Cau hamlet and killed several people and burned down some of their houses, he had become convinced of his comrades' inhumanity. That's when he had decided to change sides—but only if he could work with Tango Niner to defeat his former mates who he believed were betraying the people they claimed to champion. Huu had proven his trustworthiness by leading the Marines and PFs to the big communications center and helping them destroy it. But he'd been strangely silent since the latest enemy activities started.

"Keep an eye on him," Burrison said.

"You know it," Zeitvogel answered. He understood who Burrison meant.

Bell nodded at him. Zeitvogel nodded back. "Scrappy," he said in verbal salute, and ducked back into the radio room. "Gimme a six," he said to Lewis, who was filling in, taking a turn covering the radios for a while during Swarnes's absence.

He hadn't needed to ask; Lewis was already holding one out to him. Only a thin canvas wall separated the radio room from the commanders' quarters, and the radioman could hear nearly everything said in the other room. "Battery is new," Lewis said. "Go down by our hootch and run a radio check."

"Right." Hempen, Mazzucco, and Storey waited patiently while Zeitvogel ran his radio check. Willy and his men clustered near the main gate. When the radio checked out five by five, Zeitvogel led his Marines to the PFs. "Let's take a walk," he said to the PF squad leader. Then his eyes bored into the silent Chieu Hoi.

The eight men strolled through the wide opening in the banks of wire and down the hill, where they turned left toward Hou Ky. This wasn't a formal patrol, so they weren't in a column. Willy walked along the trail flanked by Huu and Zeitvogel. Mazzucco and Long were about eight meters ahead of them, off the trail on its left. Storey walked alone to their right and rear. It wasn't a good formation, because if there was trouble, it was most likely to come from the left front and they could be caught by enfilade fire, fire along the long axis of the group. Hempen and Butter Bar followed far enough back on the trail that if a hand grenade hit among the middle three they probably wouldn't be badly hurt by it. The Marines called the chubby PF "Butter Bar"—they had wanted to call him "Butter Ball," but the Vietnamese had some trouble saying words ending with the letter "L"; it came out more like an

"R"—because he was the only Vietnamese peasant any of them had seen who was fat. Peasants worked too hard and ate too poorly to carry much fat. Being rotund didn't make Butter Bar any less of a fighter, and the Marines trusted him to do his share of fighting more than they did some of the leaner PFs.

No one carried his rifle at the ready: both hands on it, muzzle pointing where his eyes looked. But they didn't carry them slung on their shoulders either, though Long was carrying his balanced on his shoulder like a fishing rod. They were ready. The sloppiness of the formation had its purpose. Nobody seeing them would think they were a patrol. Any enemy observing them would likely think they were just out for a walk—perhaps going to visit someplace—and maybe, just maybe, be a little careless and do something dumb to give himself away in time for the Marines and PFs to take first action. They tried not to do it too openly, but each of the eight men was carefully observing their surroundings. Their rubbernecking seemed casual, rather than deliberate. Rubbernecking was something that men who went to war in small groups did—if they wanted to survive. One way to tell a man who's been in small unit combat is the way his head and eyes keep moving, always moving, always searching. It's a habit that takes many years to break.

Most of that casualness would change once they disappeared into the cover of the trees.

Mazzucco and Long were talking quietly, telling each other what they knew of how to be an effective pointman, both teaching and taking the opportunity to learn more of how to do the job, knowledge that would help keep them alive longer. Hempen and Butter Bar were joking and laughing at each other's jokes, difficult for two men who only have a limited common language, but they knew each other well enough to be able to guess what they were saying. Sometimes their guesses were even right.

But in the middle, Zeitvogel, Willy, and Huu walked wordlessly. The dusty-sounding buzzing of insects was a background curtain to the low murmurings from Mazzucco and Long, the louder talking and laughing of Hempen and Butter Bar.

Zeitvogel broke the quiet between him and the PFs halfway from the foot of Camp Apache's hill to the trees between the Marine compound and Hou Ky. "What's happening, Kit Carson?"

Huu looked up at him over Willy's head. Willy stiffened slightly and kept his head straight ahead, though his eyes still swiveled.

Huu lifted his shoulders in a minor shrug. "I don't know," he said.

Zeitvogel lifted an eyebrow and showed his teeth in something that could have been a smile but wasn't. "No?"

"Your question is unclear." These were not the exact words they used talking to each other; they talked in broken English, Vietnamese and bastardized French, but the meaning was. "Do you mean am I glad I joined you, that I have sided with those who prove they are for the people? Yes, I am. Do you mean do I know what the Vietcong are doing?" He looked toward the trees and chewed on his lower lip. "No, I do not."

When he didn't say any more for a moment, Zeitvogel asked, "What's the matter? Don't you have Vee Cee friends anymore?"

Huu barked a short, humorless laugh. "My Vee Cee friends, as you call them, would kill me if they saw me. To them I am a traitor." He fell silent again. Zeitvogel thought he was thinking and waited for him to speak again. "I do not believe it is Vee Cee doing this," he finally said. "The local Vee Cee don't have the patience or organization to operate this way." He smiled sadly at the tall Marine. "You killed the Bun Hou Vee Cee and others. The Bun Anh Vee Cee are not directly threatened by you. The main-force Vee Cee, who used to come here from across the hills, were only passing through and could not manage the kind of attrition that has happened here the past two days and nights." He stopped talking and looked back at the trees they were almost into.

Mazzucco and Long stepped onto the trail to enter the trees. Before reaching the first bend, they looked back. Zeitvogel was now under the trees as well. He signaled Mazzucco into the trees south of the trail. The pointmen held their rifles in both hands now and soft-stepped into the deeper shadows.

"Information has come to me," Huu suddenly said in a soft voice that carried clearly to Zeitvogel's ears but not to the rest of the group, with the exception of Willy, "that strangers have entered Bun Hou." He might no longer have had VC friends, but he did have relatives and some other friends who did not hate him and who still had connections with the enemy; friends and relatives who used a network of other friends and relatives to get to him whatever information he might need to avoid being caught and killed by the VC, who would assassinate him as a turncoat.

"Where are they staying, Huu?" Zeitvogel asked.

"I do not know." Now the Chieu Hoi looked worried; he had asked, and no one was willing to tell him. That frightened him. By now all of them were under the trees, off the trail. Their rifles were in both hands now; their heads and eyes openly searched their surroundings, rifle muzzles pointing where they looked. If they had to fire at something they saw, the only delay between realization of danger and the pull of the trigger would be the length of time it took the brain's command to cross the synapses to the trigger finger. The afternoon walk was now a combat patrol. And they were loaded for bear.

Major Nghu had watched until the body of the PF lackey and those of his whore and spawn were deposited in the Hou Ky hamlet square, then, vile elation filling his heart, he assigned a sergeant to continue watching while he went to his temporary encampment. The sergeant had orders to take down the binoculars and their tripod and leave the observation post if a helicopter appeared, and to send for his commander if he saw any interesting activity in the imperialist running-dog camp. When the heat of the day was nearing its peak, the sergeant saw what he thought might be the kind of activity he'd been ordered to watch for and snapped an order at a private. The private scampered off. Minutes later, Major Nghu returned with his senior sergeant following in his wake. He was satisfied; he'd just finished demolishing a cold field meal. The sergeant watching through the binoculars could see this and felt his own hunger pangs; he wondered when he would be relieved from his post so he could eat as well.

Major Nghu sat behind the glasses and adjusted them to his own eyes, an inconvenience of having someone else use them in his absence. Perhaps he could teach this sergeant how to adjust the focus for him so he could see immediately and not have to play with the glasses. If the dolt was capable of learning such an elementary task. The peasants being drafted into the army these days and being promoted to sergeant, Major Nghu thought, sometimes seemed to have the intelligence of slow water buffalo. He studied the scene that was revealed to his eyes through the powerful glasses and immediately realized its significance. Seven men, all Yankee Marines, were leaving the back gate of the compound. The large pack slung over the shoulder of one of them told him what their mission was. The pack could be nothing other than a medical kit; they were going to Hou Cau to bac si the people. Leaving by the back gate, they could have no other destination.

Major Nghu cackled briefly, then snarled a series of orders to his senior sergeant. The senior sergeant departed, but the commander remained at the binoculars. Fifteen minutes after the senior sergeant left, he was back with his report. As ordered, ten men were on their way along the river to the woods between Hou Cau and the Marines' hill. They were divided into two-man teams, a sniper and a spotter in each team. They would split up and wait their chance. The entire area between Hou Cau and the foot of Hou Dau hill was covered; there was little chance the med-cap patrol to the market hamlet could return to the Marines' compound without passing in sight of one of the sniper teams. When it passed in sight of one of the teams, it would be in range. Major Nghu acknowledged the report with a grunt and continued watching the distant hill. The senior sergeant squatted patiently to be there when his commander wanted him.

After a time Major Nghu wished the other sergeant, the one he'd left watching while he had gone for a rest and a midday meal, would control the rumblings of his stomach; he found the noise slightly annoying. The man was probably unhappy with the situation of the company. Idiot! He should have been here with Major Nghu in the past, when they were in underground bunkers and lived in those cramped quarters with their bad air. Living hidden on the side of this ridge was certainly preferable to the tunnels and bunkers. So what if the only fires they could have were small ones during the day, and only enough to boil water for tea? The rice balls and dried, preserved foods they had with them were sufficient, if not tasty.

It would only be a few more days, then the devil Marines of Tango Niner would all be dead. Then his soldiers could go into the hamlets and sleep in the people's houses, sleep on their beds, have the village women cook hot, good-tasting meals for them. But even that would only last for a very few days before he and his men had to leave on the long trek back north. He chuckled when he thought of what would happen when the puppet troops of Saigon or their American lackeys came to Bun Hou to find out what happened to their Marines. And those troops would punish the people for their part in it. Even though the people would have had nothing to do with it. Ah, divisiveness was so sweet.

Major Nghu was beginning to consider again leaving the sergeant with the loud internal organs to watch while he himself left for a well-earned nap when he saw four PFs approaching the Marines' hill from the direction of Hou Ky. He waited. This might be interesting. He watched while the four men entered the compound and conferred with several of the foreign devils. After a time the tall black one, the one who resembled a mythical demon, left them to enter the tent with the high radio antenna. The four PFs separated from the Marines and went to stand near the main gate. Minutes later the tall one came out of the tent with one of the hand-held radios slung over his shoulder and rejoined the other Marines. He spoke into his radio, then he and three of his companions joined the four lackeys at the main gate. They departed and headed in a loose group toward Hou Ky.

How easy it would be to hurt them now, Major Nghu thought. If only I had men in that area. He watched them carefully, then through a break in the trees, saw them leave the trail and enter the scrub forest. They had been walking casually; the brief flash he had of them through the trees showed them moving more deliberately. Excited, he snapped another series of orders at his senior sergeant. The senior sergeant ran off to execute them. Major Nghu stood and stretched his wiry frame, then turned to the noisy sergeant. It would have been good to relieve the man, the NVA commander thought. He had been on watch for a long time without a break. But his noisy stomach annoyed the officer. Nghu told him to resume watch through the binoculars. He thought, but didn't say, the man needed to learn some self-discipline. On his way back to his temporary encampment he encountered his senior sergeant, returning with the report that ten more men had been dispatched, into the scrub forest this time—five more sniper/spotter teams that would set up in the woods west of the Marines' hill. Nghu's face twisted in a smile. Instead of one man, one shot, one kill, it would happen twice. Yes, this would clearly demonstrate to the people that the imperialist invaders were unable to protect themselves, much less the people.

CHAPTER THIRTEEN

Time Marches On, Here, There, and Everywhere

Corporal Tex Randall lay on his cot in the squad tent. One arm was flung over his face, shielding his eyes from the daylight. He was pretending to be asleep but was given away by his other arm, which lay along his side, fingers drumming a light tattoo on the edge of the cot.

Across the aisle that ran the length of the tent, Vega lay back, leaning against a tent post next to his cot. He was pretending to read a paperback book to cover his nervousness. Something was bothering his honcho, and he was too new here to not automatically be bothered by something bothering his fire team leader. Randall was called Tex. Probably went around telling people he was every badass who ever came out of Texas. That was common enough for the tough gringos who went by those kinds of nicknames. The thing was, Randall didn't look like that kind of shit-kicking redneck.

Vega was from the Rio Grande valley, an area that was sometimes lush with river green, sometimes parched, when the river dried to little more than a trickle. His was a Texas where, while English was the official language, Spanish was the common tongue, and nobody could survive well without speaking both. The only way you could tell there was an international border where he came from was that when you crossed the river the daily newspapers were printed in different languages and the money wasn't always the same—though merchants on either side usually accepted both currencies. Hell, in the part of Texas Vega was from, if you went out and got too drunk and too rowdy on Saturday night and weren't sure where you were when you woke up, you had to look at a newspaper to find out where you were—unless you were willing to make a fool of yourself by asking somebody. He didn't know, but he thought Randall was from a different part of Texas, farther north, where they said you could see forever. He had gone through that part of Texas once and found it depressing. It had been the wrong time of year and the grass was brown, all there was to see in all directions were blue sky and unbroken brown earth. No wonder those gringos were so crazy; that kind of landscape, where there wasn't anything friendly to be seen, had to fuck up people's minds. Maybe that's all that was bothering Randall; it's just that he was one of those Texans.

Lewis ducked under the rolled-up side of the tent between his cot and Vega's. He'd gotten Athen to relieve him on the radio. "Go find Dumbshit, newby," he said quietly. "The two of you, find a comfortable place on the perimeter and make like you're watching for Charlie."

Vega looked at the slight Marine with the asymmetrical mustache. Lewis was looking grimly at Randall. Vega knew the lance corporal couldn't really give him orders, but Lewis obviously wanted to talk to Randall, maybe about what was bothering him. And maybe Dodd had some idea of what was going on. He needed someone to explain things to him—like how come everybody called him Dumbshit.

"Right," he said. He put the paperback down on his ammo crate table; Lewis noticed that he didn't mark his place in the book. He found Dodd and quickly had a whole new set of questions. What's this bullshit about getting drafted? Nobody gets drafted into the Marine Corps. Why's this dude convinced he's gonna die? Shee-it, he didn't even say wasted, make the idea partly palatable to those who would survive him. How come this dipshit puts on this zombie act? Anybody can tell by watching him move on patrol or watch over the perimeter that he knows his shit. Vega shortly realized he wasn't going to find out anything talking to Dodd and shut himself into his own thoughts. It was obvious now why Dodd was called Dumbshit.

What the hell was going on here, anyway? Two PFs, and the family of one of them, had been killed since he had arrived, without the Marines being able to do anything about it. His honcho was acting weird; everybody was acting uptight. That spic from the DR was acting like some kind of Juan Wayne. All that was missing was for that tall splib to start acting like a pro basketball player. A lot of grunts thought CAP was candy duty, just a littler tougher than the pogues "in the rear with the beer." Vega had an uncomfortable feeling Tango Niner wasn't like that at all. He remembered when he was in boot camp, how so many of his fellow maggots had sworn when they got home on boot leave they were going to kick their recruiting sergeants' asses. He never said that or even thought it. Hell, he knew he had walked into that recruiting office on his own and said, "I want to enlist." It wasn't anybody's fault but his own. Now he was having second thoughts. He started thinking that maybe when his tour was up and he went back to The World, he'd look up that recruiting sergeant and kick ass on him for not talking him out of enlisting.

Lewis sat heavily on Dodd's cot; he made as much noise sitting as he could. "Okay, Tex," he said to Randall's hidden face, "what the fuck's bothering you this time?"

Randall didn't acknowledge him, still pretended to be asleep.

"Cut the shit, Tex. I know you're awake in there. What's on that alleged mind of yours?"

Silence.

"Tex, you don't talk to me, you'll wish you did."

"Fuck off, Billy Boy. I'm sleeping."

"Bullshit. Sleeping men don't do this." He leaned forward and grabbed Randall's hand, the one drumming.

"You want to hold hands, Billy Boy, go find yourself a boom-boom girl. Or I'll break your fucking ass in two."

"Khong the duc, no can do, Tex. A good little man will beat a good big man every time."

Randall lifted his arm from his face enough to peer one-eyed at Lewis. "Yeah? I always heard that the other way around."

Lewis lifted his shoulders in a shrug. "You beat Stilts, and he's good and big."

"He ain't as good as me, that tall-ass roundball player." He lifted his head while keeping his arm mostly over his face.

"Don't make me no never mind." He studied the one eye looking at him. "You're awake, I can tell. What's bugging you, honcho? You're so goddamn uptight you're freaking out the newbies."

Randall let his head fall back, and his arm slid off his face to lie crookedly above his head. "What happened on Christmas," he said in a weak voice.

"What about what happened on Christmas? Malahini got wasted. It's not the first time we lost someone. That ain't good enough, Corporal," he said firmly. Randall was acting like a jerk. Lewis thought he should be spoken to firmly.

"I know that," Randall said in a no-shit-you-dumb-fuck tone. "It's that Bobbie was here with her girlfriends. I invited her out here and she almost got killed. She'll probably never talk to me again." He paused long enough for Lewis to think he was through and start to say something, then continued. "She probably won't. I haven't gotten a letter from her yet."

Lewis blinked a few times. "That's the dumbest damn thing I ever heard," he snorted. "First off, there was one sniper round, and it wasn't aimed at her . . ."

"She was close."

"Shut up and listen to me. She wasn't that close, and, anyway, the sniper wasn't aiming at her. Second off, there was only one mortar round, and she wasn't even in the compound. Third off, you acted like one bad-ass Marine NCO who knows his shit and got her tail into a bunker most ricky-tick. Fourth off, you then saved some other dumb split-tail from trying to run away instead of getting under some cover." He stopped talking out loud and counted on his fingers for a moment. His lips moved while he remembered the points he already checked off. "Fifth off," he said when he found his place, "that was two days ago. We've only had one mail call since then. She could've written a letter as soon as she got back to Da Nang, but you can't have it yet because it's too fucking soon. Got that?"

Randall turned his head to Lewis. "You sure about that?"

"Does Lady Bird fuck LBJ?"

Randall smiled. "Maybe not. Maybe that's why we're here. Old LBJ's so horny he had to do something else to get his rocks off." He rolled to a sitting position and slid his feet into his Ho Chi Minh sandals. "You're right, Billy Boy. I should cheer up." His smile vanished. "Until today's mail call."

"No shit." Lewis bunched his fists in front of his face and twisted. When they came away, the left side of his mustache was a spike straight to the side; the right end was wadded into a ball.

Doc Tracker set up his medical station at a somewhat less than stable table with two rickety wooden chairs that the Hou Cau hamlet chief directed put out at one end of the large hamlet square when he saw the corpsman enter it. The Hou Cau square was larger than any of the other hamlet squares in the village, because Hou Cau was also the central marketplace for Bun Hou. The square fronted on and spread out along the Song Du Ong river to facilitate fishermen and merchants. Tracker hardly had time to begin opening his medkit and preparing its contents before he was surrounded by what seemed like all the children in the world. Every one of them wanted to be treated by the bac si, and every one of them was inventive enough to come up with something that needed his immediate attention, whether it hurt or not.

At first Ruizique ordered the five men he had with him to form everybody into lines; one line for the kids who saw the bac si's visit as a game, the other for the adults who needed medical attention—and any of the children who actually had something wrong with them. He himself stood close guard over Tracker's medkit to keep noisy children from playing with it and prevent any thefts. In not too many minutes it all got sorted out; a line of shrieking, playing children jiggled from the table in one direction, and a more sedate line of adults and children with miscellaneous ills and aches strung out in another. Satisfied that things were in order, Ruizique told Robertson to stay with him and let the others go.

Pennell, Neissi, and Knowles took Hunter in tow and showed him the sights of Hou Cau. The square sloped gently toward the water's edge, where the slant steepened just enough for boats to easily be beached or launched. At the end of the square opposite Tracker's med station, four women worked with riverbank clay, straw, long boards, and a kind of ax to make bricks. Pennell and Knowles explained to Hunter—and Neissi as well, because he was too new to Tango Niner to know this—that the women were making adobe bricks.

Knowles waved an arm at the hamlet. "See how most of the hootches are made of brick? When we first came here they were all grass shacks, like in a Crosby and Hope movie. The local economy's really going up. The people aren't paying taxes to the Vee Cee anymore, the landlords aren't allowed to charge more than they legally can for rent, and we hire some of the people to do work at Camp Apache. They got more money, so they're improving their houses. Ain't that right, Fast?" He turned to Pennell for confirmation.

"That's right," Pennell agreed.

"A month ago a half-dozen grass hootches got burned down in a Vee Cee raid," Knowles continued. "They've already been rebuilt out of brick." He looked smug, and rightfully so, because the Marines had had everything to do with the improvement of the local economy.

"The kids dress better," Pennell said.

"What?" Hunter seemed incredulous. The children were mostly barefoot and seemed to be wearing somebody's cast-off shirts and shorts. The toddlers weren't even dressed that well; the smallest girls wore short pants and the smallest boys shirts, but none of them wore both and a few were completely naked.

"True," Knowles continued. He knew the soft-spoken Pennell wouldn't want to keep talking. "When we first got here, the kids all wore rags my mother wouldn't use to clean the toilet."

Hunter looked more carefully around the hamlet and tried to compare it with other hamlets he'd been through on operations when he'd been in a regular grunt company. He didn't remember much of those earlier hamlets; he'd been looking too hard for VC and booby traps to pay much attention to anything that didn't look like it might be a threat. But now that he tried, it seemed to him that yes, the people here were all better dressed than he had seen Vietnamese peasants before. He saw almost none of the skin ulcers that Americans called "gook sores," and most of the people looked very clean. For that matter, the whole hamlet looked clean. Okay, so it didn't look like a *South Pacific* paradise, but it did look like the people were in good shape and they gave a damn.

They continued to explore the delights of the marketplace. Hunter bought a small bolt of brocade cloth—"My mother will love having this to make a dress out of"—and a doll clothed in a colorful ao dai dress, the traditional dress of Vietnamese women—"My sister collects dolls." Neissi looked wistfully at the doll. The only time he'd actually seen a Vietnamese woman wearing one was once when he'd been in a truck convoy driving through Da Nang after an operation. The ankle-length sheathlike dress, slit up the side to the hips and worn over long pants, looked so feminine and graceful he wanted to spend a lot of time with a woman who was wearing one. But Vietnamese women in the rural hamlets rarely wore them. All five Marines—Ruizique had eventually released Robertson, and he'd joined them along the way—bought some vegetables and spices to supplement their C-ration and once-a-day flown-in hot meal. This local food would be shared with the other Marines. They wandered back to the med station.

Nearly all of the people who were actually sick had been treated and most of the children who only wanted the attention as well—Tracker had alternated between the lines. "Just like a Chinese restaurant," he explained, "one from column A, one from column B." He was extracting an abscessed tooth from the mouth of a middle-aged woman when they reached him.

"Two things I never thought I'd be when I joined the Navy to get off the reservation," Tracker said, dropping the tooth into a trash receptacle and swabbing the hole with antiseptic, "a Marine and a dentist. Now look at me." He shook his head and laughed. He handed the woman a small vial of antibiotics and was carefully giving her instructions on how to use them, when they heard a distant gunshot.

Ruizique instantly picked up his radio and held it to his head. He didn't say anything into it, just listened and waved silence at his companions. He'd let them know what the shot was as soon as he found out himself. A fusillade followed the first shot.

The next playful child in line jumped onto the chair

facing Tracker. This one didn't squeal and giggle like the other children had; he was too afraid the distant gunfire meant he was going to lose his turn to laugh.

Zeitvogel and the Marines and PFs with him felt as if they'd been tramping aimlessly and uselessly. They hadn't, though. It had only been an hour, and they'd been silently gliding through the trees, managing to not disturb the fauna. Not finding any sign of Charlie, either. Zeitvogel and Willy talked it over with Huu when they entered the trees and decided to quarter the area south and west of where Zeitvogel and Hempen had found Pheet and his family. Maybe they'd find a blood trail or footprints, anything that might lead them to the place the murders had been committed. And from there maybe they'd find something that could lead them to where Charlie was hiding.

Nothing was what they found. Nothing except some insects that liked to dine on fresh, living meat.

Zeitvogel looked at his watch and saw it was getting close to time for the evening meal to be flown in. And then they had to get ready for the night's patrols. He swore under his breath, then said aloud, "Let's head on back, people. Newby, if you're going to be around here very long, sooner or later you're going to have the point at night. You may as well start learning your way around now. Lead off."

Storey swallowed and worked his mouth in an inaudible "Aye-aye." He hated point. The pointman too often found an ambush or booby-trap the hard way—by setting it off. But none of the others seemed concerned about booby-traps, and he'd heard several times in the twenty-four hours he'd been with them that Tango Niner set all the ambushes in Bun Hou. He looked up through the thin tops of the scrub trees to orient himself by the sun and headed east.

The trees became denser as they went along, until they completely blotted out the sky. Storey was afraid he'd get lost and frequently looked back at his fire team leader for direction. He always seemed to be going the right way.

After a while the tall corporal came close and told him, "Don't sweat it, newby. Once you've been here long enough you'll know this place like you do your own block back in The World."

Storey advanced a little more confidently after that.

They were a little less than a hundred meters from the open area around Camp Apache's hill and about an equal distance south of the Hou Ky trail when a single shot rang out nearby.

"Down!" Zeitvogel shouted. "Right front."

Everybody in the short column dropped, and six rifles started firing in the direction Zeitvogel indicated. The corporal didn't fire. He was looking and listening, trying to find out exactly where the shot had come from, how many VC might be out there. His radio shouted at him and he made his action report, which was only that someone had shot at them and they were returning fire. The trees and bushes he looked at seemed to be disturbed only by the bullets his own men were slamming into them; he heard only the noise of his own men's fire.

"Cease fire," he shouted. "Cease fire." Silence fell over them like falling into a bottomless lake. "Everybody okay? Count off, back to front."

Mazzucco reported he was okay. So did Long. And Huu, Hempen, Butter Bar, and Willy.

"Newby, count off," Zeitvogel ordered, annoyed at himself because he didn't remember his new man's name. Storey didn't answer. "Oh, shit." He bounded ahead and found his new man crumpled. A thin line of blood trickled from a bullet hole in his temple. "Goddamn," the tall man swore softly. His mind churned as he wracked his memory until he found what he was trying so hard to remember. "I couldn't even remember your name yet and you're dead already." He was on his knees and curled into a tight ball, tensing every muscle in his body for a long moment until he let everything relax at once and straightened up. "Homeboy, Long, stay here. Everybody else on line, let's see if we can find the bastard." He trotted to the middle of the short, ragged line, Hempen and Huu on one side of him, Willy and Butter Bar on his other. They advanced in the direction the shot that killed Storey had come from. Somehow Zeitvogel knew they wouldn't find anyone—maybe where he had fired from, but that was all. He lifted his radio to his head and gave his casualty report. They found a place that looked as if two men had lain in wait, but there was nothing positive about the location, not even a spent cartridge. No body, no blood trail, no nothing.

Unknown to the Marines and PFs, in other places in the woods around them, four more two-man sniper/spotter teams rose to their feet and trotted west without firing a shot.

Ruizique went through the "I speak, you speak" routine of radio communications when Bell called him, finished with a "Roger," waited for Bell's "Out," then slung the radio over his shoulder and told Tracker, "Pack it up, Chief. We're going back in now." Then he waited impassively while the corpsman hurried to obey the order. The Dominican didn't want to be quiet and patient at the moment, but there was nothing he could do until Tracker repacked his med-kit—and then all he could do was get his people back to Camp Apache. No point in wasting any energy.

"Ready," Tracker said.

"Fast, lead out," Ruizique ordered.

Pennell nodded and led the small column out of Hou Cau. He took a different route from the one they'd used coming in, the riverside trail this time. Neissi followed him, then Ruizique, Tracker, Robertson, and Hunter. Knowles brought up the rear. A short distance northwest of Hou Cau, the river completed its northward hairpin turn that brought it close to Hou Dau hill. Pennell left the riverside trail there and cut through the thick band of trees toward the open areas and scrub. Camp Apache was in sight and Ruizique had just stepped out of the trees when a single shot rang out.

"Down!" Ruizique shouted. "Hold your fire." He wanted to be positive of direction and maybe get an idea of how many were in the ambush they seemed to have walked into. Or maybe it was one sniper, like the one that, as he knew from what he'd heard on the radio, had hit Zeitvogel's patrol. There was no more fire. The radio spoke to him, Lewis's voice. "Wait one," Ruizique said into its mouthpiece. "Count off, Fast first," he shouted. No reply. "Shit. Chief up."

The call for the corpsman to come forward wasn't really needed. Tracker was on his feet, running forward, as soon as Pennell didn't answer. "Chest wound," he said as soon as he reached the pointman. "I want a med-evac right now." He worked frantically to stop the bleeding. The man he worked on was turning waxy; he needed to stop the bleeding in a hurry so he could start on the shock and stop it before it settled in. Maybe he could save Pennell's life. If he was good enough, if a med-evac helicopter got there soon enough.

Ruizique made his report.

CHAPTER FOURTEEN

The Rest of the Day Pheet Was Found and That Night

Randall's fire team carried Storey's body out to where Ruizique and his patrol waited for the med-evac helicopter. Pennell was still alive when the bird arrived, and Tracker thought he had him stabilized enough to make it at least as far as the operating room. The helicopter took them both, the wounded and the dead. The others trudged back to Camp Apache as soon as it took off. There was a tension about them, a tension expressed in stiff jokes.

"Damned if I'm going to give in to the fuckers," Ruizique said as he and Randall neared the south slope of their hill. "Mister Charlie is mine. I will kill him."

"Amen to that, pano," Randall said earnestly, but he looked at the other with concern. Ruizique had started taking the war personally when he'd been wounded. Now maybe he was taking it so seriously he might be inclined to do something stupid. Randall hoped not.

The helicopter that brought in the daily hot meal also carried mail. Slover held mail call while Bell set up the mess line. Tex Randall got a letter. Billy Boy saw him when he glanced at the return address and hustle away to some place where he thought he could read the letter without being interrupted. That told Lewis the letter had to be from Bobbie Harder. I hope he'll be able to eat after this, Lewis thought. He stuck his own mail in his shirt pocket and went through the chow line. The menu was overbaked pork chops, improperly rehydrated mashed potatoes, over-cooked cut green beans, and something that was supposed to be apple pie. Lewis joined Hempen and Robertson at one of the sheet-metal-on-sandbag tables.

"Stilts is taking it pretty hard," Hempen said. Usually he had some smart remark to make before he said anything serious. Not this time. "He's lost men before, but it's bothering the hell out of him he lost a man whose name he hardly knew."

"I never worked with Zeke this close before," Robertson said, concern evident in his eyes. "Man's fucking weird. Seems like all he cares about is wasting Charlie." He shook his head. "You should have seen him this afternoon. Nobody would have guessed he just had a man hit, maybe wasted." He shuddered slightly. "I only hope he isn't so wrapped up in this shit he fucks up and gets some Marines blown away."

"Ain't done that yet," Hempen said. He looked at Lewis. He and Robertson were worried about their fire team leaders. That was the way it worked. The men humping rifles in the boonies knew their lives depended on the men leading them—they wanted to keep those men with their heads screwed on right. And he knew there had to be some reason for Lewis to be concerned about his as well. "Well?" he asked when Lewis didn't say anything.

"Well what?" Lewis said back, his words muffled by a mouthful of chops and potatoes. He would have twisted the ends of his mustache, but his hands were too busy with his food.

Hempen and Robertson exchanged looks. "Well, what about Tex?"

Mazzucco and Neissi sat down with them. Their mess kits were empty—the PFCs got served before the lance corporals did, and they were already through eating.

The lance corporals looked at them. "Dee dee, junior. We're talking," Lewis said.

"That's right," Hempen said, looking as mean as he could.

Robertson was big enough that he didn't have to try to look mean. "That means now," he said.

"What the fuck?" Mazzucco asked, offended.

"You got a hair up your asses or something?" Neissi asked, equally offended. They left, throwing a few jibes back over their shoulders.

Hempen and Robertson looked at Lewis with approval. If he'd been the first to tell the PFCs to leave, that must mean he was ready to get with the program.

"Well?" Robertson echoed Hempen's question. He noticed Lewis looking away and turned his head to look in the same direction. Hempen was already looking there.

"Why the fuck are you eyeballing the shithouse, Billy Boy?" the big redhead asked.

Hempen glanced at him, amused. "If your nose wasn't so far up your ass you'd see what he was looking at, Big Red."

Robertson looked beyond the wall-less four-holer and saw Randall, sitting isolated on the lip of the perimeter trench. "So what's Tex doing this time?"

"Man's worried about his split-tail," Lewis said. "Thinks she's mad at him because Charlie hit us while her and her girlfriends were here. He's reading a letter from her."

Hempen looked at the mess line and saw a couple of men going for seconds. "Dumbass better get in gear, or all the chow's going to be gone." He looked at Lewis. "Then your ass will be grass, pano, because his stomach will be making so much noise tonight every Vee Cee in the district will be able to home in on it."

Randall suddenly leaped into the air and let out a

whoop. He ran in a tight circle a few times, then bounded toward the rifle squad's tent and into it. When he emerged he had his mess kit in his hand, and a silly smile was smeared all over his face.

"Told him so," Lewis said. "Girl's got to think he's some kind of hero because of the way he acted like he took charge." He turned back to his companions. "Now, what's wrong with your honchos? Tell ol' Billy Boy, and maybe we can get them straightened out."

"Remember, people," Bell told his fire team leaders in a hushed voice that clearly showed the strain he felt at losing two men to snipers in the past three days—not to mention two men wounded in that same time, plus two PFs killed, "be cool and go easy out there. Charlie's trying some new things, and we don't know what else he's got up his sleeve." They were in the commanders' quarters in the command hootch. Burrison sat on his cot, leaving the folding chair in front of his field desk for the sergeant to sit on.

"We are the meanest motherfuckers in this valley," Zeit-vogel said, and grinned crookedly. His voice sounded tough, but the sweat beading on his forehead betrayed his nervousness—he silently cursed himself for not remembering Storey's name and calling him by it while the new man was still alive. He sat on the cooler Bell had pulled out from under his cot. Randall and Ruizique sat on Bell's cot.

"Don't worry, Jay Cee," Randall said. "This is our village; we know our way around it. Charlie doesn't. He'll find us when we zap his ass." He wasn't sure he believed that anymore, not after what had been happening. He grinned as crookedly and looked as nervous as Zeitvogel did.

"No shit out there tonight, Tex. I mean it," Bell said. "We don't know what Charlie's up to."

"All Charlie has up his sleeve is his arm," Ruizique said. His new mustache made his grim expression very fierce. He didn't smile and showed no nervousness. It seemed to the others the loss of Pennell was having no effect on him.

"You particularly, Zeke," Bell cautioned, "you be cool out there. I don't want to be shipping your young ass back to the DR in any damn bodybag."

"Honcho, if you have to worry about somebody's safety tonight, worry about Mister Charlie's."

The look Bell gave Ruizique was short of a glare. "You be cool tonight, that's all," he said, then paused for a moment before continuing. "You've worked out your patrol checkpoints with me and how you're going to rotate through them. I don't want you making any changes after you leave this hootch. And I want you calling in each time you change location. Understand?" His words were directed at all three of them, but his eyes stayed on Ruizique.

"We gotcha, honcho," Randall said.

Zeitvogel nodded seriously.

Ruizique looked back without speaking.

"Understand?" Bell asked Ruizique again.

The Dominican dipped his head once, slowly.

"All right. If anything happens out there tonight, I want to know exactly where you are. Go get your people ready. And all of you, remember, when you come back in tonight, report to either Scrappy or me to assign you and your people to positions on the perimeter. Charlie's been hitting us during the day. If he wants to try something at dawn, I want us to have all possible hands in the trenches." Nobody mentioned the casualties Tango Niner had suffered since that day's sun had risen.

Bell watched the corporals file out, then looked at Burrison. They both wore serious expressions that on almost anyone other than a Marine combat leader would be called worry. Neither said anything; neither had to.

Burrison picked up the paperback book he had been reading, *The Two Towers*, the second volume of J.R.R. Tolkien's *Lord of the Rings* trilogy. *The Lord of the Rings* might have been the most popular reading matter for Marines in Vietnam at the time; it was somebody else's war and took place far, far away. Burrison wondered briefly when somebody would get hold of a copy of the third book and who was next in line to read the one he had in his hands. Then he lost himself in Tolkien's world of fantasy. Better to be lost in that fantasy world than to be in this reality, thinking of the men he'd lost since Christmas morning. Bell went into the radio room to relieve Doc Tracker on the radios. He hoped Swarnes would come back from the hospital soon.

Outside, in the space between the tents, Houng finished briefing his men. Tonight, for the first time in the history of Tango Niner, the PFs not on patrol with the Marines would be in fighting positions around the Camp Apache perimeter. They were there because he, Bell, and Burrison had decided to bring the families of the PFs inside the compound during the night for protection until the current threat was over. A few of the PFs talked in hushed voices when they broke and went around the tents to where their families sat or lay on reed mats brought from their homes, but most of them went silently. They were more angry than frightened. They were ready to fight the enemy and knew that every time they did, they won, even though each of them risked death every time he went on patrol. But last night the enemy had killed a woman and a child because their husband and father was in the Popular Forces. With their families safe behind the barbed wire, the PFs didn't need to be frightened; they could go out to hunt down and kill these murderers. The PFs were certain Charlie couldn't use the same tactics at night he'd used during the day to kill Mike and the two Marines and wound Pennell so badly he wouldn't be back—if he survived his wound.

No moss grew on Tango Niner. It might have taken them two whole days and nights to realize how thoroughly the enemy had changed the rules, but once they did, they changed their own rules immediately to meet the threat. The normal routine was for them to put out three patrols a night, eight or ten men in each patrol. One patrol would go

out around sunset and come back in shortly after the sun
rose—that patrol's leaving and returning times were dic-
tated mostly by the sun. A second patrol was out half the
night—it could leave anytime after dark and come back in
approximately four hours later. The third patrol was out for
something on the order of six hours—it could leave or
return either before or after the half-night patrol. The three
patrols covered different areas and, despite formally drawn
patrol routes, went pretty much where the patrol leaders
felt like going. Pretty independent characters, those three
corporals who ran the patrols; they liked to do things their
own way. They knew the land, and they knew how Charlie
liked to sneak through Bun Hou. So they tried to figure out
where he'd be and intercept him there. Until the past three
weeks they'd made contact three or four times most weeks;
some weeks, most nights; and often more than one contact
a night. Of the hundreds of encounters Tango Niner had
had with the enemy before the sniper on Christmas Day
they'd lost only one, and not a single shot had been fired
that time.

On this night, Tango Niner put out three ten-man patrols
as normal. When the setting sun kissed the hills to the
west, the first one left through the main gate of the compound and turned left. That's where the similarity ended.
Half an hour after dark, twenty men filed out the zigzag
back gate and headed briskly toward the trees south of the
Marines' hill. They reached the trees and turned east.
When these twenty men were south of Hou Dau hill, still
short of Hou Cau hamlet, they stopped long enough for
Stilts Zeitvogel to say into his radio, "Gallery, Gallery, this
is Sitting Duck One, Duck One. We are at Sitting Duck
Three's checkpoint alpha, splitting off now. Over." He
waited for Bell's terse "Sitting Duck One, roger. Gallery
out," then pressed the button on the side of his walkie-
talkie–type PRC-6 radio to break squelch, letting Bell
know he'd heard his acknowledgment. Unless something
happened, that was the longest transmission he'd make that
night. He grimaced as he thought about the warped sense

of humor that came up with the night's radio call signs. He wanted to stomp on somebody for it but suspected Burrison had come up with the call signs and didn't think he could get away with beating on an officer—no matter what the provocation. Tonight all three patrols would be out nearly all night. All three would be back inside Camp Apache before dawn.

The tall man moved through the darkness under the trees like a moon-cast reed shadow to Ruizique's side. The two patrol leaders wrapped their hands around each other's wrists and locked thumbs, wishing luck. Then Zeitvogel found his favorite PF, the tiny man the Marines called Pee Wee, and reached for his shoulder. Pee Wee's shoulder wasn't much higher than Zeitvogel's waist. The short Vietnamese looked up to where the tall American's head occluded the treetops and nodded. He shifted his BAR to a more comfortable position and turned half left, leading the patrol northeast, toward the open scrub and sugarcane fields between Hou Dau and Hou Toung.

Ruizique touched Neissi, and he and his nine men continued alone toward the heavy band of trees on the landward side of Hou Cau.

In the meantime, Tex Randall's patrol had followed the main trail west toward Hou Ky. When they reached the point where Zeitvogel and Hempen had found the bodies of Pheet and his family, they stopped for a moment and each of the ten men lost himself for a moment in whatever thoughts he had for the dead and the way they died. Then Lewis led them north to the zigzag treeline that bordered the rice paddies and turned right until they were north of Hou Dau hill. They settled down in the treeline, half watching over the still waters, half facing the black bulk of the hill on which squatted the main hamlet of Bun Hou village.

Randall waited until he heard Zeitvogel's report and Bell's reply, then keyed the button on the side of his own radio. "Gallery, Gallery," he whispered. "This is Sitting Duck Two, Duck Two. We are at checkpoint alpha. Over."

Bell acknowledged and Randall broke squelch. They waited in ambush for another hour before the round of radio reports started again.

"Gallery, Duck One," Zeitvogel said softly. "Leaving checkpoint alpha for checkpoint charlie."

"Gallery, Two," Randall said. "Sitting tight at checkpoint alpha."

"Gallery, Duck Three," Ruizique said. "Standing at checkpoint bravo. Will move to charlie in one zero."

Bell rogered the three sitreps—situation reports—leaned back on the wood folding chair in front of the radios, stretched, and rubbed his eyes. He wondered how Swarnes managed to read his fuckbooks in the dim light of the red night lamp that provided the only lumination in the bunker where the radios were kept at night. He was sharing radio watch with the two lieutenants. The other twenty-two men of Tango Niner were on the perimeter, except for Slover and Athen, who were in the mortar pit. Bell would wake Burrison in another half hour and maintain watch for another half hour while the lieutenant checked the lines. Somehow, with all those men defending it, Camp Apache felt secure, despite Charlie's recent activities. Or maybe because of Charlie's new pattern of activity. Bell idly wondered how the men on patrol were feeling.

Confused was how the men on patrol felt. Randall and Ruizique had been with Tango Niner since September, and each had run a hundred or more night patrols. They knew how the night felt, and they'd both developed that special sixth sense that night fighters must have if they are to survive their dangerous jobs. Zeitvogel was one of the original members of Tango Niner and had led twice as many patrols as either of the others. All three of them felt Charlie out there somewhere, but they didn't know where. And they didn't feel as if they were in any danger themselves. The night felt strange; it confused them.

The three patrols shifted from ambush site to ambush site through the night; Zeitvogel's Sitting Duck One sat in three places between Hou Dau and Hou Toung to protect the west approaches to Hou Toung and the east side of Hou Dau; Randall's Duck Two, the north and west approaches to Hou Dau. Ruizique's Three watched over Hou Cau. Hou Toung had already been terrorized, and so had Hou Ky. They all thought Hou Dau or Hou Cau was next, probably tonight. They were right. On both counts.

A five-man sapper team slipped into the rice paddies nearly a kilometer west of Hou Ky shortly after sunset. They waded, crouched waist low, out into the paddies until they were more than a hundred meters from the treeline that bordered the paddies, then turned east, staying in the water, rolling over the dikes when they went from paddy to paddy. Two or three hundred meters short of Hou Ky, they lowered themselves until only their heads remained above the water. At fifty meters they were almost invisible in the darkness. It was a slow and tedious method of travel, but they were in no hurry—if they needed it, they had more than six hours to reach their destination and still have time to do their work there and make their way back to safety. Each man was armed with a knife and automatic pistol with no extra clips; they didn't intend to fight when they got to where they were going. Each man also carried a tubular pack slung across his chest. A waterproof package inside each pack held a variety of incendiary devices.

A second team of six men waited patiently in a thicket on the south bank of the Song Du Ong.

The Marines and PFs on patrol slowly grew tired and their patience waned, especially those who had been out with Ruizique all night the previous night. In the normal rotation they would have the short patrol tonight. But none of them made any noise; they were all too experienced. Except for Vega, who was new at this, but he was too frightened of night patrols to be willing to make noise. When the patrols moved from one place to another, they flitted through the shadows as shadows themselves, so the only sounds in the night were crickets chirruping, night birds screeching, and the occasional cry of a hunting fuk-yoo lizard. A casual observer watching in the right place at the right time would see a passing shadow and think of high-flying clouds.

This lasted until more than an hour past midnight, by which time many of the men on patrol were thinking of how much more comfortable they would be in the trench around Camp Apache.

As soon as Big Louie Slover had heard PFC Guy Hunter's name was the third in his lineage he shouted out, "Hunter the Turd! Why would anybody go around telling the world he's a turd? Even if he is one, huh?" Hunter grimaced and tried to look invisible when he heard the hated nickname. That's what he'd been called in boot camp, the way the DIs had made him announce himself at morning roll call. At morning roll call in boot camp the drill instructors didn't call out names for men to respond to; each recruit called out his own name in turn—the same order each and every time. The idea was, if someone decided to go over the fence and had a buddy willing to take the chance of covering for him at morning roll, the buddy might be able to call out "Here" on time when the missing man's name was called but would have a harder time shouting out "Sir, Private Hunter the Turd"—or whatever name—"here, sir" right on cue. Hunter'd been able to avoid "the Turd" since reporting to Camp San Onofre for infantry training, partly through the expedient of being big enough to kick the ass of any man who called him that. But he was in a new situation here and wasn't at all feeling sure of himself. And that splib corporal was big enough that Hunter wasn't positive he could take him. Besides, Slover obviously had a lot of big friends, and was his team leader on the mortar, so Hunter didn't immediately challenge him. And immediately thereafter regretted not having done so, because just that fast everybody was suddenly laughing at him and calling him Hunter the Turd. As big and tough as PFC Guy Hunter III was, he knew when he was beaten, and he knew he was beaten now. He was stuck with "Hunter the Turd" for as long as he was with Tango Niner.

Slover had slapped a monstrous hand on Hunter's shoulder and grinned close to his face. "Don't sweat it, my man," Slover assured him. "I give the nicknames around here, and the ones I give stick like stink on shit."

"That's what I'm afraid of," Hunter muttered through clenched teeth, and tried to look mean.

Slover just laughed, and from that moment on, Guy Hunter III was Hunter the Turd.

Hunter the Turd was awake in one of the two manned positions on the steep east side of Camp Apache's hill. He was supposed to be alert, watching, but what he was doing would have been called daydreaming if the sun had been up. But it was night, so what he was doing was simply not paying attention, so he didn't immediately notice the faint orange glow to his northeast, even though that was the direction he was facing. It wasn't until shards of sharp light flickered through the glow that it caught his attention. Then he stared at it for a moment, trying to figure out what it was, then a moment longer, deciding what, if anything, he should do about it. One of the PFs was sleeping on a straw mat alongside the hole they shared. Hunter didn't know the PFs well enough to be ready to trust one very much, even though the others in the platoon seemed to treat them almost like Marines. Instead, he didn't wake his partner to ask him what the fire he was watching meant. He used the ground wire phone to call the main gate and ask one of the machine gunners there what it meant.

Kobos, the gunner, was up. He'd been watching his front and hadn't looked to his right. He found the starlight sparkling off the paddies a few hundred meters distant peaceful, and, oddly enough, it didn't make him sleepy. Instead, it helped him stay awake during his long, two-hour shifts on watch. He hadn't been with Tango Niner a long time, only a month and a half or so, but he knew right away that glow didn't belong. He also knew it was on Hou Dau hamlet's hill. "Oh, shit," he swore, and cranked the handle on his field phone to raise the command hootch. "Hou Dau's on fire," he said when Lieutenant Burrison answered.

CHAPTER FIFTEEN

The Charge of the Fire Brigade, the Wee Hours of December 28, 1966

Zeitvogel's patrol was sitting in the rice paddies, covering the northern and western approaches to Hou Toung, when the call came. Randall had an ambush set on a trail through the thick woods south of Hou Dau hill. Ruizique and his patrol were sweeping like wraiths through Hou Cau.

"Sitting Ducks, all Sitting Ducks, this is Gallery." Burrison's voice almost burst out of the radios. "There's a fire in Hou Dau. All hands, turn to. I want all hands putting that fire out. Acknowledge. Over."

"Roger, Gallery. Duck One on the way. Over."

"Oh, shit." Randall pushed his radio's button a little too soon; he hadn't meant to swear into it. "Sitting Duck Two on the way, Gallery. Over."

"Gallery, Sitting Duck Three is moving. Over."

All three patrols were on their feet, in columns, and walking briskly—walking because it was too dark to run —toward Hou Dau hill by the time Burrison said, "Roger, Sitting Ducks. Gallery out." And all three pointmen were

136

sweating more than the night temperature and the exertion of the fast walk could account for. All thirty men hoped Charlie didn't have anybody between them and the hill; they'd get caught in an ambush if he did.

Burrison immediately roused Bell and Houng. They quickly organized a ten-man force under Corporal Slover to hold down Camp Apache and had the rest of the Marines and PFs headed out the main gate to help with the fire. The PFs' families were ordered to stay behind the wire, including, most particularly including, the ones who lived in Hou Dau.

Charlie didn't have anybody between Hou Dau and the four groups converging on it. By the time Hunter noticed the fire, the five-man team that had set it was crawling north through the paddies. Three quarters of a kilometer into the paddies was a tree line. The five men then climbed into that tree line and walked east until they were parallel to Hou Toung. There they turned south to finish their night's work.

South of the Song Du Ong, a six-man squad carried its boat from the thicket they had hidden in to the water's edge and slid it into the river as soon as they saw the sky glow from the fire. These men wore black uniforms with red bands around their upper left arms. One man held on to a rope tied through a hole in the boat's bow. They squatted on the bank and waited for the fire to grow larger.

In the west, four more men also waited for the fire to get bigger. Then they would enter Hou Ky.

Major Nghu stood on his hillside. A wicked grin cracked its way across his face as he watched the spreading fire. He didn't use his binoculars now; they didn't have night lenses. A commander in the field couldn't have everything; he understood that. At this extreme range at night he knew he wouldn't be able to see any detail anyway. He rubbed a thumb along his hawk-beak nose and chortled. A little longer, that was all. Within hours all of Bun Hou village would be convinced that Tango Niner could do nothing to defend it from him and would turn against them. Then the Marines of Tango Niner would belong to him, and he would kill them. Dead. As dead as their lackey PFs would be.

"What the fuck do you people think this is, a Chinese fire drill?" Bell roared loud enough to be heard clearly over the crackling of the fire and the shouts—shouts of terrified villagers trying to find missing family members, shouts of Americans trying to coordinate what they were doing. "Let's get it organized!"

The three patrols all arrived at Hou Dau before the group from Camp Apache did. The three corporals were running around Hou Dau, trying to get a handle on the extent of the fire, get all the threatened houses evacuated, and get started putting the fire out. The villagers were scattering everywhere, screaming as they ran. Some carried large bundles of household goods; others ran empty-handed. The night was alive with the crackling of the fire. Moisture inside incompletely dried thatch sizzled; air pockets in the thatch popped and cracked. Marines and PFs shouted at one another, coordinating their actions to fight the fire and bring all the people to safety.

"I think we got everybody out of their hootches, Jay Cee," Randall gasped. He'd heard the sergeant's commanding voice and ran to it. In the flickering red light from the fire, Randall looked like a visitor from hell. He had lost his bush hat somewhere along the way; the stubble of hair on his scalp was matted and awry in random places. A smudge of soot ran diagonally across his sweaty face from left forehead, over the bridge of his nose, down his right cheek and jaw. More soot blotted his hands and arms, and there were scorch marks on his uniform. "There was some fire in a few of the brick hootches, but most of them are okay. It's the thatch ones that are burning. Zeke's got his people in a bucket brigade, hauling water from a well and wetting hootches at the edge of the fire to keep it from spreading. My people are getting the villagers together." A grin twisted his mouth. "If this looks like a Chinese fire drill, it's only because we're close to the South China Sea." He grinned wider and added, "You should show up on time next time."

"Good work," Bell grunted, not quite appeased. He looked around, and the chaotic scene suddenly appeared more organized. Villagers were still running, screaming, in all directions, but mostly they were headed toward the south side of the hamlet, an area where most of the house construction was adobe brick and there didn't seem to have been any fire—or at least not much. Marines and PFs ran among the people, heading them toward safety, helping the halt, carrying bundles for those who were trying to carry too much. Most of the fire seemed concentrated in one area where thatch hootches outnumbered the brick ones. A line of men was silhouetted against the flames, frantically passing buckets from hand to hand, tossing water from the buckets to hootches that weren't burning, throwing the empties back toward the well, where they were refilled and passed hand-to-hand back toward the flames.

Bell knew where more wells were, and he split the men who he'd brought from Camp Apache into three groups, one smaller than the other two. The small group, he sent scampering from house to house for buckets or anything else that could be used to carry water. The others, he lined up from two wells to the edge of the fire, far enough away from Ruizique's men to cover the entire south front of the fire and keep it from spreading that way. In minutes full buckets were sloshing from hand to hand to wet down hootches that weren't burning yet, to douse sparks before they turned into flames. Houses that were already burning would have to be sacrificed in order to save the rest of them.

"All the people are together," Randall reported back after checking once more. "The headman says everybody's accounted for, and he can keep them together. Scrappy and Houng are with him. Where do you want us?"

Bell put them on the fire's west side to contain it there. He was ready to concede the north side and let the fire there spread to the end of the hamlet when Burrison and Houng showed up with all the able-bodied men and women from the village. In a few more minutes the fire was completely ringed by bucket brigades and had stopped spreading. In a little while, it was being beaten back toward its core.

South of the Song Du Ong, six men saw the glow in the northern sky was probably as big as it was going to get. They piled into their boat and poled it from the bank. When the water grew deep enough that their twelve-foot poles could no longer find the bottom, they switched to paddles until the water was again shallow enough for the poles. They beached their craft on Hou Cau's wet clay waterfront and padded to a house that had been selected earlier. Once inside the house, they made sure shutters were closed and heavy curtains hung inside the windows and doors. Then their leader struck a match to light a lamp.

The hootch had two rooms. The larger one—which they were in—held a six-by-five-foot wooden platform bed, on which slept an old couple and four young children. Also in the room were a small kitchen-type table with three rickety chairs, a small open hearth with cooking implements neatly stacked next to it, two low chests, three tall wicker baskets, a household shrine, and a few other odds and ends. Conical straw hats hung from the rafters, and a few small straw mats lay on the hard-packed dirt floor. At a signal from the leader, two of the men flitted into the hootch's second, smaller room.

Sounds of a scuffle came from the smaller room, and the old woman on the bed snapped awake. The cry she was about to make drowned in her throat at the sight of the pistol the leader of the invaders held pointed between her eyes. The leader said something in a low voice with the guttural accent of the north, and the old woman reached a trembling hand to shake the old man's shoulder. He opened his eyes but didn't open his mouth; he moved nothing but his eyes.

More noise came from the small room, and two young people, a man barely of military age and a woman, were shoved into the main room by the two men who held their arms tightly from behind. He wore black peasant pants and no shirt; she wore only a light blue tunic unbuttoned half-way from the bottom. One of the red-banded soldiers said something in the same guttural northern accent the leader had spoken with, leered at the young woman, and slapped his hand on her bare crotch. She tried to flinch back, but the man holding her pressed his body against hers, forcing her onto the hand of the other.

The leader snapped something, and the soldier yanked his hand away from the woman; he looked sheepish. The soldier holding her from behind stopped pressing his body against hers.

The children were waking now, rubbing their eyes and complaining in the high voices of youngsters rudely woken from deep sleep. The old woman hushed them without being told to. They quickly picked up on her fear and huddled, shaking, against her and the still-immobile old man.

The leader snapped orders, and four of his men quickly gagged the two ancients, the two young adults, and the four children and tightly bound their hands and feet. Then they roughly seated the adults in a circle back to back on the bed and stuck the children on their laps. More rope was looped around the group, securely binding them together. The leader gave another order, and one of his soldiers knelt to shove a small pack under the bed. The soldier carefully centered the pack and struck a match to the fuse protruding from it.

"Your neighbors will soon understand this happened because your family has a man in the puppet army of Saigon," the leader told the terrified people on the bed. He blew out the lamp and led his men at a trot to the waterfront. They reboarded their boat and were in mid-channel by the time the satchel charge under the bed exploded, killing all eight people.

Northeast of Hou Dau and west of it, small groups of armed men went through Hou Toung and Hou Ky, making noise and waking the villagers. They hustled the people into the hamlet squares and harangued them. "We have proved over the past two nights that the imperialist Marines and their so-called Popular Forces lackeys cannot protect you while you sleep in your beds at night, just as we have shown during the day they cannot protect themselves from us. Right now the people of Hou Dau are learning that same lesson," the armed men shouted, and pointed to the glow on Hou Dau hill. "It is important if you want to live your lives that you stop supporting them. If you have husbands, sons, brothers, in the Popular Forces, you must convince them to lay down their arms and stop resisting the revolution. You must stop helping the American aggressors. Do not even accept medical assistance from them. If they want you to work for them, do not accept the jobs they offer you."

The harangues continued as political harangues do—they seemed endless. In Camp Apache the people dimly heard the voices in Hou Ky; they strained to make out the words. The few Marines in the compound heard the voices and wondered why anybody was awake at this hour and what they were shouting about. They decided the voices were yelling about the fire in Hou Dau and ignored them. Then an explosion from the direction of Hou Cau shook the night, and everybody stiffened.

In Hou Toung and Hou Ky the haranguers stopped haranguing and pointed in the direction of Hou Cau and shrilled at the villagers that the people of the market hamlet had just learned the folly of cooperation with the American devils and their Saigon puppets.

"What the fuck?" asked half of the Marines, who had now almost won the fight against the fire.

"I'm going to check it out, Scrappy," Bell said when he found the lieutenant. "You stay here with this situation." Then he remembered that Burrison, as an officer, was officially in charge and added, "That okay with you?"

Burrison gritted his teeth and nodded. He didn't want to stay; he'd rather go to where the new action was. But most of Tango Niner was staying in Hou Dau, and that was where he should remain, as the man in charge. Then if Bell needed him at Hou Cau, he could lead the cavalry to the rescue.

"Stilts, Tex," Bell shouted, spinning away from him, "bring your people and come with me." He didn't wait for the two fire teams, and however many PFs would join them, to form up before heading rapidly southward. He heard Zeitvogel and Randall shouting at their men and knew they were close behind. "Somebody, check that out," he yelled as he ran past a sign erected in the hamlet square, a sign he hadn't seen the last time he was in Hou Dau, one that nobody'd had the time to look at since they'd arrived to put out the fire before it could completely destroy the village's chief hamlet.

Burrison heard Bell's last shout and, curious, went to see what it was. The sign was hand-painted in black on a large sheet of rough paper attached to the front of one of the adobe brick hootches that fronted on the square. The American lieutenant could only read a few of the words, just enough to think he wasn't going to like it when he got the entire translation. He went to find Houng to confirm what he thought it was about. When he returned with the PF lieutenant, a small crowd was gathering around the sign, people whose homes hadn't been involved in the conflagration. Those whose homes had been burned were sifting through the rubble, looking for anything that could be salvaged.

Houng glanced at the sign, swore, and shoved his way through the people clustered in front of it. He screamed something in Vietnamese and tore the sign down. He rolled it into a tube as he elbowed his way back out of the crowd.

"What's it say?" Burrison asked.

"This numba ten thou," Houng said, shaking the tube furiously. "Numba ten thou." If number ten was bad, number ten thousand was a thousand times worse.

Bell nearly threw away all caution in his haste to reach Hou Cau. Whoever this new enemy was, he didn't seem to be putting out any ambushes, though this was an ideal time to lay one between the two attacked hamlets. Charlie had to know the Marines would send a team from the fire to the explosion. Maybe he didn't have enough people to make an ambush really work. But still, Bell retained some night fighter caution. He led the Marines and PFs that came with him on a circular route that had them enter the hamlet from the east, rather than going in a straight line. If Charlie had set an ambush, it was probably near the main trail leading between the two hamlets, and the circle would avoid it.

The nighttime blackout was forgotten in Hou Cau. The explosion had awakened all the villagers, and they were all out of their homes. At least one member of each household carried a lit lamp. Most of them were gathered in the hamlet square, in such tight little bunches the large square looked almost empty, despite the fact it now held more people than it did anytime except for a major market day. A quarter of the people milled around the home that had been demolished by the satchel charge.

"Fuck," Bell swore when he saw the destruction. A small fire had been started by the explosion but had been contained before it spread to any other hootches. For the first time, he looked to see which PFs had come with him. It was Willy and his squad. Might have known, the sergeant thought. Willy wants the people who did Pheet and his family. "Willy, get the chief," he ordered. Then he organized his Marines and PFs to provide security for the people around the wreckage. He noticed, but didn't respond to, the fact that the people were avoiding looking at the Marines and PFs and none of them wanted to talk to them.

Willy was back in less than two minutes. "Chief, him no come," he said. "Him say him take care of people, Ma-deen, fay epp, dee dee."

"What? Let's go see him."

"No, no see chief. You, me, all." He pointed at Bell and himself, then swept his arm around to indicate the other members of Tango Niner who were there. "We dee dee now." He pulled on Bell's arm to lead him out of the hamlet.

"No, we've got to help these people." Bell jerked his arm away and headed toward the square. People were talking when he entered the square. When they saw him, they stopped. Some stared expressionlessly at the American; most turned their backs to him. He found the hamlet chief, a middle-aged man with a wispy beard whom he knew to exchange pleasantries with.

"You, dee dee," the chief said. "Hou Cau no want you. Ma-deen, fay epp not here. This not happen. You, dee dee." He stalked off.

Bewildered, Bell returned to his men. "He seems to think this is our fault," he said. "I'll get Houng and Thien to straighten it out. Let's go back."

CHAPTER SIXTEEN

The Next Few Days

Burrison wished Captain Hasford could come out to help them figure out what was happening—or at least act as a sounding board for whatever ideas they could come up with on their own. But the captain was someplace else, and Lewis didn't know his way around the radio networks well enough to be able to contact the lieutenant colonel. They were on their own. And their own was bad.

"You, the people of Bun Hou, have been assisting the imperialist conquering foreign devil American Marines," read the sign that had been left in Hou Dau, which now leaned against the side of the command tent. "You, the people of Bun Hou, are helping the evil, despotic government in Saigon. You, the people of Bun Hou, are working in opposition to the righteous revolution of the people. The true Vietnamese, the patriots, are fighting all over the country to overthrow the oppressors of the people and to bring about the reunification of Vietnam. You have declared yourselves to be the enemy of the people. For this you must be punished, and the punishment will be severe.

"However, the revolution of the people is just and fair.

If you see the error of your ways and wish to end your punishment, you will immediately cease assisting the Running Dog American imperial Marines and their so-called Popular Forces lackeys. You will give them no aid, no information. You will not sell them goods or give them any gifts. You will not accept help from them in the rice paddies or in the cane fields or fishing on the river. You will not accept their medical attention. You will not accept from them any food or clothing. You will not accept from them any equipment for farming or fishing.

"If you show, by doing what this poster says, that you have seen the error of your ways and that you are ready to be patriots and help in the just cause of throwing out the imperialists and their Saigon puppets, the revolution will be merciful."

That's what the sign said. And it didn't escape anyone's attention that its very existence in the Hou Dau hamlet square was a clear demonstration to the people that the enemy was able to move around Bun Hou at night and do whatever he wanted. The same message had been delivered verbally by armed men in Hou Ky and Hou Toung. The people in Hou Cau had gotten the message in blood. The people were afraid. And there was something else about the sign that the Marines and PFs knew would add to the people's fear, the signature. Major Nghu had signed it in the open: "For the People's Revolutionary Government/ Thieu Ta Nghu/People's Army of Vietnam." PAVN, the dreaded Hanoi VC.

Hell, that signature scared the fighting men of Tango Niner.

Bell pondered the signature for a long time before saying, "Now we know."

"What do we know, Jay Cee?" Burrison asked.

"It's him again." He looked the lieutenant in the eye. "Before you came, a sapper platoon holed up in a bunker complex south of the Song tried to blow us away. They were good. They killed some Marines and some fay epps and scared off most of the rest of the little people. Then we found them after a whole grunt battalion looked and couldn't. The man in charge got away. It was Major Nghu."

The determined expression on Bell's face told the young lieutenant how dangerous this Major Nghu was, how bad the fighting had been before. And the sergeant's expression told something more. He looked at Houng and the corporals, and they all had the same expression. They all wanted to kill Nghu.

Thien arrived. He studied the sign, a worried expression on his face. He had good reason to be worried when he read it. He had spent the entire morning and early afternoon talking to the hamlet chiefs of Hou Dau and Hou Cau. "Them say last night happen because Tango Niner be here," he said. "Them say last night prove America Ma-deen not able to protect Bun Hou. Them want America Ma-deen to leave."

"No way, Jose," Zeitvogel snorted.

"We got us a score to settle with this dude," Slover said, nodding at the sign.

"Fucker wasted Lanani," Randall growled. "His ass is ours."

"His ass is grass," Ruizique said. He hadn't known the Hawaiian corporal; he and three other men had replaced Lanani and his men after their ambush patrol had been wiped out in the only fight Tango Niner had ever lost. Ruizique was the only one of those replacements still alive and with Tango Niner. He had no beef with Major Nghu personally; he just wanted to kill the enemy.

They were interrupted by a shout of "Company's coming" from the main gate. They turned.

Slover searched the eastern sky for a helicopter. He didn't see one and decided against going after his orange Ping-Pong paddles.

"Let's see who it is," Burrison said, and led the small group toward the gate.

A small delegation, a dozen or so people, was walking along the bulldozed road from Hou Dau. They were all dressed in white. In the other direction, a lone man walked from Hou Ky. Thien looked miserable when he saw the man from his own home hamlet.

The group on the road was closer than the lone man on the trail. When they reached the sharp turn in the road where it climbed the hill, they stopped to wait for him. Together, the baker's dozen of white-clad elders climbed the hill.

One of the old men spoke to Thien. A glimmer of hope was in his eyes, but it dimmed when Thien answered him, rapidly, forcefully. The old men shuffled themselves into two ranks, and one stepped forward of the others. He bowed to Burrison and Bell; they politely bowed back. Then he started talking. Houng translated for the Americans; Bell didn't need the translation.

"Vietcong Hanoi," the old man who was the delegation's speaker said, "they come here because America Ma-deen here. They kill hamlet chief, Hou Toung, because he talk to America Ma-deen. They kill woman, child, because husband fay epp. They burn down houses, Hou Dau, because Bun Hou help America Ma-deen. They kill family in Hou Cau because man from family in army of Saigon." He paused to breathe deeply a few times; the litany of injuries pained him. "Vee Cee Hanoi say America Ma-deen leave Bun Hou, they no longer kill people, stop burning down houses."

"That's bullshit, and they know it," Bell said. "We leave and Charlie will come back in and own them just like he did before." Then he told the elders approximately the same thing in Vietnamese.

The spokesman shook his head vehemently. "A month ago," he reminded the American sergeant, "Vee Cee come here, mortar Hou Cau. They tried to burn the hamlet down. They came because you were here."

Bell shook his head at that, more vehemently than the elder had. "They came here then because the Revolutionary Development Team was visiting. That was the first time they bothered the people in the entire time Tango Niner has been here."

The spokesman nodded his understanding of this truth. "That proves what I am saying," he explained patiently. "The Vee Cee have fought with you and found that they cannot best you in battle. So what they do now is they do not fight you directly where you can win. Now what they do is snipe at you during the day and kill you one at a time. And they come to us and destroy our homes and kill us. You must leave Bun Hou so they will leave us alone."

"But they won't leave you alone," Bell insisted, "no more than they left you alone before we came."

"Before you came they stole from us. After you go they will steal from us again. It is good that no one has stolen from us during the time you have been in Bun Hou; it has helped us a great deal. But now they destroy our homes, and they kill us. We can live with them stealing from us. We cannot live with them destroying our homes and killing us. They have proven you cannot protect us from them. You must leave." He did not bow when he stopped talking, simply turned and walked away. The two ranks behind him divided for him to pass through, then followed. The lone man from Hou Ky hesitated at the foot of the hill and looked mournfully up at Thien, then turned left and went home alone. A few people were visible waiting for him where the trail entered the trees.

On his hillside, Major Nghu watched the meeting of the village elders and the Marines. He didn't wish he could hear what they were saying; he knew what they had to be saying. There was no other reason for them to visit the way they did. He chortled softly. The foreign invaders had now lost the support of the people. His next step was to drive the Popular Forces away. It would be easy now. They had deserted the Marines when he had been here before, most of them. This time all of them would desert. Then he would kill all of the Marines at once. Vengeance is happiness, he thought. Or an idea to that effect.

Tension mounted in Tango Niner. But that's all that happened for the next twenty-four hours. After talking it over among themselves late the next morning, the CAP leaders decided to break their platoon into small groups and send all but a small defense force out into the forest and scrub woods west of Camp Apache to find some sign of the NVA hiding place. They had to be out there somewhere; it was simply inconceivable for Major Nghu to be using the same hiding place he had used before—besides, it had been destroyed by Marine engineers. Burrison, Bell, the three men of the machine gun team, Doc Tracker, Houng, and four of his PFs stayed at Camp Apache for security; the other forty-four split into four-man teams and went west. Five of the teams had two Marines in them; the other six, one each. Their paths were due west, and each had a front of close to three hundred meters to cover. If they didn't find anything today, they would look somewhere else tomorrow. Only four of the teams carried radios.

Lance Corporal Short Round Hempen took out Pee Wee, Lap, and Bay. Stilts Zeitvogel grumbled a bit; he wanted Pee Wee to go with him. It was a quiet, still day under the trees. The kind of quiet that makes the background buzzing of insects sound like Manhattan rush hour and the occasional fuk-yoo lizard sound as loud as the horn of a sixteen wheeler about to climb up your tailpipe; the kind of stillness that fills the air with dust when nothing has come by to raise the dust. It was the kind of day that is the last day for many men. Men who get overcome by it and lose their sharpness. But there was no way the Marines of Tango Niner were going to lose their sharpness.

Sweat oozed out of the men's pores and just sat there. Their noses and throats clogged and filled with dust; their skin itched from the salt of their unevaporated sweat.

Every fuk-yoo and bird cry caused their already taut, stretched nerves to thrum.

Pee Wee wanted the point; Hempen let him have it and went second. The shortest PF and the shortest Marine, who was a half a foot taller, joked about it. Anybody opening fire on the point would probably miss the small target Pee Wee presented. If he thought he was firing at a standard-sized American, he'd probably overcompensate for the range and miss Short Round, too. They told Lap and Bay to keep their heads down in case of fire from the front, fire that would miss Short Round and Pee Wee and probably hit one or the other of them. It was a fine joke that neither of the other men laughed at. This whole business was no laughing matter to Lap and Bay. They didn't understand that Hempen's and Pee Wee's joking and laughter were hiding their fear.

So they went through the quiet, still afternoon. They weren't in a hurry, and they zigged and zagged to cover half of their front. They'd cover the other half on the way back—or as much of it as they had time for. They were definitely going to be back in Camp Apache before nightfall; no fools they.

When Major Nghu saw through his binoculars what Tango Niner was doing, he thought it over for little more than a minute before convincing himself these were recon teams searching for his hiding place. He looked at his watch and smiled to himself. Unless they were coming directly to the ridge he sat on, it was impossible for them to do any searching on it today; they didn't have enough time to make a thorough search of the land between the hill and the ridge. What he needed to do was something to delay their search of the wooded land—and something to further deteriorate the morale of the PFs. He snapped an order, and his senior sergeant jumped to obey.

Hempen's team was about halfway to the western ridge when automatic gunfire erupted close to their front.

"Down!" screamed the Marine. "Spread out!" Pee Wee was eight meters ahead of him and a couple to his right. Hempen rolled twice left and let off a burst of 7.62mm ammunition to his front, then sprint-crawled forward half the distance to Pee Wee. The small PF's BAR made a terrific racket, and some small part of Hempen's mind wondered how the tiny man could possibly control the big automatic rifle—he had enough trouble with the automatic M-14, which was a much smaller weapon. The light cracking of an M-1 carbine to his left rear told him one of the others had also dropped and rolled before opening up.

The continuing clatter of AK-47s told the Marine this wasn't just a sniper shot like the one that had wasted the newby, Storey, or had taken out Pennell. He was in a fire fight for real. His mouth dried instantly at the knowledge he didn't know how many he was up against. There was a low cry of shock and pain to his left rear, and the carbine stopped firing. Then all he heard was Pee Wee's BAR and his own automatic M-14.

"Cease fire," he shouted. He shifted to see who was on his left. A stunned face that looked like Lap's stared out through the gray brain mass that drooled from his split skull. "Bay," he called, "answer up." He didn't get an answer.

"Back there," Pee Wee said in a weak voice.

Hempen and Pee Wee wanted to huddle together. Instead, the Marine got them behind cover, far enough apart that one grenade probably couldn't kill both of them. They waited. No more fire came at them, but they both knew the enemy who had ambushed them might well be circling around to hit from a spot where they were exposed. They tried not to be exposed.

A circling enemy didn't come on them. Zeitvogel arrived with Vien, George, and Traun from one direction. Mazzucco and Willard converged from the other side with Collard Green and Van. Zeitvogel got on his radio and reported the ambush and the two fatalities. Burrison answered back that everyone was to return to Camp Apache.

Collard Green and Pee Wee and the other four PFs gathered the corpses of Lap and Bay to carry back. Zeitvogel wouldn't let Hempen rest; he didn't want to give the Marine time to think about what happened. He took his fire team and Willard and went looking for adjacent teams that didn't have radios to send them back to Camp Apache.

Most of the PFs didn't want to go out on patrol that night, but they did anyway. It didn't matter; they were safe at night. Major Nghu had conceded the night to the Americans and their lackeys.

CHAPTER SEVENTEEN

December 30 and New Year's Eve, 1966

All good terrorists know what makes terrorism work, and people who fight terrorists are afraid they'll find themselves up against good terrorists. What makes terrorism work isn't continual destruction, mayhem, and slaughter. If people are subjected to enough damage, they will band together and hunt down and kill the terrorists—it's that simple. The threat is what makes terrorism work. Kill a few carefully selected people, burn down some houses, do some damage, and everybody gets scared. Better yet, do these things in such a way that they look as if they were done right under the noses of the authorities, the protectors of honest citizens—even if those protectors were someplace else at the time. Once it's proven that the terrorist can do whatever he wants, whenever he wants, wherever he wants, and to whomever he wants, people lose faith in the ability of their protectors to protect them. Frightened people start doing what the terrorist wants them to do—or stop doing what he doesn't want them to do and hope that he gets whatever it is he wants and leaves them alone.

Almost everywhere in the country, the Americans and

South Vietnamese owned the days and Charlie owned the nights. Tango Niner owned the night in Bun Hou; everybody knew that. Sure, Charlie would try to sneak supplies or reinforcements through the village, but it was awfully dangerous for Charlie to do that; Tango Niner owned the night and put a hurting on the bad guy when he tried. Whenever Tango Niner hurt Charlie too badly, Charlie would attack and try to wipe out the CAP. Charlie had tried several times, but so far it hadn't worked. Charlie fought against Tango Niner and basically left the people alone.

But now, on three successive nights, Charlie had come in and killed the Hou Toung headman, killed a PF and his family in Hou Ky, burned down a substantial part of Hou Dau, and brutally killed a family in Hou Cau. During the day, Charlie had also killed two Marines and four PFs.

The people were scared. Charlie had come into Hou Toung and Hou Ky and harangued the people, told them why these things were happening and that they'd keep happening if the people didn't stop cooperating with the Americans. A stranger came into Hou Cau, wandered around aimlessly, and talked to a few people. But the people he talked to weren't randomly selected; he explained to them in graphic detail how the family killed in Hou Cau had been selected. The people he talked to could have been selected just as easily; the stranger made sure they understood that. And there was the sign left behind in Hou Dau.

The sign told the people that what was happening to them was the direct result of their cooperation with the Americans. The very existence of the sign was a clear demonstration of the ability of Charlie to move around Bun Hou at night. And there was the terrifying signature on that sign: Thieu Ta Nghu of the dreaded VC Hanoi. Not Charlie, but Mister Charles. The North Vietnamese Army. That really scared the people.

Major Nghu knew the people were frightened, and he wanted to keep them that way without causing them to rise against him. So on the nights of the twenty-ninth and thirtieth of December all he had his men do was kill a few dogs—and put the gutted carcasses in bed with their owners. In Hou Ky they wounded a pig and dropped it down a well to drown it and contaminate the water.

Major Nghu sat on his hillside during the day and watched through his 10x50 binoculars. His lips twisted into an almost reasonable facsimile of a smile, and he cackled softly to himself as he watched the stream of villagers going to and from Camp Apache during the day damp down to a trickle and totally stop after the visit of the village elders. His shoulders shook with silent laughter when he saw Marines and PFs from the compound go into Hou Ky and be ignored by the villagers. He blessed the West Germans for their high abilities with optics; seeing the people stop visiting Camp Apache and snub the Marines for himself was so much more meaningful than receiving cold, impersonal reports from his men who went into the hamlets or watched the Marines' hill from hidden places.

Oh, yes, Major Nghu also instructed his men to avoid the Marines and PFs of Tango Niner: don't do anything to them. The people saw the Marines and PFs being left alone by the bad guys who were bothering them, and some of them got angry at Tango Niner, because the NVA were messing with the people instead. All of them got more scared.

Instead of eleven men, only nine stayed to guard Camp Apache on the thirtieth. The others, again in eleven four-man teams, headed west in late morning. They were more alert, if that's possible, on this second day than on the first. Their alertness didn't matter; they made it all the way to the ridge that was the first of a series of rising hills that led to the mountains of Laos without encountering any enemy or sign of enemy. They turned back and reached Camp Apache without incident in time for the evening hot meal. They were all hot, tired, and frustrated.

Big Louie Slover stood in his accustomed place at the white helipad circle, shirtless, back to the wind, orange paddles out to his sides to show the pilot he was level with the ground. The men of his mortar team knelt a little way outside the circle a quarter of the way around it to his left; they had their hands on the empty insulated five-gallon containers in which the previous day's hot meal had been delivered. The bird came in fast, its rotor wash kicking up white-painted dust from the circle. Slover's glossy black skin turned gray from it. The instant the UH-34 touched down on its wheels, the mortar men were on their feet, running beneath the whirling rotors to exchange the empty food containers for the full ones the helicopter's crew chief had lined up in the doorway. Halfway to the bird, they abruptly stopped, colliding with each other, to avoid running into a gangly figure who sprang out of it and tore toward them. The new arrival scrambled around them and didn't stop until he was well clear of the helipad. It took the mortar men half a second to compose themselves and go the rest of the way to the squatting, grasshopper-shaped helicopter. They threw the empties through the open door and hauled the full containers off. The bird lifted before they were clear of the pad and twisted back toward the east.

"You dumbshit, Swarnes," Athen shouted. He put down the container he was carrying and pounded the radioman on the back in welcome. The hot chow was forgotten momentarily while the others crowded around, slapping Swarnes' back and pumping his hand. They avoided his left arm; though it wasn't in a sling anymore, it was still wrapped in a bandage that showed clearly under his shirt's short sleeve. As soon as he could, he doffed his bush hat to display a two-by-two—inch bandage pasted to his shaved scalp.

Swarnes preened and puffed while the chow containers were being set up and everybody else started loading their mess kits with the hot food. He wasn't hungry just yet; he'd found a geedunk not far from the Marble Mountain helicopter facility at Da Nang while he waited for the bird that flew him to the battalion headquarters, where he trans-

ferred to the chow bird. "I ain't no fucking dummy," he
said. "I got a take-out and chowed down on the way out
here, good civilian-type hamburgers made by cunt-cleaning
fingers, french fries made by squat-pissers, and Pepsi." He
smacked his lips, partly in memory of the food, partly
thinking about the women he'd seen preparing the food in
that geedunk.

"When I was in that hospital," he told anybody he could
interrupt from their meals, "this goddamn full-fucking-bird
colonel came around the ward I was in. He stopped at
every fucking rack. We didn't even have to stand at attention. They musta been afraid we'd all shit on the deck and
refuse to clean it the fuck up, just lay there in our racks at
attention where if we shat they could just throw the sheets
in the fucking washing machine. Anyways, this full-fucking-bird colonel came to every man and asked his fucking
name. He had a goddamn sergeant major with him."
Swarnes's eyes glowed when he thought about the sergeant
major, a man who sat at the right hand of God, being there.
"That sergeant major had a clipboard and wrote down
every goddamn name and unit. This full-fucking-bird colonel said he'd heard of Tango Niner and said we was sure as
shit doing the most fan-fucking-tastic job of anybody he
knowed about. He gave us our Purple Hearts." Swarnes
pulled a small box out of his shirt pocket and reverently
opened it to display the medal it held. He was obviously
awed by having been given his medal by a full colonel—
he had thought full colonels never even looked at any enlisted Marine below the rank of gunnery sergeant, much
less spoke to them, unless it was at a court-martial. At first
everybody he showed his medal to made polite congratula-
tory noises or equally polite noncommittal grunts. Hell,
none of them thought a Purple Heart was that big a deal,
not like a Silver Star or something like that, something that
none of them had.

Then Swarnes made his first tactical error. He showed
his Purple Heart to Randall.

"Yeh," Randall said, "looks just like my Dumb Medal."

"Say what?" Swarnes exclaimed, an agonized expression twisting his face.

"Dumb Medal," Randall repeated. "I fucked up and got one, too."

Swarnes snapped the small box closed and stalked away. Zeke—Zeke's a fucking bad-ass, Swarnes told himself. He'll appreciate it. That was his second tactical error.

"The only thing to do when you get a Dumb Medal is come back and prove it was an accident," Ruizique said when Swarnes showed the medal to him. "Otherwise you wind up getting a second one and go home in a body bag."

"Bullshit," Doc Tracker interjected. "I got a second one, and I didn't go back to The World in a body bag."

Zeitvogel joined them and looked over Swarnes's shoulder. "Damn," he said softly, "they're giving those things out to just about anybody these days, aren't they." He shook his head. "Used to be a Dumb Medal meant something more than just you did something stupid."

Swarnes never had a chance to make a third tactical error, because then they were joined by Bell and Flood.

"Wow," Flood exclaimed. "I got mine when some Vee Cee threw a grenade into the mortar pit and I forgot to bail out." He nodded. "Boy, was I dumb that time."

Bell said sagely, "I got mine because I was too dumb to understand Chief when he yelled 'fire in the hole.' I stayed in the trench with that Vee Cee satchel charge and got my bell rung." He looked at Swarnes mock seriously and said, "That is how you get one most of the time, you know. You do something dumb and get zinged because of it."

Swarnes glared at them. "Fuck you," he finally said, stumped for better words, and stomped off to his radio room. He was at home here and talked to his radios, told them how everybody was ganging up on him unfairly. Hell, those others were all goddamn ground-fucking-pounding grunts; *they* were supposed to get goddamn Purple Hearts. He was a radioman; he was supposed to get shit at and missed, not get shot at and hit. It wasn't any fucking fair, he confided to his radios. The radios buzzed reassuring static back at him.

Nothing happened to any of the patrols that night, but then nothing had been happening to the patrols at night. And nothing happened in any of the hamlets, either. It was driving them mad.

There was massive frustration on Camp Apache's hill. The Marines and PFs were frustrated because they knew Charlie was out there someplace and they couldn't find him. There was also growing fear. Mister Charles, as they were coming more to call him, was clearly demonstrating that he could do whatever he wanted, when, where, and to whomever he wanted—they knew he could almost as easily be trying to do it to them. And there was anger. Most of the anger came as result of one of the two unusual radio calls Swearin' Swarnes took on the afternoon of December 31.

The first call Swarnes took didn't cause the anger.

Swearin' Swarnes hung his headset back on the nail above his head, looked at the coded message he'd just copied down, and chewed on the end of his pencil for a moment, puzzling over the code. It wasn't all that often he got coded messages. In fact, this was only the second one he could remember having received in the two-and-a-half months he'd been Tango Niner's radioman. The code was classified secret, not top secret, and Swarnes had both a secret clearance and the codebook to decode the message. He flattened the codebook next to the sheet of paper on which he had written the message, moistened the point of his pencil with the tip of his tongue, hunkered over the paper, and started decoding, frequently flipping the pages of the codebook.

When he finished he sat back in his chair, held the sheet of paper out at arm's length, and read the message. His brow wrinkled, and he read the message a second time. Then he went looking for Lieutenant Burrison. He didn't have to look far. Burrison was in the southeast corner of the compound, sitting in one of the wood-and-canvas beach chairs Hempen had brought back from his R&R in Hong Kong, looking out over the scrub toward the river. Bell sat in a chair next to him. They were puzzling over the enemy's activities, trying to figure out where this elusive foe could be hiding.

"Charlie's not between us and the hills." Bell said the obvious.

"And it's pretty damn unlikely he's coming in over the paddies," Burrison said. The paddy land north of the village was too wide and too open. Some of the NVA activity had taken place at dawn; the NVA snipers wouldn't have been able to escape across the paddies without somebody seeing them. He was glad Bell was talking to him; the sergeant had become withdrawn over the past few days.

"That leaves south of the river. . . ."

"Where Tango Niner already hit them hard."

"In the hills over there," Bell tipped his head to the west.

"We already blew the shit out of them there."

"And the east. Think they might be holed up in Bun Anh?" Bun Anh was a village a few miles east of Bun Hou where they knew there had been a Vietcong company; that company might still be there and be hosting the NVA.

"It's worth checking out. I'll see if Captain Hasford can put someone on it."

"Scrappy, Jay Cee," Swarnes said when he reached them, and flopped down in another one of the chairs, "the name Major Hoang Thanh Chuyen mean any-damn-thing to you?"

Burrison slowly turned to look at him. "Should it?"

"Got a fucking coded message from Box Top." Swarnes again held the sheet of paper out at arm's length—away from Burrison and Bell—and his brow furrowed over it again. "Says this dipshit's the new district chief cock-sucker." His face looked serious. "What happened to that guy Y? What do you think this one's like? Think he's any better?"

"Let me see that," Burrison snapped, and lunged toward the sheet of paper that Swarnes shoved in his direction.

While Burrison scanned the message, Bell asked, "Who's watching the radios?"

Swarnes shrugged. "If it's important they'll call back." But he got up and returned to his radio room anyway.

Burrison read the message more slowly the second time through, and the corners of his mouth twitched. He wanted to be straight-faced in front of his sergeant, but it wasn't easy. Yes, now he remembered who Major Chuyen was. Major Chuyen was a Vietnamese Marine attached to the intelligence section of the First Marine Division staff. They'd never met, and the young American had hoped someday they would. This Vietnamese Marine had helped get him and his NCOs off the hook when they had been charged with drug smuggling. He was hopeful this meant an end to official corruption in the district. "Jay Cee, take a look at this," he said.

Swarnes sat down at his radios and asked them if there'd fucking been any goddamn calls while he'd been away. They buzzed soft static at him. "That's what I thought," he said, and rooted through a drawer for a fuckbook. He didn't move his lips when he read the pictures, but he did lick them frequently. He was reading a particularly juicy picture and wondering if the woman in it was a real redhead when the headset hanging near his right ear crackled at him. Without looking away from the picture, he held the headset to his head and answered. A few seconds later he swore and closed the fuckbook to find another sheet of paper. What the hell's going on? he wondered. Two-and-a-fucking-half goddamn months with only one coded fucking message, then two of the bitches in one motherfucking day? He laboriously copied down the codes. After signing off, he decoded the message. He stared at this one a lot longer than he had the first one before rising from his chair to do something about it.

He didn't know it yet, but this call was going to cause anger. It would also make a very good Marine do something that, technically, was going AWOL.

CHAPTER EIGHTEEN

Then and Later That Night

"You sure you didn't screw up decoding this?" Burrison asked after reading the message. He was still sitting in the same beach chair.

"More to the point," Bell asked, "did you copy the code groups right in the first place?"

Swarnes looked pained at the suggestion that he might have made a mistake. So fucking what if he didn't get many coded messages; he knew how to copy straight, and he sure as shit knew how to translate from a goddamn codebook.

Burrison and Bell looked at each other. "You ever do this before, Jay Cee?" the lieutenant asked.

Bell shook his head.

"Well, how do you think we should do it?"

The sergeant shrugged, but he was a Marine sergeant and always supposed to know how to do things. "Zeke up," he shouted.

"Who's watching the radios?" Burrison asked.

Swarnes opened his mouth to say, "If it's important they'll call back," thought better about it, and grunted instead. He turned and wandered toward the command hootch, muttering to himself about how no-fucking-body appreciated him and if they'd have asked him he would have told them how to fucking do it and he was getting fucking tired of this chickenshit outfit and if they goddamn didn't start treating him with some fucking respect . . . Then he was too far from Bell and Burrison for them to make out what he was muttering, even if they had bothered to listen.

Ruizique appeared abruptly in front of them, almost as though he'd materialized out of the air. He squatted and planted the butt of his rifle between his feet and a few inches in front of them; both hands firmly gripped the rifle's stock: a solid three-point stance from which he could move like lightning in any direction. His stern expression, combined with his mustache and crossed bandoliers, made him look almost like a bandit chief prepared to lead his men against the enemy army. "What's up, honchos?" he asked.

"Saddle up," Bell said. "You're moving out."

"My people will be ready inside zero two. Where are we going, and how many fay epps do I take?" He stood gazing around the compound, expertly picking out his men so he could assemble them as soon as he had enough information.

Bell shook his head. "Only you, Zeke."

The Dominican looked at him curiously. "Alone?"

Bell nodded. "Pack everything you want to take with you. You're going back to The World; your tour is up."

"The hell you say."

"You're going home, Zeke," Burrison said. "Back to the land of the big PX."

Ruizique's face contorted as many emotions flurried across it. Home, The World, back to the Dominican Republic and his captain's commission. He shook his head like a dog shedding water. "Khong the duc, no can do. Charlie's fucking with the people. I can't leave until we make Charlie leave them alone."

"Sorry, Zeke. Nobody asked what you want. I've got the orders here." Burrison held out the message Swarnes had given him. "A bird's picking you up in the morning. Your tour's up."

"I haven't been here for thirteen months yet."

"When's your EAS?" Bell asked.

Ruizique paused for a moment. He hadn't thought of his EAS, end-of-active-service date, the end of his enlistment, in a while. "Twenty January," he finally said. "That's three weeks away. Enough time to get Charlie off the people's back."

Burrison shook his head. "Just enough time to process you out of country, get you across the Big Pond, and process you out of the Corps," he said. During most of the twentieth century, most Marine Corps activities had been in or near the Pacific Ocean: Nicaragua, China, the Pacific island campaigns of World War II, Korea. Two of the Marine Corps's three divisions and two of its three air wings had been stationed in or near the Pacific after the Korean War. Now Vietnam. Marines looked on the Pacific Ocean as their private waterway and called it the "Big Pond."

"I can't go. My job here isn't done yet."

"The Marine Corps says your job here is done. You leave in the morning," Burrison said. "There's a policy of taking men out of the field for their last two weeks in-country. This is your last two weeks."

"I can't go yet," Ruizique repeated.

"Corporal, I want you off my hill when that helicopter leaves tomorrow morning," Bell said. His face was stern, but his words were soft.

Ruizique glared at them, then his face turned cold and unreadable. "Aye-aye, Sergeant," he finally snarled at Bell. He started to stride away.

"One more thing, Zeke," Burrison said to the corporal's back. The Dominican stopped but didn't turn to face the officer. "You don't take your patrol out tonight. I don't want to risk you going out and getting wasted on your last night with Tango Niner."

Ruizique's back went rigid. "Aye-aye, sir," he said through clenched teeth. "I will give command of the patrol to Big Red."

"Go pack," Bell snapped. "And don't give the patrol to Big Red. You didn't make those assignments while you were a member of this platoon, and I'll be damned if you're going to start doing it now." He and Burrison watched the proud man march rigidly to the squad tent to prepare himself to leave.

"Thanks for nixing Big Red," Burrison said, looking at the sergeant. "I would have if you didn't. We have a couple of lance corporals in that squad who have TI on him and experience leading patrols. It would be bad if we made Big Red acting fire team leader." His expression was quizzical. He wondered what was wrong with Bell, if it was something other than losing a man from the platoon and losing a friend.

Something was on Bell's mind that he wasn't talking about; that was obvious. But Burrison should have been wondering what Ruizique was thinking. *I will not go with my patrol tonight,* Ruizique thought, *and I will leave on the helicopter tomorrow. But first there is something else I must do.*

Billy Boy Lewis threw a fit, of course, when Bell assigned Hempen to take out the patrol. When he started complaining about how Burrison had almost promised him a fire team of his own when there was an opening, Zeitvogel and Randall managed to take him aside and calm him down before he mouthed off so much some sort of official action had to be taken. There was fire in his eyes and steam coming out of his nose and smoke from his ears when he finally shut up. He wasn't at all mollified when Randall tried to explain how badly he needed him. "Damn it, so what if Short Round does have time in grade on me," he said. "I don't give a good goddamn if he has run as many patrols as I have. I'm the better Marine. I deserve to be fire team leader." They couldn't convince him that Bell and Burrison were doing what was right for the platoon, but they did manage to keep him from putting his ass in a sling. Hempen wisely kept his mouth shut during Lewis's tantrum.

They wouldn't let Ruizique go on patrol, but once he insisted on it, there was no way they could keep him from helping with perimeter watch. No one thought it was peculiar when he went to his post on the east side of the hill forty-five minutes before sunset and sat alone, looking down the steep slope. No more than anyone had thought it unusual that he sat in on the discussions when the patrol orders were given and when the patrol leaders decided what they were actually going to do. Everyone who knew him thought when he sat in, it was to observe and advise Hempen. Hell, any of the corporals would have done the same. And going to the perimeter early was his way of preparing himself to leave—this corporal who had originally thought he shouldn't be involved in this gringo war in Asia and then thought the Marine Corps had been making a mistake assigning him to a Combined Action Platoon. The only surprise any of them had felt was when he had suddenly become a dedicated Cong killer after being wounded in an attempted overrun of Camp Apache. Those who knew he was going to give command of that night's patrol to a brand-new lance corporal, Big Red Robertson, might have thought he was doing a little pouting about the fact that command of the patrol had been given instead to Short Round Hempen, but they weren't concerned about his feelings; they wanted him to spend the night safe behind the wire so he could go home in the morning.

But Ruizique wasn't preparing himself mentally to go home. His job here wasn't done; he had more to accomplish before heading back to The World and little time in which to do it—that's what he was preparing himself for. Neither was he pouting. He had hardly even noticed the fit Billy Boy Lewis threw when the squad was realigned to make Short Round Hempen the acting fire team leader.

What Ruizique did during that three quarters of an hour

sitting alone in his night defensive position was study the two banks of concertina wire on the hillside below him. He committed to memory each place where the coils of wire were a little farther separated from one another. He memorized the location of each mine, flare, noisemaker, and trip wire. He had paid close attention to the reports of all the activities of the northern invaders since they'd started terrorizing the villagers; he thought he knew what they had in mind next. Maybe.

The hillside was in deep shadow when Doc Tracker joined him for the night's watch. "Been a long time, pano," the corpsman said.

Ruizique grunted something noncommittal and continued examining the wire and its contents. Sure, two-and-a-half months was a long time in a combat zone. But it wasn't long compared to the four years he'd already spent in the Marine Corps when he'd joined Tango Niner. It wasn't long compared to the time he was going to be an army officer when he got home. And it certainly wasn't long compared to how long he expected to live.

"Gonna be lonely here," Tracker tried again, "being the only American who isn't white or black."

This time Ruizique did look at him, and his look almost made Tracker wish he hadn't. "I'm not North American."

"You're not Vietnamese, and you are a U.S. Marine," Tracker said with some heat. Where did this guy think he got off talking like that?

"I am Dominican," Ruizique said, and returned his attention to the hillside. "If you need an American who isn't white or black, there is that newby—what's his name?—Vega, the Tex-Mex." A small part of his mind wondered why Tracker was talking to him like this; they had never been particular friends.

Ruizique's attitude annoyed Tracker, and he wished he hadn't volunteered to spend the night on watch with him. What was his problem? He was leaving for The World in the morning; he should be happy. When the sun dropped behind the western hills and cast the hilltop abruptly into night, the two men set their rotation. There was no discussion about it; the corporal who was leaving in the morning simply told the corpsman who was staying behind who was going to have the first of the two-hour sleep periods. Tracker didn't wonder about it; it didn't occur to him to ask if there was some reason Ruizique wanted to have the last watch before dawn. If he had asked, he would have been both fascinated and appalled by the other man's reason. He would also have been surprised if he had known Ruizique had asked for him to be his partner for the night. Ruizique had asked for him because he knew Tracker was good enough and mature enough to be able to deal with the situation he was going to find himself in later. And because he wasn't good enough to prevent Ruizique from doing what he was going to do.

Ruizique studied the luminous dials of his watch. The night had been long and slow on the perimeter, but now it was 0430—time to do it. If he waited any longer, it would be too late. Any earlier and he risked discovery, which could stop him from doing it. He looked at the dark mass that was Doc Tracker lying alongside the trench. Tracker's soft, steady breathing told clearly he was sleeping. Sorry to do this to you, pano, he thought. He was sorry for how rude he had been at nightfall, and he was sorry for the rude awakening Tracker would receive at dawn—or at the next comm-check along the perimeter. He glanced quickly around for looming shadows that would indicate someone else nearby and didn't see any. Silently, he stripped off his own cartridge belt, with its bayonet and rifle magazines and first aid kit, and strapped on Tracker's. The corpsman's belt held a holstered .45 on the right hip, a K-Bar on the left, and a pouch with two magazines for the automatic. He patted his shirt pocket to confirm that the length of coiled cord was in it, then he laid his cartridge belt and rifle where Tracker could find them immediately if he woke up suddenly—but Ruizique didn't think that was likely; the nights at Camp Apache had been very quiet for a long time. He thought about it for a brief moment, then removed his crossed bandoliers as well. Belly down, he slithered out of the trench, down the hill, toward the defensive wire. In less than fifteen minutes he was running on cat feet, crouched over, away from Camp Apache, to the tree line to the east. No one saw him leave.

Once in the trees, he cut to the right and ran faster, not as concerned now with noise. He knew the patrol orders and how the three patrols were coordinating; he had no fear of stumbling into a friendly ambush and getting killed by his own people. He knew Charlie didn't have any ambushes in the area tonight either; that's not how the enemy was operating now. At 0500, little more than half an hour before false dawn would brighten the eastern sky, he settled under a bush alongside the main riverbank trail leading west from Hou Cau. If he was right, something would happen soon. If he was wrong, well, he was leaving later in the morning anyway. What could they do, kick him out of the unit?

A tree-roosting bird chirped between Hou Cau and the hiding bush. That was wrong, Ruizique thought. He closed his eyes, tilted his head back, and reopened his eyes. The sky overhead was still so dark the only way he could distinguish the treetops was the stars that showed between them; it was too early for the first bird to give its wake-up cry to its neighbors. He quickly made sure the .45 was snug in its holster so it wouldn't make any noise when he made his move, then hefted the K-Bar. He tensed, ready.

A leaf rustled to his left. A moment later a dry twig snapped beneath a soft-stepping foot. A shadow bobbed on the trail, approached, and passed him. So did a second shadow, followed by a third. All three shadows were topped by the shallow cones of straw peasant hats; they shimmered with the black of peasant pajamas; they carried the distinctive shapes of AK-47s. Ruizique waited a few more seconds without seeing a fourth shadow, then sprang like a well-oiled trap and in two bounds reached the third shadow.

In one movement, he cupped a hand over the man's mouth and nose and slit his throat to the bone with the K-Bar. He held his victim high with the hand that cupped his mouth and nose so his pounding feet didn't hit the ground and managed to catch his falling rifle with his knife hand before it could clatter to the hard-packed earth of the trail. The two NVA fading into the darkness ahead didn't notice. Ruizique eased his burden down and rushed to reach the second man. He wasn't as quick in catching the middle man's rifle, and it hit the path with a resounding thud. The man in front spun around, leveling his rifle along the trail. Ruizique threw the corpse at him; the body slammed hard into the North Vietnamese and knocked the muzzle of his rifle aside as he pulled the trigger. A spray of bullets whined harmlessly past the Marine's right ear.

Ruizique followed right behind the body he had thrown and smashed into them before the last cartridge of the burst was ejected from the NVA's rifle. All three fell heavily to the ground. Ruizique was on top; the force of his rush and the weight of the corpse knocked the air out of the man on the bottom and stunned him long enough for the Dominican to toss the AK aside and clamp a hand tightly around his throat. He used his left shoulder and knife hand to pin the enemy soldier's flailing arms. His struggles quickly weakened, and after a long minute he fell limp.

Ruizique kept his hand tightly wrapped around the throat a little longer, cutting off the flow of blood to the man's brain and air to his lungs, to make sure he was unconscious and not faking, then eased his grip. The NVA's chest heaved as his body's automatic reflexes took over to suck air into his eager lungs. Ruizique rolled far enough off to shove the corpse out from between them, then pulled the cord from his pocket and flipped his still-unconscious prisoner onto his stomach to tie his hands behind his back. A complicated loop of cord then went from the prisoner's wrists to his ankles—he wouldn't be able to run away even if he were able to get to his feet.

Then Ruizique sat with his back against a tree and waited. This wasn't part of the plan, but the gunfire surely attracted attention and someone was coming to investigate. Better to be sitting quietly, waiting, than get caught moving where somebody might pull the trigger before recognizing him.

CHAPTER NINETEEN

New Year's Day, 1967

"You know, Zeke," Burrison said when Randall's patrol brought Ruizique in with his prisoner, "this is one of those situations where if you were staying with us, I'd have to either write you up for a medal or bust you."

"Think we could go ahead and do both anyway, Scrappy?" Bell asked, straight-faced.

"That's an idea," Burrison said, looking just as straight-faced and serious as the sergeant. "Getting a medal might just take the sting out of not getting his commission because he got out of the Marines as a private. But"—he shrugged—"you know how much time these things take. By the time he got his court-martial he'd already be back in the DR, wearing whatever it is they wear there instead of railroad tracks. And then he'd have the medal for free." He grinned.

Ruizique snorted.

Bell laughed.

Doc Tracker gave the prisoner a quick physical examination. "He's just like the fake woodsman we killed back in

September," he said. "Look at him—taller than the peasants around here. His body's more filled out—that's from
a better diet; he grew up eating more than just rice and fish
heads. Look at his hands—he doesn't have the calluses the
farmers get. He's a city boy, all right. Question is, what
city?" He looked under the man's shirt and made him drop
his trousers. "Gook sores. I don't give a good goddamn if
he is dressed like a peasant, no way on earth he's a local
farmer. Our people around here don't have gook sores like
that anymore, so we know he's a bad guy. Even if we
didn't have the AKs him and his buddies were carrying,
the sores are proof of that."

Houng questioned the prisoner. The PF lieutenant first
talked to him conversationally—and got no answer. Then
he screamed and waved his arms. Nothing. He talked
harshly, fiercely. The tightly bound prisoner kept his mouth
shut and his face stoically set. Bell and Burrison crowded
in closely, trying to physically intimidate the prisoner without laying a hand on him. He ignored them. Ruizique sat in
the prisoner's line of sight and stared at him while running
his thumb along the blade of the knife he'd used to kill the
other two NVA. The soldier glanced at him once and
turned his face away—Ruizique thought he saw the prisoner's lip curl slightly as he did. Five PFs who had gone to
Hou Cau came back to Camp Apache with a tale of a pig
who had been slaughtered overnight and its entrails draped
around the door of the hamlet chief's hootch. The prisoner
looked blandly at Houng's questions about that.

Then Swarnes came out of the command hootch tent.
"Fucking company's coming," he said.

There was a lot of bonhomie when the helicopter came into
view—much backslapping, handwringing, arm-pumping,
and lots of chatter. In its seven months of existence Tango
Niner had had two dozen Marines go home, most of them
in body bags. Corporal Jesus Maria Ruizique was the first
one to leave standing on his own feet and not bleeding. It

was a red-letter day and gave hope to the rest that they could leave the same way.

"Go get 'em, Zeke!"

"Got lots of round-eye pussy where you're going, Zeke."

"Yeah, Zeke, can't let Tex be the only one to get round-eye tail."

"Make sure they pump you up with enough penicillin to cure the dose of clap I'm gonna get when I go on R and R."

"Send me a picture of your sister. I need something to jerk off over."

"You got a sister? Fuck his picture—send her to me."

A lot of the talk centered around sex, and some other things as well.

"Oh, wow! You gonna be able to get shit-faced and not have to worry about getting dinged by a dink while you're drunk."

"Don't take no shit off no MPs. They want to throw you in a drunk tank, waste their pogue asses."

"I heard some draft-dodging college students are waving Vee Cee flags. You see one, blow his young ass away. You see two, zap the second one for me."

"Am I really going to have to salute and call you 'sir' the next time I see your ugly ass?"

The helicopter landed, and Captain Hasford jumped off. He shook hands with Ruizique and shouted good luck and long life at him. Then Ruizique threw his seabag in and climbed aboard. The prisoner was roughly thrown in after him and lay quietly on his stomach on the floor at Ruizique's feet.

Bell shouted, "Make sure he gets where he's going," to the departing corporal. Ruizique nodded and raised his thumb; he'd see to the prisoner. The bird lifted off and sped away toward the east.

Silence settled on the hill; the laughter and shouting that had filled the air just minutes before was gone. Now the Marines had to come to grips with being even more short-handed. And they had to figure out how to deal with the bad guys, whose snipers were slowly whittling them down and terrorizing the villagers. The silence didn't last long, though. They'd lost men before, but this one was going home alive and whole; there was nothing to grieve over.

"Glad to see you, Captain," Burrison said, and shook the other's offered hand.

Hasford looked at the almost vanished helicopter. "I'm glad to see a man from Tango Niner go home that way." He turned to Bell, Burrison, and Houng. "You know, until today this was the only CAP that's been around for more than three or four months that didn't have at least one man rotate back to The World?" He shook his head in amazement. "Let's go talk. I want the corporals and PF squad leaders, too. Including whoever's filling in for Zeke." He headed toward the southeast corner of the compound and sat on one of the folding hammocks. The Marines and PFs he wanted to talk with arrived in his train. Hasford looked them over. "You're taking Zeke's place, Short Round?" he asked.

Hempen smiled and nodded.

"How come you, instead of Billy Boy?" Hasford had been in temporary command of Tango Niner for a couple of weeks in early November and knew from then that, though somewhat inexperienced, Lewis was a capable patrol leader.

"I got as much experience as he does," Hempen said. "And I got TI."

Hasford shrugged. Hempen wasn't the choice he would have made for acting team leader, but Burrison and Bell knew their men better than he did.

Hempen read Hasford's expression and knew what the captain was thinking. He was a brand-new acting corporal and was feeling his oats. He cracked a small grin and said, "That hammock you're sitting on, Captain? It belongs to me." Get off my case, in other words.

Hasford cocked an eyebrow but otherwise set his expression in the stone face that seemed to be issued to Marine lieutenants along with their captain's railroad tracks when they got promoted. There was sudden tension in the group; they all understood Hempen might have just stepped over a line.

"You saying you've got what it takes to be an NCO, Lance Corporal?"

Hempen maintained his grin as he said, "Yessir." He understood it was possible he was about to get court-martialed for insubordination. If he did, he might be able to convince the board he meant no disrespect by what he'd just said, but there was no way he could convince a bunch of staff officers he'd done the right thing by not saying "sir" to an officer, even in the field.

"More balls than brains, is that what you're telling me?"

"Hell, sir—" Hempen's grin widened, "—you know what they say about Marine sergeants—they got balls so big they need to carry them around in a wheelbarrow. The main difference between corporals and sergeants is corporals are tough enough they don't need the wheelbarrows."

Hasford suddenly laughed. "Yeah, that's what I thought —more balls than brains," he said, and shook his head. He turned to the others. "Now, talk to me about what's going on around here."

The tension vanished, especially when Hempen's expression told them he was going to keep his mouth shut. Burrison told Hasford about the daytime sniper attacks on three days in the past week, each attack making its mark. He told him about the Hou Toung chief and Pheet and his family being murdered. He told him about the Hou Dau fire and the explosion in Hou Cau and the harranguings in Hou Ky and Hou Toung and the dead animals. He finished with the tale of the three NVA who had just killed a pig in Hou Cau.

Hasford made a face, then asked, "And what have you done to counter the enemy?"

Burrison explained the daytime searches to the west.

"What I want to know is where's Recon?" Bell said.

"We've had trouble coming at us from the west ever since we first sat down on this hill. How the hell come Force Recon never sends anybody into those hills over there to find out what Charlie's doing? It got to the point where we—" He abruptly stopped talking, realizing he was about to say something he shouldn't: the brass—and that included Captain Hasford—didn't know that Tango Niner had run an unauthorized and extremely hazardous raid on a previously unknown Vietcong communications center hidden in the western hills a month earlier. "We've had to tango with every son of a bitch," he continued, hoping Hasford wouldn't notice the lapse, "who's wanted to come through here, and we've had to do it without knowing in advance that anybody was coming."

Hasford did notice the lapse. He studied Bell's face for a long moment before replying, but he had enough cool to not ask the sergeant what he had started to say; he knew he wouldn't get a straight answer without digging so much he'd wind up having to burn somebody. "We've been through this before, Sergeant Bell," he finally said. "Recon is a very scarce resource. We don't have enough to look everyplace we'd like to. So far Tango Niner has done well enough without having the early warning it could get from Recon."

"And we've lost a lot of men doing it," Bell snapped. "Why doesn't the Corps send in more Recon units? We need them."

"Think about it for a while, Jay Cee," Hasford said more quietly. "It'll come to you." He turned to Burrison. "What are you going to do next?" he asked.

"Today we're going east," Burrison said, glad to get the discussion away from where Bell had led it. Hasford looked where the lieutenant waved his arm; he saw most of the Marines and PFs waiting with their rifles and cartridge belts. "I don't think we'll find Mister Charles there, but we've got to look. The next place to look after we eliminate the east is the ridge. After that, south of the Song."

Hasford furrowed his brow in momentary thought. "How many are you sending out?"

"Ten four-man teams."

Hasford looked to be lost in thought for a long moment.

"Do this," he said, and his talking pace picked up. "Every time you've been hit, it's been from the west, or in some place where the bad guys could get away to that direction. If Charlie hits you today, he'll probably do the same. Have half of your teams stop inside the trees between Hou Dau and Hou Cau and wait together. That way if one of the others runs into anything from this side, there will be a reaction force in position and ready to move and block the bastards."

Bell and Burrison thought it over for a moment, a very short moment. It was a good idea. And if the reaction force itself ran into anything, the twenty Marines and PFs in it could give the enemy a very hard time.

Major Nghu sat on his hillside, studying Camp Apache through his binoculars. He mulled over the report he'd been given. A helicopter had come at an unusual time and left one new man while taking away another. His first reaction was that the newcomer was an interrogator arriving to question his man, who had been foolish enough to get captured before dawn, but that man had been taken away on that same helicopter. The departing American had taken a large package with him; he could be leaving permanently and the arrival his replacement. Were the Americans so well organized that a replacement arrived at the same time as the man he relieved left? The NVA officer doubted it. Especially since the new man carried neither a rifle nor a package of belongings. He examined the new man. His movements were different from the others'. He seemed somehow more subdued, more economical in his movements, more self-confident than the other Americans, though the others did not lack in that regard. Finally light glinted from the stranger's collar, and Nghu knew he was an officer. Was he there as an advisor? To take command, to investigate? It did not matter; the imperialist American Marines were very near where he wanted them: deserted by the villagers, their numbers reduced. Soon their Popular Force lackeys would abandon them as well.

Sudden activity in the encampment excited him. He watched closely as most of the armed men filed out the two gates and turned east. They broke into smaller groups as they neared the forest on the far side of their hill. Wonderful! Now was the time to strike another blow to instill terror into the hearts of the traitors to the Revolution. He snapped an order to the sergeant assigned to watch the Marines' hill during his absence, the noisy-stomached sergeant, whose stomach was quiet today. Then he left with his senior sergeant, giving orders as they went.

Nghu didn't know it, but the noisy-stomached sergeant had quiet digestion now because he had brought food with him to eat during his watch. While the major approved of the sergeant's silence, he would have disciplined him had he known about the food. The observation post was not an authorized eating place.

"When I go back to Division I'll try to talk someone into authorizing a flight from VMFJ-1 over the area," Hasford said after the patrols left. "If these bad guys are using radios, an electronics flight should pick it up." VMFJ-1 was a reconnaissance-and-observation squadron that had aircraft with very sophisticated electronics devices, some of which were capable of precisely locating radio transmitters. "If Charlie's using radios, they'll find him, and we can put him out of business."

"What if these bad guys aren't using radios when we get this flyover?" Bell asked.

"Then we think of something else. In the meantime, we need to cut down on your casualties."

"One last thing," Hasford said at the last minute. "Just remember, there's a truce on. That means you can't fire first, only return fire."

"Aye-aye, sir," Burrison said.

Bell grimaced.

Four men padded quickly through the scrub forest. One of them carried the tube and bipods of a 60mm mortar; one had its baseplate. The other two men carried six mortar rounds each; one of them also had a pair of field glasses. They each had a pistol. None of them bore rifles—they didn't expect to meet opposition. Five hundred meters southeast of their target, they stopped and set up the mortar, the dozen rounds stacked on the ground alongside it. The man with the field glasses climbed a tree and called aiming instructions down to the men setting up the mortar. Nice thing about mortars, he thought, the gunner doesn't have to see what he's shooting at.

When the men on the ground said the tube was aimed properly, he barked an order. The assistant gunner dropped a round down the tube and hunched away from it. The man in the tree watched through his glasses. When the round hit, he made a rapid mental calculation and called an adjustment to the gunner. The gunner twirled the cranks on his bipods and called back "ready." The man in the tree barked another order, and the assistant gunner dropped a second round down the tube. The man in the tree watched until the second round hit, called down a second correction, then climbed down out of the tree. He would have liked to see them all land, see the destruction they caused, but it wasn't necessary; they were on target. The gunner made a fine adjustment, and the assistant gunner dropped a third round. Fine adjustment, drop round, fine adjustment, drop round, until all twelve were fired. As soon as the last round was fired, they broke down the mortar and padded back the way they'd come.

Zeitvogel absently waved a hand—a hand large enough to pick up a basketball from the top—at the gnats that swarmed around his head. "Why me, Lord?" he groaned.

"What did I do wrong? I've tried to be a good boy." He sat cross-legged, with his back against a tree; he was in command of the twenty-man reaction force that waited inside the trees between Hou Dau hill and Hou Cau. The twenty men—six Marines and fourteen PFs—were divided into four-man teams, with him, Randall, Lewis, Vinh, and Willy in charge of one each. Zeitvogel had Mazzucco, Huu, and Pee Wee in his team. "It was bad enough when I had Short Round in my fire team," he continued without looking to see who was listening to his soft voice; he knew some of them were. "Then you could have spotted me Rick Barry, and I wouldn't have had a team that stood a chance of beating a bunch of junior high school girls at roundball. At least Short Round was as tall as most junior high girls. Now I got Huu—ain't got hands big enough to hold up a roundball from the bottom—and Pee Wee." He shook his head mournfully. "Pee Wee was a girl, he could give me a blow job standing up."

"Bullshit, Stilts," Randall said from where he sat under another tree a few meters away. He also spoke softly; they were keeping quiet under the trees to avoid detection by anybody who might pass nearby. Dodd sat against the opposite side of the tree Randall was under, holding a PRC-6 radio to his ear. "You've got Homeboy on your team. He can put moves on you, turn you into a pretzel. Shit, you say Pee Wee could give you a blow job standing up? Man's just the right height to stick his face in high school girls' tits standing up. He could distract them while Homeboy makes all his moves and gets the ball up court to you and you drop it through the basket. Blow out."

The tall man gazed, unfocused, for a moment, then murmured, "Shirts and skins. No uniforms. Shirts and skins. The girls could be skins. Make it a betting game; winner picks the stakes." He looked at Pee Wee. "Hey, little bro, you like suckie-suck on boobies?"

The tiny PF looked at him, confused; he didn't know the word "boobies." Mazzucco translated for him, mostly using hand gestures, and Pee Wee's face lit up. He nodded vigorously; he held his hands as though cupping the breasts of a woman facing him and made sloppy kissing sounds.

Zeitvogel leaned forward. "You're right, Tex," he said mock seriously. "How'd you do that? Who told you? Pano, that sounds like you had a thought." He ducked out of the way of a clod of humus Randall lobbed at him. He furrowed his brow in thought and continued slowly, "We wouldn't need Rick Barry. The four of us could do it by our own selves. Let me see. American girls are big enough, one of them could take care of Pee Wee and Huu, then one for Homebody. That leaves—" He counted fingers. "—three for me. That sounds about right." He smiled brightly. "I'm big enough it takes three high school girls to do me."

"You're thinking too small, Stilts," Mazzucco said, laughing. "Let's go for college girls. One of them will probably be tall enough for you. That way I get two. The redhead and a blonde."

"What, you mean I only get two?"

Mazzucco laughed again. "No way, man. You get one. If Pee Wee's doing all that distracting, he deserves one all by himself. And I'm not sharing one of mine with Huu. That leaves one for you. Unless you want to share one with him. What do you think? Is he going to want to share one with you?"

Zeitvogel started to throw something at Mazzucco. He froze in half swing at the muffled sound of a distant mortar. He turned his head to Dodd, who was now concentrating all of his attention on the earpiece of the radio.

Vega rubbed the edge of his hand over his forehead, squeegeeing sweat. He wiped his hand on his trousers and ran its back over his eyes, smearing some of the sweat out of them. The air under the trees was still; sweat evaporated slowly. He saw the deep shade lighten ahead and knew they must be near the edge of the woods, approaching the cane fields beyond it. His mouth briefly formed into something midway between a grin and a grimace. He had been in-country long enough to know the catch-22 he was about to enter; there was more air movement in the open, which would increase the cooling effect of evaporating sweat, but it was going to be hotter directly under the sun. The two were going to cancel each other out. The only way to deal with the heat was to stop moving.

He looked at the back of Billy Boy Lewis, the man in front of him, and wondered how on earth he could look so cool in this stifling heat. It wasn't as though the wiry Marine had had all that much more time to acclimate to the climate; Vega had arrived as a replacement during August, when the tropical heat was at its absolute worst. Relatively speaking, January 1 was cool. But that was only relative. He shook his head, tossing off some of the new sweat beading his face, and returned his attention to the ground around them. How were they supposed to know if anything they saw was out of the ordinary? he wondered. Aside from the main trails leading through the trees, the earth was hatch-marked with lesser pathways made by villagers who had changed their minds about where they were going or who had wanted to avoid running into other people, pathways left by village animals wandering, foraging under the trees, and game trails.

What was out of the ordinary—a scrap of cloth, a footprint, a meal remnant? How could they tell if it was out of the ordinary in a populated area? What about the remains of a cooking fire? Did the villagers ever have cookout picnics? He didn't know. Probably, he thought, the only way we'll be able to know is if we see someone carrying a rifle—or somebody shoots at us. He shuddered. Every shot the enemy had fired at Tango Niner since he'd joined it had counted.

The four-man team—Mai and Deh were also with them —broke into the open. On the right, the forest slanted away to their front; it peeled back from them on the left. Vega looked north. Four more men were a couple hundred meters away. Another team was visible beyond them. He thought he saw movement north of that. To the south, the fifth team was still under the trees. Vega wasn't paying much attention to how far they were walking. He was too new in Bun Hou to know how large the woods were; he didn't know how far they had gone under the trees. He looked at his watch and wondered how much farther they had to go before they turned around to : eturn to Camp Apache for evening chow and to prepare for the night's patrols. He also wondered who was firing a mortar to their rear and if it meant anything.

CHAPTER TWENTY

The Barrage

Carrumph, came the familiar sound of a mortar.

"Ah, shit," Bell swore. "Incoming!" he shouted as loud as he could. "Get all those damn civilians in the bunkers."

There wasn't any panic, not right away. The Marines in the compound had been mortared before and knew what to expect. They didn't hesitate or take time to pay attention to the knots of fear that formed in their stomachs; they simply started hustling the women and children into the living bunkers next to the three tents, helping old people, carrying children. Except for Swarnes, who, swearing all the way, struggled his radios into the shelter of a bunker. Houng heard Bell's shout and shouted orders himself for his men to help their families and for the families of all his men to get under cover, take shelter. He and some of his men knew what it was like to come under a barrage. For the first few seconds the children, being herded by their mothers, treated it like a game and ran, weaving and giggling, toward the bunkers. Except for the Vietcong attack on Hou Cau a month earlier, the hamlets of Bun Hou had managed to avoid being shelled throughout the war; none of the people understood what was about to happen to them.

Then the first spotter round hit, near the helipad. It erupted with a roar and spewed a fountain of dirt and debris into the air. Half of the people in the compound stopped and stared at the plume, stunned and shocked. They started screaming at the sound of the second *carrumph* and ran, panic-stricken. The Marines and PFs had to shove them toward the safety of the bunkers. The second spotter round hit north of the center of the compound. A woman screamed sharply, hit by shrapnel. A nearby Marine picked her up and carried her to the nearest bunker. By the time the third round exploded, near the tents, most of the people were inside the bunkers and the PFs warned them to stay put until told to come out. The PFs joined the Marines rushing to the perimeter trench, to try to repel the assault that might be coming under the cover of the barrage.

Eight Marines, a corpsman, and four PFs to defend a half-mile perimeter, and another Marine in a bunker with the radios. Good luck, Bell thought.

The next five rounds hit before all of Camp Apache's defenders reached the trench. Not all of them made it. Almost everybody was under cover when the last five hit.

Nguyen Thi Mo was the wife of the PF named Quot. They had a five-year-old son. Mo understood five-year-olds very well; her two other children had already been five years old, so she was experienced with them. To a five-year-old, life was an adventure with new things to be discovered every day. A five-year-old child had no built-in understanding of danger—he or she was always willing to try anything once. Only after something hurt a five-year-old did he learn to avoid it. Most things didn't hurt, and a lot of them were fun. And the ones that did hurt? Well, he survived all of them, so nothing could be too horrible. Mo understood that five-year-olds had to be protected from themselves. She huddled in a corner of the bunker and tucked her young son under her arm to protect him from himself. And, at the worst, protect his body with hers.

Le, Mo's latest five-year-old, had lived his entire life in a war-torn country, but the war had always taken place in other people's villages, other people's hamlets. He had seen people without eyes, missing limbs, he'd seen torn and mangled bodies, dead bodies, but he'd never seen what made them that way. Le was a typical five-year-old, full of curiosity and the adventure of life. He wanted to see what it was that tore eyes from heads, limbs from bodies, life from people. Outside this dark cave his mother had carried him into he heard the loudest roaring he had ever heard. Actually, he'd heard it before, but always somewhere else, never so close. It was a roaring that he knew sometimes hurt people. It sounded something like what he imagined a dragon must sound like. What did it look like?

Le squirmed under his mother's protective arm. It didn't feel protective to him; he didn't know why he needed protection. His mother's arm felt restraining and restrictive. He squirmed and struggled, and suddenly he was free of that arm. With a squeal of childish joy he darted to the patch of light that told him where the zigzag entrance to the bunker was. Behind him, his mother screamed his name, called him back. He ignored her cries. He heard her scramble after him and ran all the faster, so he could see what was outside before she grabbed him and pulled him back. A small part of his mind told him he was going to get spanked for what he was doing so he might as well make it worth it.

Le caromed through the bunker entrance, which was doglegged to prevent schrapnel from slicing into the bunker. His face lit with awe when he reached the open air. Mere feet in front of him, a brilliant flash of red and yellow let out a hideous roar that deafened him. The flash threw up a fountain of dirt and metal that filled his entire world. The flash and its fountain was the last thing he ever saw, its roar the last thing he ever heard. He never felt his mother wrap her arms around his torn and mangled corpse, never felt her tears and blood bathe him.

The barrage ended and silence fell over Camp Apache. Silence except the cries of the wounded and the keening of a bereaved mother. Burrison poked his head out of the trench fighting position he manned alone and looked out over the open land south of the hill. No one moved in his sight. He picked up the groundwire, sound-power phone in the fighting position he occupied and cranked its handle.

"All stations report," the young lieutenant ordered, and immediately cursed himself, because under the circumstances nobody knew who was in which position or in what order to report.

Bell took charge of the situation immediately. "This is Jay Cee," he said into his phone. "I'm on the west side. No one in sight between here and the trees. Vo is with me. Who's on the main gate?"

"Kobos. I don't have my damn gun," Kobos answered, meaning the machine gun, "but I don't have any targets, either. Vandersteit's with me. He needs Chief."

"Roger, main gate," Bell said. "East side, report."

"Chief here. Kobos, I'll get to you as soon as I finish patching up Hunter. I don't see anybody out there, Jay Cee."

"Back gate." Bell didn't take the time to acknowledge the casualties. How many were there? He'd know too soon anyway.

"Athen, here with Chi. Everything's cool here."

Bell thought fast. Who hadn't he heard from? "Swarnes, report."

"I'm with my fucking radios. Where the goddamn hell you think I am?"

"Graham."

No answer from the mortarman.

"Graham, report." Graham again didn't reply. "Anybody seen Graham?" Nobody responded.

"Skipper, where are you?" Burrison broke in, suddenly realizing he hadn't heard from Captain Hasford.

"I'm in the southeast corner," Hasford said over the phone. "When Chief's through with the others, I got a boo-boo that should be looked at also." Even though he was the highest ranking man in the compound, he had kept quiet when Burrison had first called for his men to report. It was best to let the men normally in command of Tango Niner take care of the situation; until they needed him in another capacity, he was just another rifle.

"This Houng," the PF lieutenant said—it had taken this long for him to figure out how to use the telephone. "Me hurt, not bad. Where Jo Jo?"

No one answered for the last PF, who wasn't located.

"Athen, Kobos, Vo, stay in place," Bell ordered. It was now a couple of minutes since the barrage had ended, and all sides of the hill had reported no visual contact. "Athen, send Chi to the east side to sit with Hunter. Everybody else, front and center."

That's when they found the carnage.

Graham hadn't answered because he was dead.

Nobody had known where Jo Jo was because his mangled legs hadn't let him reach the trench. "Maybe, if we can convince those dipshits in the rear, just maybe they can save his legs," Tracker said when he examined the badly wounded PF. "I can keep him alive until he's med-evaced, then it's up to the people in the hospital."

Out of fourteen defenders on the hill, five were wounded, one badly enough that he'd probably never bear arms again, and one was dead.

Then there were the civilians, the families of the PFs.

Mo, Le's mother, had scalp and shoulder wounds from the same mortar round that had killed her son. She'd bled a lot, but her wounds were more spectacular than deadly.

Pham's parents were dead. Both had been hit by fragments as they'd scrambled into one of the bunkers. Pham's mother had been hit in the center of her back by a chunk that had torn into her heart. His father had gotten a smaller piece in the kidney. The multiple shock of his own wound and seeing his wife die had killed the old man.

Cao's wife was probably going to lose her right arm below the elbow; Doc Tracker wasn't sure it could be saved.

Sang's wife was dead; a piece of shrapnel had neatly sliced off part of her skull.

Phoung's daughter had lost a hand to a jagged piece of metal that had torn it off as if it were made of papier-mâché.

Burrison had Swarnes re-call the search and reaction teams while the casualty count was being made. Then while Swarnes was calling for a med-evac, Tracker counseled the wounded Marines and PFs. "Your shoulder will be sore for a while," he told Houng. "I think I took care of it okay, but I want a surgeon in the rear to look at it anyway, get it X-rayed, just to make sure nothing's broken." The corpsman had given the PF lieutenant a shot of morphine, because the wound started hurting after the adrenaline rush from the excitement was over. Houng was too rocky to understand that the med-evac would remove him from action for a while.

He'd also given Jo Jo morphine, more morphine; the PF wouldn't be able to understand him, so he didn't bother talking to him.

To Hunter he said, "You know, Turd, I've heard of people trying to get out of combat, but you got to do better than an arm wound like this. They'll dope you up with antibiotics in the hospital to knock out any infection you might get and send you back here in a couple of days."

Hunter the Third flushed at being called "Turd." "You get the antibiotics and pump me up here," he said. "If this isn't enough to ship me back to The World, I'm staying right where I am." He managed a weak grin. His arm hurt something fierce, but he knew intellectually that the ragged tear in it looked far worse than it actually was.

Tracker nodded and turned to Vandersteit. "I don't want any argument out of you. You got to go back. There's blood vessel damage in your thigh that I can't repair here. You'll probably be back with us in a couple of weeks."

Hasford tried to laugh off his wound. "What is this garbage?" he asked. "I'm a staff officer, not a grunt. Staff officers are supposed to get their Purple Hearts by going to the officers club, getting blind drunk, and cutting their chins when they fall into a slit trench trying to find their way back to their billets." He had a flesh wound in his side.

"Well, Captain, look at it this way," Tracker said as he tweezed a fragment of metal out of Hasford's side. "You can keep this to show to people as proof you didn't cut yourself shaving. Not like those other pogues will."

Hasford smiled at "those other pogues" but cut his laugh short because of the pain in his side. "Is there any way I can preserve the blood stains on it?" he asked, pocketing the fragment.

"So long, pano" was all Tracker could say to Graham.

There was nothing the corpsman could say to the wounded civilians.

Zeitvogel's large reaction team arrived first, and then the search teams started filing back in. The last of them were almost back to the hill when the med-evac bird lifted off with its eight wounded people. Slover wasn't back yet by the time the bird came in; it had to land without the help of his orange Ping-Pong paddles.

Before boarding the helicopter, Hasford promised, "I'll get you replacements as fast as humanly possible. I'm sure the lieutenant colonel will help with that. And I'll get that recon flight out here within the next twenty-four hours."

The Marines fumed over the attack. The bad guys had gone a long time without messing with the people, but what they were doing now was just enough to keep the Marines and PFs uptight and off balance. They had to do something about it, but what?

Then they had another problem.

*   *   *

In Houng's absence Collard Green, the senior squad leader, was acting PF platoon leader. One at a time and in small groups many of the PFs met with him, talking in hushed tones. The Marines saw this but kept their distance and didn't try to intervene in any way. Not even when Collard Green's normal distressed-stomach expression turned very ill-looking. The Marines became concerned when the individuals and small groups around Collard Green merged into a large group. Vinh, the second squad leader, joined the group, and Willy seemed to take Collard Green's side in whatever the altercation was. Some of the Marines huddled in small groups; others wandered off to the perimeter when an occasional louder voice was raised above the hushed ones the PFs were talking in. The bodies of Quot's son, Pham's parents, and Sang's wife were being cleaned and dressed by other family members.

"This is numba fucking ten," some of the Marines said to one another. "I do believe you're right," others said back. "Are we about to be in a world of shit?" someone asked. They waited, somber, to find out how bad things really were. At last Collard Green detached himself from the PFs and walked slowly toward Burrison, who waited for what he suspected was bad news at one of the sheet-metal-on-sandbag tables. Vinh accompanied Collard Green.

"We talk," Collard Green said, and waited patiently while Bell, Slover, Zeitvogel, and Randall joined them. By this time the PF squad leader had composed himself, resigned to the worst. His sickly expression was normal for him, though his color was further off than usual. When all the Marine leaders were present, he waited politely until Burrison sat down and indicated an ammo crate chair for him to sit at.

"No good," Collard Green said in a flat voice. He talked to his Marine friends in a mix of pidgin English and Vietnamese that gradually became more Vietnamese than English. He was hard to understand, not because he spoke mostly Vietnamese—by now most of the Americans had some limited fluency in that language—but because his voice was flat and Vietnamese is a tonal language—meanings of sounds change with inflection. The Marines managed to understand anyway. "The people are afraid, very afraid. In nearly all of the time there has been war in Bun Hou and near Bun Hou the Vee Cee and the NVA have left the people alone. They have harangued the people and taxed them and stolen from them, but until the past week they have never killed them. Until the past week the only people of Bun Hou the Vee Cee and NVA killed, with few exceptions, were fay epps, those who bore arms against them. Four days ago they killed Pheet and his family. They killed the Hou Toung chief the day before that. They have killed a family in Hou Cau. They have burned down houses in Hou Dau. Now they attack the families of the fay epps. The fay epps are afraid now for their families; they must get them to safety. The men who have families are going to leave now; they are going to take their families to safety."

"They shouldn't do that," Burrison said. "Where is there safety?"

"If those men leave this compound with their families they are playing into the enemy's hands," Bell told him. "Those NVA out there probably want exactly that. They want to split us up. If they can hurt us inside Camp Apache, think of what they can do to those families if they catch them outside the wire."

"No," Vinh objected. He was one of the PFs with a family. "They will not attack us. They are not brave enough to attack two squads of fay epps. They are cowards who can only snipe at small patrols and murder unarmed women and children. They will not dare attack us." He shrugged. "We will come back when our families are safe. Then fay epp and Ma-deen work together. We will find and kill these cowards."

Burrison looked at Collard Green, a silent question: How many of the PFs leaving? The PF leader shook his head slightly. Half of the PFs in the platoon had families to

concern themselves with. "Only those with families will
go. Not all of them. My family and I will stay here."

"If you go," Burrison said to Vinh, "the Vee Cee will
attack Camp Apache while you are gone, when we are at
very low strength. When you come back, they will attack
and kill you."

Vinh shook his head adamantly. "They will not know;
they will not attack. We must go, take our families to
safety." A shout made him turn his head. One of the other
PFs shouted at him that they were ready. He stood up. "We
go now. When our families are safe, we will come back.
Maybe tomorrow, maybe the next day. Our families have to
be safe." He bowed to the Americans and left them. He
was shouting orders to the PFs who were going to escort
their families before he reached them. When they first took
shelter in Camp Apache, they made as many trips as they
had to to bring as much as they thought they would need
from their homes. Now that they were leaving, they took
only as much as they could carry in bundles slung over
their shoulders or balanced on yokes across their necks.
The PFs rigged litters to carry their dead. With four men to
each litter bearing an adult body and two carrying the one
with Le's body, there was only one armed escort who
wasn't burdened.

Wordlessly, the Marines and remaining PFs watched
them trudge eastward until they disappeared into the woods
south of Hou Dau hill. It was going to be a long, lonely
time until those fifteen men returned.

Zeitvogel stood at the western edge of the compound,
looking in the direction the mortar had fired from. He kept
his head pointed that way and shifted his eyes farther west
toward the ridge. After a moment he lifted his head and
looked full at it, then back at the trees where the mortar
had been and back again to the ridge. He nodded firmly to
himself and turned back to the command hootch.

"Bet I know where Mister Charlie's hanging his hat,"
the tall man said to the group of Marines he found there.

"Where?" Burrison asked.

Bell stared at him blankly; he was lost in his own dark thoughts.

Randall looked up at him expectantly.

"Mister Charlie's got to have an OP on the ridge. His camp is probably over there someplace that we can't see from here."

"What makes you think he's on the ridge?" Burrison asked.

"Think about it. They knew when we had company on Christmas and hit us just right. Two days later they had sniper teams in position to waste Storey and hit the Fast Talking Man." His expression didn't show anything, but secretly Zeitvogel was glad he now remembered his dead newby's name. "Two days after that, they had people in position to ambush Short Round's team. Today they hit Camp Apache when most of us were out, when they were sure they could hit the people."

Bell stared hard past Zeitvogel's shoulder. To a distant observer, he looked as if he were looking up at the taller man's face. "I'll bet you're right, Stilts. Let me think on this for a while."

Randall grinned at his squad leader. "You got to think about it, Jay Cee? Shee-it." He turned to Zeitvogel. "How come we're always ahead of him and he's got more stripes than we do?" He knew what the other fire team leader had to be thinking.

"How many stripes you got?" Zeitvogel looked down his nose at the short, husky corporal.

"Two." A deep, thinking V formed between Randall's eyebrows.

"So do I. How many's two and two?" Zeitvogel continued in the kind of tone he might use explaining things to a slow child.

"Four."

"How many's Jay Cee got?"

"Three."

"Who's got more stripes, us or him?"

Randall's brow smoothed, and he grinned. "Gonna get us some," he said, then his face turned serious. "Gonna get us some bad, gonna put those mo-dickers so deep in a hurt locker their mamas and papas gonna wish they never came here to fuck with the people."

Hempen stepped close between them and held his hand out palm up. "You ain't doing nothing without me."

Lewis glared at Hempen, then faced him from the other side of the corporals and slapped his hand on Hempen's wrist. They locked hands. "I'll be there to make sure you don't do anything too stupid, Short Round."

Zeitvogel and Randall slapped their hands on top of the other two.

"Seems to me I've seen this somewhere before," Robertson muttered, and shouldered his way into the group to add his hand.

Mazzucco had played too much basketball not to know what it meant. He joined them. Willard and Neissi crowded in as well.

Vega swallowed deeply. Where the fuck do they think they are, Texas Stadium? he wondered, then pushed in to add his hand.

Dodd shrugged. It didn't mean a damn thing, but at least he was going to be in good company when he died. He prayed a silent prayer, begging forgiveness for seeming to act like some kind of John Wayne, and joined hands with the rest.

Slover signaled his remaining mortar men to circle the others. They clasped hands around the group and hugged them all tight. "You find 'em and fix 'em, my men and my tube'll fuck 'em," he promised the riflemen.

Major Nghu drank a leisurely cup of tea and munched on a rice ball after his senior sergeant dispatched the mortar team. When he finished his snack, he returned to his observation post and watched patiently for the barrage to begin. His heart leaped for joy when he saw the first explosion inside the Marine compound; it raced with excitement when he watched the panic that ensued. The sight of people lying on the ground with their life's blood gushing from broken bodies warmed his soul. Less than an hour later his planning was rewarded by a line of people filing out of the main gate of Camp Apache, headed east. He rubbed his hands in glee. A little more, he told himself, only a little more, and I will let you die, Tango Niner. It was as solemn a promise as he could make. He returned to his camp.

The sergeant who was left watching through the glasses saw the Marines huddle, chest to shoulder, but paid it no mind. He thought they were clumping together like frightened cattle; it was nothing to report to his commander.

CHAPTER TWENTY-ONE

The Same Time, Heading East and North

Everybody was surprised when the helicopter taking Ruizique on the first leg of his trip home landed; it brought Captain Hasford out for an unexpected visit. He shook hands with Ruizique and wished him well. Then Ruizique threw his seabag in and climbed aboard. The prisoner was roughly thrown in after him and lay quietly on his stomach on the floor at Ruizique's feet. Bell shouted something at him, but Ruizique couldn't hear over the roar of the rotors. He could guess what the sergeant was saying, though. He nodded at him and flashed an uplifted thumb. As the bird lifted off, Ruizique placed a foot firmly on the prisoner's back between his bound arms. He looked at the crew chief and mouthed the word "Mine."

The crew chief looked at him blankly and shrugged, then turned to look out at the landscape, hands ready on his machine gun. The flight was short, only about fifteen minutes. Two MPs armed with Buck Rogers—looking rifles of a kind Ruizique hadn't seen before—somebody told him they were M-16s, the new rifle the Army had been using for a couple of years but was just now starting to get into the hands of Marines—met the helicopter and took the prisoner away. A warrant officer pointed out the battalion headquarters, a narrow, rambling wooden building that had open screens in the upper half of its walls, and told him to report to the gunnery sergeant in S-1, personnel.

Ruizique plodded across the dusty red earth to the HQ building. A Marine in clean, pressed utilities and spit-shined boots, with PFC chevrons on his collars, sat at a typewriter on a field desk just inside the door. He looked too well bathed to be a grunt, and his tan was too even for a man who spent any real time in the field. Ruizique looked around for someone who looked as if he might be the gunnery sergeant.

The PFC paused in his typing and looked leisurely at Ruizique. He saw a man with skin dark from spending too much time in the tropical sun and ground-in dirt from living too long without enough soap and hot water to scrub it out. His eyebrow lifted slightly at Ruizique's threadbare, though clean, uniform, which was many times patched, and his scuffed boots. He ignored the M-14 slung over this stranger's shoulder. "I help you with something, Private?" he asked imperiously. He was pissed off about having to work on New Year's Day and didn't like grunts anyway. What the hell, he'd demanded when told he had the duty, there's a truce on. Why should I go to work when there's a truce on? Because there's a goddamn war on, his section chief had told him. Truce or no truce, wars don't take holidays—you got the duty. He was grateful for the presence of this dumbass grunt to take it out on.

Ruizique didn't cooperate. He looked down at the clerk and decided this pogue wasn't worth bothering with; he didn't correct him about his rank. "I'm looking for the gunny."

"'Cher name and yer business." The PFC acted as if he was too busy to waste time on some dumbass grunt. He looked back at what he was typing but didn't start working the machine; he was waiting for an answer.

"Corporal Ruizique. I'm fresh in from the field, and I

was told to find the gunny. I'm going back to The World."

"Okay, so you're going back to The World," he said, annoyed. How come this crud got to go back to The World, and he had to stay in this stinking country, where he could only get ice cold beer and a movie a couple of times a week and the TV in his barracks didn't seem to work half of the time and the air conditioner was always on the blink? He looked up again and examined Ruizique's bare collars. "As a private," he snapped in what was meant to be an official-sounding voice. "Around here, you don't look like a corporal, they make you a private." That'll show him, the PFC thought.

Ruizique leaned forward, one fist resting on the desk next to the typewriter. Pogues did have a use, he was sure, but at the moment he couldn't think of one. "Don't give me any shit, PFC. I asked you a polite question; you *will* give me a polite answer."

The PFC looked into Ruizique's eyes and saw what he thought were the blank, flat eyes of a killer. Now the rifle this grunt had slung on his shoulder meant something more than just decoration. He swallowed and forgot about having the duty during the truce. "Ah, yeah, uh, Corporal, uh . . . Right through there." He pointed to a slatted fence deeper into the room. "Go through the gate. The gunny's desk is the last one on the right, right where he can eyeball everyone in this office." He watched Ruizique stand straight and look where he had pointed. He decided against warning this badass to get some chevrons on his collars if he wanted to keep his rank. Serve the son of a bitch right if he got busted, coming in here and acting like some bad-ass John Wayne or something. The gunny was a real hardass; he'd straighten this dumb grunt out most ricky-tick. He went back to his typing and swore a moment later; he'd made three typos and had to start the form all over again.

Ruizique headed deeper into the narrow building. It was wide enough to accommodate one desk on either side of a narrow aisle; only about a quarter of the desks were occupied. He brushed through the gate in the slatted fence and headed toward the far wall, his eyes on the lean, hard-looking man sitting at a desk with more space around it than the others had. He ignored the typing and paper-filing pogues he walked past; they pretended to ignore him.

"Gunny?" he asked when he reached the back desk. He didn't have to ask. The man wore his insignia on his collars, and there was a plate on his desk that gave his name, McGowen—the name was flanked by a Marine Corps emblem and the three up and two down of a gunnery sergeant's rank insignia.

Gunny McGowen looked up. His face was furrowed from a hard life spent in the field before he'd gotten this staff assignment, and his eyes were the eyes of a man who'd been in the shit and come out tougher. "Yeah?"

"I'm Corporal Ruizique. They told me to report to you."

The gunnery sergeant's eyes paused on Ruizique's collars on their way back to the papers on his desk. He shuffled a few and came up with one sheet. "Yeah, you're on it, all right," he said. "A CAP Marine, huh." A wry smile curved his mouth. "What CAP's doing out there is almost enough to make me wish I was still a grunt, instead of sitting at a desk. I'd kind a like to join you, get some. But they don't let gunnery sergeants go into the villes with you." He shook his head ruefully. Then he snapped at a Marine sitting at a nearby desk, "Schwartz, you got those cut CONUS orders yet?"

"Right here, Gunny," Schwartz said, and tapped a thick stack of papers on the corner of his desk.

"Give Ruizique here his, and dig out his SRB. Man's a short-timer, headed back to The World. Point him in the direction of transportation to Da Nang." He glanced at Ruizique again, then added, "And tell him where he can get some chevrons. Be a goddamn shame, a man be a combat NCO and get busted because some dumbfuck staff officer didn't like him not wearing his rank."

He turned again to Ruizique. "Corporal Schwartz'll take care of you. You'll be out of this shit in time to have evening chow in Da Nang. Probably be good, too, because of the holiday." He shook his head at the thought of a holiday meal in Da Nang. What was his Marine Corps coming to, coddling pogues this way while the grunts were in the field, eating C-rations? And he'd spent too many years as a grunt himself to let some rear-area pogue fuck with one without him giving the man a fighting chance, especially not getting screwed by some dipshit boot-brown bar without combat experience who was pissed off because he had the duty on a holiday. Shit, the grunts didn't have today off. Why should the pogues? "Pin some stripes on your shirt if you want to keep them."

"Thanks, Gunny." Ruizique went to Schwartz, who handed him a stapled sheaf of paper—his travel-and-transfer orders. Schwartz took a copy of the orders himself, open to the page with Ruizique's name and service number, and pawed through a wooden horizontal file cabinet for a couple of minutes until he came up with a heavy manila file folder—Ruizique's SRB, service record book. Schwartz tried not to let the gunnery sergeant see him glance in his direction—he knew it was pointless; the gunny had eyes in the back of his head, and probably the top and sides, too, and never missed anything that happened in his shop—as he opened a drawer in his desk and pulled something out. "Take these," he said. "I got more where they came from, and you probably can't find any place around here right now where you can get any."

Ruizique took the pair of metal corporal's chevrons along with the SRB. "Thanks, pano. Maybe you aren't too bad for a pogue," he said with a friendly smile. Schwartz smiled back. Ruizique pinned the chevrons on his collars while the clerk gave him directions to the helipad, where a bird would be heading to Da Nang sometime within the next hour. "Thanks, Gunny," he said before leaving. McGowen waved a negligent hand at him while not seeming to look up.

The directions were good, and Ruizique didn't get lost on his way to the helipad. Three other Marines rotating out of country were already there, waiting next to a UH-34, the ubiquitous workhorse helicopter of the Marine Corps. Ruizique let the others talk among themselves as much as they wanted; he kept to himself, brooding about the job he had left undone. After a while the copilot and crew chief came along and inspected their aircraft. The pilot joined them, and they went through the preflight warm-up and checkout. By now five more Marines had joined the group waiting for a ride into Da Nang. The crew chief looked at the nine waiting men and the seabags some of them had. He spread the fingers of one hand and held up one finger of the other; his bird would only take six of them.

Ruizique slipped to the rear of the waiting group. Maybe if he missed his Freedom Bird he could go back to Tango Niner for another week or two, help make Charlie stop fucking with the people. Then he could leave with a clear conscience.

The crew chief looked at the nine Marines more carefully and pointed at three of them to wait. They weren't carrying manila folders; five of the other six had seabags. He figured the three he pointed out were headed for R&R. The five with seabags were probably on their way back to The World; he'd take them.

Not long after that the helicopter touched down in Da Nang close to a Marine administrative area. A staff sergeant met the group, sent the one headed for R&R in one direction and made the other five get into two ranks. "Any time three or more Marines go anywhere together, the senior man gets the others into a formation and marches them," he explained between the screams of jets on the nearby airfield. His was the barking voice of a career staff NCO. He had them balance their seabags on their left shoulders and marched them to a clapboard building, where he had them stack their rifles—the weapons didn't belong to them anymore. Then he handed them over to another staff sergeant and two lance corporals for initial processing.

Ruizique held back behind the others. They crowded forward, all eager to be done with whatever had to be done now so they could head to geedunks and clubs and eat and drink—or, better yet, get liberty passes for Da Nang city, find whores, and fuck their brains out. Until the staff sergeant had to order them into a line. Ruizique quietly got on the end of the line. He was trying to figure a way he could return to Tango Niner for another week or two. How soon did his plane leave? The shortest time he could extend his tour for was ninety days. What he needed to do wouldn't take that long. He didn't need to extend for that long; he only needed a week or two. He had that much time left in his enlistment. This first-step processing didn't take long; it seemed like only a couple of minutes before Ruizique sat in a chair at the side of the staff sergeant's desk.

The staff sergeant compared Ruizique's face with the photo on his ID card to verify his identity, scanned his orders, and riffled through a thin stack of papers on his desk until he found what he was looking for. Inside the building, the jets on the airfield weren't as loud and didn't interrupt conversation as much as they did outside. "You leave on Pan Am flight oh eighteen on eleven January," the staff sergeant said, and sighed. He had sighed just like that four other times already with this group. How come they never sent him anyone who was leaving today? he asked himself. "That means I got to assign you to a transient barracks and to casual company. Then I got to keep track of your ass for the next ten days and make sure you get on that Freedom Bird in one piece." He grimaced and shook his head.

"The eleventh! You mean I'm not going today?"

"You must be hard of hearing, because I know I didn't mumble," the staff sergeant growled. "That's what I said."

Ruizique leaned back in the chair and thought furiously. "Staff Sergeant," he suddenly said, earnestness in his eyes, "what happens if you don't assign me to a transient barracks? I mean, what if I have something I want to do for a few days? I promise to be right here or wherever else you say at oh eight hundred sharp on the eleventh."

The staff sergeant studied him for a long moment before

saying, "You've been out in the field a long time, haven't you?"

Ruizique nodded. "I had R and R in November. I've been in a CAP since September and was on battalion operations before that." He rolled his eyes up in thought. "Six months ago my company had perimeter duty guarding the Hawk battery on Red Hill at Chu Lai. That was the last time I was out of the field. Except for R and R."

The staff sergeant kept his eyes pointed at Ruizique, but he wasn't really looking at him; he was pondering the situation. A lot of grunts asked if there was some way they could skate these last few days in-country, and he usually told them no. But he had been at a New Year's Eve party the night before, and his hangover was mild enough that he felt mellow instead of hardass. "You come through Da Nang on your way to R and R?" he asked.

Ruizique nodded again. "And on my way back, too."

"Anybody grab your ass for any shit details yet?"

"No."

The staff sergeant unfocused his eyes past Ruizique's shoulder and said slowly, as though to himself, "Probably found yourself a little mama-san when you were here." Ruizique didn't deny it. The staff sergeant leaned his elbows on his desk and became more businesslike. "Tell you what I'm going to do, Corporal. I'm going to mark you down as assigned to a transient barracks and to casual company—they're real casual around there—" A smile crinkled one side of his mouth at the wordplay. "—about holding roll calls. I'll file the carbon here, but the original will be lost on its way to casual company. That way, if you don't show up in the front of this office at oh eight hundred on the eleventh, my ass is covered. You're UA and it's on you." *UA* is "Unauthorized Absence," an offense similar to, but somewhat less than, AWOL. "If no one's grabbed you for a shit detail yet, they won't miss you." He smiled and finished with "Some grunts voluntarily extend their tours here, Corporal. If you miss that formation, your tour will be extended for you, but I don't think you want to spend six months at LBJ." Long Binh Jail, the notorious Army stockade outside Saigon, was rumored to be worse than any brig the Marines ran, and the Marine brigs were supposed to be the toughest in the Western world.

"I will be here, Staff Sergeant," Ruizique promised. "Where can I stow my seabag?"

The staff sergeant told him where to put the seabag and gave him directions on how to get into Da Nang city. Ruizique stored the seabag and went in a direction different from the way to the city. He felt naked without his rifle and was glad he'd brought a knife in his seabag. He had the knife in its scabbard stuck inside his shirt—it wouldn't do to have some junior officer or an MP see the knife and confiscate it. He watched the sky for a moment and saw most of the incoming helicopters seemed to be headed in the same direction.

The Marble Mountain Helicopter Facility was across the Song Han River—better known to the Americans as the Da Nang River—from the main base at Da Nang. Ruizique skirted the airfield; the roar of jets constantly taking off and landing numbed his ears. On the other side of the airstrip, he headed in the direction the helicopters were going. Sampans poled up and down the waterway. Eventually Ruizique saw one close enough to the bank he was able to hail it.

"*Chao, ong,*" he called out. "Hello, sir."

The Vietnamese poling the boat looked at him with considerable surprise; it wasn't that often one of these foreign giants addressed a man politely.

"*Lai day.* Come here."

It is a strange accent, the boatman thought. It sounds like a country dialect. He poled closer to shore.

Ruizique squatted on the bank and talked with the boatman; they used a few words of Vietnamese, some English, a couple bastardized French, a lot of sign language. In the end the boatman agreed to ferry the Marine across the river for one hundred piasters, less than one dollar American. Normally the boatman would have charged more for such a service, but this American was polite and had taken the trouble to learn a few words of his language, so he should not be taken too much advantage of. But still, it was a good price for the boatman—he would only have charged a Vietnamese a few dong.

Ruizique wandered along the helicopter flight line when he reached it. Every time he saw a bird that didn't look too polished, he stopped and talked to the Marines working on it. He didn't bother with the really clean ones, because he figured they were command and control, battalion commanders' helicopters, or were used to ferry staff. A C-and-C or staff bird wouldn't do for him.

"Yeah, we're headed out that way," the crew chief of a med-evac helicopter finally told him. "That battalion has a company in contact with the bad guys. They want someone standing by close for when they need us." He didn't say "if"; he knew when a company was in contact with the bad guys they were going to need a med-evac. "You must be on your way back from R and R and can't wait to rejoin your buddies and tell them about all the sideways nookie you got, right?"

Ruizique said something noncommittal that sounded like yes.

"Stand by." The crew chief glanced at his watch. "We're supposed to leave in about one zero. If the docs and the pilot are here in time, we will." He shook his head at the corpsmen and officers who couldn't be counted on to be where they were supposed to be when they were supposed to be there.

The pilot and corpsmen were on time despite the crew chief's misgivings, and the bird lifted off. It was on its approach to the battalion combat base when it got a call to go to collect wounded Marines. First it took time to hover long enough to let Ruizique jump down ten feet to the ground. He asked someone for directions and headed straight for the mess hall. He went to the mess hall only in part because he hadn't eaten since morning chow and it was now mid-afternoon. Mainly he went to the mess hall

because that was where he could find out when and where
to catch the flight for the next leg of his journey. He got the
information and had time to wolf down a sandwich and
gulp a glass of reconstructed milk and half a cup of real
coffee before he headed back to the helipad. This time he
didn't walk; he rode in a Jeep that carried four five-gallon
insulated food containers. He helped load the containers on
the helicopter and climbed aboard.

Fifteen minutes later he jumped off the helicopter and
dashed out from under its whirring rotors. "Hi, guys," he
said to a very surprised Sergeant Bell and Lieutenant Burrison.

CHAPTER TWENTY-TWO

New Year's Night

They held a council of war over evening chow, those twenty-one Marines and fourteen PFs who were left. Bell had figured out on his own the basics of what Zeitvogel and Randall knew they were going to, had to do. He dropped enough hints to Burrison that the lieutenant quickly picked up on it and thought it was his own idea. Burrison asked the three fire team leaders if it was all right with them, if they didn't think it was maybe too dangerous. Randall and Zeitvogel shot looks at Bell that said, "Who's he kidding?" Ruizique barely smiled; he was going to do it anyway—with or without authorization.

"Scrappy," Zeitvogel said, a twinkle in his eye, "we got a goddamn truce on. Do you really think going on a camp-out in our own little village here will have any danger to-night?"

Randall snorted. "Where the fuck you been, Stilts?" he said. "After what Charlie did today, you really think he got the word on the truce?" None of them doubted their foe knew about the truce; they all thought Major Nghu was going to ignore it.

"Little bro——" Zeitvogel started, but Randall interrupted him.

"That's the fucking problem with all you too tall dudes," Randall said, flexing his weightlifter's shoulders. "You think everybody else is too small."

"Next to me you are."

"Want to compare shoulders?"

"Shitcan the grab-assing, people," Bell said sharply enough that the two corporals shut up and looked at him in consternation.

They continued with the business at hand and finally decided on five four-man killer teams. A little deception was necessary, in the possible—they now thought it was probable—chance someone was watching them through high-power glasses. That would leave fifteen men to hold Camp Apache overnight—a very normal number to have in the compound at night.

One eight-man team—four Marines and four PFs— would leave through the back gate shortly before nightfall and head southeast, as though they were headed toward Hou Cau, until they were under cover of the trees. The others would leave in one group after dark.

Randall drew the first patrol. Once under the trees along the river, his patrol would take a hard right and head west until they were about halfway to the ridge. Zeitvogel had command of the larger, later group to leave via the main gate. They were going to head to Hou Ky but cut into the scrub before reaching it. They also would go about halfway to the western ridge. Nobody was going to come back to Camp Apache until the mission was accomplished—or Camp Apache was in danger of being overrun.

"Let's get this show on the road," Randall said a little later. "It's time to tango. Tonight we're going to find those bad little bastards and give them some of their own."

Huynh, Tho, and Chi rose from the cot they sat on side by side and tittered nervously.

Huu nodded imperceptibly from the entrance to the tent and looked at Lewis.

Lewis balled his fists in front of his face and twisted. He nodded and released his mustache—its left end pointed down and out at a rakish angle, and its right swooped in a curlicue. The Chieu Hoi could take the point. Lewis would be right behind the former Vietcong. If there was any treachery, he'd make sure Huu was the first one to die.

Vega tried not to look as nervous as he felt. What they were doing felt too much like both an ambush and a listening post, but it was too damn small to be a good ambush, and he'd always hated night-long listening posts, because there were never enough men in them to put up a successful fight if the bad guys came along.

Dodd stood impassive, ready to go when ordered. He was prepared mentally and, he hoped, spiritually to meet his fate. He certainly hoped he hadn't offended the God his parents and aunts and uncles prayed to, or any other gods, with his minor show of bravado earlier, clamping his hand on top of the others. He didn't want to suffer much when he died his inevitable combat death.

"Huu, go," Randall said.

Huu stepped out of the tent, closely followed by Lewis. Huynh came next, then Randall, Tho, Dodd, and Chi. Vega nervously brought up the rear.

Burrison, Bell, and Slover stood near the back gate to wish them good hunting. Zeitvogel was elsewhere preparing his own men for their night out.

"See you tomorrow," Randall said.

The others grunted or made other nonword noises. Except for Dodd, who knew there was no luck for him, not since he'd been drafted into the Marines. The Marines? What on earth was he doing in the Marines, a nice, pudgy suburban kid like him who should have been an accountant or a used-car salesman or something? Vega hoped there would be a tomorrow. Maybe there would be. Randall was sometimes too moody, and Lewis was too damn gung ho, but they both must know what they were doing—or else they wouldn't have survived so long doing the kind of things they did.

The patrol stretched itself out moving down the hill, each man going slower than the man in front of him until there was an interval of ten meters between them.

Huu looked back at Randall when the sun was halfway behind the ridge. They hadn't reached the river border trees yet. Did Randall want them to continue in the same direction? He did. Huu kept going southwest. He would intersect the band of trees halfway to Hou Cau. They proceeded on cat's feet and listened to the evening change of sounds from day animals, insects, and birds to the sounds of night dwellers—sound changes that didn't take place near them; they were making too much noise of their own, startling the quieting down day fauna into abrupt silence, holding up the cries of the night fauna. Everything sounded normal. The stars came out and gave plenty of light for them to see their way in the open area the patrol traversed. Somehow they felt more exposed under the stars than they had with the sun still out.

They reached the deeper darkness under the trees, and the column automatically closed up. There was no way they could maintain a ten-meter interval in the near black under these thick trees. Huu didn't bother to double-check with Randall now; the time for changing plans was when the sun went down. He found the main trail that paralleled the river a few meters from its bank, and turned right. The next question wouldn't come until time to turn off the well-used path—unless they met someone coming from the other direction. Huu walked faster along the trail than most Americans would walking point at night; he felt confident the Marines and PFs still owned the night in Bun Hou, regardless of the morning sniper fire they'd recently received. And the rest of the enemy action, day or night, had all been directed at people other than Tango Niner. The NVA in the area wouldn't be using the trails in Bun Hou this early in the evening; he was positive of that. A hole of silence in the night noises surrounded them and traveled along with them, but it didn't matter, not yet.

Lewis was perturbed. He was accustomed to being on point himself, where he could let his mind go blank of all conscious thought, let his senses absorb the sights, sounds, smells of night, and funnel the data to some backwater of his mind, and where it could be analyzed. Ever since he'd discovered this sixth sense, which told him somebody was near, and had learned not to try to control it, he'd never been wrong. At any rate, every time his sixth sense told him someone was there, someone was; no one had ever fired at him or his patrol when his sixth sense hadn't warned him of the stranger's presence. His sixth sense also worked when he wasn't on point, when he could still let his mind go blank with only a small portion of it making sure he was following the man to his front. But now he had to keep a sharp eye on Huu. He didn't fully trust him; he thought the Chieu Hoi should have some information about what was happening out here.

He knew intellectually he should trust Huu; his reason for having turned was good enough. The Marines had demonstrated their basic humanity by treating a bullet wound in his leg without turning him over to the ARVNs; the VC had demonstrated their basic inhumanity by ruthlessly attacking Hou Cau while a Revolutionary Development team had been visiting. Then Huu had changed sides on the condition he be a Kit Carson scout for Tango Niner, as though Tango Niner, with all its PFs, needed one. For his first job, he told the Americans about a secret Vietcong communications center in the hills two days march west of Camp Apache. He had led a reconnaissance there, and after that had led Tango Niner on an assault that had completely wiped out that communications center.

Since then things in Bun Hou village had been quiet—until Christmas Day. Lewis wondered if they were being set up and if Huu was a diversion to distract them while Charlie got ready for some big hit against the Marines. But if that was the case, why had Huu led them to the communications center? Lewis knew the VC base had been real and now was gone because he had helped destroy it. Still, he felt queasy about trusting a man who so recently had been on the other side and more than willing to kill him.

Lewis was paying so much attention to Huu, he wasn't sure his sixth sense would work if they were being led into a trap. But how could Huu do that? What they were doing was not part of any pattern Tango Niner might have established in their nightly activities, and there was no way Huu could have gotten word to anybody about their plans. Lewis shook his head and scowled at himself, told himself to stop worrying about it; Huu wasn't leading them into a trap.

It was a quiet night, with nothing but the passing of the eight men in this patrol to disturb the buzzing, whirring, and chirruping of the night insects, the squawks and cries of night-hunting birds. An occasional surface-feeding fish in the river jumped for a fat insect that wouldn't settle on the water, adding its falling plop to the background noise. There was no wind; the air moved in vagrant wifts rather than a steady breeze. The gentle, almost unnoticeable air currents brought the smell of decaying leaves, the odor of human and animal waste, the rancid aromas of river and land life. Nobody noticed the smells; even the American with the least amount of time in the country had been there long enough to have become accustomed to the aromas. The dark under the trees was so complete, if it hadn't been for the occasional glimpse they had between the trees on their left of light reflecting off the river, they might have been in a tunnel. The big trees muffled sounds.

An hour after turning onto the main path, Randall passed word for the point to stop. They waited while he radioed in his report that they were at the breakaway point and proceeding. Proceeding: it was a good word in this context. If the NVA were monitoring Tango Niner's radio frequency, proceeding could mean heading to the next check point, going into an ambush site, or whatever. They wouldn't expect the eight-man patrol to do what it did next —they hoped.

Randall tapped Vega, Huynh, and Tho on their shoulders and pointed to the riverbank. They nodded and settled by the water's edge to await his return.

He then led Lewis, Dodd, Huu, and Chi away from the river to a convenient clump of thicker brush in the scrub forest beyond the band of thick trees that bordered the river, some two hundred meters north of where the others waited for him. Then he returned.

Randall set Vega and Tho to watch the trail; it was less than ten meters from the water at that point. He sat with his back against a tree, almost in arm's reach of the riverbank. Huynh sat nearby. They had the river and the trail covered. His men were set. Now all they had to do was wait: the infantryman's curse. He radioed a terse "Engine, Engine. Boxcars four and five on line." The radio crackled back at him when Swarnes broke squelch and said, "Roger."

An hour after sunset, Zeitvogel raised his right hand to his shoulder and dropped it, pointing one long finger at his favorite PF, the tiny man they called Pee Wee. Pee Wee saw the pointing finger, a finger that sometimes looked as if it were the size of his whole hand, and nodded. He stepped through the main gate and led the column of six Marines and six PFs down the hill. He turned left and walked off the trail leading to Hou Ky, paralleling it a few meters to the right. The little man felt uncomfortable; Zeitvogel had made him give his BAR to one of the PFs staying at Camp Apache and carry a captured AK-47 in its place. The giant American had explained that the camp needed the heavy fire power from the big automatic rifle, that the AK provided more than they would need for their mission. Privately, Pee Wee thought the real reason was Zeitvogel didn't think he could handle the big weapon, the automatic, which was almost as long as he was tall. He tried to feel resentful about this seeming lack of trust in him, but he trusted the huge Marine too much and knew he was trusted in return, so he briefly turned his annoyance in a different direction.

He wondered why, on night patrols, the Marines never walked on the trail leading to Hou Ky, a trail that went through open land and was under constant observation, but walked on trails under the heavy band of trees along the river, trails that could not be seen from Camp Apache. He understood the reason for not walking on trails was the trails could be booby-trapped, but nobody would know where to put a booby trap off a trail. It hadn't occurred to any of the Marines to explain to the PFs that they didn't walk on this trail in the hope that an enemy would see them not walking on it and think they avoided paths all over the village and, therefore, not bother setting booby traps. Maybe the Marines' idea worked; they rarely encountered booby traps.

They entered the thin forest north of the path to Hou Ky, but didn't stay north of the path for long. When Pee Wee estimated he had gone fifty meters into the trees, he turned sharply left and soon crossed the path. He kept going another hundred meters and turned sharply right. It seemed they walked through an enchanted landscape; the ground was level, but the trees and bushes created a nocturnal illusion of a violently rocking and rolling earth, intersected by a maze of faint foot and animal paths. Starlight glinted off small leaves, and made them seem to silently tinkle; the softly moving air currents brought reflecting leaves together, pushed them apart, gave the image of silent crystalline shattering. The sounds and aromas in this northern reach of the scrub forest were the same as near the river, except the smell of the river was distant, and there were no plopping fish. The sounds, fragmented by the multitude of bushes and small trees, came at them from confusing and unexpected directions.

When Pee Wee thought they had gone far enough, he stopped and knelt, looking and listening to his front.

Zeitvogel knelt at his pointman's side, bent low, and still towered over him. The tall Marine looked this way and that, satisfied they had gone far enough—he knew where they were. He said a few quiet words into his radio, let

Camp Apache know he was splitting his men into their night-watch positions. A short distance ahead and to the right was a well-concealed rise with a defile behind it where a waiting man could safely watch the trail from a finger ridge where the long hill on the west formed a gentle path down from the hills to the Song Du Ong flood plain.

He signaled the rest to wait for him and led Ruizique, Neissi, Vien, and George to the rise to cover the trail. It was a continuation of the same trail that ran from Hou Dau to Hou Ky. He rejoined the rest of his men and led them south. Two hundred and fifty meters south, he stopped and told Mazzucco, Pee Wee, and Butter Bar to wait for him. Farther south, he stationed Hempen, Robertson, Hien, and Doung at the edge of a clearing. Alone, he flitted back through the scrub growth, impossibly ghostlike for so tall a man. He was back in the midst of the others before they realized he was close. His smile could be clearly read in the night by Mazzucco, a smile that shone with the shine of what looked like too many teeth. I'm a night fighter, Homeboy, his smile seemed to say. Stick with me, and when you grow up you can do the same. He stationed his team overlooking a place where several tracks came together, merged, crossed, and set them in place to watch this busy intersection. Then he murmured a few soft words into his radio.

The next step was up to Mister Charlie.

CHAPTER TWENTY-THREE

January 2, 1967, Dawn

The night seemed endless to the twenty men waiting in the brush west of Camp Apache. Inside the compound, at least the twelve men on the perimeter had periodic comm checks to make and were visited occasionally by Bell or Burrison to break up the monotony of the long night. In the bush all they had to do was wait; only Randall, Zeitvogel, Ruizique, and the men who relieved them had radios to make hourly reports. To ease the tedium and subjectively shorten the time, they took turns sleeping, one man awake, one man dozing, in two-hour shifts. It wasn't a lot, but anything that broke up the long, interminable night was better than nothing. Randall and Huynh had the boat lights of the fishermen on the river to look at during the long long night—it helped them. Now and again during the night an occasional dog barked somewhere. None of the barks were the barks of dogs disturbed by strangers intruding on their territories; they were the bored barks of dogs who had slept enough for the moment and called out to see if anybody was awake to keep them company for a while.

Eventually the blackness overhead lightened into a

darker-than-dark gray, and the stars blinked out, first one by one, then whole bunches at a time, as that predawn gray slowly lightened to a washed-out gray-blue. The buzzing of night insects and cries of nocturnal hunting birds was interrupted by the shriek of a day bird sentry, the first of its flock to respond to the warming rays of the rising sun. Somewhere else, a territorial bird started awake and cried out its presence, warning off all rival birds. Another territory hoarder answered with its keep-away-from-me-too. A second flock sentry woke its brothers and sisters and aunts and uncles and nieces and nephews. A cacophony erupted as the day birds greeted the dawn and one another and warned rivals off. The night fliers dropped into trees and bushes and ground burrows, called their good-days, and settled in to sleep until time to hunt again. A fuk-yoo lizard shouted out its first hunting cry, and the cicadas stilled their vibrations and hunkered down for their sleep. The sounds changed totally with the arrival of life's day shift and departure of its night shift. Light filtered down through the trees, allowing night-blind eyes to see as far as the trees allowed. In the scrub, a thin, cloying dust seemed to hover in the air, a dust not noticed during the endless night.

The ambush units had an informational call from Swarnes at 7:00 A.M. "Boxcars, all Boxcars, this is the Engineer, Engineer," Swarnes said over the radio. "Count off, Boxcars. Over."

"Boxcar Two. Go," Zeitvogel said, his voice husky from too long silence.

"Boxcar Five. Yours," Randall responded, equally thick-voiced.

"Boxcar One. Over," Ruizique answered. His voice was low but clear.

Usually Zeitvogel was call sign one, Randall was two, Ruizique three. Because there were five positions on a line this night and morning, they were numbered from north to south.

"Boxcars, the New Year's truce is over as of this moment. You are no longer under any they-must-fire-first constraints. Do you understand? Over."

"Two, roger." Zeitvogel's voice snapped with excitement.

"Five, gotcha." Randall's voice crackled.

"One, I understand." There was a distinct pop in Ruizique's tone.

Regardless of what their call sign numbers were, they still spoke in their usual order. And as for any NVA eavesdroppers, hey, they knew the truce was over anyway.

"Engineer, out."

The excitement didn't last long. They were still just sitting out there, waiting. So they sat or lay quietly, as motionless as they could, through a morning that promised to be as long as the night had been. Being able to see gave them something very minor to focus their attention on and cut the heaviness of the boredom, but that was countered by the mounting hunger—none of them had brought food. It wasn't an oversight; they'd left food behind deliberately. It wouldn't do to have a passing enemy hear the scraping of a John Wayne can opener on a C-ration can or be alerted by the smell of food where they didn't expect anybody to be waiting for them. Wait and wait some more—that was all they could do until somebody came to them or someone else decided there wasn't any point in them waiting any longer. Goddamn, but sometimes being a mud Marine sucked.

Major Nghu was at his hillside observation post well before dawn. Long before he could see anything through his binoculars, he was listening for a distant gunshot that would tell him one of his snipers had just reduced Tango Niner's numbers by one more, had driven another nail into the coffin he was burying the imperialists' morale in. It caused him no particular concern that he didn't hear a gunshot. That only meant none of the patrols returning to the small hilltop encampment had passed close enough to any of his sniper teams. No problem. Another patrol would most likely return to the hill at dawn; it would be vulnerable from a much greater distance and could not avoid losing a man.

From his high vantage point he saw the eastern sky lightening before the day animals on the plain did; he watched the sun begin its rise before the plains fauna woke. Once the sun touched the top of the running-dog Marines' hill, he shoved his hawk nose between the eyepieces of his binoculars and observed it. A few men flitted from the perimeter trench to the bunkers, but not many, maybe a half dozen, maybe fewer. He swept his view from side to side, deeper and closer. He saw no patrol return. He watched patiently for half an hour without seeing anybody move on the plain. On the hilltop he watched men go from bunker to trench, duck down out of sight, arise and go back to the bunkers. He suspected the men he saw go back were not the same he saw come out but wasn't certain. If they were the same, Camp Apache was only defended by a half-dozen men; the rest were out in the forest somewhere. But that did not seem likely. He raised his face from the binoculars and wondered if none of the Marines were out, if all of Camp Apache's complement was inside its defenses.

Yes. He nodded to himself. It was entirely possible the patrol that had gone out to the southeast before sunset had returned early, before any of his snipers had reached that part of the flatland, and that no others had gone out after dark. But that would be very unlike these Americans and their lackeys. The North Vietnamese officer knew his tactics were having their effect on the Popular Forces traitors, but he wasn't certain the American invaders were yet properly affected. He looked at his watch. It was well past time for the last patrol to return to base. Another look through the binoculars and he was almost convinced the cowardly foreigners and their few remaining traitors had set a trap. All right, he decided, let them bait their trap with only a few men visible while all the others were hidden. Let them think he thought now was a bad time to do anything because most of them lay in wait elsewhere. Major Nghu would not be fooled; he knew they were all waiting, hoping he would launch an attack against their encampment, thinking he thought only a few men were manning it while most of them stayed hidden in its perimeter trench. A master tactician was impossible to fool.

Major Nghu stood and snapped an order at a sergeant, the same sergeant who had led the mortar team the day before, the team that had wreaked so much havoc on the families of the PFs. A reward for this sergeant was to let him watch through the binoculars and see the discomfort his actions had wrought on the hill. He strode rapidly to his camp to dispatch a runner with orders for his sniper teams —the men in his sniper teams were all good at what they did, well-disciplined soldiers. He knew they were all waiting for their targets that hadn't come and would all wait until they had new orders. Or until two hours after dawn. He now sent them new orders: to each fire one shot at the hill's defenders, each team to make one kill, then return. He chortled, pleased with himself for having seen through the Americans' subterfuge. A pot of tea would taste very good right now, along with a few dried fish and a rice ball to break his fast.

Zeitvogel sat cross-legged, his back leaning against two young trees growing too close together for both of them to reach their full height. If the trees to his front had been thinner, he could have seen the long hill that made the Song Du Ong's western horizon. He rotated his shoulders and flexed-relaxed-flexed his back to ease his upper body stiffness. He bunched his thigh and calf muscles, doubled and relaxed his hands for the same reason. Behind him were several thick bushes that effectively screened him from view from his rear. Close to one side was a thinner bush that he could see through but effectively shielded him from sight. A similar bush was between him and the bare ground where the many tracks came together. On his right side, an isolated, unexpected strand of bamboo formed a wall that couldn't be seen through. Mazzucco lay prone next to the bamboo, his left hand under the rifle extended in front of him, his right resting on its pistol grip, his chin on his right hand. Neither man wore his cartridge belt. Pee Wee and Butter Bar were at the other side of the thick bush behind them, lying underneath them, watching in the direction of Camp Apache.

"I'm bored, Stilts," Mazzucco said in a low voice. "Bored and hungry. You bring a book with you?" Bored and trying to find something, anything, that would relieve the boredom for a moment or two.

"When'd you learn how to read, Homeboy?" Zeitvogel answered in an equally low voice. He didn't look at his companion but kept his eyes on the area they were covering.

"Shit, when'd I learn how to read," Mazzucco said, smiling. He paused a beat or two and said, "Don't want to read it. I'm part billy goat. Gonna eat the fucker." He didn't look at the other man.

Zeitvogel snorted softly. "Pretend that's a nudist beach out there and we're waiting for some naked girls to show up. That'll cure your boredom."

"That's an idea. Ever see one?"

"Nudist beach? Nah."

"No, not a nudist beach, a naked girl."

Zeitvogel shot a look at him. "Go ahead. Keep that up, Homeboy. You're aching for a hurting, saying that kind of shit. Ask the mothers of my children, did I ever see a naked girl." He snorted again.

Mazzucco thought hard for a moment, looking for something more to say that wouldn't make his fire team leader laugh out loud and compromise their position if somebody was out there. It had to be something that wouldn't piss him off, either. Suddenly he saw something black flit through the trees on the other side of the clearing with the trails. He shifted both arms a couple of inches and rested his cheek against the thumb of his right hand, trying to see it again and aim his rifle at it at the same time.

Zeitvogel saw Mazzucco's movement in the corner of his eye and rolled onto his knees, leaned forward with his left hand supporting his torso, his rifle gripped in his right. Now he saw it, too.

A man in peasant pajamas entered the clearing, following one of the game tracks. He wore a military-looking hat on his head and carried an AK-47 slung on his shoulder. His angle was going to bring him within ten feet of where the Marines hid.

Zeitvogel laid his rifle down and motioned to Mazzucco. He tapped his own chest and pointed rapidly out. Then he pointed at Mazzucco and held his hand as though he held a rifle to his shoulder. I'm going to jump him, his gestures said. You cover me in case I judge it wrong. Mazzucco nodded and sighed on the man. Zeitvogel uncrossed his ankles and rose into a sprinter's stance. He picked the place the man had to be at when he made his spring and tensed. The man abruptly stopped a foot short of that spot and turned his head in the direction of the hidden Marines; the radio had made a noise, Swarnes calling to tell the patrols to continue sitting tight.

No time now to wait for the man to get into position; he was already reaching to unsling his rifle. Zeitvogel plunged outward from his tight crouch, and his reaching hands were more than halfway to the NVA messenger before his feet left their starting point.

The NVA was a professional soldier, a good one. He didn't shout or cry out when he saw the strained black face that looked as if it belonged to a demon burst through the bush he was staring at. He pivoted and stepped back and tried to unsling his rifle to bring it to bear on this man, who he knew must be the very tall American. But Zeitvogel was too close; the soldier had his weapon in his right hand but didn't have enough time to point it before he reached him. So he spun to the side to avoid the onrushing American. The northerner didn't allow for the length of Zeitvogel's arms; the tall man swept one out and slammed a huge fist against the side of his head as his body thrust through the spot he'd aimed at.

The blow staggered the soldier, sent him sprawling to the ground, but he was still a good soldier; he didn't drop his rifle. He was scrambling away, far enough to turn and drop on his attacker, when Zeitvogel pounced a second time and landed with all his weight and force in the middle of the much smaller man's back. He flicked out one hand to knock the rifle away from him and slapped the other on his mouth to keep him from crying out to any of his companions who might be close. Then the hand that knocked the rifle away grabbed the soldier's arm and yanked it far up his back, almost dislocating the shoulder.

A tiny yelp of pain burped from the soldier's throat, then he silently tried to twist out of Zeitvogel's grasp. He stopped struggling when Mazzucco droped to his knees and poked him in the face with the muzzle of his rifle. The blow drew blood from his forehead.

Zeitvogel kept the pressure on the arm he held tight and sat up, straddling his prisoner. His chest heaved as he drew breath to calm himself. He used his free hand to work his belt free of his trousers, then grabbed his prisoner's other hand and jerked it up and tied the two wrists together with his belt. When the man was secure, he put his hands on his knees and leaned his weight on them. He looked at Mazzucco.

"When this fucker started to turn his weapon on me, why the fuck didn't you blow his young ass away?" he demanded.

"You should have seen yourself, Stilts," Mazzucco said, awed by the struggle. "You looked like the Spiderman. You were about to be all over his young ass like white on rice." He shook his head. "You were so goddamn fast I knew he wouldn't be able to shoot before you reached him, and you looked so big I didn't think I could hit him without the bullet going through you first."

Zeitvogel looked at him hard for a moment, then sucked a last, deep breath into his chest. "Right," he said. "Use your belt to tie his legs, then stick something in his mouth." He stayed on the prisoner, pinning him to the ground, until Mazzucco had his legs secured. Then he went to his radio to report the capture.

"As long as you can keep him quiet, stay in position," Burrison ordered after getting the report. "Let's see if any of his buddies come looking for him. Engineer, out."

Zeitvogel grunted. He wasn't thrilled with the order, but it could work—as long as the Marines and PFs kept alert and not too many of the bad guy's buddies came around to find out what happened to him.

Major Nghu waited long enough for his runner to reach the sniper teams around Camp Apache and returned to his observation post. He wanted to be watching when his snipers brought down the imperialist defenders, showed them they could not fake him out, punished them for what they were trying to do to him. No matter what their trickery, he would hurt them as he wanted to hurt them. He settled down with his nose between the eyepieces and watched the camp. Still he saw no more than a half-dozen men on the hilltop, all going between the bunkers and perimeter trench. Soon he would see them start to fall. His lips bent in a caricature of a smile.

Time passed. Major Nghu lifted his face away from the binoculars and twisted his back. His forehead furrowed in thought. Something seemed wrong. He looked at his watch. It was now more than two hours past dawn, and no one had fallen on the distant hilltop; no shots had been fired at it. He wondered why none of his snipers had yet done their new duty; the Americans had surely given them many targets. By now the sniper teams should be well on their way back to his camp. He bent back to his binoculars. After a few more minutes he heard distant gunfire and smiled again. The smile vanished almost immediately. In the same instant he realized nobody on the hilltop had fallen, and he should have seen someone fall before he heard the gunfire. Then he saw the men on the hilltop gather at its western edge, more of them than he had seen earlier on this day. Finally, he realized the gunfire was not near the distant hill; it was near the river, about halfway between the hill and his observation post. Then more gunfire broke out a distance east of the foot of the finger ridge.

CHAPTER TWENTY-FOUR

January 2, 1967, Mid-morning

Tex Randall was getting edgy. He'd been sitting in this ambush for more than twelve hours, and that was too damn long. He was as good as anyone else at being patient and motionless in an ambush, but the typical ambush he and the other men of Tango Niner sat in lasted no more than four hours, and most of them were less than two hours long. Tex Randall, corporal, USMC, was a twenty-year-old American male. Make a twenty-year-old American male sit still in one place for twelve hours and he gets fidgety. He watched the boat traffic on the river: some fishermen out with their nets, but not many, they mostly fished at night; market traffic, but not to and from people living upstream, because nobody lived upstream on the navigable part of the river—instead, it was people who went upstream to forage for wild foodstuffs, and a few hunters and wood gatherers. None of the boats gave him any impression they were anything other than what they looked like; none of the people in the boats seemed to be disguised VC or NVA.

Here and there, now and then, a plink on the water

surface—and a soft plop if the sound was close enough—
indicated a fish catching a dragonfly or other surface skim-
mer. Within a few feet of the bank, Randall watched small
mud-colored fish, three or four inches long, dart about
close to the surface. These small fish were thicker through
the body than anybody would expect such small fish to be,
and their pectoral fins were much chunkier than most.
Once in a while one of them came close to the bank and
jumped out of the water at it. The mud-colored fish were
some sort of lungfish; their bodies were thicker so they
could hold lungs and their pectoral fins chunky with muscles to pull themselves along the ground. But the bank here
was too high for them to get onto the ground, and every
time one jumped, it bounced off the bank and fell back in
the water. Maybe if one of the fish had made it to the bank,
Randall could have watched it walk around and been less
bored for a while.

His stomach growled. Not loud, not hard, just enough
to remind him—as if he didn't know—it had been a long
time since he had last eaten. He thought of how some people said CAP was the Marine Corps version of the Army's
Green Berets. If that was so, they should have been taught
how to eat snakes and bugs like they taught the Green
Beanies, he thought. Then he remembered hearing somewhere that there were ninety-three species of snake in
Southeast Asia and ninety-two of them were venomous.
And the other one was a man-eating python. He changed
his mind about wanting to eat snakes.

Damn it, he thought, the only thing that's happened
since we've been out here is that runner, or whatever he
was, that Stilts captured. I wish something would happen
somewhere so I could go back in and get some chow.

Huynh was older and more patient than Randall; he lay
in his position a few feet from the Marine, where he
quietly watched the river and as much of the trail as he
could see. He was glad to be in one place, rather than
expending energy walking around in the heat of the day.
That's one of the things you learned as you got older, to

conserve energy during the heat of the day. So Huynh was content to lie, watching the river and trail to the east. Hunger didn't bother him; that was something peasants learned to live with. Before nightfall, though, he'd want to leave this quiet, comfortable spot by the river and eat something. Or have someone bring some food to him. At any rate, his attention wasn't at what anybody would call its sharpest.

Ten meters away, Vega and Tho lay under some bushes on the other side of the trail, watching it in both directions. Vega was younger than Randall and less accustomed to sitting overnight in an ambush, much less sitting in one for more than twelve hours. Vega didn't have the distraction of boats to watch; he was paying less attention to watching than Randall was, and more attention to his stomach.

A thin line of tiny red ants scurrying from one place to another passed near him. The line seemed to be a writhing cord until Vega looked at it closely. Then he could see the individual ants dashing to one side, darting to the other, turning back to race an inch or so against the tide, crawling over other ants, before getting turned back in the right direction. He recognized these ants from the one encounter he'd had with them before—they were small enough to get inside any article of clothing, no matter how tightly worn, and their bites stung like fire. He decided to keep a wary eye on them, make sure none detoured to him.

Tho was bored, not as much as the Americans, but still bored. He wasn't married, but he did have a sweetheart in Hou Dau whom he hadn't seen in a few days. He was daydreaming about his girlfriend and trying to ignore his hunger pangs.

Neither man was watching real closely.

That's how two of Major Nghu's sniper/spotter teams managed to walk all the way through this four-man ambush without being spotted.

If Huynh hadn't picked that very moment to twist around to scratch an itch, the four NVA might have made it without anybody knowing anything. But Huynh did decide to scratch an itch low on the back of his left thigh. He half twisted around to get to the itch, and his gaze swept across sandaled feet headed west along the trail. Every fiber in his body wanted to twitch at the sudden sight; he knew in his gut that somebody had just walked by that close without him being aware of it and could just that easily have killed him. He didn't twitch, though; his military discipline took instant control, and he froze in position.

Randall wasn't looking out over the river at the moment, and out of the corner of his eye saw Huynh freeze. He wasn't moving, but he froze anyway—except for his eyes, which searched for whatever had startled his partner. His ears told him before his eyes did; he heard the faint pitter-patter of rapidly shuffling feet. Then he saw a flicker of black through a break in the surrounding brush and knew what had happened. At least he hoped he knew; the alternative was something he didn't want to think about.

It was possible that Vega and Tho had been discovered and silently killed, but Randall didn't think it likely that those two could have been killed without making some kind of noise. And he knew it was even less likely that the soldiers he saw would have found and killed those two without searching the area for anybody else who might be around.

Randall waved a hand at Huynh, telling him to get ready. The PF slipped the index finger of his right hand through the trigger guard of his rifle and tensed to spring the rest of the way around and open fire. Randall put his rifle in his shoulder, pointed it at where he thought the enemy soldiers were now, and filled his lungs.

Simultaneously Randall started pulling the trigger of his rifle and shouted, "They got through! West of us. Fire! Fire west!" He dropped into a prone firing position and moved the muzzle of his rifle with each shot; he tried to make his shots hit a couple of feet away from each other where he thought the soldiers who had passed through were and tried to keep his rounds from going more than a foot above the ground.

At the first sound from Randall, Huynh spun to face the opposite direction, flicked his safety off, and opened up. His aim wasn't as disciplined as Randall's was, but his bullets flew through the right area.

A few meters away, Vega and Tho were caught by surprise. They were almost as surprised as the NVA. Tho was already facing in the right direction, so when he heard the first cry of alarm and scream of agony from the snipers, he fired at them. Vega had to scramble around before he could shoot. Instinctively, he fired the same way Randall did—keep 'em low and spread 'em around.

The four NVA hadn't gotten very far beyond the four-man ambush before they were fired on. Their closeness to the Marines and PFs caught them in a crossfire—had they been closer, the ambushers might have been firing at one another as well as at the bad guys. Randall's first shot didn't hit anybody, but it did galvanize the enemy into action. The action one took was to run. He made it one step —his leading foot planted itself on the ground and all of his weight went onto it just as Randall's second bullet went through the same space his shin occupied. The bullet shattered the shin bone, and the leg collapsed under the northerner's weight. He screamed once as he fell, but the agony of the splintered bone shredding through the flesh of his leg overloaded his system, and he was unconscious, dropping into shock, by the time he hit the ground. He never felt the bullet from Vega's rifle that shattered his temple.

Two of the northerners whipped their weapons into their hands and started firing back at Randall and Huynh, advancing toward them. The remaining one dropped to the hard-packed earth of the trail to fire on the same level as the attackers. One of Huynh's first rounds hit him in the middle of his face on his way down, and he died instantly. The two still on their feet were charging at an angle from the trail to the river when Vega and Tho opened up, catching them in the crossfire. One of them jerked his head to the side, at the new fire pouring at him and his companion, and turned to run away. One of Vega's low-flying bullets tore through his calf and threw him off balance. He staggered and bounced off a tree. He stumbled on his wounded leg, trying to regain his balance, when another bullet hit his other leg and knocked him down. One of Huynh's bullets slapped onto the middle of his back and ricocheted off a rib. A bullet from Tho's carbine splashed between two ribs under his out-flung arm and smacked into his heart, killing him. The one remaining NVA burst through the last bush between him and Randall.

The Marine raised the muzzle of his rifle and rapidly jerked the trigger three times. Two bullets flew out of his muzzle; the bolt was locked to the rear when he pulled the trigger the third time. The two bullets Randall fired into this last sniper were tracer rounds that he'd loaded into his magazines to let him know he was at the bottom and needed to reload. The phosphorus-coated bullets didn't start to ignite until they rasped against bone going into this last target; they were almost completely glowing when they exited his back. Some of the phosphorus stayed inside the NVA's body and burned, momentarily increasing the mortal pain he screamed from. His momentum carried him forward, and he tried with his dying spasm to point his rifle and pull the trigger, but Randall rolled out of the way of the falling body, and it didn't matter whether he fired or not.

Both Marines had twenty-round magazines in their M-14s; the two PFs had fifteen-round magazines in their carbines. All four of them, because they had opened fire at different times, emptied their magazines at almost the same time. In the brief silence when some were reloaded but hadn't yet fired again and others were knocking the empty magazines out of their rifles, Randall noticed that he didn't hear anything from the enemy.

"Cease fire," he shouted. "Listen up. Anybody hear anything?"

Nobody heard anything but their own rasping breath.

Then Randall heard his radio squawking at him for a situation report. He looked around for it, saw it lying next to the tree he'd been sitting against, reached to pick it up, but before he could push the speak button on its side, he heard gunfire from the north.

Ruizique and his men didn't have the same problem with divided attentions as Randall and his squad. First, they were all together in one small group overlooking the east–west trail from Hou Ky to the hills. Second, Ruizique knew he had very little time left to deal with the enemy and couldn't afford to let his attention wander. Third, while George had sent his family to hoped-for safety away from Bun Hou, he had stayed behind and wanted the problem cleared up fast so he could get his wife and children home, where they belonged. Fourth, Neissi was somewhat awed and a little freaked out by the way his fire team leader had come back after having left and didn't want to risk getting the Dominican angry at him—anybody crazy enough to go UA into the field, instead of away from it, was capable of doing anything. Vien went along with the rest of them on staying alert.

They all stiffened when they heard Randall's ambush set off. All but Ruizique wondered about the staggered opening of the fire; the corporal guessed right away what had happened and let himself smile at it—it was something to rib the Texan about later. When the fire fight south of them reached its end, they were only vaguely aware that the last firing they heard was the heavy booming of an M-14. Their attention was too occupied by the four skittery men they saw coming toward them on the trail.

Ruizique gave George a perfunctory glance to confirm that these men, armed with SKS rifles and AK-47s, were strangers, then, since he was on the left end of the line, the farthest from the approaching men, lined his sights on the lead man. He didn't bother giving any orders on how to react when he fired; he had told his men that the previous night, before they had left Camp Apache.

The four NVA, in peasant pajamas and North Vietnamese Army pith helmets, were trotting along the trail and looking into the trees on their left more than they were looking ahead. They weren't looking for an ambush in the trees along the side of the trail; theirs were the looks of men who listened to distant fire fights and knew friends of theirs were involved in them, that it could just as easily have been they who walked into the ambush. They felt danger for themselves for the first time since they'd arrived on the Song Du Ong flood plain. Even though they had had the success operating during the day that Major Nghu had promised them, they still weren't comfortable to be moving about during daylight in an enemy-held territory. They wanted to get back to their hillside camp before any roving Americans and PFs found them. They knew Tango Niner had to have people out here someplace. They had watched the camp while waiting fruitlessly for the patrols to return and only seen a few people in the compound. They were close enough to it to make out some individuals. It wasn't so much who they had seen as who they hadn't seen that told them many of the Americans were still out here someplace. The second man in the line, the senior man in this quartet, grunted something at his men and they picked up their pace. It was too late.

Ruizique didn't want to risk a miss, so he drew a sight picture on the middle of the torso of the first man in the short column and slowly squeezed the trigger. The bullet as it was aimed would go through the man's solar plexus; even if he moved suddenly in a different direction, the bullet should hit him. Ruizique's target did move suddenly; he trotted faster. The faster forward motion startled the Marine and made him jerk his shot. If he hadn't jerked, the bullet would have hit the NVA in his left side, not in a vital location. The jerk sent the bullet high and to the left; it slammed through the man's breast and sent a shard of the broken bone through his heart.

The other three men in the ambush fired in the instant after Ruizique did. Vien, on the other end of the line, was leading his man slightly, so his sudden faster movement didn't matter; his bullet drilled through his chest, piercing both of his lungs and his heart. George didn't take chances; he cranked off three rapid shots—two of them slammed his man to the side, and he fell down, a broken doll. Neissi missed because of the man suddenly speeding up, but he recovered fast and put a bullet through the middle of of his back before he finished turning away to run from the ambush.

"Dumbfuck," Neissi said. "Didn't anybody ever tell him if you run from an ambush all you do is give somebody one ass-kicking target?"

Ruizique looked at him patiently, slight amusement in his eyes. "It didn't matter," he said. "He was dead anyway." He picked up his radio and waited. Randall was through making his report. Then he made his own. Bell ordered them all to come back to Camp Apache. An order all of them eagerly agreed to; they needed to eat and get some sleep. Zeitvogel tossed his prisoner over his shoulder. Randall and Ruizique left the corpses where they'd fallen and just took their weapons—none of the dead carried any documents.

In between the two successful ambushes, a third four-man group managed to go through the space between Lewis's and Hempen's ambushes without being detected. Major Nghu had sent out six two-man sniper/spotter teams to hit the returning patrols. Only two of them made it back to his camp.

CHAPTER TWENTY-FIVE

Homecoming

"Put it back," Bell said. "Pick a different one."

"What?" Tiredness made Dodd's voice slower and duller than normal.

"I said put the fucking ham and limas back. Take a different one."

Dodd looked dull-eyed at the sergeant, too tired to be puzzled. During the night Bell had broken open three cases of C-rations and placed the thirty-six one-meal boxes upside down along the side of the command hootch, mixed up and upside down because the top of each box had the entree it contained printed on it. Usually he only put out twenty-seven boxes, one for each Marine in Tango Niner. As the Marines came in from patrol, they each blindly picked a box; the perimeter watchers picked theirs when they left their defensive positions after the sun came up. The reason the boxes were upside down and mixed so nobody knew what any box held until he picked it up and turned it over was that some C-rations were edible and some were so bad you'd wish them on your worst enemy only if you really and truly hated him—with a passion.

C-ration ham and limas were the most universally hated meal in the entire U.S. military cuisine. One out of twelve men got stuck with the ham and limas out of every case of C-rations. Randomly picking from the mixed-up boxes was supposed to ensure that each man had an equal chance of getting the good meals and being stuck with the ones no-body wanted. It was no fair peeking to see what was in a box before taking it; the rule was, you touch it, it's yours. Last night he had put out one box for each of the Marines and PFs who were there, plus one more just because there was one left over in the three cases.

Bell normally tried to make himself and Lieutenant Burrison the last ones to pick. He cheated this time; he took two of the three boxes of ham and limas, kept one for himself, and gave the other to the young officer. Burrison tried to conceal his grimace of disgust. He somehow seemed to get more than his fair share of ham and limas as it was; it hardly seemed fair to stick him with one on pur-pose. That left one ham and limas among the remaining thirty-four boxes waiting to be picked over. Somehow, thirty-two men had picked before Dodd, and thirty-two men, without cheating, had managed to avoid picking the ham and limas. Bell knew none of them had cheated, be-cause he watched the selection like a hawk. Today he didn't want one of the men who had been out waiting to ambush the snipers to get stuck with the ham and limas.

There were two boxes left when Dodd picked his. He picked the wrong one.

"Put it back," Bell said again. "Pick a different one."

"But there's only one left."

"I can see that, Dumbshit. Take it."

"But that's cheating." Dodd didn't like ham and limas and he was too tired to be able to think clearly, but he knew what the rules were and didn't want to cheat.

"I said pick a different one," Bell shouted, exasperated. He snatched the box from Dodd's hand and slammed the other box into it. "Hell, the one you picked probably even has Viceroys in it." Each C-ration box included a miniature pack of cigarettes; either Salem, Winston, Pall Mall, Lucky Strike, or Viceroys. Almost nobody who smoked liked the distinctive taste of Viceroys. Nonsmokers used the cigarettes as trade items; Viceroys didn't make good trade goods.

Dodd turned the new box over and stared at it. Slowly his face brightened. "Motherfuck," he said softly, "it's breakfast." The last box was ham and eggs. Canned, reconstituted scrambled eggs with fatty chunks of ham embedded in it. Not very appetizing, but it was ham and eggs, a proper breakfast. "Hey, thanks, Jay Cee. Let me know if I can do something for you sometime."

He already had his mess kit and field stove in hand, so he wandered away in the general direction of the sheet-metal-on-sandbag tables, where the other men from the ambushes were already settled for their first meal since the afternoon before. Real breakfast food, Dodd thought, pleased with what he now had. I can heat up the food and some hot cocoa and have a real breakfast. He didn't care that C-ration ham and eggs wasn't something his mother would allow anywhere near her kitchen, much less serve at her table, or that C-ration cocoa was something that could only be stomached in the field. The contents of a C-ration ham-and-eggs can had started off as breakfast food, no matter what it might be now.

"Did your mother have any children who lived, Dumbshit?" Bell muttered at Dodd's back. "I want you to wake the fuck up, asshole." In a loud voice he shouted, "Anybody got a starving dog?" He still had a can of ham and limas to get rid of, and he certainly wasn't going to get rid of it by eating it himself.

Bell and Burrison let the men who had been out all night and half the morning sleep until mid-afternoon before waking them. Actually, Bell tried to wake only the three corporals, but a helicopter that landed a couple of minutes earlier had disturbed the others enough that they were already half awake. When they heard why he was waking the corporals, everybody got up. Wall McEntire and Doc Rankin were back from R&R. Captain Hasford was with them and had information. Everybody wanted the information. And they all wanted to find out if McEntire found out which end to stick it in. One look at McEntire's glazed eyes and silly grin told them all he'd stuck it in the right end so often, he wasn't likely to forget again for a long, long time. But he couldn't take the time to tell them about it until after Captain Hasford's briefing.

Hasford did a good job of hiding his dismay about half of the PFs having left the compound to take their families to safety. He did it by favoring his right side and making puns about the stitch in his side. He encouraged remarks about the wound, which Hempen said made him "an honorary real grunt, fully entitled to eat cold C-rations in the rain and get eaten up by mosquitoes and leeches and go on operations where he got to change clothes once every month or two if he was lucky." Hasford told them it hadn't been easy, but Jo Jo's leg was saved; he'd be able to return to farming even if he was so crippled he couldn't be in the Popular Forces anymore.

"When do you think Houng will be back?" Bell asked.

"If he can hitch a ride, maybe this afternoon. Maybe tomorrow. Anyway, he's okay except for a sore shoulder that's got his arm in a sling. Nothing was broken. He'll be back soon—and probably meaner than ever."

"How's Vandersteit doing?" was the other thing they wanted to know right away.

"I don't know," Hasford said, and shook his head. "He had some blood vessels pretty badly busted up in his leg. He might have to go to Japan, maybe even back to The World for grafting."

When he thought everybody was relaxed enough and ready for the news he had for them, he led the Marine officer and NCOs and the two remaining PF squad leaders to the southwest corner of the compound and sat on the lip of the trench, facing west. In a way it made sense, but it certainly increased the vulnerability of the men left at

Camp Apache. The others gathered around, facing in the same direction. "The man Zeke caught the night before last hasn't said anything yet." He had looked deeply into Ruizique's eyes when he'd first seen him but hadn't said anything to him and, after that one look, didn't acknowledge his presence; he knew he'd have a very hard time explaining to somebody how a man supposedly being processed out of country at Da Nang was in fact in the field with a combat unit. "Not even his name, rank, and service number. I did manage to get a recon flight to pass over that ridge, however."

"When?" Burrison asked. "I didn't see any aircraft except for helicopters coming here." He turned to Bell. "Did you?" He included the corporals in his question.

The sergeant shook his head; the others did nothing.

"It was a high flier," Hasford said, "real high. Not much point in letting the bad guys know we're scoping them out; they might get some bright ideas about moving their base someplace we don't know about. All they picked up on any radio frequencies was a couple of snatches from you. You must have been maintaining radio discipline. They got something else on infrared photography, though. Right on the other side of the hill over there"—he pointed at the hill to the right of the cleft the Song Du Ong river flowed through—"they picked up a lot of heat speckles. It looked like more than a couple hundred men scattered over so large an area it would take a Rolling Thunder strike to get them all." Rolling Thunder was the code name for B-52 bombing missions. "And there were a bunch of brighter spots that looked like small cooking fires. Of course, nobody would authorize a Rolling Thunder strike without somebody making an eyeball recon to see who it is. It could be some refugees settling in what they think is an unpopulated area free of Vee Cee and government forces. Unlikely, but possible." He paused for a moment, visualizing what the infrared had shown. "If it is the bad guys, a whole battalion could sweep that area and probably not catch many of them, because they're too spread out. Something else was found in infrared that indicates it's not something as innocent as a refugee settlement, though. I'm not going to point this time. I'll show you on a map. There was a spot on this side of the hill that looked like two or three men. Could be an observation post. Make sense?"

"Don't anybody look," Bell said, and moved to sit on the opposite side of the trench. "If Charlie does have an OP over there, he sure as shit can see us here—and if he's got some good glasses, he can see us all looking in his direction. So let's don't look at him."

Slover hefted his bulky body across the trench and sat next to Bell. "Jay Cee's got a good idea," he said. "But if old Luke the Gook is paying attention, he already saw the captain point in that direction." Mentally he started computing how far he'd have to move his mortar to get it close enough to take out the observation post—if he knew where it was. He didn't particularly like the answer he came up with.

"Now, I want you to fill me in on exactly what happened this morning," Hasford said. "I want to know everything. How many men you saw, what direction they were traveling in, exactly where you saw them, how they were acting when you first saw them, how they fought back, what kind of weapons they were carrying, what documents they had on their persons, what other equipment they had. Everything." He looked Zeitvogel, Randall, and Ruizique each in the eye while he listed the things he wanted to know. "Damn, but you've changed since the last time I saw you, Short Round," he said, looking at Ruizique. "I think you've grown a bit."

Ruizique grinned at him and said, "They made the mistake of letting me pick my own shit detail while I waited for my Freedom Bird."

"Anybody got a map?" Hasford asked, looking around.

"I thought you might need one of these shitrags," a voice said behind him, "so I brought you one."

"You know, Swearin' Swarnes," Hasford said without looking back, "if this war ever ends and they let you go back to The World, somebody's going to have to teach you how to talk around officers, or you'll be in the brig for so long you'll be too old to collect Social Security when they finally let you out."

"Shit," Swarnes snorted. He held the map out for anyone who wanted it. Zeitvogel reached out a long arm to take it. Swarnes went back to his radios before anybody could ask who was watching them. Sometimes he got the impression nobody believed people really would call back if their message was important and he didn't answer when they called the first time.

"Me first," Zeitvogel said. He held the map on a knee with one hand and held out the other. Swarnes had laid a clean sheet of acetate over the map. "Who's got a grease pencil?" Burrison handed him one, and he carefully marked where his ambush was. "I can't give you the exact time," he started. "I didn't look at my watch until it was over. . . ."

When Hasford was satisfied the three corporals had told him everything relevant—he didn't push Randall too hard for any of the embarrassing details of how the soldiers he ambushed had managed to walk through his men before being spotted—he marked the map with the position of the suspected observation post. Then he turned to Collard Green and talked in rapid Vietnamese. "What about the new prisoner? Has he said anything?"

Collard Green shook his head, then paused briefly and nodded slowly. "He said one thing. He said if we were going to execute him, to hurry up and get it over with."

Hasford blinked a couple of times. "Why did he say that?"

Collard Green shrugged. "I think the North Vietnamese commander told his men Tango Niner doesn't take prisoners, that we kill everybody."

"You didn't the last time this Major Nghu came around. You took a couple of prisoners that time."

"I don't think Major Nghu knew that; he escaped before

we caught any prisoners. We did kill most of them."

"And then and now he's killed every one of our people he's caught," Hasford said, nodding. "The bloodthirsty son of a bitch probably thinks we operate under the same rules he does."

Collard Green looked at the American captain straight-faced. "We give our prisoners to the Arvins," he said. "Would you like to be a prisoner of theirs? What do you think the chances of survival are for prisoners of the Arvins?"

Hasford had heard tales of the prisoner-of-war camps maintained by the Saigon government. He didn't know if the stories were true, but they told of gruesome, inhuman treatment of prisoners. This was one area where the South Vietnamese tried to have things both ways. On the one hand they claimed they were being invaded by a foreign country, North Vietnam, and that a foreign country—North Vietnam again—was fomenting a violent revolution in their country. On the other, the Saigon government often also claimed the prisoners weren't soldiers, subject to being treated according to the terms of the Geneva accords, but rather domestic criminals who could be treated any way the government wanted to treat them. Hasford knew this was a two-edged sword that could damage the South Vietnamese position in world public opinion.

"He said nothing else?"

"Nothing," Collard Green confirmed. "Not even his name."

Hasford looked, unfocused, into the distance. "That's two," he said after a moment in English. "Two prisoners, and neither one will even give us his name. I think this Major Nghu has some very good troops under him."

"Well disciplined, at least," Burrison agreed.

"At least." Hasford looked lost in thought for another moment, then abruptly shook himself out of it and said, "Okay, you did something different last night and it worked. What is your next step?".

"What I'd like to do is go over to the other side of that hill and kick ass," Randall said.

"An admirable sentiment, Tex," Hasford said dryly, "but not very practical. They've got you too badly outnumbered, and they're probably very well camouflaged as well as dispersed. Realistically, what are you going to do tonight?"

They hashed it out, the Marine lieutenant and sergeant. The corporals and the PF squad leaders and the captain interjected their comments occasionally. Eventually they had a plan. It might not work, but it was different enough from anything else they'd done to counter Major Nghu that it might. If nothing else, it reduced their chances of receiving more casualties overnight tonight or at dawn tomorrow. The only certainty they faced now was one each side had learned the hard way—if you do the same thing two days in a row, it's liable to hurt you.

"Who wants to do it?" Bell asked once the plan was formed. It wasn't the kind of mission he was willing to send anybody out on; somebody had to volunteer.

Zeitvogel snorted. "Shee-it, Jay Cee. You got to ask a question like that? Who the hell you think is the biggest, baddest, night-fighting, card-carrying little guerrilla killer in this rinky-dink outfit?"

"Don't tell me. I know," Randall said. "Just let me think for a minute." He looked up and away, seemingly lost in thought for a long moment, chewing on his lower lip. "That's it," he finally said, looking like a canary-eating cat. "Short Round."

Zeitvogel leaned far forward, one long arm draped across one long knee. "Think you can kick my ass again, Tex? Fuck a bunch of Short Rounds. He can be second best. I'm the biggest, baddest mo-dicker in this valley." His expression was fierce.

"Man, if looks can kill, I want to bottle that and use it on Charlie," Slover said.

Ruizique laughed. "Stilts, you're so ugly you should

never look like that around friends. You might wind up without any," he said.

"You really think he's got friends?" McEntire asked.

"You've got a point there, Wall," Ruizique said, and laughed again. "But there are friendly forces in the area. Somebody might want to land a BLT on his ass, the way he's looking." He didn't mean a bacon, lettuce, tomato sandwich; he meant a Battalion Landing Team—an infantry battalion reinforced with armor and artillery.

Zeitvogel drew his wallet from his shirt pocket and showed them a card he carried in it. "I'm for real, dudes. I got training," he said with a certain irony. The black-bordered card had a cartoon Pancho Villa figure on it shooting a popgun that displayed a sign that said "Little Warrior."

"Short Round's got one of them, too," Randall said. Both Zeitvogel and Hempen carried cards they had earned by completing the First Marine Brigade's Guerrilla Warfare school in Hawaii.

"No shit. He can come with me."

So it was settled. Zeitvogel, Hempen, Mazzucco—if he agreed—and four volunteer PFs would run the night's one patrol.

"One last thing," Hasford told them while waiting for the evening chow bird that was going to take him away from Camp Apache. "I want Stilts and Athen to saddle up to leave for R and R tomorrow."

"Say what!" Zeitvogel yelped.

Hasford put on his captain's stone face and stared, hard-eyed, at the tall corporal. "You and Athen are the last of the men who have been here from the beginning," he said. "The two of you leave for R and R tomorrow."

Zeitvogel fumed and opened his mouth to argue, but Hasford's expression was one that didn't allow discussion. The tall man shut his mouth with a snap.

"I don't make the rules, Stilts," Hasford said firmly. "I just enforce them. The current rule we are operating under is all members of Tango Niner who have been in-country more than six months will go on R and R. You and Athen are the last of the ones who come under that rule. There's no one you can pass it on to this time. You will go. Tomorrow."

Zeitvogel's jaw was clenched. His eyes blazed, and he said, his teeth still clenched, "Aye-aye, sir."

Athen didn't say anything; he just packed his civvies and a khaki uniform in his seabag and made sure he had a clean uniform to wear the next day when the helicopter picked him up.

Major Nghu sat on a folding chair at his tiny field desk. The chair and desk were under the camouflage netting he used in place of a tent; it couldn't keep out the rain, but it did conceal him from aerial observation. The netting was strung between two trees six feet apart and pulled out to the sides by cords attached to other trees. A hammock hanging between those two main trees and a pack with changes of clothing were the only other furnishing he had in his shelter. He was fine as long as it didn't rain. An open map case hung from the side of his field desk; he had removed a map, tracing paper, and colored pencils from the map case and was drawing on tracing paper overlaid on the maps.

He could not again risk sending out the sniper or harassment teams that had worked so well so many times already, not after losing eleven men that way in the past thirty-six hours. The imperial running dogs had found a way to counter them. And the visitor to Tango Niner had pointed in the direction of his camp; the Americans might have somehow found out where it was. Had one of his men been captured and told them its location? He needed to make his move before the Americans could send in a larger force to attack him where he hid. Not that they could do much damage to his troops, of course. But an infusion of a large number of troops would disrupt his plans, delay his destruction of Tango Niner. Also he had the morale of his own men to consider. If the Americans had more success against his forces, his men might start to fear them. It was now time to administer the coup de grace, while half of the so-called Popular Forces traitors were gone. Major Nghu was ready to tango. All he had to do was figure out how.

CHAPTER TWENTY-SIX

Well, It Starts on the Second, Ends on the Third

When the briefing and planning were finished, Wall McEntire mulled it all over for a few minutes, very serious. Then he shrugged it off before he could start brooding over things. After all, there was nothing left to do at this time except wait. He stood up and went looking for Kobos. He thought of what he was going to tell his gunner, and he beamed in anticipation. When he found Kobos, he threw a massive arm around the smaller man's shoulders, staggering him, and started talking.

"You remember what end to stick it in, Kobos? Let me tell you about it. Now, I know you ain't been in-country nearly as long as I have, and you've probably had round-eye tail since the last time I did, but, by gawd, I sure as shit stuck it into the right end of some women more recently than you did—don't matter none it was sideways, instead of fore and aft. Now, I want you to listen up good so one of these days when you get your R and R you'll know what to do. . . ."

Doc Rankin had had an appreciative audience of junior enlisted men and PFs while Captain Hasford was giving his briefing and the CAP leaders were making their plans for the night. The PFs, being simple rural people who occasionally listened to local radio, seldom read a newspaper, rarely saw movies, and had never seen a television, could be excused for not believing everything he told them.

Doc Rankin told them of the wonders of Hong Kong. What it was like living in a hotel for four nights, only drinking water that was put in a pitcher for that purpose, and never drinking faucet water. How cold and delicious Heineken beer was at fifty cents a bottle in the hotel bar. What it was like eating a steak fresh-cooked to order, with vegetables that weren't overcooked, and being served by waiters who paid such close attention to their diners that someone wanting an after-dinner smoke didn't even have to light his own cigarette.

He told them about the street people, families either too poor to be able to afford an apartment or far down on waiting lists, who staked out portions of sidewalk and, at dusk, spread their sleeping mats on them for the night. He told them about all the stores, and how cheap their goods were, and displayed the two suits and five shirts he'd had tailor-made for less than a hundred dollars. He regaled them with tales of riding the Blue Star ferry between the Kowloon mainland and Hong Kong island, of double-decker buses, of excursions in taxicabs whose drivers weren't happy unless they were driving at high speed with their car hoods tucked under the tailgates of trucks. He vividly described the tram ride up Mount Victoria and the pre–World War II defenses on that peak, and how he'd analyzed it with an infantryman's eye, both as an attacker and a defender, and how he now understood why the Japanese had to hold the civilians of Hong Kong hostage in order to force the British soldiers defending Mount Victoria to surrender rather than continue the fight they could have fought for a long time. Rickshaw drivers got their share of his story-telling, too.

All of which might have been very entertaining, especially to the newer men who hadn't had R and R yet and didn't know when they would, except that what everybody really wanted to hear about was dark bars and bar girls and hookers and getting some.

Doc Rankin was just getting around to telling them about the dark bars and the bar girls and hookers and getting some when McEntire started talking to Kobos.

McEntire said, "Bangkok is the best-named city in the whole wide world. Now, anybody who's been there can tell you all about the pagodas and the canals and the restaurants and the shopping and the brightly dressed, friendly people. But, hell, you can say most the same thing about any big city in the Far East, so I'm not going to tell you about those things. No, I'm going to tell you what it really is about Bangkok that makes it special, and why it's the best-named city in the world. You go to Bangkok and that's exactly what you do—you bang your cock."

Doc Rankin suddenly found himself talking to himself. Everybody knew McEntire would give them all the juicy details that they wanted, instead of all this sight-seeing bullshit.

"Well, don't that beat all," Rankin said to himself. "I might have known. Damn jarheads don't give a good goddamn about culture. No, all they care about is getting laid, and talking about getting laid when they can't get laid." Then he lay back on his cot with his arms crossed under his head and happily remembered those four glorious nights when *he'd* been getting laid in Hong Kong.

Lieutenant Houng came back on the daily chow bird. His arm was in a sling, but his spirits seemed high.

"You're not going to win anything at Camp Perry with that arm," Bell said.

Houng smiled broadly, even though he had no idea of what or where Camp Perry was and had never heard of the national shooting matches held there every year. He knew Bell meant well, and he was glad to be back home, where he belonged.

"Where are the women and children?" he suddenly

asked after the Marines and his two remaining squad leaders greeted him.

Collard Green answered in Vietnamese too fast for any of the Americans to follow exactly, but they knew what the PF squad leader was saying. The two jabbered back and forth, and Willy was reluctantly drawn in to defend Collard Green, to explain how the platoon had been divided down the middle and the two of them hadn't really been able to do anything to stop the others from taking off with the families. Abruptly Houng said something that sounded very final, and the discussion ended.

"What do we do now?" he asked his friend J. C. Bell.

Bell told him. Burrison helped with the explanation. When they were through, Houng nodded at the wisdom of the plan. Like the others, he didn't know if it would work or not, but it was clear they had to do something different from what they had done before. He changed the subject and told them about Jo Jo.

"The hospital bac si wanted to cut off his leg," the PF lieutenant explained. "But Dai uy Hasford was there and argued with him. He told the bac si Jo Jo is a farmer; he needs to have his legs so he can tend his fields and paddies. The bac si argued back; he said he didn't have time to do the work that would save Jo Jo's leg. Dai uy Hasford said I am your next patient. I will wait in the operating room while you fix Jo Jo. When you have saved his leg, you will fix my side. Dai uy Hasford still had his pistol on his belt; he patted it. The bac si turned red in the face; he did not want to do that much work on a Vietnamese farmer, not even one who was a fay epp. Dai uy Hasford told him you will fix his leg so he can walk again or you will never fix another patient. The hospital bac si stopped being red; he turned very pale and he shook. Then he fixed Jo Jo's leg. It took five hours, and Dai uy Hasford was in the operating room the whole time before he let anybody fix his side." Houng nodded emphatically. "Dai uy Hasford boo-coo numba fucking one."

The Marines looked at one another and a silent vow

passed among them; if any doctor ever refused to do his best to treat one of their little people, his career was over. Their admiration for Captain Hasford grew even higher than it had been.

"Everybody saddled up?" Zeitvogel asked shortly before dusk. "Homeboy, you've got the point," he said when he saw his two Marines and four PFs all had their rifles and cartridge belts. "Lead out."

"But, Stilts," Mazzucco objected, "you haven't checked anybody for noise." He hopped in place to show his gear was all secure.

"Cut the crap, Homeboy. We don't need to do that tonight. Ain't nobody dumb enough to go out there unless he's got everything down tight. Go."

Mazzucco grinned, lopsided, and headed toward the main gate. "Way to go, Wall," he said to McEntire, who was already at his night position at the main gate with Kobos and the machine gun. The gun was in its position. The two machine gunners were sitting on the overhead designed to give them some protection in a fight.

McEntire belched loudly and grinned.

"Come on, Wall," Kobos urged, ignoring the departing patrol. "Tell me about the one with the honey-covered snatch again."

"Oh, *man*," McEntire said, "she was delicious. I met up with her in this bar—the Flaming Dragon, it was called. . . . " McEntire's voice faded into the background as the patrol descended the hill. Over the next twenty minutes a dozen other Marines and PFs could be seen on the hilltop, drifting toward night-defense positions.

Mazzucco cut to the right, off the road, before he reached the bottom of the hill and headed across the open ground in the direction of Hou Dau hamlet. Past Camp Apache's hill, he angled slightly to the right to enter the trees south of the break in the trees where the bulldozed road entered them. Inside the trees, he was going to turn right and continue in a half circle around the Marines' hill until he was south of it.

The sun had been down for close to an hour when Zeitvogel stopped the patrol and talked into his radio. "Dugout, Dugout, this is Outfield. Over."

"Outfield, this is Dugout. Go," Swarnes said immediately.

"Dugout, we're in foul territory at your first base side, ready to do our thing. Over."

"Roger, Outfield. You are at our first base and headed toward the bleacher seats. Gimme an ETA. Over."

"We turn in our tickets in about one zero, Dugout. Over."

"Go for it, Outfield. Dugout, out."

Ten minutes later, Zeitvogel stopped his patrol again. This time he didn't use his radio; he had already made his early report. He set his men in an outward-facing circle fifty meters inside the trees to the southwest of Camp Apache's hill. They would stay there all night, or until something happened.

The thirty-one men left inside Camp Apache spent a very nervous night. It was a tedious night, during which nothing happened except nobody got more than a couple hours of sleep. Bell, Burrison, and Houng stood radio watch; Slover and Hunter manned the mortar position; the other twenty-six men hold down the half-mile perimeter. The defenses were much heavier than on most nights around the compound, but on most nights they didn't expect to get hit. They didn't necessarily expect to get hit tonight, but anything was possible—and those who had been in Tango Niner in September knew that Major Nghu might do just that, and wished they had more people watching the wire. Twenty-six men in ten two- or three-man positions were strung out around the perimeter, close to ninety meters between positions. A hell of a front for two or three men to cover.

Once an hour Zeitvogel radioed in a terse sitrep. Then

Randall made one, then Ruizique did. So what if Randall and Ruizique were close enough to the CP bunker that they could have stood up and yelled in their reports. They were doing it not to make situation reports but to make anybody monitoring their radio frequency think there were three patrols out there and fewer than half the number of men who were actually there inside Camp Apache's wire.

"I'm going to check the lines," Bell announced about half past two in the morning. He started at the back gate. Ruizique held it with a PF.

"He is out there. I can feel him," Ruizique said grimly.

"Do you see anything?" Bell asked. "Hear anything?"

Ruizique shook his head in the dark—it didn't matter if Bell didn't see him do it. Anything other than a verbal yes meant no. The Dominican didn't want to talk about it anyway. This position was where he had been two months earlier when Charlie had come in force to throw the Marines out of Bun Hou; it was where he was when he'd been wounded and the gringo war he had thought he had no business being in had become very personal.

Counterclockwise from the back gate, Neissi watched tensely with two PFs, both of whom were wide awake, staring down the steep slope of the hill.

"I thought I heard something a little while ago," Neissi whispered. "Sounded like some kind of soft metallic scraping."

"Did you hear it again?" Bell asked into Neissi's ear.

"Negative."

"Stay sharp."

Knowles, Doc Rankin, and a PF held the far end of the steep eastern side of the hill. They had nothing to report.

"I ain't felt nothing like this since the last time this dude Nghu was here," McEntire said when Bell reached the main gate. The machine gun team leader forgot his sexual exploits in Bangkok for the night. Bell was half surprised to find him, Kobos, and the PF with them under the roof of the machine gun position, rather than on top of it, as the man on watch at the main gate usually was. All three were awake. None of them had heard or seen anything, and it was only McEntire who felt anything.

It could simply be first-night jitters back from R and R that had McEntire edgy, but Bell wasn't going to bet anyone's life on it. He told them to stay alert.

It wasn't until Bell reached Lewis at the northwest corner of the compound that he was certain the hill was being observed.

"You just tell Big Louie to be ready to fire his tube," Lewis said. "Mister Charlie's snooping and pooping out there." He looked at the silhouette of Bell's head in the darkness. "I bet if Louie dropped a light about a hundred meters out there, we'd catch some bad guys in the open."

Bell thought hard for a moment. If the NVA were massing for an assault against the northwest corner of the compound, Zeitvogel's patrol was in the wrong area to counterattack. If they were just scouting or probing, firing a flare from the mortar might give them information about the heavier-than-normal defenses of the compound without giving the defenders any advantage in return.

Bell decided against doing anything for the moment. "Keep me posted," he told Lewis, and moved to the next position.

"I wish to hell I was out there someplace," Randall told him.

"Why for?"

"Because if I was out there, I'd have a better chance of finding Charlie than he had of finding me. This way he knows exactly where I am, but I don't know where he is." He paused long enough that Bell thought he wasn't going to say anything more, then added, "Except I know he's right out there someplace where I could zap some seven-sixty deuce into his ass if I could see him."

After he finished the complete circuit of the perimeter, Bell stopped at the mortar pit. Slover and Hunter were talking their way through the drill they'd use if they had to fire in support of the east side of the hill. Every half hour they talked their way through the drill they would use for one side or another.

"You might get the chance to show us just how good you really are before the night's over, Big Louie," Bell told the big mortarman.

"Tell me about it."

"If I can believe everything I hear, Mister Charlie has us surrounded."

"Oh, shit." When Bell left to go back to the CP, Slover and Hunter started talking about what they would do if the compound got hit from all sides at the same time.

Less than half a kilometer from the command hootch, the men in Zeitvogel's patrol sat quietly in their circle. No one slept; no one dared to. If any of them had been superstitious, he would have sworn ghosts were out that night, drifting transparent through the night, slipping unseen but felt through the Marine and PFs in their circle, the ghosts' dead touches on their living skin spidering tendrils of fear up and down their backs. But none of them were willing to admit to being superstitious; all any of them would say was they weren't alone out there.

CHAPTER TWENTY-SEVEN

January 3, 1967

Tango Niner's normal morning routine was for the overnight ambush patrol to return within a half hour after sunup and then, along with the men who'd spent the night on perimeter watch, head to their squad tents and crap out for a few hours of uninterrupted sleep. At dawn everybody was tired and ready for some sleep; they had all been up for most of the night.

That was the normal routine, and it normally worked pretty well. The Americans and South Vietnamese owned the days, even the Vietcong conceded that.

There was a break from the normal routine this morning, in that the all-night patrol didn't come in at first light. Neither did anyone stand up and leave the perimeter right away, despite being tired from the night's vigil.

After a while Flood muttered to Tracker, "I gotta piss." His voice was heavy with sleepless fatigue. He got out of the fighting position he shared with the corpsman on the south side of the hill and walked to the piss tubes, which were halfway between there and the helipad. He voided his bladder into one of the tubes sticking out of the ground and went to the mortar pit to pass some time with Slover and Hunter. "How's the arm, bunkie?" he asked.

Hunter gently kneaded his left arm. "Sore, about like a toothache. Nothing I can't live with." He sounded more tired than Flood did.

Slover snorted; he was the only one of the three who sounded more than half awake. "Only kind of wound you can't live with is the one that puts your young ass in a body bag," the big man said.

Hunter cocked a droopy eyebrow. "How many Hearts you got?"

Slover snorted again. "I ain't never been dumb enough to stand up in front of flying shrapnel."

Hunter turned to Flood. "You think the man's saying he doesn't have one?" he asked slowly. "What do you think? Is he jealous?"

At that same time Neissi stood up and leaned against the parapet of his fighting position on the east side of the hill. He looked down the slope and, because he was tired and a bit groggy, didn't immediately understand what it was he saw, only that something was odd. He saw a Claymore mine. It was turned around, its convex face—the one that said "Front/Toward Enemy"—was facing him and a thin wire trailed from it down the hill and into the grass surrounding the hill. His sleepy brain suddenly realized this was the source of the metallic scraping he thought he had heard during the night, somebody turning the mine around. His realization came too late. The Claymore exploded, set off by a hidden NVA soldier at the far end of the wire, and sent its seven hundred steel balls flying uphill, spreading their cone as they flew. So many of the balls hit Neissi that nobody later bothered to count the wounds.

Some of the hill's tired defenders stood to look in the direction of the blast. Some others leaned forward in their positions, rubbing their eyes, looking out over the areas they were supposed to cover, searching for enemy. More of them, abruptly wide awake, ducked deeper into their holes, checked their weapons and waited for someone or some-

thing to tell them what direction the attack was coming
from—they were the smart ones.

Seconds later, four more explosions ripped across the
hill as more of the Claymores went off, mines that had
been turned around during the night by sappers who had
crawled naked except for loincloths into the wire and gotten away without being spotted. The Marines and PFs had
a little bit of luck; the NVA didn't know there were ten
positions being manned that night; the sappers had turned
around as many mines as they thought they safely could,
but they only set off one in front of each of the five positions usually manned overnight.

At the back gate, Ruizique was one of the defenders
who looked out over the surrounding land. There was sudden flame and billowing smoke in front of him, then he
was hit with a sledgehammer blow in the head and fell
back.

At the southwest corner of the hill, the PF the Marines
called Hank stood up and looked toward the first blast.
Then he yelped and clasped his side. This corner position
wasn't exactly where night defenders usually sat; it was
offset about twenty meters. That offset was enough to
place Hank on the edge of the Claymore's cone of flying
steel, and only one pellet hit him.

In the northwest corner, Lewis and Willard both ducked
down when the first mine exploded. Lewis curled up and
leaned against the forward wall of the trench. Willard flattened himself against the back wall and watched for someone to come over it from the front. Lewis bunched his fists
in front of his face to twirl the ends of his mustache. A
Claymore erupted directly downhill from them. The bottom of its cone gouged the earth, tore up chunks of dirt,
sprayed powder into the air. Some of the pellets scythed
through the concertina wire on the hillside, broke pieces
from it, and sent those pieces flying uphill. The dirt and
debris flew almost as fast as the pellets kicking it up. They
reached the lip of the trench and, because they weren't
going quite as fast as the pellets that had gouged them up,

cascaded over and across it. Dust and sand grains splattered over Willard's face, filled his mouth, and clouded his eyes. He slapped his hands over his blinded eyes and spat furiously until his mouth was clear enough for him to scream.

Lewis didn't immediately hear Willard's scream, because he was screaming himself—he felt a nip on his thumb and jerked his hand away from it. A chunk of metal had gouged his hand. When his hand came away from his face and he looked to see how badly he was hurt, he saw pinched between his thumb and forefinger the left end of his mustache; the chunk of metal had clipped it cleanly off after cutting his thumb. Lewis screamed not at the small pain in his hand but at the loss of the end of his mustache.

McEntire, Kobos, and their PF were still under cover at the main gate. There wasn't a Claymore directly downslope from them; the sapper who'd turned one around had to do it at an angle and wasn't able to see the aperture to aim at. A lone pellet managed to ricochet into the covered machine gun pit. Kobos had the butt of the gun's stock in his shoulder, his cheek was planted against the stock, and he was looking out for a target. Not much of his right side was exposed, but that ricochet found it. The jagged pellet tore off the top of his right ear.

Vega took care of Hank for the moment, and McEntire bandaged Kobos's ear while Doc Rankin ran to aid Willard. Tracker was closer to Ruizique and headed toward him.

The Dominican corporal was stunned by the blow to his forehead, but it was only a couple of seconds before he was able to shake his head to clear it. His bellow was terrible when he opened his eyes and only saw streaks of light through blackness. Then Tracker was at his side.

"Hold still, Zeke," the corpsman ordered. He used a field dressing to wipe at the blood that covered Ruizique's face; he needed to see where the wounds were before he could do anything to control the bleeding. A flap of skin hung loosely on the corporal's forehead. Tracker worked as gingerly and as quickly as he could to put the flap in place and tie a bandage over it. Then he daubed at the blood pooled around Ruizique's eyes.

"I can't see!" Ruizique shrieked at him.

"Does this hurt?" Tracker asked, daubing at his eyes.

"No. But I can't see, Chief."

"Hang in there." Ruizique's eyes were closed; the corpsman didn't see any injury to the lids when he got most of the blood wiped away. "Open your eyes. Let me see them." Ruizique opened his eyes, and Tracker grimaced at the bloody redness he saw there. Then he noticed the blood was just lying there, not flowing or spurting. "Blink," he ordered. Ruizique did, and Tracker told him, "Squeeze them shut." He wiped away the blood that came out from between the lids. "Tighter." More blood welled out, and he wiped it away. "Open your eyes."

Ruizique did. He shook his head, blinked a few times, grinned, and shouted out. He could see again; the blackness he'd seen was blood that had run into his eyes from the cut on his forehead.

"How's your head feel?" Tracker asked, assured that his patient's eyes weren't injured.

"It's okay," Ruizique said, and raised a hand to the dressing on his forehead. His hand stopped before reaching it, sort of hovered for a brief moment, then lowered. "Where's my weapon?" he asked, looking around for his rifle. He found it and picked it up.

"And here I was afraid you didn't really want to go back to The World, Zeke." The corpsman could joke now that he knew Ruizique was all right. "You came back so you could pick up a couple more Hearts, get sent home that way. Right?"

"Right," Ruizique said dryly.

Tracker looked at the bandage on Ruizique's forehead; it was rapidly turning completely red from the blood it was absorbing. He tied another field dressing on top of it, tied it as tightly as he could. The new bandage quickly started turning red also. "I don't know, Zeke. I might have to tie a tourniquet around your neck to stop the bleeding," he said half-seriously.

"Don't sweat it, Chief. I'll stay upright. That'll slow the blood from coming out."

"I think you're right. But if it does keep bleeding, don't take off the dressings that are on it, because some blood is clotting under them and you'll make the bleeding worse. Put another one on top of them if it doesn't stop by the time I get back. Okay?" He put a hand on Ruizique's shoulder.

"Aye-aye, Chief."

"I got someone else to take care of. Be back as soon as I can." The corpsman pushed himself off Ruizique and ran almost doubled over back the way he'd come, beyond where he'd started from, to where Hank was babbling in relief that his wound was as minor as it was.

Tracker examined it and hoped it was minor. He couldn't tell how far in the pellet was, only that it wasn't lodged in the muscle, and it hadn't been a glancing blow where the pellet cut and kept going. He gave Hank a tetanus shot. "You did a good job," he said to Vega after he replaced the field dressing. Then he returned to check on Ruizique again.

Diagonally across the compound, Rankin was having more trouble with Willard. First he blew as much of the dirt as possible away from his eyes. Then he made Willard lie on his back and poured the water from his canteen between his eyes to wash dirt away. He succeeded in washing it away from the eyes, but there was dirt impacted under his lids.

"Open them wide," Rankin said. He grimaced when he saw how much dirt covered the eyeballs. "Keep your eyes open until I tell you to close them." Then he poured the water from Willard's canteen slowly onto the bridge of his nose. That washed some of the dirt away, but now he was concerned about the surface of the eyeballs getting scratched. Worse, he feared permanent damage to the cornea. He started using cotton swabs from his medkit to clean the eyes and hoped Charlie would hold off long enough for him to finish the job. He wasn't surprised when he got part of one eye cleared out to find it was badly bloodshot. He was only glad he didn't see any cuts on the eyeball. "You'll be ogling the round-eyes next time you see one," he said.

"What next?" Bell said when the complete casualty report was in. The NVA's pattern since they'd moved in and started hitting Camp Apache had been to hit the compound with a few rounds and let it go at that, but this time the defenses had been badly weakened in the process. Was the blowing of the five mines all Major Nghu's men were going to do, or was this merely a prelude?

"What does Stilts say is going on out there?" he asked the lieutenant.

"He says he thinks he saw someone slipping away after the Claymores went off, but not close enough to try to get him," Burrison answered. "He hasn't seen anyone else, but he's pretty sure there's more of them there."

Bell grunted and picked up the field phone that connected the defensive positions with the command bunker. "Everybody stay where you are," he ordered. "Mister Charlie might have something else in store for us, and I want us ready if he does. All positions acknowledge."

One at a time, eight reported they understood the order to stand by in place. Two positions didn't reply. One of them was where Neissi's death left two PFs; the other had a lone PF because of Flood's visit to the piss tubes and Tracker tending to wounded men. The PFs didn't know how to use the field phones.

"Me tell them," Houng said, and ducked out of the CP bunker.

"Get Swarnes in here," Burrison told Bell. "I want to talk to Box Top, and I'm not sure of how to raise them."

A minute later Swarnes was sitting at his radios, looking very relieved at being there. "What the fuck you need, Scrappy?" he asked. He rubbed his sore arm.

"Get me Box Top."

Before Swarnes could raise anybody on the command net, someone outside shouted, "Incoming!" The crashing of mortar rounds that started a few seconds later provided a background sense of urgency to Swarnes's voice when he did get Box Top. Houng wasn't back yet.

"Box Top, we have an unknown number of bad guys out here," Swarnes explained once he made contact. "They have us under a mortar barrage right now. Earlier they—" He decided he didn't want to let the radioman at the other end know someone had sneaked into the wire during the night and reversed some of their Claymores. "They hit us with other explosives. They ain't storming the trenches yet, but they might."

Box Top wanted to know how long they'd been under attack, if they thought they needed any help, and if they had casualties.

"The first hit was about five minutes ago, Box Top." He looked to Burrison for an answer to the request for help and a casualty count. Burrison told him gunships and held up fingers for dead and wounded. "We have reason to believe we are surrounded by more than two hundred bad guys. Send gunships. Also we have one Kilo India Alpha, four Whiskeys." Kilo India Alpha were the phonetics for KIA, killed in action; Whiskey meant wounded.

"Stand by," Box Top ordered, and went off the air.

While Swarnes was on the radio, Bell was on the phone, talking to the men on the perimeter. He ordered them to stay down until he gave the all-clear. This time every position acknowledged him. Houng had quickly instructed the two PFs who had been with Neissi on how to use the field phone, then headed toward the other position. He was in the open, halfway to it, when the "incoming" cry was sounded. The PF lieutenant dashed to the trench and ran, bent over, along it until he reached the lone, frightened PF. He stayed with him and answered when Bell gave his stay-down order.

The two earlier mortarings of Camp Apache had concentrated in the middle of the compound—they'd been aimed at the visiting women on Christmas Day and at the families of PFs on New Year's Day. This time the barrage was aimed at the defenders; the rounds exploded around the perimeter close to the trench. Fortunately, a trench is a hard thing to hit with a mortar. And the trench was zig-zagged to prevent bullets or shrapnel from going any distance along it. Twenty mortar shells exploded around the edge of the compound without causing any real damage before, suddenly, twenty were fired at the mortar's highest rate of fire into the perimeter wire on the west side of the hill. Then it started firing at the west-side trench. Every fourth round was white phosphorus. The burning chemical kept the Marines and PFs down, because they were more frightening than the antipersonnel rounds; they also put out smoke.

"Outfield, Dugout, go," Swarnes said into the radio when the barrage shifted to the west trench; he was responding to an excited call from Zeitvogel.

"General Custer, it looks like all the Indians in the world are coming down on you from the west," Zeitvogel said.

Bell overheard the message and grabbed the handset from Swarnes. "Say that again, Outfield," he said. "Say it clear."

"There's at least a reinforced company of bad guys coming at you from the west under cover of that barrage," Zeitvogel answered.

Bell swore under his breath. There were only seven defenders on the west side, and two of them were already wounded. And the smoke put out by the Willy Peter prevented them from seeing their attackers very well, even if they'd had enough Marines on that side to successfully hold off a reinforced company.

CHAPTER TWENTY-EIGHT

Do You Think Maybe We Should Have Named This Place Camp Alamo?

"Get Box Top back and tell them we're under assault by at least a reinforced company," Bell ordered Swarnes. "Tell them we need those gunships on station most ricky-tick." He grabbed the phone and cranked the handle to get the mortar pit. "Louie," he said when Slover answered, "start putting them out to the west, one hundred and fifty meters from the foot of the hill. Stilts can see them. I'll relay his corrections to you."

The *carrumph* of Slover's first shot seemed to come almost before he acknowledged Bell's order. "One thousand one, one thousand two, one thousand three," Bell counted. The mortar *carrumphed* again—three seconds to reaim and drop another round down the tube.

"Roger," he said into the radio when Zeitvogel reported the attacking force was advancing at a trot. He relayed that information to Slover.

While the Marine mortar was beginning to fire at the assault infantry, Zeitvogel moved his patrol to the edge of the trees they waited under and set his PFs facing the flanks and rear.

"You fired Expert, right, Short Round?" he asked.

"Two forty-five," Hempen replied.

Zeitvogel whistled through his teeth. Expert was the highest level of marksmanship—a score of 245 on the scale of 250 was very high indeed. "How about you, Homeboy?"

"Sharpshooter," Mazzucco replied. Not as good as Expert, but still very respectable.

"What we're going to do is something Marines are famous for," Zeitvogel told his two Marines. "We're going to use aimed fire to try and stop those sons of bitches. Slow fire—try to make every shot count."

Hempen and Mazzucco looked at him soberly. They didn't believe the NVA they saw advancing in the open almost six hundred meters away were the only enemy soldiers around Camp Apache. When they opened fire, they would probably attract some very unwelcome attention. And moving targets at that range would be very hard to hit.

"Aim about ten feet in front of them at waist level," Zeitvogel continued without returning their looks. He knew as well as they did the danger of alerting other soldiers to their presence. He also knew how thin Camp Apache's defenses were and that the mortar barrage hitting along the trench was preventing the defenders from firing at the NVA with anything other than the mortar. No matter how good Slover was with his tube, there was no way one 81mm mortar could stop a reinforced company before it reached the wire.

He carefully sighted his own rifle and squeezed the trigger. He waited to see if he hit anybody before firing again. The couple of seconds the bullet took to travel the distance seemed to stretch into eternity before he finally saw someone in the line stagger under the impact, then fall down. At his sides he heard Hempen and Mazzucco fire also. Another of the attacking NVA dropped.

The assault force wasn't expecting to receive any flank

fire; they weren't spread out as much as they should have been. If the bullets were aimed at the right height and didn't go in front of or behind the line of attackers, each bullet had at least a fifty percent chance of hitting someone. Three men firing at them at this range couldn't stop the attackers, Zeitvogel knew, but they could slightly even the odds for when the NVA reached the hill. Damn, I wish we had a machine gun, he thought.

Mortar rounds burst among and near the assaulting troops, and more of them went down. But not nearly enough. The NVA mortar shifted its aim and fired a counter barrage at the Marine mortar to silence it. Slover, Flood, and Hunter dove into depressions dug into the side of the mortar pit—they were probably safe from anything except a direct hit inside the pit.

"They're warming up two shitbirds now," Swarnes told Bell and Burrison when Box Top told him help was on its way. That was the same time the NVA mortar shifted its aiming point. "They'll be here in about one five." Sweat glistened on his forehead, and his voice trembled. Fifteen minutes might be too late for most of them, and if Box Top said fifteen minutes, maybe they should figure on twenty or more before the gunships were close enough to do any harm to the enemy.

Bell swore; he understood the time element better than Swarnes did. He spoke into his phone. "Zeke, grab those two fay epps on your left and get over there to help Tex." Now that the enemy mortar wasn't firing at the defensive positions anymore, the men in the trench could rise up and fire at the assault line. They had to, now that the mortar couldn't fire.

Ruizique dashed to his left to get the two PFs who were crouched down by Neissi's body; neither one was looking out over the ground to the east. "Come with me," he ordered them. They scrambled to follow him. It didn't matter to them where they were going; being in a fight with a live Marine was better than being someplace relatively quiet with a dead one. The PF Ruizique left at the back gate joined them on their way past him. One of the PFs ran standing upright in the trench, exposing his head and upper body to view.

Major Nghu was watching from a new observation post he had set up in a tall tree near the river, a half kilometer southwest of the hill. He liked this new observation post; the powerful glasses at this range allowed him to see the expressions on the faces of Tango Niner's Marines and PFs. Those expressions told him the Americans and PFs felt fear. He would make them feel more before they died. He saw the southeast defenders move to the west side. That was what he was waiting for. His radioman sat on a branch a few feet below him. Major Nghu would wait just a little longer before radioing the order to his second assault force.

"Stay with Big Red," Ruizique ordered Tracker as the small group he led passed Robertson and the PF with him. A short distance farther, they passed Houng and another PF. The Vietnamese officer watched with anxious eyes as they passed.

The smoke from the enemy Willy Peter rounds dissipated quickly after the mortar started firing at the Marines' 81mm. Randall looked out over the open. "Holy Christ!" he swore. A hundred NVA soldiers were almost at the foot of the hill. More than a dozen others littered the ground behind them, mortar casualties and hits made by Zeitvogel and his Marines. Worse, he saw that the barrage that had hit in the wire had broken it in many places.

"West side, fire downhill," he bellowed, and dropped his own sights onto one soldier. He pulled the trigger, and the man in his sights fell. He shifted aim to another and pulled the trigger again. More rifles opened up at his sides, more of the attackers fell, but there were too many of them even when Ruizique and the three PFs with him joined in. Still, the defenders might have been able to hold, because the breaks in the wire were narrow and the attackers had to bunch up to file singly through them. But some of the men in the assault carried boards which they threw over the wire where it wasn't broken to make bridges to cross. They were coming over and through the wire in too many places for eleven men to be able to stop them. And the enemy mortar shifted its aim again once the assault line reached the wire. A string of white phosphorus rounds hit along the west side of the hill, blinding the defenders and forcing them back down so they couldn't fire. Someone screamed somewhere. So did Randall.

Slover and his mortarmen rolled out of their cover and started dropping rounds into the wire.

"West side, pull back," Bell ordered over the field phone.

On the left flank of the hill's west side, Ruizique gathered his three PFs, Vega, and Hank and pulled them back along the south trench. In thirty meters they were clear of the smoke from the Willy Peter, and he started positioning them to fire when the NVA broke through the cloud of smoke. By the time he had everybody set, his defenses included Robertson, Tracker, Houng, and two more PFs.

"Hold still," Dodd ordered Randall. It was the sharpest he had ever spoken to anyone in his life. He didn't try to think about what to do; he just let his mind remember on its own what he had learned in first aid classes about treating white phosphorus wounds. He jabbed his bayonet in along the side of the burning crater in Randall's right forearm and twisted it in a circle around the wound to dig out as much of the burning chemical as he could. He ignored the grating he felt through his knife when its point dug into the bone of Randall's forearm. Then he tore off the waterproof covering from the field dressing in Randall's first aid kit and slapped it over the wound. He tightly bound the bandage on top of the covering; he hoped it was tight enough to keep air from getting inside. White phosphorus is very active; it will act with the oxygen from anything to burn. Water won't put it out, because it can use the oxygen in water; the only way to put it out is by smothering it.

"Let's go." He slung his rifle over his shoulder, picked

up Randall's, and grabbed the corporal's unwounded arm to pull him by. He glanced once quickly at his team leader's face; it was enough to tell him he had to get him to the corpsman as fast as he could. Randall's face was contorted with agony from the burn. Dodd hoped he wouldn't go into shock.

They found Willard at the northwest corner; he wasn't exactly whimpering, but he was clearly incapable of doing almost anything. He sat erect in the middle of the trench, groping the air with both empty hands; his eyes were bandaged. "Help me, help me, somebody please help me," he repeated over and over in a moaning voice.

Lewis sat a few feet away, ignoring Willard's cries. He had cut off his left boot and was grimly packing mud onto his bare foot. A clot of something bloody on the floor of the trench showed that he had dug out most of the Willy Peter.

"You two get Willard out of here. I'll take care of Billy Boy," Dodd said.

The sight of the two helpless men snapped Randall out of the daze he was in from his own wound. He looked sharply at Dodd and decided not to say anything about who was supposed to give orders—he knew the draftee was right. "Give me my piece," he said, and took his rifle from Dodd. He turned to the blind man. "Let's go, Willard," he said, and helped him to his feet. He handed him his M-79 and grenade pouch. They left Dodd and Lewis behind.

"Let me in there, Billy Boy," Dodd said, kneeling at Lewis's side.

Lewis's jaw was clenched too tightly from the pain for him to respond with words, but he took his hands from his foot when Dodd told him to. The draftee went to work. When he was satisfied he'd done everything he could at the moment, Dodd straightened up. "Let's get the fuck out of here."

The NVA mortar barrage shifted from the western perimeter toward the middle of the compound. The Marines' mortar was silenced again.

"Wall, get your gun turned around," Bell ordered over the phone.

"Got ya, honcho," McEntire replied. He had already turned his machine gun to cover the hill where he expected to see the attackers appear. He was going to feed belts into the gun and act as spotter for it. He had the PF with them, watching the north flank to give warning if somebody came from that direction.

When the remainder of the hundred assaulting NVA grouped themselves to lunge onto the top of the hill, the expected gunships were still at least ten minutes away. Ten Marines and PFs, two of them wounded and one still recovering from an earlier wound, held the south side of the hill, facing the assault. Seven more were spread out on the north side of the hill—three of those seven were wounded, and one of the three was blind. McEntire had moved his machine gun to the east trench, facing west. Three Marines huddled helpless in the depressions in the sides of the mortar pit; three more were in the command bunker. One Marine and one PF were left to hold the east side of the hill.

Then Zeitvogel radioed in more bad news. "Alamo, Santa Ana and the whole fucking Mexican army are headed toward the back gate. You got about eighty or ninety more bad guys coming that way." He didn't wait for an acknowledgment; there wasn't time to if he was going to give any help.

"On your feet, people," the tall corporal shouted. "Line of skirmishers, go."

The NVA crossing the open ground toward the back gate were walking fast but not running. Zeitvogel had time to cut the distance between his patrol and the new assault unit down to a reasonable firing distance before it was halfway from the trees to the hill. He got his men down on line inside the trees.

"Blow the fuckers away," he shouted, and he and his six men opened up on the NVA.

Eight of the NVA were hit before their commander realized they were under fire from their left rear—the din of battle on the hilltop disguised the direction of the gunfire they were taking. He shouted orders to turn his men around to face this new threat. Five more of them were hit before they got down and started returning fire.

"We got them pinned down," Zeitvogel reported on his radio. "You take care of the ones you already got, and don't worry about these." Bullets sang their death songs through the air above the heads of the seven men desperately trying to pin down the second assault force; bullets thwacked into the trees that gave them partial shelter.

The officer commanding the first assault force listened to the amended orders that came over his radio and spoke his understanding and obedience into it. He looked to his flanks and saw his men had suffered greater casualties than he had expected in reaching the crest of the hill, but then there were fewer Americans and PFs on the hilltop than he had expected. He shouted to the sergeants controlling the elements of his force, raised an arm above his head, and dropped it forward. The hundred soldiers under his command rose from the cover the hill crest gave them and surged forward into the rapidly thinning smoke directly in front of them. In seconds they would be sweeping across the hilltop, killing everyone in their path. The mortar barrage stopped so it wouldn't hit any of its own men.

The defenders on the north and south sides of the hill didn't form a U type of formation, but that didn't matter; the U was most effective when the enemy was completely inside it and could be hit from three sides. They could still hit the NVA from two directions.

"There they are!" McEntire screamed when he saw the NVA burst through the smoke that still hid the west trench. He clapped Kobos on the shoulder, and the gunner started putting twenty-round bursts into the line of attacking soldiers. Ahead of him, four other Marines and two PFs opened up with their rifles. Ruizique bellowed orders at the men in the south trench, and the eleven there raked their fire across the front of the assault line.

The NVA hardly made it all the way through the concealing smoke before fifteen of them were down. Their commander shrilled his whistle and waved his arms. They dropped back into the trench they had just crossed.

Bell looked out of the CP bunker to assess the situation. "Tell them to hold their fire," he told Swarnes when he saw the NVA in the trench were keeping down and not returning fire. The gunfire on the hilltop stopped, leaving the sound of Zeitvogel's patrol pinning down the secondary assault force below the hill on the west as the only noise of battle. Bell suddenly realized if the NVA were ballsy enough and their commander thought fast, the bad guys could stay in the trench and roll up his flanks. The defenders would hurt them, maybe badly, if they did, but that maneuver would win the battle for the hilltop for the bad guys. He looked back into the bunker. "Where the fuck's John Wayne when we need him? Scrappy, I got to get grenades to the men in the trenches."

"Think you can make it?"

"I better." He turned to Swarnes. "You showed off your Dumb Medal like some kind of hero, Swearin' Swarnes. Well, I'm going to make one out of you." Or kill you in the attempt, Bell thought. "Come with me."

"But who's—" "Going to watch the radios," he was going to say, but Bell interrupted him.

"Scrappy knows how to talk on the radios," the sergeant said. "You and me are going to the ammo bunker. Now." He ducked back out of the CP and ran the fastest fifty meters he'd ever run in his life across the open hilltop to the ammo storage bunker. Swarnes dove into it on his heels. Nobody fired at them.

They couldn't get all the way into the bunker; it was small, and fully packed with ammo crates. There was no light in the bunker, but Bell knew its layout well enough that it didn't pose any problem. He grabbed the rope handle of an ammo crate and yanked it off the stack it was on, then pushed it back toward Swarnes. "Get this out of here," he ordered, then reached for another crate, a few feet to the side of the first one, and pulled it out. He crawled out of the bunker, dragging the second crate along. The two Marines stacked the two crates on top of each other. "You ready?" Bell asked.

Swarnes looked at him, wide-eyed, and swallowed. "You're crazy, Jay Cee. You know that?"

"On three," Bell said. "One, two, three." The two Marines lurched to their feet with the crates between them and ran, staggering, a hundred meters to the north trench. Again, they made it without anybody shooting at them. They jumped into the trench where Doc Rankin had his impromptu med station set up. The corpsman was talking to Willard, assuring him his eyes were going to be all right as soon as he got to a hospital.

Bell saw the bandages on Randall and Lewis and realized Athen and Dodd were the only other Marines left on this side of the machine gun. "Who's in charge over here?" he asked.

Randall grimaced from the pain in his arm, but the pain was less than it had been. "I guess I am," he said.

The sergeant didn't have time to discuss it, and there was no one else on that side with leadership experience— unless he pulled McEntire off the gun. "If those fuckers have any sense, they'll stay in the trench and try to roll up our flanks. Here's a case of grenades and a case of Claymores. Stop them."

"Aye-aye, Jay Cee." Randall grinned crookedly. "No problem." He looked at the men he was with. Lewis shouldn't try to walk with his foot in its condition, and Willard was still blind. "Dodd, give me a hand with these?"

Dodd nodded and helped the wounded corporal pick up the crates to carry them forward.

Bell and Swarnes didn't see them leave the med station; they were already headed back to the ammo bunker.

Major Nghu's lips almost disappeared as he drew them in in an angry grimace when he saw the toung si and another man carry munitions to the north trench and run back for more. By now the smoke over the west trench had cleared enough for him to see the assault force huddled in it not doing anything. The fools, he thought, furious. He snapped orders at his radioman. The idiot commanding the troops on the hilltop would never lead troops in combat again; he would see to that later. They could not stay there; they had to move, move along the trench on both sides to roll up and destroy the few defenders. He snarled more orders when the radioman finished instructing the first assault team commander to move up the trenches. The mortar would lead the two lines entrapping Tango Niner. From where he was, he could not see the second assault force, the one that had been stopped by a unit of unknown size. He instructed his radioman to order that unit to dispatch a squad back into the woods to flank the unit that had it pinned down, then continue its assault on the hill while there was still no one defending its front.

Bell and Swarnes reached Ruizique with a load of grenades before the enemy mortar started dropping more rounds into the compound. It only took three hits for Bell to understand what was happening.

"Stay down below the top of the trench, and crawl to the back gate," he ordered Ruizique. Then he got on the field phone and tried until Randall finally answered. He gave him the same instructions, except the men on the north side were going to the main gate and the machine gun nest. He headed toward the ammo bunker for more grenades.

Vinh squatted in the trees east of Camp Apache, trying to decide what to do. He couldn't tell how the battle was going, but from the number of men he saw pinned down south of the hill and the mortar barrage on top of it, he knew the defenders, his friends and neighbors, couldn't hold on too much longer. Not without help.

CHAPTER TWENTY-NINE

To the Rescue

The PFs who'd elected to transport their families to safety had to take them all the way to Phuoc Nam town, the district capital. They stopped once along the way at a hamlet where several of them had relatives to whom they handed their dead for safekeeping. The bodies were too heavy to carry all the way—and in the tropical heat it wouldn't be long before they started smelling. Phuoc Nam was a long day's walk from Bun Hou; it was near dark by the time they arrived. Then they had to find someone to shelter their families in the shantytown that was building up on the outskirts of town. By the time they were through, it was far too late to head back. First thing in the morning on the second of January, several of the PFs decided to construct rude huts for their families before heading back, so it was mid-morning by the time the small column of PFs started their return trek. Still, the journey was long enough that night caught them before they reached Bun Hou, and, rather than risk walking into a Tango Niner ambush and getting killed by accident, they decided to stop for the night. They were on the road again at the crack of dawn.

The fifteen PFs were still more than a mile away from Camp Apache when they heard the distant Claymore mine explosion that was the first shot fired in the assault. They cast worried glances at one another and picked up their pace—it wouldn't do to reach Camp Apache after the VC Hanoi had overrun it.

Vinh couldn't think of any way to get to the hill without too great a risk of being spotted and fired on by any enemy he couldn't see from the trees he watched in. After another minute's rumination he decided their best course of action was to join whoever it was who had the NVA pinned down in the open. He rose from his squat and joined his men, who were waiting a few meters away. He briefly explained the situation—as much of it as he had been able to figure out—and told them what they were going to do. None of them liked Vinh's plan very much, not without any of their Marines to lead them, but the only alternative any of them saw was to run away. If they ran away, they could never go home again; they would have to join the torrents of refugees and probably wind up in the ARVN. None of them wanted to be Arvins. They followed Vinh through the trees, toward the river, and west to the fire fight.

Vinh heard the sound of someone moving through the trees on his right. It didn't sound right to him; he and his men were now midway between the two firing groups. He looked in the direction of the sounds in the deep shade under the band of trees along the river and saw movement. He dropped to one knee and held his rifle ready to fire. The other PFs followed suit.

The PF squad leader gathered himself and shouted out in a strong voice, "Ai do, Ma-deen, fay epp." Who's there? Excited voices that he didn't recognize came to him, and the sound of people moving stopped. He threw his rifle into his shoulder and called out again, "Ai do." He was answered by a fusillade of fire. The PFs opened up and heard a scream when one of their bullets found its mark.

Vinh shouted orders at his men. Ten of them stayed

down, firing at the enemy through the trees, and the other four jumped up and followed him. More than fifty meters farther, he stopped and said a few hushed words. The four men with him put full magazines into their rifles and nodded their readiness. The sounds of the firefight they left behind were reassuring—the PFs were putting out far more fire than the enemy group they were fighting. They moved away from the river until they were parallel to the NVA fire, then they advanced until they could see where the enemy fire was coming from. Vinh signaled his men to get down, waited until they were all ready, then opened up.

The fire from a second direction caused consternation among the NVA. Two jumped up and ran—or tried to run; they didn't make it far before they were gunned down. Only three were left. Then there were two. The last one tried to give up; he should have thrown his rifle away and shouted out his surrender before he stood up. The squad sent to flank Zeitvogel's patrol was wiped out.

Vinh called to the rest of his men to join him; they continued toward their destination. "Ma-deen, fay epp, this Vinh," he shouted when he thought they were close enough. Now reinforced to triple its previous strength, the part of Tango Niner in the trees was much better able to deal with the eighty NVA still in the open.

"Short Round, stay here and keep those fuckers pinned down," Zeitvogel ordered. He left the four PFs with his automatic rifleman and gave him three of the men who had come back with Vinh. Then he led Mazzucco, Vinh, and the others back to a place where they could fire more directly on the enemy they had pinned.

On top of the hill, the NVA were advancing slowly along the north and south trenches. As soon as the enemy mortar started its prep fire, Randall realized he wouldn't be able to use the Claymores the way Bell wanted; if they stayed in positions to trigger the directional mines when NVA came in range of them, they ran too great a risk of getting killed by the enemy mortar. He kept the Claymores and backed off along the trenches. Sooner or later, he realized, the enemy soldiers would be so close to them the mortar would have to stop firing. Then maybe he could use the Clay-mores.

After Burrison moved the CP from its bunker to the east trench and Slover and his mortarmen joined them, all the defenders of Camp Apache were on the east side in an arc running from the main gate to the back gate. The lieuten-ant, being the last man left in the CP when he moved it, only took one radio with him—the PRC-25, which was their communication with Box Top, the same radio he'd use to communicate with the helicopter gunships when they arrived. Burrison looked out over the hilltop and saw the middle of it being ignored by the attackers. He decided to take a chance and ran back to the CP bunker for a whip antenna for the radio; it was no longer connected to the twenty-foot antenna that towered over the bunker. He'd just had time to screw it into the radio's top when he heard a transmission.

"Apache, Apache, this is Lightning Lead, Lightning Lead. Do you hear me? Over."

"Lightning Leader, this is Apache. I hear you. Over," he said into the headset.

"We have you in sight, Apache," the radio voice said laconically. "What is your situation? Over."

Burrison blew out hard, a huge sigh of relief. "We are being overrun, Lightning," he answered. "What can you do for us? Over."

"Let me get closer and eyeball you, Apache. Stand by."

Bell and Swarnes dashed across the open hilltop and thudded into the trench next to Burrison.

"They're here," Bell said, looking at the two helicopters coming at them from the east.

"I fucking hope they're not too goddamn late," Swarnes said.

"Apache, this is Lightning Two. Who are those people on the ground to your Sierra? Over," the radio asked. Sierra was the phonetic meaning south. Lightning Two, the second bird, was flying toward the south side of the hill; the other was several hundred meters away from it, on the north side.

"Those are bad guys, Lightning Two," Burrison said. "We have people in the trees, pinning them down."

"Roger, Apache. The people in the open are bad guys; the people in the trees are yours. I'll give your tree dwellers a hand." The bird on the south fired a brace of rockets at the exposed NVA, then turned broadside to them so one of its machine guns could fire at them. "Hoo boy, Apache," the radio voice said, "I hope you got boo-coo people in the trees. The baddies we just blasted are making for the shade." The helicopter kept its machine gun firing at the running NVA until they were all under the trees. They left behind a string of broken bodies that showed the path they had taken to cover.

"Oh, shit," Bell said. There was nothing the Marines and PFs on the hill could do to help Zeitvogel and his people. He didn't know they had been reinforced by the missing PFs. He turned his attention back to the situation that faced him. Stilts was on his own for now. The nearing mortar explosions showed him the progress of the enemy along the trenches.

"Apache, Lightning Leader," the radio said again. "We got to do something serious about that mortar before we can get close enough to you to help with your problem. Hang tight until we get it done." The two helicopters buzzed off to the west in search of the mortar.

"Hot damn, we got help," Zeitvogel exclaimed when he saw the helicopter headed toward the men in the open. He watched while the helicopter slowed almost to a hover and fired two rockets at the pinned-down NVA, and let out a whoop when he saw the rockets hit among them, spewing out plumes of earth, making newly wounded and dying men scream in agony. The helicopter turned so its crew chief could fire his machine gun on them. "Let's give that bird a hand," the tall black corporal shouted. He and his baker's dozen men poured fire into their enemy. Then he said, "We got trouble," in a soft voice when he saw the NVA suddenly jump up and run to the cover of the trees. He knew the enemy escape route had to be to the west— through him and his men. "Let's dee dee out of here," he shouted, and started running back to where he'd left Hempen and the other PFs. Hastily, he organized his men into a tight defense. As many men as the NVA had left behind, his force was still out numbered by at least three to one.

They waited tensely for the enemy to appear.

One of the helicopter pilots thought he saw where the mortar was and fired a rocket at it to mark the position for the other bird. They zoomed in, firing more rockets as they approached. Even though they were firing at the right place, none of their rockets were exactly on target, but they were hitting close enough that the mortar squad leader decided to cut and run while he still could. They took the tube and as many of the rounds as they could grab in their haste. They had hardly reached a safe distance when one of the rockets hit the pile of mortar rounds left behind. The explosion knocked down trees and bushes all around the small clearing the mortar had been in and showered dirt and debris more than a hundred feet into the air.

"Apache, Lightning Lead," the lead helicopter pilot called. "Any survivors are on their way back to Hanoi. We're coming back around." Soon the two birds were flying low past the hill, one north of it, the other south. Once they passed it, they wheeled around, and the leader called again, "Apache, give me some smoke to mark your forward positions."

"Roger, Lightning," Swarnes answered. "The birds want us to pop some fucking smoke so they'll know where to drop their shit," he said to Bell and Burrison.

Bell cranked the handle of the field phone and ordered, "Front and back gates, throw smoke at the bad guys so the birds will know where they are."

At the main gate, Randall's arm hurt too much. He told

Dodd to throw the smoke. It's not easy to throw something far or accurately from under a low roof. Dodd only managed to toss the grenade fifteen feet to the next bend in the trench. The NVA were still more than fifty feet away—but at least the smoke was between the good guys and the bad guys. Ruizique didn't have the same throwing problems at the back gate; he was able to lob the gray cannister well beyond the closest approaching enemy soldiers. That was okay, too; most of the bad guys were on the other side of it.

The two helicopters aligned themselves on the zigzag trenches and roared over them, firing their rockets. Half of the rockets hit outside the trenches, but the ones that hit inside did their damage to the enemy. The birds spun away from the hill after making their pass and lined up for another pass, one that allowed their crew chiefs to fire their machine guns into the trenches. The cacophony of the M-60s streaming out their long bursts was clearly heard above the roar of the rotors. The Marines and PFs on the hilltop heard the death screams of hit NVA above the machine guns. The helicopters twisted around to make another pass.

There's something that all very well trained and well disciplined soldiers know almost instinctively, something that allows them to win every time they fight against less well trained and disciplined troops: advance toward fire.

Major Nghu's NVA were very well trained and well disciplined soldiers; they didn't panic when the helicopters started strafing them. But there's no way infantry could advance against aircraft, so they did the next best thing. They fired back at the helicopters, big, slow, vulnerable planes.

The pilots started jinking up and down, side to side, to throw off the aim of the men on the ground. Suddenly the trenches worked to the advantage of the NVA. The trenches gave them some protection from the gunships' fire—the helicopters had to stand off to the side of the hill in order to bring their machine guns to bear. A burst from an automatic rifle stitched a line of bullet holes in the front side of

Lightning Lead's cockpit, and the bird swerved away from the hill and climbed for altitude. A lucky shot from the other side of the hill drilled the crew chief of the other helicopter through the middle of his chest, and that bird stopped firing and pulled out of range of the ground fire.

"Apache, Apache, this is Lightning Lead," the radio spat. "My copilot has been hit. I've got to get him out of here. I can make one more pass on the way. Lightning Lead out." The helicopter circled around the hill to the south. Its machine gun rained fire onto the trench as it went. The two gunships linked in formation over the river and headed east. "We'll get somebody else out here ASAP, Apache," the gunship leader called back. Lightning Lead switched to a different radio frequency to alert Charlie Med he was coming in with wounded. Then he changed to a third frequency to let someone know there were Marines out here who needed help—they needed some fast fliers. Two UH-34s with rockets and machine guns weren't going to be enough.

Major Nghu screamed loudly and waved his arms wildly when the two helicopters came into view and attacked his men pinned in the open. He tried to order the mortar squad to stay in place and continue its bombardment of Tango Niner's hill when the helicopters started to fire their rockets at it, but came to his senses—if the rockets hit, he would lose his artillery. Then he became more virulent when the gunships rocketed and strafed his men on the hilltop. So much so his radioman blanched and held tighter to his own perch; if the commander gyrated so wildly he fell out of the tree, the radioman didn't want to be knocked down with him. The hawk-nosed NVA officer cheered when the two helicopters were hit, and he lost his balance but recovered in time.

When the injured birds trundled off, he snapped orders to his radioman: continue the advance on the hilltop; attack and kill the Marines and PFs in the trees.

* * *

There weren't as many NVA left on the hill as there had been ten minutes earlier, but there were still more than twice as many of them as there were Marines and PFs of Tango Niner. They were there to tango, and determined to win. They started advancing along the trenches again. There were also fewer NVA under the trees south of the hill then there had been before, though there were three times as many of them as Zeitvogel had with him. Their officer had his orders; he shouted instructions to his men to form to assault the men who had pinned them down until the helicopters had come.

CHAPTER THIRTY

Coffee, Tea, or Bodybags?

Randall took advantage of the helicopters pinning down the NVA attacking along the north side of the compound. "Someone give me a hand with these things," he said, and grabbed two of the Claymore mines with his left hand. He tried to pick one up with his right hand, but sharp pain flashed through the burned part of his arm and he dropped it.

"I've got a couple, and I'll bring my rifle," Dodd said. "Let's go, honcho."

Randall glanced at him, then looked at the other men in the machine gun nest; Lewis, Willard, Athen, and two PFs. "Billy Boy, take Willard to the CP while the bad guys aren't shooting at us," he said.

"Fuck you, Tex. I'm staying right here, where I can get Charlie one at a time."

"Point me in the right direction," Willard said grimly. "This is an area weapon. I don't need to see what I'm shooting at to hit it." He hefted his M-79.

"Bunch of fucking John Waynes," Randall snorted, but he was proud of the wounded men who wanted to stay and continue the fight. He tried to keep his injured arm from hitting the side of the trench as he scuttled forward to the next bend in it. He set up one of the mines facing along the next trench section and attached a wire to fire it. Then he started to climb out.

"Hold it, Tex," Dodd said. "Your arm's too fucked up. Tell me what you want to do, and I'll do it."

Randall looked at him hard, briefly. The draftee's expression was that of a man who wasn't going to be argued with. "Okay, Dodd. I want one of these suckers on the top facing down the next piece of trench. Plant the other two between here and there. We see anybody stick his head up, we blow them away with a Claymore."

Dodd grunted and scrambled out of the trench with the mines. He left his rifle behind. Even though he worked fast, he took time to carefully align each of the mines so they would throw their pellets where they were most likely to be useful and so the backblast wasn't directly aimed at the gun position. He started crawling back toward Randall, then stopped and looked at the wires trailing from his hands to the mines. "I'm going back overland," he said. "That's the only way I can avoid getting these wires tangled up." He looked up and added, "Charlie's too busy with the birds; it's safe for me to go that way," and started crawling backward without waiting for an answer. He played out the wires as he went and kept them well separated.

"You think people come down hard calling you Dumbshit now, Dodd?" Randall said to himself. "Wait till people hear about you making like a hero. Then they'll really call you Dumbshit." He took Dodd's rifle in his good hand and headed back to the rest of his men.

Then the helicopters made their final circuit of the hill and headed east. There was a long moment of deafening silence on the hill before the North Vietnamese officer commanding the troops on it started shouting orders at his sergeants. Whistles blew, and the advance along the trenches started again.

Dodd squatted behind the protection of the wall of the gun position. His head was exposed as he watched the hilltop; the wires leading to the mines were in his hands. "I know which one is which," he told Randall. "If I pull them, there won't be any fuckups." The corporal grunted agreement. He also watched. Thirty meters away, the NVA pointman made the mistake of standing up to see if he could spot where the Americans and PFs were. Dodd saw him. "Down," he shouted at Randall. They ducked behind the wall, and Dodd jerked one of the wires. The middle mine exploded, and the NVA disappeared in a hail of pellets—he didn't even have time to scream before they tore his head and shoulders to shreds. When the dirt and debris kicked into their position by the backblast stopped cascading in, Dodd and Randall stuck their heads up again.

They heard excited voices jabbering where the enemy pointman had been. One voice rose above the others, a commanding voice. The other voices quieted down.

"I think they're coming again," Dodd said.

"I think you're right," Randall agreed. "Do you think they can see the Claymore you aimed along the trench?"

"Maybe. But if they can see it, they might not know it's armed and I'm holding the string."

Randall grunted. He thought for a moment, then said, "As soon as I see one of them at this bend"—he pointed to where he had set the Claymore in the trench—"I'm going to fire it off. You let the one aimed at the trench go at the same time. If we're lucky, we might get two squads at the same time. Slow them down."

Dodd nodded. They waited tensely. In a moment they heard another excited voice; it sounded as if it came from the bend in the trench opposite the mine Randall had set.

"They must have seen it," Randall said.

There was a pause before the commanding voice spoke, then silence again. After a moment a face appeared at the end of the trench zig the Marines were watching. The face was covered by a sheen of sweat, and its eyes were locked on the mine. A hand tentatively reached out from under the face toward the mine.

"Now," Randall said. He ducked down and pulled the wire he held. Dodd also ducked and pulled the wire to the mine facing into the trench. The two Claymores went off at almost the same instant, their two roars sounding like one. This time they heard screams from the trench. The commanding voice didn't speak to counter the excited jabbering that followed the screams; the NVA sergeant was one of the casualties. The mines had stopped the NVA advance on the other side of the hill. For the moment.

The situation on the south side was a bit different. Ruizique didn't have any Claymores to put out; he had two cases of hand grenades. And he had nine men with him to fire at anyone dumb enough to raise his head above ground. The grenades he was throwing were holding up the NVA advance.

"Let me do it," Vega said the first time Ruizique threw a grenade and it didn't drop into the trench, but instead spewed its fragments harmlessly through the air. "I was pitcher on my high school ball team."

Ruizique gave the new man a show-me look and handed him a grenade. Vega held the grenade in an unorthodox manner, with the spoon held down by the web where the thumb joined his hand, and pulled the pin. He crouched sideways to the direction he was going to throw and held his hands together at chest level. He stood, looked quickly where he wanted to grenade to go, and give it a half-push, half-overhand throw. The grenade sailed in a low arc and hit inside the far lip of the trench section. Someone screamed in a high register. Ruizique shoved the case of grenades at him.

"They're yours. Make sure they're all as good as that one."

Vega grinned at him and got another grenade ready. This time he held it the way he was supposed to, with the spoon under his fingers. "Airburst," he said, and released the spoon. Then he stood and threw the grenade with the same motion he had thrown the first one. It exploded above the trench, and more screams came from under the explosion.

"Lucky," Ruizique said.

Vega shrugged. "Want to see it again?" He didn't try for another airburst, though. He knew as well as Ruizique did that the grenade fuses weren't that well calibrated—most of them went off four or five seconds after the spoon was released, but they could explode in as little as two seconds or as much as seven seconds after being armed. That's why a grenade is supposed to be thrown hard—make it bounce around a little when it hits so whoever you throw it at doesn't have a chance to grab it and throw it back at you. He got another grenade ready to throw, but before he could stand up, a torrent of bullets flew overhead.

"Oh, shit," Ruizique said when the fire didn't stop. He figured out that a squad or more had stood up in the trench and was firing to keep them from standing up to throw more grenades, so the rest of them could continue the advance.

"No sweat," Vega said, nervous sweat beaded on his forehead. "I know where the trench is." He pulled the pin on the grenade in his hand and lobbed it without any part of him other than the hand that threw the grenade going above the top of the trench. More screams answered the explosion of the third grenade. The gunfire at them didn't seem to be affected. "I wonder if I can hit the bad bastards who are shooting at us." He quickly raised his head so his eyes were above the lip of the trench and ducked back down again. He swore, then explained, "I saw them. They're too far back for me to reach them unless I stand up. And I ain't wearing bulletproof skin."

"Big Red," Ruizique ordered, "you get right here and waste any motherfucker you see poking his head around that next corner." He stationed Robertson and his automatic rifle at the far end of the trench section they were in.

Vega threw another grenade at the trench where he knew the enemy had to be. Nobody screamed this time. The

NVA advance on the south side of the hill was slowed, but the soldiers still moved forward; the advance hadn't been stopped.

"There they are. I see them," Hempen said below the hill. His voice was low and even, but it was edged with fear.

Zeitvogel looked where Hempen aimed his rifle and made out dim movement through the trees. "Hold your fire, people," he ordered in a voice that carried to the ends of his defensive arc but wasn't loud enough to go through the trees to the NVA walking at an angle across their front. "Don't anybody fire until I say to."

Vinh repeated the order for the PFs, who might not understand the English words in their excitement. Each of the twenty-two men lined his rifle on a target—some of them were too nervous to see straight enough to actually aim; they just pointed. Their mouths dried; they licked dry lips, tried to ignore the sweat dripping into their eyes. Many of them wondered how many more minutes they had to live.

Zeitvogel watched the enemy until he thought enough of them were in easy range. He wanted to open up before any of them were past his position, because he knew they could send a flanking element on his left side and he didn't want anybody in a position to hit him on the right flank as well. "Get ready," he ordered. A few of the men he saw through the trees seemed to stop and look in his direction.

"Fire!" Zeitvogel screamed, and opened up with his M-14. The line of Marines and PFs erupted in blazing gunfire.

Half of the NVA they could see dropped immediately, some hit, some taking cover to fight back. The rest took a split second longer to dive for cover. The NVA officer and sergeants started shouting orders, and the company under the trees quickly got organized. In half a minute the men of Tango Niner were under much heavier fire than they were putting out.

*   *   *

If anybody had looked in that direction, they would have seen two specks low above the horizon in the eastern sky. The specks grew rapidly until one of the riflemen keeping Vega from standing up to throw his grenades accurately saw light flashing from the white bodies of the aircraft, which had grown too much to still be specks. That northerner stared, slack-jawed, for a few seconds before screaming out something almost unintelligible. Then he jumped out of the trench and ran away. The others on the firing line looked and panicked.

But for most of the people on the hill, the first they knew of the fast-flying jets was when they flashed low above it. For an instant their delta wings seemed to blot out the sky, then the roar of their engines drowned all sounds of the battle. The two jets climbed in a sharp-turning arc to the right and headed back toward the hill.

Burrison grabbed the radio handset from Swarnes when the two A-4 Skyhawk attack bombers zoomed overhead and waited for the flight to contact him. The lead pilot's first transmission came before the two aircraft completed their turn. "Blue Ball flight," Burrison answered, his voice filled with hopeful excitement, "we are on the east side of the hill. I say again, friendly forces are Echo on hill. Everybody else on the hill is bad guys. Over."

"Roger, Apache. You willing to clean up crispy critters? Over." "Crispy critters" is what bodies burnt to death by napalm were called.

"Not if we can avoid it, Blue Ball. Do you have anything else? Over." Having to clear burned bodies off the hilltop was one thing, but napalm would probably destroy the squad tents and a lot of personal property of the Marines—and if any got into the mortar or small-arms ammo bunkers, it could cook off the ammunition, and nobody could predict what that might do to the defenders.

"Do we have anything else? Watch this, Apache." By now the two A-4s had completed their turnaround and were flying toward the hill from the east again. They were low, only about fifty feet above the top of the hill, and so slow they looked as if they were about to stall out. The A-4 Skyhawk couldn't carry as much armament as the F-4 Phantom jet, but it could come in low and slow and drop its ordnance exactly where it was needed. Because of that, the Marines on the ground loved to see Skyhawks come around to help. A-4 pilots said their jets were friendly little aircraft that they didn't get into; they just sort of strapped one on and went flying with it.

Blue Ball lead came in over the north trench, his wingman fifty meters behind and over the south trench. Two large objects tumbled off the bottom of each jet, 250-pound bombs. The pilots hit full thrust as soon as they released their bombs and peeled up and out. One bomb landed in the middle of each trench; the others hit toward the western end of the trenches. The hilltop roared with incredible force and noise from the explosions of the thousand pounds of high explosives. Dirt, smoke, and debris rose higher than the jets had been when they'd dropped their lethal cargo. Broken and mangled bodies were thrown out of the trenches, some landing in the barbed wire surrounding the hill. Agonized screams from the wounded rent the air as soon as the din of the bombs rumbled away.

The Marines cheered when the A-4s dropped their bombs; the PFs gaped in awe at the blast clouds raised by the explosions. The surviving NVA were still well-trained, well-disciplined troops, but they didn't have any weapons that they could use effectively against attack bombers; no matter how low and slow the A-4s came in, they were a lot faster than the helicopters. The trenches gave them protection from fire from the men on the ground and from the helicopters, but they weren't any help against bombs dropped from directly above. The NVA bolted from the trenches and ran—some of them threw their weapons away so they could run faster. Maybe they could make it to the cover of the trees before Skyhawks made it back from their turnaround. It was a vain hope.

"Blue Ball, they're on the run," Burrison shouted into

the radio. "Make some crispy critters in the open below the hill."

"Roger your last, Apache," the A-4 lead replied. "Got your marshmallows ready?" The two delta-wing jets lined themselves up on the flat south of the hill and flew in just as low, but not quite as slow, as on their first bombing run. Before they reached the running men, they released the napalm bombs and peeled up and away on full thrust. The cannisters tumbled down out of the air and erupted in huge balls of flame that rolled along the ground, incinerating everything in their paths. Shrill screams were cut off in mid-breath as burning men inhaled flame and collapsed, suddenly turned to charcoal. Fewer than a third of the soldiers who had assaulted the compound from the west made it to the cover of the trees.

The firefight under the trees was fierce before the Skyhawks arrived. The NVA used their superior numbers to advance on Zeitvogel's small pocket of men; they leapfrogged, two men firing while one dashed or rapidly crawled a few meters forward. The rapid booming of Hempen's automatic drew a lot of fire, and he was bleeding freely from a hit on his thigh. Linh was dead from a bullet that had crashed through the side of his skull. Tho's left shoulder was shattered, but he kept firing his carbine with one hand. A bullet had drilled Duc in the left shoulder next to his neck and shattered his shoulder blade—he was unconscious from shock.

"All things considered, I'd rather be in Philadelphia," Mazzucco shouted. He lined his sights on a rapidly advancing figure and pulled the trigger. He didn't wait to see his target fall; he looked for another one.

"You and me both, Homeboy," Zeitvogel shouted back. He cranked off two tracer rounds at a prone man firing at him and reloaded.

"Can I come, too?" Hempen asked weakly. He was on his fourth magazine and wondered if he'd be alive long enough to empty his seventh, and last, one.

Then the A-4s roaring over the hill blotted out the noise of the firefight under the trees. The NVA kept shooting but stopped their advance. The A-4s dropped their 250-pound bombs, and a few of the northerners in the trees shouted their fear to their companions; they broke and ran. The rest of them bolted when the Skyhawks came back and dropped their napalm.

Major Nghu screamed his fury when the A-4s made their first pass over the hill. He shouted an order at his radioman to have the soldiers fire their rifles at the two jets. The radioman looked at him, dumbfounded. Everybody firing rifles at attacking jets was nice in theory, he thought, but he doubted it would do any good in reality. He flinched when he saw Major Nghu's hand go to his holster because of his delay in making the transmission, and hurried to relay the order. By then the jets were making their second pass, and their bombs exploding on the hill overrode his radio voice so no one heard the order—not that they would have obeyed it anyway. Major Nghu screamed again, cursing the authorities who had sent him here without any anti-aircraft weapons. He did not curse himself for not thinking of the possibility. When he saw the napalm spread across the flatland, charring his fleeing troops, he knew his campaign was ended and scrambled out of the tree. He led his radioman to a position where they could intercept the retreating survivors and join them.

CHAPTER THIRTY-ONE

We Got Them on the Run

"Who do we have wounded?" Bell asked into the field phone after the napalm had sent the NVA survivors staggering into the forest. Tracker reported Ruizique and Hank were with him; Rankin had worse news: Randall, Lewis, Willard, and Kobos. Bell ordered Tracker to send Ruizique and Hank to Rankin. "Everybody else, form at the back gate." Ruizique met him there.

"You going in pursuit, Jay Cee?" Ruizique asked.

"You better believe it, Zeke."

"I'm going with you. This won't hold me back." He pointed at the bandage on his forehead.

Bell didn't answer. He looked around to see how many men he had. Thirteen Marines, Doc Tracker, and nine PFs stood, waiting for him.

"I don't care how bad my arm hurts," Randall said. "I can still fire my weapon. And I want a piece of that son of a bitch."

"I only lost a chunk of my earbone, Jay Cee," Kobos said. "That ain't near enough to keep a Marine down." He hefted his machine gun.

Bell grunted at them; he wasn't going to say no to men who wanted to fight. He nodded approval at Athen, who had Willard's M-79 grenade launcher.

Burrison and Houng joined them; the Marine lieutenant had the PRC-25 radio. "You forgot something, Swearin' Swarnes," he said, and handed the radio over. Swarnes muttered curses under his breath as he hefted the radio onto his back. The twenty-six men filed rapidly out of the gate and headed toward where Zeitvogel stood at the edge of the trees.

Burrison talked to the Skyhawks as he trotted across the flat. The jets agreed to remain on station even though they couldn't see any targets and couldn't fire into the trees, for fear of hitting the men of Tango Niner. "If they come out in the open anywhere," Blue Ball Lead said, "we'll blast 'em with our guns." The A-4s were armed with 20mm cannons. Then he switched to another frequency and requested help from a second flight of A-4s. He also asked for a med-evac.

"I got one fay epp dead and two others badly wounded," the tall man reported as soon as they were close enough. "Short Round's been hit—not bad, but it's his leg, and he can't walk." He looked to the west. "There's about eighty or ninety of those little bad bastards out there."

"Let's go get them." In seconds Bell had the platoon organized into three groups, with five Marines and eight PFs in each. One group headed toward the main path along the river; one stayed inside the trees near the scrub, the third in between. The half-dozen men left formed a command group that followed close behind the middle group. They moved west as fast as they could.

Major Nghu quickly realized the two jets were still in the area, flying high and waiting for someone to come out from under cover. When his men reached the cleft where the Song Du Ong came out of the hills, he tried to make them stop to form a defense that the Marines and PFs that he knew had to be pursuing them would break itself on.

Unless more infantry came in, they could stay there until nightfall and then retreat up the cleft. The cleft was too dangerous in the daylight; there was no overhead cover, and the jets would see them and could fire on them, destroying them.

The soldiers were reluctant to obey, but they stayed under the trees, out of sight of the circling attack bombers, and waited for their foe to show up. They didn't have to wait long. The arrival on station of a second pair of Skyhawks helped them decide to sit tight.

"Hold up," Bell shouted. They were a hundred meters from the cleft. He looked at Swarnes, who had been in constant contact with the A-4s.

"They been eye-fucking that cunt slot up there and ain't seen no-fucking-body come out there or no goddamn place else," the radioman told him without being asked.

"They're right in front of us, then," Burrison said.

"You got that right, Scrappy." Bell said. "They're just waiting for us to come into their killing zone." He looked, steely-eyed, into the trees ahead. "I think we should drop in place right here and recon by fire, set them off before they're ready. When we know exactly where they are, we can call in the Skyhawks and have them blast 'em with their cannons."

"Do it."

Bell shouted more orders; he didn't care if the enemy heard him now or even if they understood what he was saying. Tango Niner had the bad guys right where they wanted them; there was no escape for them now. Everyone got on line across the band of trees and took what cover they could. They waited for Bell's next command. He did it by the numbers, just like on a qualification range back in The World.

"All ready on the right," Bell shouted. "All ready on the left. All ready on the firing line. Commence firing!"

Thirty-eight rifles, the machine gun, and the M-79 opened up, shattering any remaining semblance of tranquillity under the trees. Return fire came, spotty at first; it built up fast until more bullets were flying at Tango Niner than they were sending at the enemy.

Bell and Burrison put their heads together and agreed the bulk of the enemy soldiers were on a line twenty-five meters from where the trees butted against the foot of the hill. Burrison took the radio handset and gave that information to the A-4s.

The four Skyhawks swung north, then spun around and flew south as close to the steep side of the hill as they dared. They flew a level two hundred feet off the ground until they were within can't-miss range, then, one at a time, fired long volleys into the trees. The 20mm rounds blasted through the foliage of the trees and splintered small trees, tore gouges in the earth, ripped living bodies apart. The soldiers trying to fight Tango Niner knew the jets had their position marked and were coming back to do it again —they couldn't take another pass like that.

"Charge them!" Major Nghu shrilled. "Attack, attack! The aircraft won't dare shoot if we close with them." He stood and waved his arms and his pistol at his men. They ignored him in their haste to get away from the sky-borne death. Even when he shot one of the retreating soldiers in the head, they still ignored him, still fled for safety. Into the mouth of the cleft, which was about to become the mouth of death.

Major Nghu had no choice; he had to go with his men.

"Tally ho!" Blue Ball lead shouted over his radio. "They're headed up the cleft." He ordered the second flight to go into the cleft first and drop its bombs; he and his wing man would follow with their cannons.

Now that their part of the battle was over, the Marines and PFs were able to feel how they felt; they were exhausted from far too many hours without sleep, from too many days fighting this enemy, who stayed elusive until he closed in for the kill. They slumped; their very bones ached.

The *boom-bang* roaring of high-explosive bombs erupting in the cleft cascaded down at them, followed by a buzz-saw whirring of Blue Ball flight's cannon. They heard the jets overhead spin around and come back on another run. This time after the explosion of the bombs, a wall of heat from the napalm washed over them. They didn't care; they were too tired to care. All they could do was rest and hope the jets were doing enough damage to Major Nghu and his men to keep them away for a while, long enough for Tango Niner to recuperate and replace its lost men, regain the confidence of the people. They were too exhausted to think of their losses.

Eventually the guns stopped firing and the bombs stopped exploding in the hills, and the two teams of A-4s screamed past on their way back to Chu Lai. Through a break in the trees, some of the men on the ground saw one of the Skyhawks do a victorious barrel-roll.

A message came over the radio. Swearin' Swarnes looked around, then replied. He waited for the rest of the message, rogered it, and signed off. "Company's coming in, Scrappy," he said. "Gonna land outside the trees over there in zero three." He pointed away from the river toward the scrub. He was too tired to swear.

"Get 'em on their feet, Jay Cee," Burrison said. "We got to provide security for that LZ. Just in case Charlie's still got a few people around here." He brushed a hand through his hair, tried to make himself presentable for the lieutenant colonel he expected to get off the bird when it landed.

Painfully, Bell worked his aching joints until he was standing. "Saddle up, people," he croaked. "We got to provide security for a bird."

Grumbling, the Marines and PFs rose to their feet and held their weapons more or less at the ready. They trailed out of the band of large trees bordering the river and formed a loose, wide circle in the scrub around a grassy patch where the visiting helicopter could touch down.

Two helicopters circled them. One landed, and the

other, a gunship, continued orbiting. A tall, raw-boned man with a stone face bounded off the bird. Burrison had been right; it was Lieutenant Colonel Tornado. Captain Hasford pulled along in his wake. They ducked under the spinning blades and trotted to where Burrison, Bell, and Houng stood waiting for them.

The lieutenant colonel looked briefly into the eyes of each of the three CAP leaders, then his gaze swept the hills to the west. "Probably nobody left," he said without preamble. "All aircraft expended all ordnance before departing." He looked back at them. "And they reported they didn't see any more movement or other sign of life long before they finished firing." He turned in a slow circle, looking at the worn Marines and PFs of Tango Niner who were securing his landing zone. "Give your people another hour's rest. I'll have two gunships on station then. When they arrive, I want you to go up there and see what you can find. Probably just a lot of dead meat. I'll come back myself with your evening chow. Carry on." He turned sharply and trotted back to the waiting helicopter.

Captain Hasford, who hadn't said anything until now, said, "You did good," popped them a crisp salute, and rushed after the lieutenant colonel. Then they were gone.

"Let's get back under the trees," Burrison said. Wordlessly, the Marines and PFs straggled into the shade.

Bell, Randall, and Zeitvogel sat almost leaning on one another under a large-boled tree overhanging the river. The flowing water quietly sloshed against the bank. A muffled bump came from the water, and they leaned toward it. A khaki-clad corpse jostled its way along the bank, shifting about in the small eddies that momentarily formed and as quickly disappeared. A Sam Browne belt supporting an empty holster crossed the body's chest. Wavelets splashed over the hawk nose arching from the face; blank, cruel eyes stared sightlessly through the water. A wide red hole in the corpse's chest showed where a cannon round had hit. They looked farther out over the river, and they looked

upstream. There were more bodies, many of them black-
ened from napalm, than they felt like counting bobbing
along the current.

"I guess it's true, what they say," Zeitvogel said.

"What?"

"If you sit on the riverbank long enough, sooner or later
all your enemies will come floating past."

In the distance they heard the *whumpa-whumpa* of approaching gunships. They knew they wouldn't need that
support when they went into the hills.

ABOUT THE AUTHOR

David Sherman served as a Marine in Vietnam in 1966, stationed, among other places, in a CAP unit on Ky Hoa Island. He holds the Combat Action Ribbon, Presidential Unit Citation, Navy Unit Commendation, Vietnamese Cross of Gallantry, and the Vietnamese Civic Action Unit Citation. He left the Marines a corporal, and after his return to "The World," worked as a library clerk, antiquarian bookstore retail manager, deputy director of a federally funded community crime prevention program, manager of the University of Pennsylvania's Mail Service Department, and a sculptor. He has also written on the Combined Action Program for the *Marine Corps Gazette*.